Nothing Happens Until It Happens to You

Crown Publishers / NEW YORK

Nothing Happens

UNTIL

IT

HAPPENS

TO

YOU

A Novel

T. M. Shine

Copyright © 2010 by Terence Shine

Published in the United States by Crown Publishers, an imprint
of the Crown Publishing Group, a division of Random House, Inc., New York.
www.crownpublishing.com

CROWN and the Crown colophon are registered trademarks of Random House, Inc.

Library of Congress Cataloging-in-Publication Data
Shine, T. M.
Nothing happens until it happens to you: a novel / T. M. Shine. —1st ed.
p. cm.
1. Middle-aged men—Fiction. 2. Self-perception—Fiction. 3. Unemployment—
Fiction. 4. Florida—Fiction. 5. Domestic fiction. 6. Psychological fiction. I. Title.
PS3619.H576N68 2010
813'.6—dc22   2010011023

ISBN 978-0-307-58985-9

Printed in the United States of America

Design by Jennifer Daddio / Bookmark Design & Media Inc.

1   3   5   7   9   10   8   6   4   2

First Edition

For my people

Nothing Happens Until It Happens to You

manwich . . . all over the walls

love this part. Everyone is busy, occupied, happily employed. One person is even working.

The office is split into three distinct divisions—sales, editorial, administrative—and as I cut across the billing department to use the fax machine I'm reveling in the snippets of disjointed conversation bombarding me from every direction.

Josie, who writes a fashion column, "Glamazon," for our South Florida weekly—she's freakishly tall and glamorous—is relating to the temp receptionist how she fainted at the Muvico movie theater over the weekend. "And, of course, 1 get the one uncute paramedic on the planet," she says. "I'm sorry they even revived me."

Our new intern is nervously pacing around a small conference table and talking into his cellphone. "Yeah, this place is lame but that's not the worst of it," he's saying. "My pants are driving me crazy. They won't let me sit still."

I enjoy these walks. My desk is off in its own little Siberia in a corner right beside a storage closet. When the big oak door is carelessly left open—

about a thousand times a day—I'm totally obscured from the rest of the employees. I used to constantly reach over and shut it but that gets old around the four-hundred mark. So, to keep from feeling too isolated, I create reasons to get up and cruise the office, like a Peeping Tom in a cul-de-sac of cubicles.

I take an unneeded detour through the art department because I relish glancing at their workstations to see half-finished sketches and experimental photo layouts that the public will most likely never see. There's a small crowd around illustrator Gregg's desk. I stop to peek over the huddle and see he is excitedly putting the finishing details on . . .

"A commuter roller coaster," Gregg says. "I took the Tri-Rail one day last week and everybody is sitting there zonked out, taking baby sips of coffee and doing sudoku. Then I envisioned them all on a roller coaster heading to work—newspapers flying in the air, coffee splashing into people's hair, laptops crashing off treetops. This beast could take you from here to Miami in eleven minutes."

"I like the four-mile corkscrew between Boynton Beach and Delray," a coworker with her chin resting on his drawing board says.

"Check out this facedown drop into a fog-filled hole right out of the gate in West Palm," Gregg says, trailing his finger across the route.

Gregg's pencil is splintering under extreme creative pressure, adding curves and loops as he spits out the details. It's as if the whole image is busting out of him. He couldn't stop it if he wanted to. I know this is just one of Gregg's fleeting ideas that will never appear in our publication, but I can see it. I can really see it. Where does talent like that come from? It's just not in me, I know that, but I'm still buoyed by seeing it in others.

I feel like I'm soaring and swooping as I approach my true destination: the fax machine. Nicole, whose desk butts up against the copier, spots me briskly walking toward her and says, "It's hard to keep a good man down."

"I'm the exception," I say.

That's our exchange. I mean, really, that's it—for the past six years. Nicole is sweet but she's one of those people who constantly repeat lines in the realm of "Working hard or hardly working?" It took me three years to come up with my comeback, so I really shouldn't talk.

"Jeffrey," Eileen says, stopping me as I begin to circle back to my desk. "What should I do tonight?"

"Regina Spektor at the Cameo," I say without skipping a beat. "Costs twenty-eight fifty. Doors open at eight-thirty. For more information visit cameoconcerthall.com."

"Awesome, I love her," Eileen says.

I guess that's my talent. I'm the go-to guy if you want to know what's going on in town—from samba lessons to what ex–sitcom star is appearing at the Improv to what time the Coral Gables Health Clinic is scheduling skin cancer screenings. My title, which I received in lieu of a raise four years ago, is Universal Calendar Editor. I know, it sounds grand and intergalactic but it's really pretty mundane. Still, I like being the go-to guy, even if it's only for someone who needs to know where to get her cat spayed on a Tuesday night. (Paws City, 1222 Belevedere Road, Margate. The first Tuesday of every month.)

I stop just before my desk to close the storage closet door, but get a quick "Hey, leave that open. I'm hiding."

Gillian is sitting cross-legged on the corner of my desk, which is not a surprise. I actually keep the one area clear for her visits, so she'll always feel welcome. A couple of years back I put out a coffee mug full of Slim Jims in that exact spot and all the employees began coming by to say hi, and make some obligatory small talk. I eventually ran out of meat sticks and that was the end of my massive popularity, except for Gillian. She continues to stop by periodically, sitting on the end of my desk crunching on carrot sticks, guzzling Diet Coke, and basically complaining about her day.

She is so comfortable with her own beauty you almost forget about it. But our art department never does. Whenever they need a model on the cheap for a photo illustration, they turn to Gillian. I think I still have a copy of the special food issue where they have her in thigh-high waders, fly-fishing for Chilean sea bass off a diner's plate in a crowded dockside restaurant.

"I think my head is going to explode," she says.

As copy editor Gillian is in charge of correcting all the punctuation and grammatical errors before they go to print, so I immediately try to envision the shrapnel from the blast—commas boomeranging off the walls, asterisks hurtling through the air and cutting our throats like ninja death stars, clouds of periods bursting over our cubicles and unleashing a dark, nasty, prickly rain. And everyone covered in Diet Coke.

"The sales department is having their big awards dinner tonight," Gillian says. "They have, like, six of the actual awards on display outside the director's office. It's called the Excalibur. It's very regal—a miniature sword that looks like the most expensive martini-olive skewer you've ever seen, imbedded in a rock, and it's all encased in a glass cube. Nothing like the slabs of Lucite and the Target gift cards the company pawns off on editorial."

As I'm talking to Gillian I see Artie coming toward us with an odd grin on his face. Bearded, disheveled, and wearing shirts that should have been retired in 1984, Artie is one of those beloved characters who endear themselves to everyone by just being themselves. When my eleven-year-old niece and a friend visited the office, they simply said, "We like Artie. He reminds us of Jack Black."

Artie stops by regularly, too, but it's just part of his MO. He lives by the philosophy that if he visits everybody at their desks and "regales" each of them with identical anecdotes for twelve minutes twice a day, he can automatically cut four and a half hours out of his workday. He forced me to try it once, but I fizzled out after two stops and six minutes. I'm just not that good a talker, especially if it involves regaling.

Oh, Artie's the talented music writer who is forever trying to profile some old blues hound playing the Bamboo Room when he is supposed to be getting an eight-minute interview with Fall Out Boy's Pete Wentz. If his head suddenly exploded, the shrapnel would certainly include bottom-shelf whiskey, hash browns from a twenty-four-hour diner, varnish from a stage-worn stool, and at least a bucketful of highway dust from the mythic crossroads where people sell their souls to the devil for unearthly musical ability.

"What's with the face?" Gillian says the second she sees Artie.

"I moved somebody," he says.

"Where to?"

"No, emotionally," he says, holding up a small postcard adorned with a picture of a bird outside a cage looking in. "A reader wrote in that they were totally moved by the story about the street performers."

"I wish I could move somebody," I say. "Other than into a new apartment or something, I mean."

"I told you that story was heartbreaking," Gillian says. "That's great."

"Anyway, that's not why I'm here," Artie says.

"The Excaliburs, right?" Gillian says, lowering her voice.

"Right out in the open," Artie says excitedly. "I bet we could send Jeffrey over there to swipe one and they wouldn't suspect a thing."

I want to question why he picked me, but I usually don't get included in stuff like this, so I act as if I'll go along.

"Yeah, I bet he could pull it off," Gillian says.

The salespeople are flighty—always deep in conversation with some transsexual who owes money for placing a personal ad, or out back smoking More menthols and throwing rocks at squirrels—so I think I can do it.

"Artie, can I see you for a minute?" our boss, Mark, says from across the office.

"Sure," Artie says, heading off. "You guys got this, right?"

"Oh yeah, we got it," Gillian says.

"What do you think would come out of the boss's head if it exploded?" I ask Gillian.

"That one's easy," she says. "Manwich . . . All over the walls."

Gillian hops off the desk, looks around, and says, "Ten minutes and we do this."

"I don't know," I say. "Let's wait until . . ."

"Eight minutes. I'll meet you by the marketing partition."

I stare at the clock for eight minutes and then walk over to the marketing partition. "Are you coming with me?" I ask Gillian.

"No, but I'll be the lookout. And one thief tip: Wherever you are, act like you belong."

For me, that really will be an act. I hesitate, but then, right on the other side of the wall, the delivery manager starts repeatedly banging a stapler on his desk. "Damn this thing. It's the goddamn staples. And they're from Staples! How the hell do you name your company Staples and then serve up the shittiest staples ever created?"

I can't let the unplanned diversion go to waste. I round the corner and am *this close* to acting like I belong when I hear Artie's voice about ten feet behind me loudly announce, "OK, it's been nice working with everybody."

I turn and all I catch is his back heading toward the front door; he is awkwardly waving to everyone as he exits.

What the . . . ?

Normally, I'd just assume it was Artie, regaling us all with nothing more than a mundane departure. But there was something in the throatiness of his voice, an awkward gulp at the back of his words, that made me cringe. Clearly I wasn't the only one who'd heard it. Several employees in our department instinctively flow into the parking lot, drifting along on Artie's uncertain wake.

"They told me not to say anything, that I couldn't even go back to my desk, but I'm not going to work with people for thirteen years and not wave goodbye," Artie says as coworkers surround him on the blacktop before he even reaches his car.

What the . . . ?

The media company we all work for owns two large and eleven small papers in the Southeast (the kind that lie on people's lawns until they're soaked by the rain and then shredded by lawnmowers) and has not been impervious to downsizing. But it has been happening so slowly and subversively that the rest of us simply spent our days lingering in denial. Most of us didn't even notice until the vending company came and took the snack machines out of our break room because there weren't enough employees in our bureau to make it worth the trouble anymore. Hadn't Artie just said this morning, "I miss my Twizzlers"? So we've been sitting here while positions slowly evaporated around us, but the usual MO involved the doomed employee getting a call at home to report to our main office on Green Road, aka the Green Mile, where one would be disposed of quietly.

This is something new. I feel a gulping vacuum where my stomach should be.

I focus on Artie as if I'm taking a final snapshot. More of a "why not me?" than a "why me?" guy, Artie seems to be graciously accepting his fate along with several languishing parking-lot-in-broad-daylight farewell hugs from the office ladies. As I wait my turn (just to shake his hand), I think of how he is made of the good stuff. Whatever they use to puff up those unbelievably comfortable Natuzzi couches or cram into the extraordinarily delicious grande burritos at the Mexican place down the road, that is what Artie is made of. His interior is high-grade.

But before I can blurt out, "Artie, you are one high-grade SOB," the boss is yelling out the front door of our office complex. "You all need to get back inside," he barks.

What? We can't talk to Artie now?

What an absurd thought. That's all we do most of the time.

Artie smiles and tells us to go inside, he'll call everybody later. But as we file back in on command, the boss plucks Gillian out of the line with a clipped "Gillian, can I see you for a minute?"

It takes only a second for the realization to set in: If they can dispose of Gillian, who would have been last on everybody's hit list, no one is safe. Instantly we are gazelles at the water hole after lions take down a buck. Multiple brainstems pulse with a single primal thought: *Who's next?*

We're engulfed by whispery screams. *They don't let you come back to your desk! They don't let you come back to your desk.*

The herd bolts. It's all going—family photos, thermal coffee cups, knick-knacks from the trip to Amsterdam, Thai takeout menus, SpongeBob action figures . . . We are frantically sweeping off our desks into makeshift boxes, cloth sacks, and plastic shopping bags.

Thumbtacks pop off cubicle walls as faded magazine shots of Bradley Cooper's smile and 50 Cent's abs are stripped away. Two employees race to the bathroom to split a mini bottle of tequila that had been smacked out of a monkey piñata at a holiday office party two years ago, then get right back to it—loading plastic crates, making runs to the car, returning for more. A life-size promotional cardboard cutout of our regional VP cradling a penguin in his arms is knocked to the ground and spiked by coworker Josie's purple high heels—a quick casualty of a corporate stampede.

Everyone is preparing for the worst. "I'm glad I wore my cargo pants today," Gregg says, climbing over his own desk to get to the stockroom. "I'm swiping Post-its. You know how much Post-its cost in the real world? You don't want to know."

"I was specifically told I had to be here today," says Eileen, a longtime employee who usually works from home on Wednesdays. "If I had to be here, it must be because . . ."

We are all going down. The human resources department doesn't have time to be subtle anymore. They are not concerned that an employee will make a scene or set off the fire sprinklers on the way out the door. No, this time the cuts will be swift and multiple, consequences be damned.

"Oh, I know the company doesn't really need me. I don't want to go into that little office," Josie mutters as artifacts swept from her desk pile up at her feet.

Does the company really need any of us? Couldn't we all be replaced by a

Bangalore phone bank? "You're right," I say. "Let's disappear." (Who wouldn't want to disappear at a time like this?)

"Yeah, why make it easy for them," Eileen says, pumping her tiny fist.

In seconds, we are all back in the parking lot, slapping a stolen Post-it on Gillian's car—"Meet us at Rotelli's"—and fleeing a quarter mile down the street on foot. When the boss comes back out, there will be no one to fire.

"Run! Run! Run!" Josie is screeching hysterically. We have to cut along the shoulder of the main highway and, even now, I wonder how drivers in passing cars are summing us up—this weird band of nine-to-five refugees trying to escape the corporate ax.

"Gregg is strong," Eileen shouts as we drop down a grassy reservoir gully and he swiftly pulls everybody up the other side. As I reach for Gregg's outstretched hand he shouts, "Go! Go! Go!" Jack Bauer–style, and we're frantically trailing up the sidewalk half scared, half doubled over from exhaustion.

"I'm not in good enough shape to be fired," Eileen says. "Someone carry me."

By the time we make it to the front doors of the Italian restaurant, Gillian, who always carries herself regally, is getting out of her car, beaming and primly clutching the severance package to her chest as if it's an award for valor, which in her case it may very well be.

"They made short work of me," she says.

The walking papers quickly become a placemat for a Diet Coke, and we laugh at the thought of the boss coming back out to an empty office and marvel at Gillian's full-of-glee Mary Poppins attitude at being terminated. We half expect her to break into song, but instead she breaks out a sheet from the packet that reveals the job description and age of every employee being fired today. "I only had a chance to look at it quickly," she says, putting her finger on the list.

There's Artie. There's Gillian. There's . . . me.

No one else.

"Now that I know I didn't get fired I'm kind of sorry I drank the tequila," Josie says. "I don't feel so hot. Maybe they'll let me go home early."

My cellphone rings. The boss. I ignore it, but I know this is a summons I can't escape for long. Instantly I am separated from those who fled here beside me. Those sitting directly across the table are now simply workers on lunch break arguing over pizza toppings—mushroom or pepperoni?

I am a fugitive.

the smell of fresh-cut grass

I don't want to go home. It's all a blur, but somewhere between helping Josie carry a pile of office-worn Bratz dolls to her Audi and recovering from smacking my head directly into Gregg's during our getaway, I had made an erratic cellphone call to my wife, Anna. Blurting the words "They've come for us. All of us!" and her responding, "Who? Who's come for you? What the hell are you talking about?" is vivid in my memory, but beyond that I'm not sure what I said. And now I don't want to say anything.

I drive away from the office building but only travel about two miles down the road before I pull over, park beneath a huge banyan tree, and start walking toward a small shopping center. I am a master at stalling, even in moments of crisis. I have done this before, allowing procrastination to cushion me from the inevitable.

When my two children were younger I was bludgeoned by a phone call at work from the sheriff's office, notifying me that there had been a car accident "involving your wife and son . . . and daughter." The lieutenant spoke in generalities—where the accident occurred, what hospital they were transported to—but didn't reveal specifics. I asked no questions beyond directions. The hospital was thirty minutes away and I wanted that extra half hour of not knowing. I stayed behind the slowest cars. I prayed for lights to turn yellow. I wanted to stretch the highway like taffy, but no matter how much I tried, the hard facts were not going to allow me a soft landing. My mind was racing. *Anna had been taking them to pick strawberries. She would have driven the only single-lane highway that goes out west of town. She would have been flying. She had been talking strawberries with a passion all week. She is passionate when it comes to fruit.*

We survived that. We will survive this. This is not that kind of bad, I keep telling myself. But how is Anna going to take it? I've felt our marriage teetering as it is. We've never had a ton of money to go out on the town with, but we've made up for it by doing everything together, even if it was just shopping for produce at the Green Market every Saturday morning or slaughtering overgrown shrubbery in the backyard on Sundays. We even sorted the laundry side by side. But lately Anna seems to be always racing. She writes the lists of what we need to accomplish in any given week, rips it in half, and it's

"OK, you go this way and I'll go that way" with a kiss on the cheek. And even that kiss has become more fleeting. We are still a team, but now it's more like a relay team full of well-timed handoffs and speedy getaways. We've changed, even from the way we were a year ago. But don't get me wrong; neither of us behaves as if we are stewing in some sort of misery. If I suddenly pulled Anna aside and blurted some soap-opera line like "What has happened to us?" she'd certainly only laugh and say, "What the heck are you talking about? Finish putting the groceries away, you goofball. I've got to go online and pay bills."

Our relationship has become steeped in the action of what needs to get done next, but if some chore isn't written on the erasable board on the fridge our relationship starts to lose its energy. Things rarely come spontaneously anymore. When it comes to sex I always have to initiate it now. She hardly ever turns me away but I just wish the need would come from her on occasion. In bed, I sometimes lie there in the dark fighting the urge to reach over and touch her. I lie still, just hoping she will come to me, but she never does.

Anyway, if I had to sum it up, I'd say that on good days, ours is a union that is settled in for the long haul despite our differences. On bad days, I feel our marriage is set to autopilot on an aircraft that's skipped a few maintenance checks. The AP knob is a bit iffy and unreliable and if the captain spends one more minute reading a Fareed Zakaria essay in the lavatory, we're going down.

Anna is so analytical. Will she immediately see nothing but dollar signs and financial collapse? She works as a tech for a solid family-owned medical lab but they offer lousy benefits and my pay made up almost two-thirds of our total income. Our debt far outweighs savings, and both our children are now in their teens and extremely needy. I can still hear Kristin's voice from this morning, going on about how she's been accepted for the high school's dual enrollment program and will be able to get college credit for two classes. "Dad, all I need is a hundred and sixty-eight dollars for this macroeconomics book." Ahh, I'm afraid we're all about to get the economics lesson of our lives. Gregg is right. I don't want to know what Post-its cost in the real world.

When I get home, do I walk in the door and make some kind of royal announcement? Stand atop the stool in the kitchen we all use to reach the cinnamon on Sundays and say, "Gather 'round, family, I have some big news"? Do I let it creep up on them like the cat-on-the-roof story? "The economy has been awful and . . ." No, they would guess too soon. I'd barely have the economy tripping over the gutters before Andrew, my fourteen-year-old son, would blurt, "Dad, you lost your job, didn't you?"

When the boss ushered me into the office to face my demise I immediately started to go through a checklist in my head, trying to decipher why I was chosen. Age? In context, I'm only a little older than Keanu Reeves but not nearly as old as Prince. Performance? I could see my Lucite "Staffer of the Year" trophy from where I was sitting. Money? All things considered, I thought I came pretty cheap.

The strip mall is new, too new for someone who just lost his occupation and wants to stare at window decorations for forty-five minutes while getting up the nerve to go home and face his family. Half the space is unoccupied and the few open businesses are small eateries already winding down from the lunch rush. I stop to read a menu, but I can't get past the potato vichyssoise, leek, and butternut squash soups before I start zoning out. My eye catches a HELP WANTED sign two doors down and I immediately skip to coming through the door at home with a good news/bad news scenario. The bad news: Lost my job today. Good news: I start hostessing at Sushi Rock on Monday.

A waitress clearing outside tables looks at me suspiciously and I don't blame her. I've got sort of an exceeding hairline that makes me appear sinister. People are afraid I'm going to reach up and pull my woolly mop down like a ski mask and stick them up. They really are. Two women told me that in a bar once.

I also have these spindly chicken legs. Well, they're actually more like free-range chicken legs, which are a little more muscular than chicken legs because they're . . . you know . . . running free. I sometimes think I'm a bit of an odd-looking earthling, but I'm probably just being self-conscious because people have said that once they get used to the sight of me (takes about two weeks) I'm actually "vaguely attractive." Still, I always give people who eye me warily the benefit of the doubt, especially if I sneak up on them.

The sidewalk ends. As I round back behind the shopping center toward the car, I am mesmerized by a heavy-equipment operator chiseling away at a slab of concrete. The iron claw he's commandeering is gently nicking at the stone, barely breaking off a quarter-inch at a time. A tall, bushy-haired worker standing cross-armed about ten feet away puts a hand up to halt me. "It's not a safety thing," he shouts. "You just need to watch this guy work. You don't want to miss this. He's a marvel."

"I was already admiring his skill," I yell back.

"Nobody handles the J784 Skit-Kat like this guy. I'd let him make love to my wife with that thing," the worker says, his protruding belly jumping with glee, as if to celebrate a wonderful remark by its owner. I like when bellies are friendly. I've encountered far too many angry ones in my lifetime.

When I get back to the car, it is circled by three landscapers with blowers raging. And my windows are open. Even on one of the worst days of my life, I love the smell of fresh-cut grass, but not on my steering wheel.

I lean up against the tree and slide down to the ground, the jagged bark scraping against my back. My knees are touching my chin when I get a phone call. I spring up and see it's a company number. "Maybe they want me back," I say aloud, and honestly believe it. But it's only Eileen, curious about my disappearing act from Rotelli's and wanting to know, "Are you still alive?"

I am.

bed of confusion

Anna is standing at the closet, still dressed in her work clothes, when I find her in the bedroom. Her eyes immediately go to the stack of papers gripped in my hands.

"It happened" is all she says.

Between the erratic phone call and my early arrival home, no doubt remains, no big explanation necessary.

"What are we going to do?" I say.

Her expression softens and she walks over to where I'm frozen in my tracks, takes me by both arms, and sits me down on the end of the bed. I have seen her do this with our children when they are so stricken with emotion they appear as if they are about to seize up.

She flops down beside me and before you know it we are flailing the papers back and forth. It is like one of those scenes when a couple on the run pulls the heist of a lifetime and they empty a sack of cash onto a hotel bed to roll around in the dough, only we are steeped in the massive paperwork of my "involuntary separation."

To protect themselves, the company smothers you with details and it is hard to navigate toward what really matters. We are flopping about and sloppily attaching clothespins to any documents that seem as if they may be pertinent to the immediate future. This will be my instruction manual for the next several months and we are actually the antithesis of the renegade couple on the run. Our life is about to come to a complete halt.

But there is still so much motion—stuff falling on the floor, pulling and tugging—"Let me see that." "You already saw it." "Give it back."

Long-limbed and coltish with penetrating blue eyes, people say Anna looks like a shorter or taller Amanda Peet, but no one seems to know how tall Amanda Peet is, so they're not sure which. Honestly, they could even be the same height for all I know.

"What does this even have to do with us?" Anna says, holding up a blue sheet titled "Required Taxes You Must Pay in North Dakota and Rhode Island."

"Who even knew Rhode Island and North Dakota had something in common," I say.

"Here's the date for the last day dental will be covered," she says, high-lighting the day with a pink marker. "It's coming up fast."

"I'm going on that exact date."

"Looks like the medical will last a little longer."

As I roll over, one of Anna's clogs digs into my back and I almost fall off the side of the bed. When I right myself, all I see is color. Stretched across the bed, Anna is still wearing her lab scrubs emblazoned with starfish, octopus, sea turtles, the friendliest-looking moray eel you've ever seen in your life, and bubbles, hundreds of bubbles. She is passionate when it comes to fish. We have an aquarium in almost every room of the house and the cranberry gravel in the one on her bureau matches our bedroom carpet. Her wardrobe is awash in bright pinks and greens and blues.

"Your closet looks like a clown's closet," I say, looking across the room at the rows of hangers.

"Clowns don't have closets," she says. "They have trunks."

There was a time when Anna wore black to work on Mondays as sort of an inside joke, but it didn't fit her personality. "And it was scaring the ducks by the lake behind our building," she said at the time.

Her work with blood and specimen handling always sounds like a grind to me, except on that rare occasion when she calls to tell me something like "We just got Jimmy Buffett's blood in for a test. Everybody's holding it up to the light like they expect to see cheeseburgers and coconuts floating in it."

As Anna flings a handful of papers in my face I flinch, but she laughs. I feel like I'm drowning in this mess, but she's swimming in it. All I want to do is follow her upstream. That's all I ever want to do, but I can never match her colors. Maybe I'm paranoid, but I think deep down she's come to that realization. Or perhaps not so deep?

I'm suspicious of Anna's initial reaction to my job loss because she can often be all sunny and accepting of things on the surface, but then make an abrupt turn. Maybe this is a bad example, but at a wedding reception in the fall of 2006 she purposely tripped this guy Tim McCardle. McCardle is one of these guys that not only make racist remarks but also have to try to bring you in, like we're all on the same side. Simple stuff like "Hey, Reiner, one more Haitian comes out of the kitchen and we're out of here, right?" Most people just ignore him, but Anna, who had been all smiles up to that point, decided to stick out her foot and send him reeling onto the parquet floor with a splat that split his nose open. We fled before McCardle even knew what hit him, but when we got outside I saw our car had been moved to directly in front of the catering hall. It was all premeditated and planned. Right down to the getaway. "Damn straight. I've been setting that up for two years," Anna said. She really seemed to get off on it. On a side road, only a couple of miles from the catering hall, she abruptly pulled over and we ended up having sex in the car. It was kind of a turn-on for me, too, having your wife trip a bigot. But, like I said, this isn't the best example because these calculated moves of hers aren't always so righteous and honorable. A better example will come to me.

I'd had this job even before I knew Anna. I was about eight months in when I first encountered her at a bus stop and saved her from one of those parrot guys—you know, the ones who walk around with a macaw on their shoulder that's crapping down the back of their shirt. They're just hoping, praying, that some pretty girl will walk up and ask, "What's the birdie's name? What kind is it?" They're all over down here in Florida, these guys: bus stops, the beach, McDonald's. It's very sad the way loneliness walks around in warm climates. All-year sunshine and efficiencies with no AC make this place a petri dish for desolation.

On that afternoon, Anna was wearing flat shoes and a ground-scraping gauzy dress and I could spot from fifty paces away that she was obviously a bird lover. Maybe not the big, squawking, talking Polly-wants-a-cracker kind, but certainly a fan of the more elusive of the species, the ones that skitter through the brush giving you a quick glimpse of a yellow chest or a burnt orange plume. She was smiling at the macaw guy but was obviously trapped, so I stepped in and asked the requisite questions. They hate it when a dude asks the questions. I blocked Anna from view and asked, "What's the birdie's name? What kind is it? Why do you let it crap down the back of your tropical shirt like that?"

And off he went, disappearing quicker than you can say, "For my next trick, I'll need a volunteer." When I turned to nod at Anna, she was giggling and said—I do not lie—"You're a lifesaver."

In all my years, no one else had ever said to me, "You're a lifesaver." Half the time the people I save from the macaw guys look at me as if my pitiful rescue act is less than a step above the birdman's lonely cry for help, but not Anna. She was not only appreciative of my valor; she wanted more. She asked me if I could pull the top of her water bottle up. It had been driving her nuts. She'd been pulling and tugging at it, and there were actually these two tiny drops of sweat at the border of her ginger-colored hairline from the struggle. As I watched, they slid down to the middle of her forehead and then stopped running as if they'd crystallized. When I reached for the bottle, she said, "Thank you. Thank you."

She shouldn't have. I couldn't get it open.

I lie back on the bed. I'm exhausted. "A half day of unemployment and you're going to become an afternoon sleeper?" Anna says.

"And now we've got Andrew in that private school," I say. "I can't stop thinking how everything adds up."

"We'll deal with it."

"I'm just . . . I know so many people are going through this but . . ."

"Nothing happens until it happens to you."

"Yeah."

"Just clean this mess up before you fall asleep," she says before heading to the kitchen to boil up some tea. "Put the pages back in order and I'll put it all under the microscope after dinner. I want to go through all the fine print."

Propping myself back up on one elbow, I scan through three pages of Outplacement Services and then skip ahead to something called ISP Funding Rights. I don't know what ISP is, but the people who head it up are called "fiduciaries of the ISP." And they operate under the ERISA. What the hell is the ERISA? If we as a people were at some point to draw the line at using an acronym, I would think it would be at ERISA.

I feel a little dizzy and one arm is shaking. I'm not sure if it's from the awkward way I'm propped up or a fear that this is not just the end of my job, but of other things, things I don't even know about yet.

The whole situation reminds me of the sensation parents go through when they lose track of a small child in a large department store. The heart immediately gallops, the sweat pours. It takes only a second before you think you will never see that child again. I swear that's how I feel, that I will never find a good, decent job again.

I make a slick but sloppy airplane out of a 1-800 twenty-four-hour-a-day mental health service brochure and send it crashing toward Anna's open closet, then lie flat on the bed, my mind racing again. I do all kinds of crazy calculations in my head, methodically trying to decipher where we're at financially and emotionally. Mortgage, utilities, cable, landscaping, two car loans, Andrew's tuition, the home equity loan . . . What am I forgetting? The deposit we put down on new window installation. How are we ever going to make good on the balance? Life insurance, car insurance, Florida windstorm insurance, COBRA. You know things are going to be bad once you're forced to get health insurance named after a deadly snake. What else? *Food.* We eat so much damned food between the regular grocery store and Costco, Sam's Club, BJ's . . . Why the hell do we belong to all three? And that Best Buy card and the Rooms To Go with no interest until 2010? It's 2010! Damn.

The big company sets you free with enough severance to cover short-term debts, a bookload of financial advice, entrée to a high-priced career planner, and mental health counseling to feign off "the blues." I know I'm at the beginning, but where does it end? Being thrust out into the job market after eighteen years is akin to suddenly having to take your driver's license road test all over again. You thought you were good for life, and now he's back, this bespectacled guy in a skinny tie shaking his head and checking off all the wrong boxes. You just know you are going to fail.

I fall into a feverish sleep and when I wake up I am sweaty, it is still light, and stuck to my face is a green 401(k) form that has three words highlighted in bold lettering: "Expanded Rollover Options."

I frantically start putting the papers back into a neat stack for Anna, but I'm afraid that the more fine print she reads, the more I will begin to appear a liability. At her work everything is analyzed, even stool samples. Sooner or later she's going to get around to putting *me* under the microscope. I know it, because everything is going to crap.

triple backflip

You know, I still think I'm going to do something magnificent one day, something that will culminate with three triple backflips and a bear hug from Bela Karolyi. Just for that instant I'd be a man in triumph; Bela coming out of retirement to put those big hands around my tiny waist, lifting me up high where everybody could see me even though I'd be too overwhelmed by my own achievement to see anybody else."

Our dog Alonzo—two parts collie, one part Burmese mountain dog— listens to these little soliloquies of mine but then he just laughs that gruff, kennel-cough laugh of his.

Whenever I get distraught, which I believe is pretty much going to be every second now, I hear a voice in my head say, "You better do a little func- tioning." What does that mean—walk the dog? Take out the garbage? Usually, the last thing I do at night is take Alonzo for a stroll. We circle around out front, trying to find the moon through the high trees. "Where is it? Where is it tonight, boy?" Then I sit down on a patch of grass and throw him a wish like I'd throw him a bone. He usually listens patiently.

But not tonight. Even he's not buying my false bravado. I'm just a talking stool sample. Insulted, I tug at his leash and pull him toward the sidewalk, back up the edge of the driveway.

"Zo. Hey, Zo." A voice rises up from the other side of the car.

But there's no one there.

Alonzo pulls me in the other direction and on the stoop next door, half camouflaged by the shrubbery, I see the tip of a lit cigarette and then a tiny hooded girl.

"Hey," I say just as Alonzo jerks me across a small patch of grass and up to her concrete steps.

Her head down, she cups Alonzo's face in her hands and rubs noses with him. "Ooooh, I love a chilly nose. Your nose is a big, wet ice-cream cone, isn't it, Zo?"

"I take it you know Alonzo," I say.

"He gets loose from your daughter once in a while," she says, glancing up at me. Jagged pieces of black hair spill out of the hood. She is thin-lipped with a pointy nose and big round, angelic eyes that captivate the second they widen.

"Yeah, he does like to escape once in a while," I say.

"Alex," she says, holding a hand out limply but pulling it away and tucking it back into her sweatshirt before I can get anywhere near it.

I've only ever seen this girl from a distance. Since our home is on the corner, Alex's family is our closest neighbor proximity-wise, but I barely know them. The dad always seems a bit ornery and rushed and the rest of the flock make themselves pretty scarce. Anna tried to give me a rundown once—a daughter, Alex, I guess, about twenty-three or twenty-four; a son, Troy, I think, who's a little younger. Mom operates a small spa near the airport.

"Your daughter's kind of a snob, huh?" Alex says in a tone that doesn't seem harsh, only matter-of-fact.

"She's just better than the rest of us," I say.

"On rainy, dreary days your wife looks like Mumbai," Alex says. "All that color running through a drab day."

"Oh, OK. I get it. I think. That's her thing. Colorful."

"Not a bad thing," Alex says, looking away.

I'm not sure I like seeing all of us through Alex's discerning eyes.

"You're kind of scary-looking in the dark," she says.

"Yeah, I've heard that before. All right, nice meeting you," I say.

"You work from home?" she says, looking directly back at me. "You have one of those businesses where you can just jack on the computer all day?"

"Actually, I just lost my job," I say. "Today."

"Bumma, all those mouths to feed," she says, mockingly jutting her lower jaw out and gaping her mouth open like a baby bird.

"It's turning into the longest day of my life. I fell asleep when I got home and now I'm never going to be able to sleep tonight."

"I can grab you some Ambien. Two bucks apiece," she says.

"No, no. I'm fine," I respond, but she's already turning her head away again.

I realize she's been looking off toward the brightly lit minor-league base-ball park a few miles west of us.

"Game tonight," I say.

"Yeah."

She puts a fresh cigarette in her mouth but doesn't light it and it bounces delicately as she continues to talk. "I like that the game's far enough away that you can't ever hear the crowd or the crack of the bat at all," she says. "But if you stare long enough you can catch the sight of a ball when someone hits a high pop or a home run. It's like watching for shooting stars."

"Only the odds are better."

"Yeah, right-o. The odds are better," she says, pulling Alonzo close, grip-ping him tightly enough that he'd have to fight to get away. "Oh, Zo. You're a big hairy quilt. Listen, I know a guy who runs five businesses. He hired me to answer his phone once, but it got crazy. I never knew how to answer be-cause he had so many things going on. Maybe I could hook you up with him."

"What are the five businesses?"

"I forget them all," she says. "One is pressure cleaning. And he caters Jamaican food. Oh, and car detailing. He has all the stuff for that. And he does the Pergo flooring but everybody does that. I don't know if he counts that as one of his five. The businesses are always changing. People subcon-tract him for a lot of stuff. Oh, he's into bootleg movie sales big-time. He's a very enterprising dude."

"Does he also, by chance, sell weed?"

"A little, I think—Blueberry Kush. But I don't think he counts that as one of his five, either. He doesn't even use a phone anymore, but I can prob-ably put you in contact with him if you're interested in some work."

"Let me see how things go," I say.

"Pays under the table so it won't screw with your unemployment."

"That's a plus. You attending school now, college?" I ask.

"No."

"Working?"

"No, not this week."

"Does that mean . . ."

"Oh, there," she says, pointing the unlit cigarette toward the horizon. "There goes one."

watering down the Gatorade

That girl's disturbed," Kristin says.

"I don't know about that," I say.

"What, is she your *Lost in Translation* girl now?"

"I talked to her for two minutes. She knows a very enterprising dude. He may be a good contact. But let's not change the subject."

I've finally gotten Kristin and Andrew to sit still. Anna is in the other room hunched over her calculator, so this family meeting is being taken off course by Kristin's apparent disdain for our neighbor.

"I didn't even know you knew her."

"Well, now you know."

Earlier, when I announced my job loss to the kids, they seemed totally indifferent, like it wasn't really their problem. I don't want to frighten them, but I need them to know this could affect them enormously and I need their help.

"Dad," Andrew says, lying down across the couch. "Do you just have a list or something you can give us?"

"Try to stay upright," I say. "Your mom will just be a second."

"I have to be at work. *I* have a job," Kristin says.

Kristin looks like her mom, only stringier. Her hair's stringier, her gangly arms and legs are stringier. When she's curled up on the couch, she looks like an exhausted ball of yarn. Every time I call her, she answers the phone, "What now?" I'm not sure if that greeting is for everybody or only me. She drives this ancient VW Scirocco that must be 101 years old. I was going to help her buy a car but she insisted on paying for one herself with the money she makes working at a bath shop downtown. Know two things about Kristin: (1) After she blew out the candles at her fourteenth birthday party, she turned to Anna and me and said, "OK, you two have done what you could. Parenting ends at fourteen. I'll take it from here." And she pretty much has. (2) She has a 4.7 grade point average.

"I'll take notes," Andrew says, stretching his long arm over to the desk and pulling out a pen and a scrap of paper. His loose, curly hair flops over his oddly angular quarterback's face (I don't know where it comes from). I'm amazed at how big he's getting and frightened by how much food he can consume. I hate looking at my own children as consumers. Andrew has so many good traits—earnest, athletic, generous, master of Call of Duty: Modern Warfare 2—but all I'm looking at right now are his massive incisors, and I know he's capable of devouring everything in sight.

"OK, while we're waiting for Mom can we at least talk about the laptops? There's no reason for them to always be plugged in," I say. "I know you don't want to deal with recharging but that's how they're made."

"You don't know how laptops are made," Kristin says.

"And the phone chargers."

"Why didn't you just retire before they fired you?" Kristin says.

"Is this why you watered down the Gatorade tonight?" Andrew asks.

"I didn't do it consciously, but maybe subconsciously I added less powder or more water," I say.

"Or both," Andrew says.

"Just because you don't have a job, don't act like you're our boss now," Kristin says. "That's not going to fly. You're not some overlord now."

"Overlord. I like that," Andrew says.

"Thanks," Kristin says.

"Don't team up against me," I say, even though I like seeing Andrew become an ally for his sister. There was a time, not that long ago, when he'd go mum and barely speak his mind.

He is often quiet but he is not shy. When he was younger I made the mistake of thinking he was genetically inhibited, that he'd inherited my social reserve and tendency to withdraw. But one afternoon we were at the skating rink and there was a race for a prize. An intimidating array of older boys assembled on the starting line, as did Andrew without hesitation. Lost by a mile, but he went for it. The reserve was off. I was never like that, no matter how big the prize. I just cowered back and watched. These days, when irritating relatives corner Andrew and say, "Why are you so shy?" he responds, "I'm not shy. I just don't have anything to say at the moment. Check with me later." He seems to know who he is, even if everybody else—including me—isn't privy to exactly who that is quite yet.

"Can we keep Showtime? I have to see *Dexter*," Andrew says.

We don't live that high to begin with, so when we set out to prune our list of meager luxuries, we have little choice but to hit the movie channels. They're always the first to go.

"Maybe we can just get Showtime for the twelve weeks when *Dexter* is on and then cancel it."

"I want it when *The Tudors* are on; then you can cancel it," Kristin says.

"There are other things," I say. "We can really make a dent if we all use the same shampoo. I counted six different in each bathroom. You can buy one kind in bulk and—"

"I'm not using shampoo that comes in a pail," Kristin says, getting up.

"Where are you going?"

"To make a point," she says. "I'll be right back."

"One cereal each?" I say to Andrew. "Can you live with that?"

"Cinnamon Toast Crunch," Andrew says.

"I'll eat that, too," I say. "I'll eat whatever is there. That's going to be my attitude. My needs will be met by whatever is already available."

Kristin comes sauntering back in wearing a pair of yellow rubber gloves that extend up to her elbows.

"Look where being cheap and cutting costs got you before," she says, raising one arm and giving me the stilted wave of a princess on parade.

OK, when I needed to repair some stucco near our side door I hired these suspect-looking guys going house-to-house offering labor on the cheap. The job looked perfectly fine when they finished but they must have somehow put the grating for the stucco up against some wiring in the wall because every time someone touches the door now they get shocked.

"Electrocuted," Kristin says.

Now we keep a pair of rubber gloves in the flower box near the door to avoid electrocution, and it's been working out fine. (Unless you're barefoot and don't know about the rubber sandals we stash there.)

"I admit, that was foolhardy of me," I say. "But that's not the kind of cost cutting I'm talking about now."

"Foolhardy," Kristin says.

"I like that. Foolhardy," Andrew says.

"I'm also looking at the Go-Gurts. I think we can get a big tub of yogurt and then put them in those little Tupperware cups we already have with the snap lids."

"Auck!" Kristin says.

"What? I'll set it up. In a year's time, how many do you think you eat? We have to start multiplying this stuff out. You'd be shocked at how much we could save."

"I really don't feel like multiplying my Go-Gurts by fifty-two right now," Kristin says.

"I want to start having a hamburger night," I say. "I know it's not all that healthy, but when McDonald's has the thirty-nine-cent burgers on Wednesdays we really should be taking advantage of being able to feed a family of four on a dollar fifty-six. You multiply that by fifty-two and it's . . ."

"Eighty-one dollars and twelve cents," Kristin says.

"What about fries?" Andrew says.

"No, that would blow it," I say. "And we get drinks at home, too."

"What about cheeseburgers? They're only forty-nine cents on Wednesdays," Andrew says.

"No, that would cost a dollar ninety-six."

"So?"

"That doesn't sound as good," I say.

"How does a dollar ninety-six not sound as good as a dollar fifty-six?" Kristin says.

"Dad's right. It doesn't sound as good," Andrew says.

"I'm going to buy my own shampoo and just nobody else touch it," Kristin says.

Andrew sits up and glares into the bubbling fish tank at the end of the couch. "How much energy do these fish tanks use?" he says.

"I don't know. Probably too much," I say. "I don't know why your mom has to light them up every night. They get plenty of natural light in the daytime."

"They're not even pretty fish. They look like lake fish," Andrew says.

"I know."

"You guys are idiots," Kristin says, before shouting, "Mom, the idiots are going to turn out the lights in your fish tanks!"

"What's going on?" Anna says, rushing into the room.

"Dad wants to shut down our computers and all the fish tank lights and have us all dipping into a community pail of shampoo," Kristin says.

"Get away from the tanks," Anna says, stepping in front of me.

"We were just talking about things we could cut back on and . . ."

"It's not like the fish are reading in there," Andrew says.

"Is this your idea of a family meeting?" Anna says.

"I'm trying," I say.

I can't quite put it into words for them, but, to be honest, I just want to break away from the fear that all the responsibility is on me. I like the idea of us all pulling together, even if it's just to survive in the short term. I want to make the kids realize a big chunk of the money coming into this house was from my paycheck and now that has stopped. It's that simple. They have to understand that in these harrowing times, in order to stay alive, we may have to water down the Gatorade.

"Hey, if nothing else, I just want this meeting to make the point that we're all in this together," I say.

"Got it." Kristin gets up, heading for the kitchen.

"And I want to have a garage sale to make extra money. Everybody start gathering up things."

"You're on your own with that," Anna says.

"Here," Andrew says, handing me a sheet of paper that reads NOTES across the top, but then there's all white space except for a single word: "OverLord."

Anna drags me into the den. "You're scaring them," she says.

She's still in her work clothes and her hair is a frizzy mess, stray tips wet from sucking and chewing on them while she crunched the numbers. "OK," she says, running her finger across her notes. "It's imperative that you sign up for unemployment within twenty-four hours, so do that tomorrow. But the good news is—"

"I didn't expect this day to end with good news."

"Relatively speaking," she says. "I'm going to go over this ten more times before I go to bed tonight, but it appears to me that once the unemployment checks start coming—by the seventeenth if you sign up right away—and with the severance that should be arriving by the middle of next month we'll be OK on income for twenty-one weeks."

"That's a lucky number."

"That's how much time you have to find a job, to figure out exactly what you want to do."

"That's a lot of time."

"It's enough."

"So I can stop shaking? I can relax?"

"Well, I don't know about relax," Anna says, already punching at the numbers again. "But you can allow the children to have cheese on their burgers for a little while longer."

avett brothers at the parker

Signing up for unemployment benefits online puts it all into perspective: I'm screwed.

After getting the twenty-one-week reprieve, I was planning to turn the first days of this mess into a mini-vacation. Spurred on by Gillian's report on her first official day of unemployment: "I slept till 10:30 and watched two hours of *Will & Grace* reruns on Lifetime. Ate Doritos for lunch!"

Trying to relax, I sit outside on the porch, reading *Spin* magazine.

But it doesn't take.

Eat some blueberry pancakes.

Doesn't take.

Put *Mermaid Avenue* on the iPod.

Doesn't take.

When Anna headed off to work at seven-thirty this morning she threw me a wave and said, "Have a . . ." before stopping short. I certainly wasn't expecting a "Have a great day" or a "grand day" or even a "good day." I would have accepted "nice" but she just stuttered, giggled loosely, and settled on, "Have a . . . day."

I can do that.

Even though there's this constant mix of the excitement of being liberated from the routine and the dread of not knowing how I will ever make a decent living again. One second I'm elated about going on to other things in life—doesn't everybody dream of being set free? No boss. No deadlines. And the next I want to puke. I can't seem to get into that vacation mode, so I follow Anna's mandate and go online to fill out the state unemployment form.

I'm shocked by the math: Even the maximum amount allotted is barely milk money. I'm not sure if Anna figured that into her calculations. And the thought of having to report to the state where I applied for a job "each week" does nothing to ease my nausea.

People have already started asking me, "So, what are you going to do? How are you going to make money?"

All newspapers are in a state of severe contraction, if not death throes. Looking for a job there, or in any other part of the industry I committed my career to, would be more of a sick joke than an act of hope.

I had the bad fortune to be in the not-very-creative end of a creative enterprise, so I had two strikes against me right there. I used to pitch human-interest-type story ideas to get a byline but it rarely worked out. Once in a while I'd get to juice up a listing with a little flair. Like for *The Life and Music of Celia Cruz* I wrote, "Take a journey through the career of the 'salsa queen' as a large cast of singers and dancers bring to life the . . ."

I could do that all day. And I did.

But what employable skill did that represent? In retrospect, it was both too specialized and too unspecial to help me now. I always seem to be hard to characterize. When Gillian and Artie and I imagined what would come out of the exploded heads of our colleagues and it got to me it wasn't that easy. Everyone just sort of went silent and then changed the subject. I guess a lot of people thought I was a dud but I was always listening to every word they said and on the day of our exploding heads I had hoped someone had noticed and would blurt out, "If Jeff's head erupts the entire second floor of this building will look as if it is the dump for everything meaningful in our lives that ever fell behind a couch and was never retrieved. People will be scavenging through the debris and come across some personal scrap of paper or trinket they thought was lost forever, eternally intertwined with cat hair and stuck to a melted Sugar Daddy. And as the survivors step and crunch over all the little pieces of themselves that have been discarded and forgotten, they will suddenly get it. 'Man,' they'll say, 'all this time, he's been storing all this. That's what Jeff's been doing. He's been collecting *us*.'"

I always think of amazing stuff that other people could say about me, but they never do. That will probably hurt me when it comes to getting references.

"Focus. Focus," I say aloud to myself. I try to block out memories of the old job and concentrate on getting my unemployment benefits established. The one saving grace of this online unemployment form is that at the very end you have to pick the occupation that most resembles yours from a list provided. It is in alphabetical order so the first one is "Able Seaman."

The job title stops me cold, and the description sends me: "Stand watch at bow or on wing of bridge to look for obstructions in path of vessel. Turn wheel on bridge as directed by first mate."

Further details, which describe rig overhaul and running gear, make me a little nervous but, since I'd have the first mate supervising, maybe that wouldn't be a deal breaker. I could start tomorrow.

My brother-in-law says, "Jeez, you have a little severance. At least take it easy for a couple of months. Give yourself the summer. Let's play some golf." I love the summer, but I would rather be the main course of a lone cannibal dining in a gnat-infested ravine than play golf with my brother-in-law.

I picture Gillian lying around, singing the "Happy Not Working Song," her cats brushing her hair, finches painting her toenails. Artie is probably bowling.

Perhaps I'm the type who does have to wallow in this a little bit. That's my form of vacation. But I desperately want to lighten up, bring a more cavalier attitude to the situation, at least for today.

There is one thing that brings me a glorious sense of relief. You could corner me and demand to know what is going on around the metro area tonight, but even with a gun to my head I would have to declare: "I have no freaking idea."

Eat Doritos for dinner.

Doesn't take.

loons over the black water

No, no, no. That can't be what I think it is. Damn!

A three-man crew is putting up a DEAD END sign right on the southwest corner of my yard. All three men are thrusting it into the ground as if they are staking the territory once and for all.

"Why?" I ask the town worker wearing the cleanest shirt.

"Because your road's a dead end," he says.

"No, why now? It's always been a dead end but we never had a sign. Why now?"

"It's been on the docket. We're finally getting to it," he says. "We're planting them on the whole south side this week. From here to Seacrest Boulevard."

I ask him if there's any way they could skip a sign on this block because it sits right in front of my house and things aren't going so well as it is, and to have a big blaring dead-end sign greeting me every day is just . . .

They laugh.

"I hear you, brother," the worker with the dirtiest shirt says.

"Do you think you could at least put it on the opposite corner?" I ask.

"Why?"

"Because we're brothers and you hear me," I say.

They laugh again.

"It's going to face the other way," clean shirt says. "Once it's in you won't even see it from your front porch."

"Don't take it personal," dirty shirt says.

But how can I not?

As they dump a sack of cement mix into a wheelbarrow, the dust of it floats up and lightly covers all of us. I look at my bare arms turning gray and can't help thinking I am covered in loser dust.

I'm overreacting to everything and I need to cry. I almost think I have to. I'm OK during the day as I tend to the mechanics of dealing with employment, but I wake up at first light with such a sense of doom that my face scrunches up as if I'm going to bawl like a baby and then—nothing.

I think it's because I do all my crying during *Extreme Makeover: Home Edition.* The arc of emotion is overwhelming. I weep so prolifically during the heartbreaking stories and eventual revelation of new appliances that I have nothing left for the basic tragedies of my own life. It does not seem fair.

In surveys I've been reading, experts state that if you've been terminated from a job you've had for more than five years you need to grieve. Certain things I can do. I can put tinfoil up on windows and sleep late. I can lie in the dark and listen to Nick Cave and the Bad Seeds drone on about loons over the black water. I can fold up into the fetal position with relative ease. But when it comes to weeping, I'm caulked up like the seams of a brand-new six-jet master suite tub.

I pick up the phone to call the free mental health counseling service the company provided with my walking papers, not because of the crying problem, but because of a glitch with their online depression screening. To gauge your stability during the past week, it has statements such as "I did not feel like eating," "my appetite was poor," and "I could not 'get going.'" And then you pick from the multiple-choice answers, which include the easy-to-grasp extremes of "rarely" and "most of the time." My problem is with the other two alternatives: "sometimes" and "occasionally." I just don't know the difference. Am I sad "sometimes" or "occasionally"? I'm stumped. And I'll get a grade on this, so I don't want to guess.

"I need to know which is better," I tell a phone counselor named Elizabeth. "'Occasionally' or 'sometimes'?"

"Well, it would depend on the question," Elizabeth says.

"I hate my life. Occasionally or sometimes?" I say, trying to simplify the situation for her.

Elizabeth starts giving me some gobbledygook about how specific words—like *sometimes*—are used in the evaluation for a reason. Apparently it's extremely scientific and perhaps beyond my level of comprehension.

I think she's either messing with me or, like a sex-talk operator, she gets paid by the minute. There's some goateed supervisor over her shoulder prodding her on to meet her quota: "Lizzy, if you got him hooked on *sometimes*, run with it. Keep him on the line. Throw some metaphysics at him."

To stop her, I ask if she watches *Extreme Makeover*.

"Oh, yes," she says, as if I've suddenly brightened her day. "It's fantastic what they do for people."

"I know I should cry, but I think I use up my allotted crying during that show," I confess.

"It is sad, but it's also uplifting," she says.

"Maybe if I thought of my own problems during the show, I could piggyback—"

"What?"

"Piggyback. Piggyback my own emotions onto those the family on the show is experiencing."

"No," Elizabeth says. "You need to release your emotions during your own personal time. Or you can share it with others close to you."

"Mark didn't even give me a thank-you."

"Who?"

"The boss. Eighteen years with the company and I didn't even get a simple 'Thank you for your service.' Nothing."

"Eighteen years. Wow."

"After I'd signed all the papers Mark stopped me at the door and I thought he was going to say something sincere but all he wanted was my security code for the front entrance."

At the time all I could think was where are the kind words? In the end, even death-row prison guards get a little sweet on their condemned prisoners, go soft and pamper them in those final moments. In the movies the predator that killed forty-two innocents ultimately gets a "Hey, you're not all that bad, Jimmy Ray" before they shave his ankles and strap him down.

"It's a business decision. You can't take it so personal," Elizabeth says.

"Forty-seven hundred."

"What?"

"That was my secret code."

I explain the unemployment situation I'm in. I mean, I could get all kinds of counseling, but there is really only one cure for this—getting a job. Otherwise I'm just fooling myself.

"Only you know the magnitude of your situation, and it sounds as if you have good reason to be frustrated," Elizabeth says. "But you can't let it overwhelm you. You don't want to unravel."

"But until I get a job, I should be a wreck, right?"

"You need to address these feelings," Elizabeth says. "Would you be more comfortable meeting with a counselor in your area?"

"Are you trying to get rid of me?"

"Not at all."

"They put up a dead-end sign in front of my house today."

"Who did?"

"I don't think I want to see anybody face-to-face right now, but can I call *you* back?"

"Yes, but I can't guarantee that you'll always get me," Elizabeth says.

"Good. I'm just going through the checklist of everything my company is offering. I'm going to the job counseling and the finance classes first thing next week. At least my company is offering some help; I know a lot of others are—"

"It's not your company."

"What?"

"You keep saying 'my company, my company . . .' It's not your company anymore. You're going to have to start thinking that way. These are only services for the transition. Are you only going through the motions or are you actually getting anything out of the transition plan?"

"I'm not sure. I guess occasionally something clicks. I mean, *sometimes*. But I mainly called just to see if you were really there."

"Oh, we're here all right. Just not me. Not all the time, anyway."

"Well I'm here twenty-four/seven," I say. "I guess that's part of the problem."

jarred sauce

I can overhear Anna talking to her aunt Rosie on the phone in the kitchen and I don't want to get out of bed. She is laughing and retelling a humorous story about a woman at the deli. I've heard the tale before, but I like lying here, a cool blue sheet pulled up to my chin, listening. It's Saturday, which is a relief, because I'm not the only one who isn't working. I enjoy hearing Anna's voice so full of life and, in a way, I feel as though I'm spying on her. Because when you're ill or sleeping at an odd time, you might as well have disappeared, right?

Years ago, I was coming out from under a twenty-four-hour bug and woke up sweating. I was in the throes of knocking the heavy blankets away when I heard Anna on the phone relaying the details of a sweet-corn festival we'd attended the previous weekend. In her telling, it sounded a lot more fun than I'd remembered and I suddenly grew curious about what she might say about me when I was nothing but a sweaty fever victim locked away in delirium. And then I heard it: "He's awfully sick, the bum. . . . Oh, I know, I know, he's great that way. I am lucky."

"Great that way . . . lucky . . ." I said in my own raspy voice as I hunkered back down for one more feverish dream.

During a period when I was working nights, it had become a habit for me to try to take a nap on Saturday afternoons. I guess Andrew and Kristin were about eight and eleven when I heard them downstairs talking with their mother about everything from how they could get to the milk in coconuts to whose arms were longer. My name was sprinkled everywhere—Dad would measure their arms. Dad would try to drill a hole and shove a straw into the core of the coconut.

I recall having put one foot on the cold tile floor when I heard Andrew say to his mom, "When's Dad getting up?"

"Soon," Anna said.

"Good, because things are different when he's up," Andrew said.

I put my foot back under the covers. I wanted more. I wanted to enjoy the near distance of their voices a little longer.

But today, paranoid that every change in the timbre of Anna's voice, every muffled phrase is something horrible about me, I can't hop out of bed quick enough.

"Hey, Aunt Rosie says not to worry about being laid off," Anna exclaims as I step into the kitchen.

"Tell her thanks," I say.

"What?" Anna asks into the receiver. "Rosie says, 'Sometimes, God has a strange way of getting his soldiers some rest.'"

Anna's aunt is a big believer in those old adages like "Everything happens for a reason" and—this one really gets me—"Everything that goes around comes around." I know so many backstabbing creeps that should have molten karma raining down on their souls, but the only thing that seems to come around for them is forty-one-foot boats, ski trips to Steamboat Springs, housekeepers that make them Belgian waffles in the middle of the night, five-car garages, and kitchens that are perpetually being remodeled even though the stuff they're tearing out is ten times better than what's in my kitchen.

"Your cousin wants to talk to you," Anna says, holding out the phone.

I didn't even know I had a cousin.

"Gerald. He's at Aunt Rosie's having breakfast."

"Hello. Yeah, how have you been?"

Gerry tells me he left his teaching job and it's the best thing that ever happened to him. He's taken a full-time position with a company that puts jars of spaghetti sauce into boxes for shipping to Olive Garden restaurants.

"Olive Garden uses jarred sauce?" I say.

"All I do all day is pick up a jar, put it in a box, and then pick up a jar and put it in a box and then pick up a jar . . ."

"OK, OK!" I say. "But doesn't that get to you?"

"It's who I am now," he says. "It's the mundane and repetitious that I crave."

I guess there is some solace in that, isn't there? The repetitious and mundane can form a sweet island, especially after you've been fired.

"Yo, I wasn't fired," Gerald says. "It was my choice."

"Oh, I only talk to people who get fired," I say with a laugh, handing the phone back to Anna.

"What'd he say?" Anna asks.

"Olive Garden uses jarred sauce."

"Hey, don't rest too much, soldier boy," Anna says, covering the phone. "You promised to check with Sal about the garbage disposal."

Sal is the type of neighbor who, on a whim, will decide to build a utility shed from scratch one Tuesday, and when he's done (on Thursday), it is slightly larger than his house and appraised at twice as much.

The last time I needed help (to light a gas water heater) I called Sal and he blew me off. I was stunned, but then thought he must be fed up with me constantly taking advantage of his neighborliness. Anna says I shouldn't call, that I need to "put in an appearance." She's always been big on getting me to be more social. About a month after we moved into this neighborhood she accused me of ruining her life. "Because of you," she said, "we have no friends."

She decided to take a stand when she saw two neighbors across the street playing what she said was horseshoes. "Go over there," she demanded, "and talk to them."

"But what would I say? They're playing a game. What am I going to do, ask them the score? I don't even know if people keep score in horseshoes."

"Find out!" she yelled.

I grab an apple off the kitchen counter and start heading out the door to Sal's, but I'm only halfway out when Anna says, "Oh, and stop at that hospital administrator's house—I think that's what she does—on the way. She may have work for you. You know, like you said Artie was doing."

That work she's referring to involves Artie's sideline of doing PR releases for a hospital in Broward County. I recall him telling me about doing one on a doctor using robotics during gastric surgery, but Artie's prose can make anything sound interesting, even a urinary tract infection. I can get a poetic flourish going here or there, but that's about it.

"Hey, does Sal know?" I say, popping my head back in the doorway.

"Know what?"

"That I lost my job."

"Why?"

"I don't like people to know."

the wayward neighbor

Well, look who it is. The man of leisure," says Sal's wife, Peggy, as she flings open the double doors to their home.

This isn't the type of neighborhood where you'd expect to find massive double doors, but Sal had a doctor's appointment fall through one afternoon in 2008, so he "refaced" the entire front of his house. And Peggy never singles it. She always thrusts both doors open at once, as if they're the gates of Narnia.

"Making an appearance," I say.

"Sal was just saying how he bets now that you're not working, you're taking long baths and reading ladies' magazines. Those're his words, not mine. Are you and Anna still going to Orlando to see the dolphins? I know Anna was excited about it. You're not going to let your layoff spoil that, are you?"

"Actually, I had forgotten about that," I say. "But I'm sure nothing is going to spoil that."

"Don't sound so excited," she says, leading me into the house and then taking the first exit into the kitchen. "Sal's by the pool putting in an outdoor shower. I don't know who's going to use it. Not me."

Peggy wears these pointy bras that, along with her tiny waist, make her look like a Jetson mom. For her fortieth birthday there was a big party and all the women wore pointy bras. It was supposed to be a big joke but I have to confess, I found it erotic. Peggy's as pretty as any soap-opera extra, the only person I know who still cheerily wears polka dots, and as perfect a mate as any man could hope for. But I'm currently much more jealous of Sal's station in life.

"I told you civil service, didn't I?" Sal says, jumping up, his hands covered with grout. "You don't see the government laying off anybody."

Sal is all of forty-three years old and collecting a pension. "Didn't you do the math when you got out of high school?" he says. "You're eighteen, you put in twenty, and you're thirty-eight to thirty-nine retired. Boom! The twenty-in pension is the poor man's lottery. I told you that."

When I was first out of high school and had friends signing up with the postal service and the nearby national cemetery, I used to shake my head and think, "Man, who wants to sort mail or dig graves for the rest of his life?" But today I would give up both my elbows to be collecting a pension and still have my whole future ahead of me. Why couldn't I have had the wisdom to think pension first, life second?

Why couldn't I be more like Sal, who now only takes what he refers to as "goofball jobs" such as driving a nursery school bus or staking off turtle nests at the beach? "All my jobs are summer jobs," he says.

Lately he's been operating a small ferry/water taxi that shuttles tourists over to the JFK bunker on Peanut Island, which is about a quarter mile off the coast of Palm Beach.

"Hey, now you can be my first mate," Sal says, getting down on his stomach near the base of the shower stall, trying to limbo his head under a crossbar. "Damn mustache!"

Sal is compact—more jockey than bulldog—and built for tight spaces. But to offset his close-cropped hair he has a bushy mustache that still manages to get in the way during projects.

"No, really. How you taking it so far?" Sal says. "Anything I can do to help?"

"You know what the acronym ERISA stands for?"

"Man, I don't even know what YMCA stands for," he says, shimmying eel-like across the tile. "Once you get past FU and BBQ I'm not interested."

"Well, there's also the matter of our garbage disposal."

"That's more like it. Hand me that dowel. Not the towel! The dowel rod."

"This?"

"Yes, *that*."

Sal often gets short with me when it comes to the mechanical stuff, and I understand. He's always doing some project for me and I never have anything to offer in return. I've known people who switch back and forth with home projects. One weekend Ryan helps Nick put in an electric garage-door opener, and the next Nick helps Ryan hang a new back door at his place. But with Sal and me, it's all one-sided. No one in his right mind would want me to help out with a home-improvement project.

In my own way, I tried to do what I could to show my appreciation. I did always give Sal's chili big props. That's his specialty. Peggy always says, "Sal makes the best chili." To me, it tastes like the usual slop you'd throw on a hot dog, but I like to build a guy up, and what does the common man have to live for if not the recognition of his specialties?

So, whenever I got a taste, I burst out with a big, "Mmmm, this is the best chili this side of the Rio Grande." Or sometimes I'd switch it up with "this side of the Mason-Dixon Line."

Sal always seemed grateful for the chili kudos. Now, whether he considered it compensation for spending six hours ripping through the plaster walls to rewire my bathroom lighting is another question altogether.

"You know, you don't seem all that tense for a guy who just lost his job," Sal says. "I pegged you as a guy who'd immediately go all fetal."

"Well, Anna's got it all figured out how I have twenty-one weeks to get into something new."

"Anna, yeah, I bet she's going to write up a daily regimen for every one of those weeks. I've seen those housekeeping charts and graphs on the fridge at your place. Looks like something you'd see at the Pentagon."

"She seems to understand it's going to take some time."

"Listen, make yourself useful and take the hose and just add water to that bucket of grout until it's about the consistency of pancake batter," Sal says. "Be my handyman for a change."

"Sure."

To be honest, I have no desire to be called "handy." I want to be referred to as dynamic, effervescent, and righteous. I've always wanted to be known as strapping, electrifying, and uncompromising. But "handy"? No thanks.

"Were you only helping me because Anna would bug you otherwise?" I ask.

"No, but the alarm was when she would be on the phone with Peggy and say, 'Jeff's going to try it himself.'"

"That's an alarm? The words 'Jeff's going to try it himself'? Be honest, if you see my name on the caller ID tomorrow, do you pick up?"

"Well, when your name comes up, I treat it like a 911 call, something I can't ignore. But don't worry about it. You can call me anytime," Sal says. "I'll always help you out. Especially now. One more rejection and you're likely to crack. It's not easy not having a full-time job. I'll tell you, sometimes I'd kill for one more hour of OT."

Sal's four-year-old son, Graham, walks about two feet in front of my face and burps.

"Bless you," I say.

"Don't bless him for that!" Peggy yells at me.

"I was burping right at you," Graham says proudly.

I quickly grab him. "Don't you be aiming your burps at me. Don't you be using me for burp target practice," I say as he squeals and slithers away.

"You know," Sal says, standing up. "We should hang more, especially now that you've got twenty-one weeks to kill. That might make me feel better because right now you're like the wayward son who only comes around when he needs money. Only you need home repairs. You're like . . ."

"I am the wayward neighbor."

"Jesus," Sal says, looking down in the bucket at my side. "I said pancake batter, not diarrhea."

dear leena or lyra . . .

I don't know the exact house, but I know the car of the hospital administrator. I used to think she was a prostitute because she drives a burgundy-colored Corvette with a sparkly license plate frame, has radiant hair, and I once saw her wearing nightclub-style clothes in the daytime.

Historically, our neighborhood has constant turnover. It's lined with mostly cinder-block starter homes and, except for a handful of us who have decided it's not in our best interests to move up in the world, young families come and go every year. Of course, Sal is the exception to all of that. His starter home is now three times the size it was when he moved in and has twice been highlighted in the Home & Patio section of our local paper.

The Corvette isn't out front, but I spot the glitter of the license plate frame and the taillights poking out of the open garage. I kind of nervously walk past the house and then linger. Anna didn't even sound completely sure that the woman *is* a hospital administrator. To just show up on her doorstep on a Saturday morning seems like the move of a desperate unemployed man three months and change in, not on day three—or is it four?

"Reiner." A voice comes up behind me. "What are you doing roaming the streets?"

"Hey," I say, recognizing the big Irish face. Patrick or Thomas, I think.

"I haven't seen you since the meat wagon," he says.

"Right." A guy who worked for one of those meat delivery services had an overstock at the end of one week and pulled down our block to see who wanted T-bones, three for fifteen bucks. I declined and I think I recall this Patrick calling me an asshole for not taking advantage of "the chance of a lifetime."

"I hear you lost your job. Jesus, that's tough. Bessie and I were talking about it last night. I don't know what I'd do. What are you going to do?"

"I don't know."

"Yeah, Jesus. Well, we'll keep thinking of you."

"Thanks," I say.

"There is no work, you know. But I guess you know that."

"I guess I do now."

"Hey," he says as he's heading back to his driveway, "don't turn into one of those Cheeveresque guys lurking in our bedrooms at night and stealing change off our bureaus."

"I'll try not to."

I can't stand that part of this. Some people will say there is currently no stigma attached to being unemployed because it's "just the times; business is bad." But I will tell you straight-out: Twenty minutes into unemployment, everything changes. The taint rolls over you in waves of pity, from the way people look at you in the street to the subjectless emails from people you haven't had contact with in ages that need no explanation: "Sorry to hear it, man."

Even the "hello" has become excruciating. Three times this week I have gotten boisterous "top o' the morning" greetings while riding my bicycle. I'm not even counting the nods or car-horn toots, the friendly kind. You know how hard it is to tap the horn in order to release a friendly "tweep"? Well, people have mastered it at the sight of me. They can smell my desperation, and the effervescent "howdy do" is their version of putting money in my cup on a street corner.

It feels like all your insecurities and eccentricities are magnified when unemployment is added to the mix. Even my bicycle has taken on a new identity. About a month ago the spokes started to pop and snap in half and the rims began caving in slightly, but I thought it was funny. When the spokes popped, they made a plink-plinking sound that made me feel as if I were commandeering a rolling music box. I kidded that if Mr. Bojangles had turned in his sole-peeling shoes for a bike, this is the two-wheeler he'd have used to cruise through the foggy bayou and lean outside jailhouses as he slept off the burdensome drunk of the roving entertainer. Now add "unemployed" to that scenario, and everything changes. The bike while I was employed: big goof. Unemployed: the saddest goddamned thing you've ever seen in your life.

That first night in bed, surrounded by my papers of involuntary separation, Anna said, "At least I know you're not too proud to take any kind of job." But the last thing I want to be is someone who makes the best of things. I've always hated that cliché of someone dying and a family member recalling, "Oh, his spirits were high. He was flirting with the nurses, joking right up till the end."

Not me. The joking stops now. I don't want any of you SOBs saying, "Oh, I ran into Reiner at the mall and he was laughing and spouting one-liners. Making the best of things." No—I looked miserable. I hit you up for twenty bucks. That's the story you take back to your cronies.

And Patrick isn't the first person to tilt his head like an Irish setter and ask, "What are you going to do?" That's the real question that keeps nagging me.

"You just need to get a blog going," Anna's mother told me. "I hear you get money every time somebody clicks on it." I've always thought blogging is for people who aren't having sex, but I guess I'd be willing to abstain, too, if there is some money to be made.

What are you going to do?

I find myself semi-excited about getting another opportunity and applying for positions I may not be completely qualified for, but what the heck, right? I've already spent hours online reading the small print in the job requirement sections and checking them off one by one. *"Must be fair and balanced and able to provide lively copy."* Whoa, I'm all about the "lively." Boom!—my application and inflated credentials are off to *Stars and Stripes*.

"Promotional writer to work on everything from quarterly magazine to fliers." Fliers, that's one medium I've never been published in. Boom! One application to Liberty University. Wait, make that two in case one goes directly to junk mail.

"Willingness to contribute to both print and online products." I'm willing, I'm willing . . . *"Desk skills are a plus."* I can clear a desk out quicker than you can say, "Artie, can I see you for a minute?" Boom! My name is in the running at the *Northern Virginia Daily*.

The Tennessean—Boom! *Amarillo Globe-News*—Boom! *The Decatur Daily*—Boom! *The Martinsville Bulletin*—Boom!

Where the hell is Martinsville?

I know I need to jump-start myself, up my game if you will, and work the odds. If it's 30 to 1, I need to get thirty applications out in a single morning and start preparing my acceptance speeches. What if the *Amarillo Globe* actually does call back?

But they don't. Nor does anyone else. No one even acknowledges receiving the applications. I don't want to whine to Anna about that. It's hard to even talk about it out loud. I really do believe that if you keep throwing stuff out there, maybe, maybe just by mistake something hits. I don't care if it's from interaction with some stranger on the street. I don't mind being branded. *Here I am. Have you got something for me?*

What are you going to do?

I keep racking my brain over what else I could be qualified for but that time between high school and my attempts at college was only crammed with odd jobs—retail clerk, preschool van driver, junk mail bundler at a sweepstakes company—and short flights of fancy, like attempting to poach clams with my cousin Eric on Long Island's Great South Bay. I wonder what the market price for littlenecks is this time of year?

What are you going to do?

They say all the jobs are in health care, but the only position I think I could handle is surgical tech. I hear it's just like prepping a salad bar, only you get to wear scrubs.

What are you going to do?

I mentioned to Anna how I once wanted to be a UPS or FedEx guy (mostly because I once found a UPS worker's pay stub in a parking lot and it was astronomical, even without the OT) but never thought I could make the grade. The drivers all seem too energetic, healthy, and incapable of getting lost.

"The UPS guys that pick up at the lab look great in brown shorts and all have really well-defined calf muscles," Anna muttered, sort of agreeing with my theory.

Before they went out of business I did think I could be a DHL driver. They always seemed a little rough around the edges, like maybe they drank orange soda for breakfast, dodged paying child support, and were indifferent about whether their girlfriends ever bother taking their tops off during sex. And got lost . . . a lot.

What are you going to do?

It's perplexing to me how I ended up here in South Florida to begin with. I got in a car one day. And it wasn't even my car. It was one of those deals where you drive somebody else's car because they're too old to drive. I forget what they called it in the ad I spotted in *Newsday*. I think it was Southline. "Make a beeline for the Sunshine State on us. All gas and tolls covered."

I'd been listening to that old Billy Joel song, the one that goes, "Your sister's gone out, she's on a date, and you just sit at home and masturbate." I couldn't completely identify with that part because, you know, I don't have a sister. But then there's that line where he says the guy is twenty-one and his mom still makes his bed and "that's too long . . . that's toooo long."

I turned twenty-four somewhere between Chevy Chase, Maryland, and the border of South Carolina, alone at the wheel of a Chrysler Imperial, which probably wouldn't have been too bad if not for the fact that it was stuffed top to bottom with every personal item Mr. and Mrs. George Altiner of Lindenhurst, Long Island, couldn't take on the plane with them to West Palm Beach, Florida. I'd had about five boxes of stuff I wanted to take to my new life, but I had to leave it in the driveway when I found out there was not one square inch of space left for my belongings among the Altiners' valuables, which included four ice buckets and a three-foot-high ceramic of a Lhasa apso. Isn't that bigger than life-size?

The morning after I dropped the car off I went to the state employment agency and they sent me directly to the media company because I had "some word processing skills." The paper hired me and I stayed until they told me to leave. That's it. That's my whole story.

Eighteen years.

How the hell does that happen?

I don't want it to happen again, but I am baffled by the fact that I don't know what I want to do today any more than I did then.

What are you going to do?

A car coming down the street pulls me out of my daydream and I look back up at the taillights of the garaged 'Vette. Maybe I should leave a note on the hospital administrator's door. I think her name is Leena or Lyra, something like that. "Dear Leena or Lyra . . . or something like that."

One time, at the paper, there was absolutely no one left in the newsroom so an editor who didn't know any better sent me out to the home of a guy who had just been killed in a helicopter crash. It was before MapQuest or GPS and it took me forty-five minutes to navigate through the gated neighborhood of identical homes and find the right address—4012 Ulster Place. Funny, I remember that. Anyway, I was just about to get out of the car when the editor radioed to notify me that "the family might not know yet. They might be getting the news from you, so take that into consideration when you start the interview."

I took it into consideration, all right. I immediately restarted the car, drove around for another twenty minutes, and reported back, "No one home."

I take a few steps in reverse, toss the empty AriZona Iced Tea can into the yellow recycling bin at the edge of the Corvette lady's driveway, and race home.

What am I going to do?

the scent of failure

Dad, I've got this great . . . wait a second," Kristin says with her mouth full. She's standing in the kitchen wagging three-quarters of a frozen banana in my direction. She hides away entire bunches until they go absolutely black, then peels them, pops them in a jumbo storage bag, and stashes it in the far back of the freezer. Days, weeks, months later, she pulls out the bag, pries lose one of the 'nanas, and gnaws on it, like a Popsicle. Or uses it to make a point.

"I picked up this great card," she says, gulping. "I want you to give it to Grandma when you go tonight."

"Oh my God," I say. "I completely forgot." Not to mention, this is the last thing I need right now.

Tonight's the night I have to pick up my older brother, Lawrence, so we can visit our mother, who lives in an assisted-living facility in the next county. We do it religiously—every fifth Thursday—but with everything going on I totally blanked out. My first thought is to cancel, to make up some excuse, but then I think about how Artie's been sheepishly bragging about hitting up his parents for money here and there. "I'm no good to them underwater," he rationalizes.

I'm doing nothing if not sinking fast, so why shouldn't I get some maternal assistance? Maybe my mom would like to buy me a little more time. It's not like she's saving for a cruise.

Even Anna used the phrase "safety net" this morning. I hate that Anna's been working fourteen-hour days in preparation for some government contract her lab might get. Two out of the last three days she has come home after I was asleep. It's as if she's already existing without me.

When I came up behind her at the kitchen sink this morning, I started to massage her neck and shoulders. I usually do it for a few seconds and then flit off to groans of "Don't stop now. Why'd you even bother if you're just going to run off?" but this time I lingered, kneading away while staring into the school of clown fish cascading down her back. Anna left the water running and rotated her neck as if she was in ecstasy. I kept at it until my fingers cramped, but the second I released her she turned to dry a coffee cup and hurriedly gather up her stuff for work.

She's working late again, so I give her a call. She picks up on the third ring and sounds slightly irritated, like she's in the middle of something, probably pouring off a double urine sample.

I quickly tell her how I forgot about Mom, that I'm heading out now and planning on bringing up the idea of financial aid.

"That's probably good—talking to your mom," she says right away. "Just in case—you know, a safety net. Maybe at least mention Kristin's college tuition coming up."

"I will, and I'll tell her you said hi."

"OK, just don't tell Lawrence I said hi."

One thing you need to know about my brother right now: He smells.

I hate to even use my car to pick him up because the interior stinks for days afterward. If I had the money I'd get a rental for the day but, of course, I no longer have that luxury.

Since he stopped working at his eleventh job in four years, Lawrence has been downsizing. First it was a two-bedroom apartment and then a one-bedroom and now . . . His current place is hard to describe. They call it the Orchid Hotel or the Orchid Bed & Breakfast, but it has been a long time since anyone came down for the blueberry pancakes in this place. Now there's just sort of a communal dining area and the constant ding of a lone microwave.

The first time I came by the Orchid, I think there were a handful of Norwegian tourists who didn't know any better, but every time since, it just seems to be inhabited by a bunch of single men in borderline shoes. I want to call it a flophouse just to irritate Lawrence, but that would be unfair to the Orchid since, despite the clientele and tiny rooms, they always keep it freshly painted and neat as an Englishman's garden. Plus Lawrence would only use it as an excuse not to show any irritation. Lately his thing has been not showing me anything, not revealing anything that I may later use to analyze him. So he gives up no emotion, no anecdotes, no goals, no complaints, and no conversation. I drive him over 150 miles both ways and the most I get in return are remarks such as "sure," "no thanks," "if you think so." And the universal "yeah, right."

I can smell him through his front door.

I can never tell if his odor has actually permeated the grain of the wood or if it's steadily seeping out with the light through the crack at the bottom. But either way, his stench is unmistakable.

He always acts as if he doesn't know why I'm standing at his door, and today is no exception.

"*What?*" he says.

"You know we're supposed to go to Mom's. Are you coming or not?"

"Sure," he says.

He has recently shaved his head and I think he thinks it makes him appear menacing. All I know for sure is that it wasn't his hair that was caus- ing his horrible odor, because he still stinks.

On the ride, since he won't respond to even simple questions, I just drive and think of ways to deal with the smell. I crack the windows, trying to kill it with an arctic chill from the AC. I wonder what exactly it is I always see coroners in movies dab under their noses before autopsies and if it's available over the counter. I often breathe through my mouth when the smell becomes suffocating but it makes me feel as if I'm swallowing whatever it is that is him, which then causes me to only exhale. I blow short puffs of air outward but, as you probably know, man cannot exist doing that.

About halfway, I stop for a fountain Coke and he always says the same thing: "You and your fountain Cokes."

There is a kitsch shell factory and gift store in the same shopping center and I step in to buy a little something for Mom. She gets a kick out of shell people and they have them riding shell horses and shell surfboards and wear- ing aprons and cooking in shell kitchens. Lawrence doesn't come in. He stands out in the parking lot smoking and having long, animated conversa- tions with anyone who happens by. I think he just wants me to know that he will talk to anyone but his brother.

There is always some kind of theme going on here at this assisted-living facility and today is "Cowboy Day." The tables in the eating area are covered with checkered hoedown cloths and when we get to my Mom's room, where she always leaves her door wide open, she is watching a *Judge Judy*–type show featuring a male judge and wearing a ten-gallon straw hat that someone has stuck on her pint-size head.

Lawrence races to hug her first, as he always does, so by the time I get to her, she has little strength for me. I squeeze her but get next to nothing in return.

I notice that my mother smells, too.

Mom often talks about the good old days in Detroit now, even though none of us has ever been to Detroit. When we tried to explain that to her, she said, "Well, you best check it out. It's the greatest city in the world."

I try to talk around Detroit but it's not easy, especially since Lawrence has embraced the city himself. He even bought Mom an I LOVE DETROIT T-shirt and studied up on the early days of industry in the city and its current economic struggles.

Sometimes they sit and talk for hours about growing up in Detroit and how much they miss being able to go to Canada for lunch. To escape such nonsense, I usually walk downstairs and try to play with the two overweight cats they keep in the recreation center. They say petting animals is supposed to help old folks relax, but so far, three seniors in this building have been taken to the hospital after allergic reactions.

Today, as the fat cats run away from me, I begin to sense that I, too, smell. I am in desperate need of assisted living myself, aren't I? If Anna ever kicks me out I should drive straight here.

I want to go up and ask Mom about the money the moment Lawrence goes outside to smoke a cigarette, but it's kind of tricky. Don't get me wrong; I've no problem with accepting money or lavish gifts. I know if I had a bunch of money I'd be giving it away all the time. Sure, we all say that, but I really mean it. I kind of abhor luxury now. It makes me a bit ill, frankly (once in a while I do think it would be nice to have one of those outdoor kitchens I see on HGTV). So I'd love giving people handouts. I'd be giving my accountant fits. "You can't be giving cash to every Tom, Dick, and Harry who puts his hand out," he'd complain. "At this rate, even with your substantial fortune, you're going to be broke in 2042."

"I can't think about that," I'd tell him. "I can't dwell on 2042. My fellow man needs me too much right now."

You can tell I'm stalling, huh? The main complication with borrowing money from my mom is she's not all there. When my dad died the funeral bill was $8,650. She wrote the check for $68,404. Just now, as I was leaving her room to come down here I saw her checkbook lying open on top of her armoire. The help probably takes Caribbean day cruises with it but . . . I guess what I now realize is, I've waited too long to borrow money from my parents. Let that be a lesson to all of you.

I pass Lawrence in the hallway on my way back up to the room, and he nods at me in a way that says, "Don't forget you're going to have to drive me home."

The complex is similar to a huge hotel with endless hallways, and many of the elderly can't tell one room from another so, to individualize them, on little ledges outside the doorways, residents have put everything from models of the Santa Maria to chunky hand-carved Buddhas. I stop at the oversize ceramic Oreo cookie that Lawrence brought Mom on his second visit.

Mom is sitting on a pale love seat about two feet away from her TV and I sit down beside her. The last time I visited, she bit me. She grabbed my arm and just sank her teeth into it. It wasn't the first time. We're not sure what the little nips mean but we're used to it. I sometimes joke with Anna that I can identify more than most with the vampire craze in this country. Lawrence even wears three sweaters sometimes in hopes there will be no perforation. It's sort of a homemade version of those bulky, padded things dog keepers attach to their arms to train attack dogs.

"Lawrence tells me you have no work," Mom says.

"I'm between jobs," I say.

"Sometimes it's good to be between things."

I'm not sure where Mom stands when "her boys" show up. When you grow up in the same small bedroom together, as Lawrence and I did, you feel so connected by the bunk beds that literally stack you on top of each other, by the same dim desk lamp, by the shared drawers of frayed underwear and socks. But once that is left behind you realize how different you are. There was never any big blowup between my brother and me, nothing specific I can point to that has created this wall between us. We simply set out on different paths that, over time, led to different interests, different ideologies, different goals, different smells. We have settled inside a bubble of toleration, which isn't so bad. Aside from sharing a branch on the family tree, we are nothing alike, so why try to fake it, right? At certain moments Mom eyes us up and down in a very curious manner. To watch your own children grow is one thing: To watch them age into peculiar adults must be something else altogether.

I leave her watching a different TV judge. Lawrence is already sitting in the car waiting for me. As I'm putting on my seat belt, I ask him if he remembers our dad ever giving him wise advice. "Did he have any sayings?" I ask. "You know, like when people always say, 'My daddy always said . . .'"

"My daddy always said . . ." Lawrence says, leaving the expression dangling in the air as if it might trigger a memory. But it doesn't.

After about a half hour, Lawrence clears his throat and says, "I may go to Tampa for work. Have you thought about moving?"

"Everywhere but Tampa," I say.

I look over at Lawrence, the way his hands lie limply in his lap as if they never picked up a thing without being forced. It's odd, because we grew up with such a strict work ethic. Dad used to take us to work with him on Saturdays and give us chores around the office. Then he'd print up actual paychecks for us with odd little amounts like $5.67 or $7.54, not unlike the odd-numbered paychecks we'd all collect in real jobs someday.

He was a grand example, Pops was, and as reliable as a hinge on a door, but his two boys turned out a bit odd and the only explanation I've ever been able to come up with is the mercury.

I was raised on mercury. I probably should have mentioned this earlier.

My father was an accountant at a company that made blood pressure instruments. He'd often go into the office on Saturdays to catch up on paperwork and drag us along, especially in the summer months. Mom would say, "Take the boys with you. All they're going to do around here is ride their bicycles behind the town utility truck as it dispenses glorious, billowing clouds of pesticide" (she didn't make it sound quite so wonderful, but it was).

After Dad gave us some busywork on Saturday mornings, the adjacent factory became our playground. And these were the old blood pressure instruments—the ones with mercury like a thermometer. Some doctors still use them as the gold standard. I assume at this time nobody knew how dangerous mercury was. But everybody knew how much fun it was—how it splatters into a million little balls but then congeals into a giant puddle—and we had an unlimited supply. We'd have mercury wars, ricocheting blobs of it around giant metal tables. The Saturday before the Super Bowl, long before there was a Bud Bowl, there was a Mercury Bowl in a factory in Copiague,

Long Island. I would actually bring mercury to school and bat it around my desk. So if you need an explanation for why I am the way I am, this is it. This is my excuse. And when I see my irritating brother Lawrence, I know that we both have at least one single thing in common: We've both had fistfuls of mercury shoved down our pants. Mercury . . . was our Play-Doh.

And, to top it off, every day my mother made us sandwiches for elementary school. And every day it was tuna fish, loaded with mercury.

"You should look like the Silver Surfer," I say to Lawrence.

"I think about that all the time," he says. "I almost broke a thermometer about a month ago just to play with the stuff. Man, those were good times. Remember racing the office chairs through the factory and that soda machine?"

I did. When Dad wouldn't give us any money we'd reach up through the vending machine's trap door, stab the cans with pens, and try to drink the soda as it sprayed down the front of the machine.

"Black cherry," Lawrence says. "And the paychecks . . ."

Lawrence clicks open the glove compartment and hands me a tissue that I dab and press against three little punctures on my left forearm. Then he snaps the glove box shut, leans back, and gazes out the window.

"That was the best job we ever had," he says. "It's been all downhill since."

feel the click

"What the heck are you doing?" Anna says the second she sees me standing in the center of the bathroom naked.

"I just got out of the shower. I'm drying naturally. I read that after a shower it's good for your skin to dry naturally a couple of times a week."

"Oh, where'd you read that, *Shower Digest?*"

"I'm just giving it a whirl."

"Well, whirl around and get a towel. Today's the day."

"I know, D-day."

"Don't start with that. This has been planned for weeks. We're going. Sure, if we'd known you were going to be laid off, this wouldn't be happening. But my brother has it all set up. Plus it's not costing us anything. Who knows when we'll get a little vacation again."

"I really can't enjoy the leisure world right now," I say.

"Yes you can," she says, her voice dropping down in tone, the way always does when the time for debate is over. "We just need enough stuff for one night. I already threw some things in a bag, if there's anything you want to add."

"I really can't enjoy anything right now. I can act like it, but I really can't. You don't understand."

"Oh, I don't understand. Like this uncertainty isn't having an effect on me. You better think about what you're saying," she says, throwing a towel at me. "And you're riding the dolphin whether you like it or not."

"Ride? Who said anything about ride? You said swim with the dolphins."

"They let you ride it, too. Everybody gets to ride a dolphin to shore. What's the big deal?"

"Sorry. But I'm definitely too out of sync with things to be riding a dolphin. You need to be loose and in the flow to—"

"Just block all that bad stuff out. Just *block* it out."

This is supposed to be a treat from my brother-in-law. "Unemployed men need plenty of treats," he keeps texting me since he heard the news. My brother-in-law is one of those people that everybody likes but you can't figure out why. He also keeps texting me stuff like "Mr. Unemployed: Wanna hose down my boat for 20 bucks? I'll throw in another 10 if you wash my golf balls. LOL." He made a ton of money in pay phones about two years before pay phones became extinct. I know, I don't know how he did it. But he paid cash for a huge house on a PGA golf course in Port St. Lucie and just had a second home built on the waterway near our home. Now he just spends days tapping at the icons on his iPhone and dabbling in several endeavors at once.

"Don't worry, everything will be comped," he told Anna a few weeks ago. But everything on this trip to Disney's Discovery Cove in Orlando is comped for him, too, so it doesn't really count as a big favor, does it? While there, he's going to be filming it for some glorified infomercial he calls Travelrama. It's a highlight reel of pseudo-adventures such as this, strung together and sold in half-hour blocks to be run at 3 A.M. in places where people dream about riding a dolphin or cave diving with belligerent ex–Navy SEALs. I'm trying to think if there's anything else important you need to know about him. Oh, he's one of those people who get upset if you don't call them by their proper name. Michael. "Mike" sets him off. If you're already anticipating that I'm going to use it, don't. It's too easy.

"I'll pet the dolphin's snout," I tell Anna as we load up the car. "I'll rub its belly. But I'm not grabbing onto it and going for a ride. And even if you try and make me ride it, I could slip off 'cause dolphins aren't like snakes where they look slippery but then you touch them and they're rough and dry-skinned. Dolphins look slippery and they *are* slippery, so if I can't hold on and lose my grip, I don't want you thinking it was intentional. I'm telling you that now. Don't count on me being able to hang on to a slippery dolphin racing for the shoreline because . . . because they're not as easy to ride as you think."

"Are you on something?" Anna looks at me quizzically. "You haven't strung that many words together since you tried to sing that superfast Bare-naked Ladies' song to Alonzo on New Year's Eve."

"I'm not on anything. I'm just . . . uneasy."

"What is it, some animal rights thing or something? You don't think people should be riding dolphins?"

"I couldn't care less what people do with dolphins. They could change every dog track in South Florida into a dolphin track, slap numbers on their backs, and have them chase a mackerel on a stick for all I care. I just don't want to be riding one myself. I don't want to be a guy . . . skimming across the top of the water . . . with a big goofy grin on his face while riding a chubby fish. It sabotages my cool."

"What cool? Oh, when you ride the dolphin they snap a picture and afterward, at the souvenir shop, you can have it put in a snowglobe."

"I don't know if I want to be in a snowglobe."

"Here," Anna says, handing me a printout to look over during the three-hour drive north. At first glance I think it's from the theme park, but it's an itinerary she's prepared that includes details from the temperature of the water in the man-made snorkel park down to how much lunch for four will cost at the outdoor snack bar versus the inside restaurant.

"I thought the lunch was comped, too?" I say.

"It is," she says. "But I just wanted to work out the differential. For fun."

Anna is a bit of a contradiction. Like I said before, there's this odd mix of regimentation and spontaneity. Her dad was a military man who specialized in sonar engineering but her mom was a photographer for novelty catalogs (the first person to capture Big Mouth Billy Bass on film), if that helps explain anything. I'm not sure where the influences of her parents begin and end—she has her mom's brow and her dad's feet. She can be playful, a great teammate in a pillow fight against the kids, but she also seems to find "fun" in places I just don't understand. I couldn't begin to tell you what might stick to the walls if Anna's head suddenly exploded. I like—no, I love that I can't figure her out.

But to be completely honest, I sometimes think there might be something missing in her makeup—a screw loose, even. It's the only way I can comprehend why she ever would have agreed to marry me. She never said yes when I proposed to her. I caught her off guard as she was heading toward the door, taking three large black trash bags full of clothes and shoes to Goodwill. I suddenly couldn't let one more second go by without knowing we would always be together. (At that moment we didn't know it—at least I didn't—but she was already pregnant with Kristin.)

She could barely even see me when I popped the question. She dropped the bags, revealing a strange grin that stayed plastered in place, like a façade to give her mind time to run through all the pros and cons. I held my breath trying to think like she might think—*We are definitely at that point in time. We're both settled with our jobs, settled with each other. Why not?*

If I close my eyes now I can still see the moment the corners of the grin wilted and I was left with a look of glazed acceptance. I should probably be thrilled she didn't say, "Why not?"

She said, "All right," as in:

"Will you . . . Will you . . . Will you marry me?"

"All right."

She said it with a tinge of trepidation but my mind was eased when I overheard her telling her mom, "We're a good match." And in the weeks we spent planning our wedding she would often look up at me and say, "I think this will work. We like the same things," as if love was as simple as that.

I gaze at her profile now, wisps of hair fluttering over her face, and then look back to the itinerary. "The dolphin encounter is at twelve-eighteen?" I ask. "Did you decide that?"

"No, no," Anna says. "They've got it down to a science. People tell me the place is so organized. I can't wait to study how well organized they are. I wonder if they have a behind-the-operations tour."

See, she gets off on organization.

We stop for gas and, after going inside the Mobil Mart, Anna comes out with two bottled waters, hurdles over the gas line, and leans into me. The sun hasn't hit a harsh peak yet and there is no sweat between us. Her warmth settles comfortably against my body. I feel as if we're standing at the end of a pier gazing out at the morning breaking, even though all we can see is a truck driver using a pressure hose to remove the goop of smashed love bugs off his windshield.

"Sal says twenty-one weeks isn't really that long," I say.

"Will you stop already?" she implores.

"It's really only a few months or whatever."

"Try days. There's seven days in a week and we're talking twenty-one weeks."

"Aren't we actually down to twenty already?"

"OK, twenty weeks and a day. Do the math."

To Anna's credit she does wait a few seconds before saying, "You want me to do the math?"

"Yes."

"One hundred and forty-one days. Does that sound better?"

"Yeah, I think I'll go with days instead of months."

"You know what I forgot to tell you. It looks like that government contract is a done deal. Handling all the blood work for the army reserves in Palm Beach and Martin counties. There's going to be bunches of overtime. That will be a big help."

"You shouldn't have to . . ."

"Why not? I've got this all figured out. We're not upside down in our house—we're in a better situation than a lot of people. As long as you get some kind of half-decent job, we can deal with the debt and we can downsize everything—simplify. Go to one car. Rent a second-floor walkup. Go to the one plate, one spoon, and one towel mentality."

"Really, one towel?" I ask.

"Of course, we have two children but we'll figure something out with that." She laughs lightly.

"Kristin will be going off to college."

"What do we really need?" she says. "We could miniaturize our lives."

I do like the idea of living a tiny—monklike—existence. I've always liked miniatures of almost anything—miniature stereos, miniature screwdrivers. Oh, I love when they did that thing where they miniaturized the Bible onto the head of a pin.

"Renee at work was talking to her cousin, the one that just moved to

Montana," Anna says. "They just picked up and got out of here. People do it. I think there are nine people in the town she's at. While Renee was talking to her on the phone a llama poked its head in her kitchen window. With my job in medical I can work almost anywhere."

"But what would I do? I can't be a fishing guide."

"Why do you say that? Maybe you could be. No, you're right, you couldn't."

"In theory, I like the idea of a small town but I think I'd feel like I'd left the planet. I'd feel so distant from everything."

"Would that really be so bad?" Anna says.

I feel so distant now, and I don't like the feeling.

"God, enjoy this," Anna says, swinging her hips into me, trying to knock me out of the doldrums.

It does, for an instant, but there's this new nagging voice in the back of my mind insisting that tomorrow is too uncertain to enjoy today.

"Is the tank almost full?" Anna says, putting her hand over mine on the gas nozzle. "I want to feel the click."

sea donkey

The water is freezing.

"That's the way the dolphins like it," Michael says. "The temperature's not for us. This is the dolphins' environment."

Of course, he and his wife, Hania, are wearing $350 wet suits they bought at the gift shop four minutes ago and Michael is toting a bulky waterproof camera for his infomercial.

"J, don't look at the camera. Look into the camera. [I know, everybody has to call him Michael, but I'm J.] No, naturally, like the camera isn't here," he says, shifting it to his other shoulder. "Never mind, I take it back. Don't look at the camera."

The last thing I said to Anna before we entered the water was "I know this is something you really want to do. I will help you get on the dolphin. I'll give you a big boost right onto its back. But when it comes time for me to ride, I will bow out gracefully."

Earlier, I nervously watched other riders in the distance and it appeared as if you have to hang on sideways and hook your hand up around the top and you could easily get your thumb stuck in the blowhole like a bowling ball. "I bet it happens," I said. But Anna looked at me as if I was crazy and told me to rub my sunscreen in better. "It looks like somebody threw a glass of milk in your face," she said.

Now I don't even see her. She might have bolted off into a more dolphin-friendly group.

"There you are," Anna says, rising up from the deep right in front of me. "We're supposed to be over there by that trainer."

The trainer, a frizzy-haired woman with toned arms, gathers us in a circle of chest-high water and then the dolphin, named Thelma, pops up in the center of our group. It is kind of exciting. Everyone pets Thelma, everyone rubs Thelma's belly, everyone kisses Thelma's bottlenose, even me.

At one point, it seems as if the dolphin trainer is about to give us a dissertation on the plight of the dolphins in the North Atlantic, but then she suddenly switches gears and asks Anna and me to swim into the deeper water. We quickly oblige, and before I know it, the trainer has me spinning around in the water while Thelma mimics my moves. I actually get into it, and the trainer has to grab me and say, "OK, you can stop spinning now. You're making Thelma dizzy."

Then the trainer says, "OK, Anna. I want you to go first and then your husband."

I clear my throat and say, "Thanks, but I wasn't going to be riding the dolphin today."

"He thinks it will sabotage his cool," Anna says and snickers.

"It's just not something I want to do," I say.

"Don't worry, he's riding the dolphin," the trainer says to Anna. "Let's go, put your right hand here and your left . . ."

And off Anna goes.

Her goldish-brown hair looks great streaking between the plumes of water. The sight is wondrous, and I'm truly glad she finally got her wish but . . .

"Let's go. Now," the trainer says.

The trainer is so commanding. She talks to me just like I'm a smart fish. I hesitate, but I'm thinking, *Is this really where I want to make a stand, in the middle of a man-made cove beside a dolphin named Thelma?* I can't remember anything I'd ever taken a stand on, so why this and why now? If I were to croak tomorrow, people would say the only thing I ever took a stand on was not riding a dolphin named Thelma. What would that really say about me? If nothing else, I desperately want to be with Anna and the quickest way to get to her is . . .

I grip the dorsal fin and close my eyes, imagining I'm effortlessly soaring above the waterline, my profile set for my snowglobe snapshot, but then the spastic ride whips me out of the daydream. I really did hope it would be similar to riding a missile . . . a big whoosh and I'd be gliding and skimming into shore quicker than you can say SPF 30. But it's the complete opposite. The dolphin is struggling, trudging as if it were a burro trying to go up a rocky incline—a sea donkey.

No one had told me what to do with my legs exactly, and Thelma's tailfin going up and down is whacking me in the legs to the point where . . .

"He's kicking the dolphin!" a woman from another group screams as I near shore. I try to yell back, "I'm not ki—" but I get a mouthful of water. The next thing I know, the trainer is pulling me off and people are huddling around saying, "What happened?" And everybody is explaining, "That man started kicking the dolphin."

I try to laugh about it and tell those who haven't ridden yet how awkward riding a dolphin actually is, and that a good tip might be to keep your legs toward the front of the dolphin. But no one is hearing any of it.

"I swear, fighting back was just natural instinct."

"I got it all on tape," Michael says, tapping the side of his camera.

Hania peers at me oddly. "Nobody else had a problem."

"I know. I told Anna I was out of sync. I shouldn't even have been attempting something like this right now."

I hurry up the shoreline to where Anna is standing alone and whisper, "I did it for you."

"I didn't tell you to kick a dolphin," she says.

wannado city

'm off.

Sal was right. Anna gave me a printout this morning that looks like something a SWAT team leader would hand to his men before trying to negotiate a hostage situation—locations, times, driving distances. The only difference being that the SWAT captain's order sheet probably wouldn't have little happy faces in the margins and a "luv you" in orange Highlighter on page two or targets such as job fair, cattle call at a Kohl's department store, and an open admissions session for adults at the junior college.

"All polished up," Mrs. Dupont, the neighbor across the street, says when she spots me in my one sport coat. "You can't keep a good man down."

"I'm the exception," I say, and wave back.

I have the feeling this is going to be the second-longest day of my life so I'll simply run down the action in the same order Anna has it. She also has a few errands on this list but I'll spare you.

1. I arrive early at Kohl's, but obviously not early enough. A disorderly line snakes out of the front of the building and into the parking lot. It reminds me of those mob scenes you see on TV when Best Buy advertises a Toshiba laptop for $229, except the only unbelievable deal we're looking for is a decent job and a fresh start.

"Dad, nobody shows up in person for a job. Just fill out the application online," Kristin told me. And she was right. When I went by Total Wine and Target earlier in the week the managers wouldn't even talk to me. When I snuck up on a manager at the Muvico movie theater, he acted so startled you would have thought a half-naked winged Bruno had just landed on his face. But when I saw this Kohl's listing I was like "Nice. An invitation to appear."

I'm in the thick of the line, taking baby steps, and trying not to drip sweat on the one-page résumé I quickly pieced together.

"I've been working since I was fifteen so it's been forty-one years now. Shouldn't that be enough?" a slender man says as he pulls at a striped shirt that appears to be tucked too tightly into his new trousers. "I have to keep going? People keep telling me I've got to move on—'Move on!'—but I've got no move-on left. Period."

"Can you move up? The line's going," the impatient woman behind me says.

A gentleman near the first turn in the line is wearing a tattered suit and I keep looking down at everybody's shoes to see who will stand a chance today. Most of us are dressed decently but it's like when construction workers put on a new dress shirt for the company's annual Christmas party—the collars itch, the sleeves bunch up in all the wrong places. Everyone is ill-fitted.

I've waited in line for free samples of toffee popcorn. I've waited in line for Tony Hawk's Boom Boom HuckJam tickets. I've waited in line for doughnuts. I've waited in line to rent the fourth season of *The Wire*.

I have never waited in line for work.

"This is where you come when you're out of options," a gruff guy says, turning to me as if I will jump on that bandwagon, but I just smile politely.

I have options, I tell myself. This is just one more thing to keep in mind. When it comes right down to it I don't regret any of the jobs I've had. Oh, except the one where I had to apprentice for a drunk guy who fixed heavy machinery in Queens. He insisted I eat his homemade sandwiches, which always had traces of thirty-weight industrial oil mixed with the mayo.

The line is so long that some people have brought lawn chairs. Toward the front I can hear little bursts of singing, some choral-like. Out of boredom, one robust guy takes out his wallet and starts doing card tricks with a stack of credit cards and his license and whatever else is in there. Some of the credit cards still have activation stickers on them. "Look, I'm unemployed and companies are still sending them to me," he says.

"Pick a card, pick a card," he tells a woman nearby as he shields his eyes with one hand.

The woman plucks one out and he says, "Don't tell me, don't tell me. Visa. Wachovia."

"Yes!" she says, and applause breaks out in our little circle. A chorus of "We Will Rock You" also trickles down the line, but I think it's unrelated to our credit card tricks.

I appreciate the camaraderie. We're all in this together. If my life has to blow up, it's comforting having everyone else blowing up with me. On the other hand, it haunts me a little that when I ask the people in line with me how long they've been out of work, they don't talk in weeks or days. They talk in months—five months, nine months, eighteen months. Some are simply speechless.

"Can I have everybody's attention please?" A booming voice strikes up right beside me.

The prim woman in a navy blue pantsuit introduces herself as Kohl's regional hiring supervisor. She smells very fresh. She's so close that it feels like I'm in an elevator with someone who just took a hotel shower. She's all honeysuckle and minty dewdrop.

She has our attention. In fact all 424 people in line are trying to make eye contact just as their career counselors taught them. To her, it must look like a thousand beady cartoon eyes peeking out of the darkness.

"We didn't expect this turnout," she says.

None of us did, did we?

We should have.

But we didn't.

"I'm going to ask those of you who haven't received a number yet to sign up on the sheets near the south entrance," she says. "And we will be in touch with each and every one of you. I promise."

She smells like her promise would be good, so I step away from the line. After leaving my information, I stroll outside and walk around the perimeter of the building to the rear of the shopping center. Anna's home this afternoon, so I don't want to race back to the house with nothing but a handful of anecdotes. I already know that as soon as she asks how it went, I'll quickly reach for my wallet. "Pick a card, any card."

2. The job fair starts with a seminar called "Working the Room." Susan, the host of the motivational talk, charges into the conference room. "Who here is absolutely fabulous?" she shouts.

No hands rise.

"Do you want to meet fabulous people?"

Some members of the audience admit they do, but I'm not one of them. I never, ever want to meet fabulous people. In fact, up to this point I have engineered my life in such a way that the odds of my meeting a fabulous person are about 18 million to 1.

"Did you ever notice that all the fabulous people get the fabulous jobs?" she asks, keeping the theme going. But she's losing us here. Except for a few rare exceptions, I think she's way off on this one. Most of us would agree it's the backstabbers, the phonies, and the assholes who get the fabulous jobs.

Susan switches gears and has us get up and introduce ourselves to a nearby stranger. I meet Sarah, a red-haired woman with matching fingernails, who's looking for an accounting position.

"I'm sorry to hear that," I say. And she laughs as if she really needed to.

"A first impression is made in twenty-eight seconds," Susan tells us. "Eye contact, people! 'Hi' is good but I'd rather you say 'hello.' And the key is 'likability.'"

I don't know if I can fake that.

"Likability can be a powerful thing. People hire people they like," Susan says. "Do you like the person you just met?"

I like Sarah. She's my type—earnest, unassuming, attractive without working too hard at it, a natural openness about her.

"People fall in love with the people they first like," Susan says.

I think I'm falling in love with Sarah. It never lasts but I am capable of falling in love several times a day when I meet people that are kind and friendly toward me and have fetching red hair cut into diagonal points that brush across a delicate chin every time they lean in to talk.

"When you get out there to work the room, you've got to be prepared. You've got to be a thirty-second infomercial advertising yourself," Susan continues.

The job fair is set up like your typical convention, with rows of employer tables and draped interview booths that look similar to the VIP areas of night-clubs with names like Purge. Applicants snicker when they pass the Dollar General booth, but I wonder how many days away each of us is from regretting that laughter.

Unlike Dollar General, the Tri-Rail booth has a bit of a pileup, so I linger and notice from the posters that the commuter train company is trying to fill mostly administrative positions. A dark-haired gentleman with taxidermy eyes turns his attention toward me for a second, and I immediately say, "Hi, I mean, hello."

I quickly explain that I know his company doesn't currently have such openings, but I wonder how to apply for driving one of the trains.

"Driving?" he repeats.

"You know, at the helm."

He looks me up and down, lingering a little too long on my questionable shoes, and then says, "No."

I wait for a "but" or a curt explanation, but nothing. Just, "No."

I start circling, and the only other option I see is a booth recruiting for prison guards. I like having lots of keys, and it pays decently. A GED is good enough and an illustration shows that the main qualification is being able to carry what looks like a forty-five-pound sack of grain meal twenty-two yards.

I see Sarah coming out of one of the VIP rooms in a huff. "*This*," she says, "is work."

I'm so over her.

The thing is, I'm not seeing any of this as real work. Not far from here, up at the Sawgrass Mills Mall, there's a place called Wannado City, a role-playing theme park for kids. Eight-year-olds sign up for the day and play doctor or airline pilot or mayor or . . . train conductor. It's all very realistic—the pediatric ward has real incubators!—and at the end of the workday the kids are paid in currency called "wongas." That's what this job fair feels like to me. There are so many roles to play out there, but it's a game. I can't actually see myself transitioning into any of them. I may have good intentions, going from booth to booth, but I'm really an overgrown outcast with my head down, hands in my pockets, roaming the empty streets of Wannado City in search of a fistful of wongas.

3. No way I'm going by that junior college.

dog knees

When I pull into the driveway, Andrew is hovering over Alonzo and frantically waving his arms.

"Dad, Dad . . . At first he was only limping—I didn't think it was a big deal—but now he won't even get up."

"Why's he all dirty? What the hell hap—?"

"I had him in the woods at the end of the block."

"We have a woods at the end of the block?"

"And he tumbled into this ravine."

"*Ravine.* We have a ravine?"

"It's his right back leg."

"Up boy. Up boy," I say.

Alonzo just stares at me and then starts nudging his nose at the clumps of sticks and debris still clinging to his fur.

"He was walking when you brought him home?"

"Yeah, yeah."

"That means it's not broken. That's good."

"But he won't move. He won't move."

"Did you try to coax him up with the string cheese?"

"Of course."

Sargento string cheese is Alonzo's favorite treat in the world. We have often used it to lure him out the door or away from cornered cats. If he won't budge for Sargento's, there's a definite problem.

"OK, let's get him in the car," I say.

We've lifted Alonzo like this before when he ran across a neighbor's driveway while they were having it blacktopped. He was gooey all the way up to his knees (do dogs have knees?) and Andrew and I had to carry him around for a week like he was a boy prince. He was so traumatized by being stuck on the Hayses' driveway that he refused to take a single step outside to go to the bathroom.

Our vet, Gordon McKenzie, and his wife, Carol, are in the parking lot in front of their clinic when we pull up, about to call it a day.

I can see Carol, who acts as his trusty assistant, smiling and already getting the keys out to reopen the doors she's just locked.

"Do you want me to get the gurney?" Gordon says.

"No, we've got it," I say.

We're not great when it comes to regular checkups for our pets. I know Alonzo isn't up-to-date on his heartworm pills and shots, so I'm hoping we can just deal with the problem at hand and not have to go through his entire history. The McKenzies can be sticklers and this could get costly.

"I think it's just a sprain because he was walking," I say.

"That's not always the case," Gordon says.

"Initially there's shock," Carol says. "He may not have felt a thing for the first couple of hours."

"It was my fault. He fell into a ravine," Andrew says.

"Ravine?" Gordon says, digging his hands into Alonzo's fur up and around his hips.

Alonzo rests his head on the cold steel of the examining table and aims his eyes up toward Andrew and me before shuddering and letting out a piercing yelp.

"That's the spot. OK, boy. Calm down," Carol says, stroking the top of his head.

"Several ways we can proceed," Gordon says. "I'll give you the same speech we've been giving everybody these days. We treat this on a scale of how invested you are in the dog. Is he only a watchdog or—"

"He barks in the middle of the night," Andrew says.

"But is he more than that? Is he a companion?" Gordon looks me in the eye as if to say, the adult is going to have to make a decision here.

"Companion. Yeah, I mean, we talk," I say.

"We love him. We need to do whatever it takes to make him better," Andrew says, but Gordon looks directly at me again to get a read on how to proceed.

It is my decision to make. Even Anna always says, "That's your dog. You deal with it. I've got fish to take care of."

"Is it just a sprain?" I ask.

"No," he says. "It could be a fracture and not a total break, but if it is a fracture I'd like to break it and reset. That's always better. Then he'll spend three to four days here and then we like to send them home on an outpatient basis. Do you have a kennel-size cage? You'll need a kennel-size cage. You can buy that through us if need be. Then, over a period of eight to ten weeks you'll need to take him out of the cage and exercise for ten- to twenty-minute intervals every two to three hours."

"And don't worry, you won't be alone during the rehabilitation process," Carol says, picking up the spiel the second Gordon pauses to take a breath. "We still want you to bring him in every two to three days so we can monitor progress. We can preset those visits now to alleviate any long waits. I'm sure your time is valuable."

"So you're absolutely certain it's a fracture?"

"Well, we'll need to X-ray," Gordon says.

This keeps getting better. "Uh, how much is an X-ray?" I can feel Andrew's eyes boring into the side of my face.

"We don't do them here," Carol says. "You'll need to take him over to the Four Paws Radiography Clinic up on Lucerne Avenue. It'll cost between three and four hundred dollars."

The pair is making me dizzy and I don't want to be cold but I'm not the type of person who makes his or her pets a priority over all else. I mean, we need to do what we can, but right now I don't know what we can do. I'm starting to add things up in my head, and it's not even hundreds. It's thousands—initial operation, overnights, a *cage*. Where am I going to put that cage—in the living room? And then string-cheesing him out of the cage every two to three hours. All for a "maybe fracture."

"Let me get his file to see if he needs anything else while you're here," Carol says.

"I think we better think this over," I say abruptly.

"Dad?" Andrew interjects.

"It's not going to heal itself. That's my professional opinion," Gordon warns. "Is it financial? We have payment plans for up to sixty months."

"It's a lot of things," I reply.

I'm trying to play down the severity of Alonzo's problem, but the fact that we are physically carrying him back to the car doesn't support my attitude. "We should probably give it a day. See how he's doing tomorrow," I say, directing my thoughts to Andrew.

"Why?" Andrew asks.

"Oh my," Carol says. "You're actually leaving. Let me get you something to give him if the pain becomes too excruciating in the middle of the night. No charge. Just please take them."

"We'll definitely check in tomorrow to give you an update," I say in such a wavering tone that Carol can't hide her disdain.

"I'm concerned about infection," Gordon adds, following us out the door.

"I am, too," I say.

We leave the McKenzies standing in the parking lot shaking their heads fretfully. We hit a speed bump and Alonzo lets out another frightening yelp.

"It's just tender right now," I say to Andrew. "We just need to think about what we're going to do."

"The doctor told us what we need to do."

"I know but—"

"Dad, it's Alonzo. He can't walk."

ongoing argy-bargy

How many people here own their life?" Grace, the career counselor, asks.

Gillian and I look at each other across the table as if we've just been beamed down from a spaceship.

Dressed in power red, Grace is rangy with a swanlike neck and wiry arms that flutter about as she speaks.

"Well?" she says, hovering over us like a highly motivated pterodactyl.

I don't even know if I'd want to own my own life. When people preach about shredding all your personal papers so you're not a victim of identity theft, I immediately think, *My identity? Take it. Let somebody else have a shot with it. I'm not really doing anything with it.*

Anyway, no one raises a hand, and I guess that's Grace's point. The company is paying for this transition service to help us former employees prepare for the job market, and Grace is our designated life coach, career coach . . . "CEO of fun," she says.

Although I was going to skip this job-coaching nonsense, I've never had a detailed, professionally prepared résumé in my life, so I figure I can at least get them to do that for me. Plus I told Anna this would take up my entire day so there would be no need for an itinerary.

"What we're not going to do is write a bloody résumé for you," Grace begins.

Grace lapses into a lazy stance, her arms drop to her sides, and her body seems to be leaning against something that isn't there, but her language is still stern and full of harsh realities. These days you're only going to have a job for five or six years tops, so get over it, is her creed. "You have to become 'Me, Inc.,' straightaway," she says, and she talks about how the goal is to not be dependent on income and to earn your first million. What kind of company fires you and then sets you up with a guru to talk about having a million dollars?

Sitting around a large conference table at this introductory seminar— Gillian is directly across from me, Artie's a no-show—are about a dozen un-employees from various professions, and several look at one another as if to say, "My goal isn't really to become a millionaire. My goal is to find a decent job that I enjoy, maybe do some good in this world, and eat lunch out at Pollo Tropical every other week or so."

"For most of you, this is the first time you've been redundant, isn't it?" Grace says.

I join in a collective shrug, a chorus of shrugs that is interrupted by a bulky guy in a suit entering the room, sweating profusely and carrying a clunky brief-case. "Stuck on the motorway, were we?" Grace says. "You're lucky this wasn't an interview. Take a seat."

"How many of you are aware of the secret?" Grace asks.

This time several people raise their hands. "Good," she says, and that's that. She moves on. And what have I become that I don't stop the process and shout, "Hey, I want to know the secret, too!"

Oh well.

Grace insists we all introduce ourselves. We've got quite a crew—two workers from an aeronautical manufacturing plant west of the county, a graphic designer, a young woman who was laid off by Tri-Rail (I'm guessing locomotive engineer), and several members of a financial firm that has a very pedestrian name. They keep mumbling but it sounds like Douglas & Ingram or something. When it's my turn Grace asks me to elaborate. "Wow, *universal*. Go on . . . Do you have a degree?"

I don't have any education to speak of (I have fifty-four days of community college—for accounting—but I don't want to say that out loud) and she says, "Lovely, lovely, so you're self-skilled."

The supervisor who originally hired me at the paper seemed awfully rushed during the interview. He only glanced at the application I'd filled out and said, "Well, you look dependable and you look like you know how to abbreviate. We can teach you the rest."

Yes, that's what I plan to put on my résumé under "Education": self-skilled.

"You don't even have an AA degree?" she asks.

"What is that?"

I wish Grace would just write my résumé.

"OK," Grace says, doing this thing where she snaps her fingers and knocks her knees together simultaneously. "Got to keep it zooming. Some of you are getting a bit scatty on me. The first weeks of unemployment are the most tumultuous. Don't let it get away from you. Stay on the toppity-top-top of it."

I disdain taking part in organized things like this, so I've set up a little reward system for myself. Today I brought jelly beans in my pocket—the good kind. I've been here for thirty-nine minutes now.

Eat peach jelly bean.

"So, some interesting occupations have revealed themselves here. Does anyone want to do a switcheroo? Could you see yourself leaving the financial world and leaping into aerospace engineering?" Grace says looking at the D&I bunch. "Would you like to be someone with different talents and skills and grand opportunities? Do you ever wish you could be somebody else?"

I don't really want to be anyone else; I don't think anybody does. I mean, I'd like to make funny faces similar to Jim Carrey and still be considered a fairly handsome man and make $22 million a film before taxes. And I've thought about being Mr. Bruce Springsteen or someone of that ilk who can throttle the frets of a guitar and create anthems for a generation. That would be nice, but it's not like you'd want to step into someone else's boots, right? The average person doesn't want that. We want all the adulation and cash that many others have accumulated, but we want it to be due to our own grand accomplishments, not those of some scruffy guy from the Jersey shore.

If you think about the specifics, it might be fun to be the Boss for a day or two. But then, during a big show in the middle of a sold-out three-night stand, Little Steven would come over and want to share your microphone, and you know how he gets worked up over "Glory Days"; spit's flying everywhere. That would get old fast. And what about the part of the show when everybody onstage squishes together into a sweaty knot to prove how united they are after a marathon, four-hour concert. Honestly, at that point I don't think Patti would smell any better than Clarence. Plus, you know how years ago it seemed so great when the saxophone stepped in? Now the saxophone just sounds stupid to me. I couldn't deal with that thing honking away every night. Anyway, when Grace asks, I don't get into all that. I just say, "No."

The bulky guy looks up for the first time and says, "Yes."

"Well, here's a news flash for all you teeter-totters, you may very well have to become someone else if you're going to . . ."

A skinny, bright-haired man is standing in the open doorway, clumsily trying to get Grace's attention. "If you're going to create a . . . OK, I've got an ongoing argy-bargy going with this dodgy buster," she says, nodding toward the character in the doorway. "Let me step out before he goes all mental. Right back."

As soon as Grace exits, Gillian and I look at each other and blurt, "I can't believe Artie blew this off."

The whole room comes alive. "Do you think her British accent is for real or is it just a motivational tool?" someone at the far end of the table asks.

"I don't think she's English. I thinks she's an Aussie," the railroad girl says. "When I first came in I heard her say 'cheers' to somebody. I think the British say 'cheerio.'"

"She looks Canadian," the briefcase guy decides.

"All I know is I definitely prefer unemployed to redundant," the more handsome of the two aeronautical workers says glumly.

Gillian is reapplying lip gloss and up and down the table people start talking over one another and we're getting a nice little bitchfest going. I thought the firing at our company was a bit surreal, but the bulky guy says they fired so many people at his company on a single day that they set up banquet tables in the lobby and had to hire a temp service to come in and handle all the paperwork. "I actually got fired by a funeral director who had his hours cut and was doing temp work on Tuesdays and Thursdays," bulky guy says.

"I guess if you have to get fired it's nice to have someone who specializes in sympathy," Gillian tells him.

"He did have a nice touch."

"Our company actually made us stand in line to be let go," the graphic designer says. "A bunch of us sat on the floor and played Boggle while we waited. I was winning when I got called. I didn't want to get up. Plus I had my left leg tucked under me while we were playing so I had to hobble in. The whole time they were going over my paperwork I was jabbing a pen in my leg. I was totally determined to walk out of there on my own two feet."

By the time the other aeronautical guy is telling us about how the head of HR followed him into the bathroom to fire him I'm thinking maybe this is my blog—the tales of the dismissed . . . At this rate I'll never have sex again.

As if this is a competition, the graphic artist says she's already been called back into work twice to fill seats. We think she's kidding. "No, they're down to like a half dozen employees, so when clients come in they have to make it look like somebody works in the freakin' place," she says. "I sit there and call my cousin in Toronto."

"Do you sit at your old desk?" the bulky guy asks with a tone of longing.

"No, I actually sit at my old supervisor's desk. He was terminated three weeks after me."

"Is he too proud to be a seat filler?" the handsome aeronautical guy asks, laughing.

"I'd like to think I'm too proud to be a seat filler," Gillian says.

I'd like to think that, too. But I'm beginning to wonder if a seat filler is all I've ever been.

parking garage epiphany

G illian and I are standing in the parking garage adjacent to Grace's counseling office still trying to digest the seminar. "For some reason I feel *less*
motivated," Gillian says, and laughs.

I love watching Gillian laugh and it can easily become contagious. When
she first started paying attention to me in the office it kind of made me nervous, but the more I got to know her the more I realized that she's a little
flirty with just about everyone. Of course, then I was disappointed.

Gillian is clearing her throat ("OK, you ready, here it comes . . .") in preparation for her first attempt at doing an impression of Grace when all of a
sudden a former employee of our company—a woman I barely know—pops
out of the car we've been leaning against for fifteen minutes.

"I was just sitting in the car getting myself psyched up," she says at the
sight of us.

"Beverly!" Gillian exclaims, apparently more familiar with the woman than
I am. "You look like you're holding up well."

She really doesn't. I mean, I don't know what her appearance was like
before the job loss, but her hair is unkempt and her top is hanging on her like
a clumpy slicker with no sheen and no mercy, as if she's waiting on the deck
of one of those *Deadliest Catch* ships, hoping for a rogue wave to put her out
of her misery. Plus, I would swear her shoes are on the wrong feet.

"This is my second session. Did you guys have the sweet Welsh lady?"
Beverly says.

Mmmm. We're not sure.

"So, I guess you're finding the seminars helpful," I say. "You think it's worth
coming back."

Beverly lowers her voice. "Can I be real with you guys?"

"We are nothing if not people to be real with," Gillian says.

"In the car just now, I was praying. In the nights before I was fired, when
I knew there were going to be layoffs, I was getting on my knees and praying
that I'd be on the list. I didn't know if I wanted to be part of this company
anymore."

"I hear you, sister," Gillian says.

As an employee, Gillian was different from me in that she always had a lot of complaints about our upper management. "A regiment of doofuses," she often called them. I just kind of ignored all the bureaucratic crap and never really understood the constant griping. Our work environment often reminded me of that movie *Monsters, Inc.*, where the factory was fueled by screams, only our office ran on whining. But maybe Gillian just knew better. Maybe it's a lot harder to tolerate fools when you have a master's.

"I was asking God what to do," Beverly confesses. "I did not want to be complacent in this. The atmosphere they were creating was becoming intolerable to me. I mean, morally, ethically . . . I have too much respect for myself and the people I work beside to accept being treated like that."

I can understand where Beverly is coming from. In the months just before the company was taken over by a corporate raider type, our ranking officers battered us with a motivational campaign tagged "Transformative Change," based on Harvard Business School author John Kotter's *Our Iceberg Is Melting*— a B version of *Who Moved My Cheese?* Skim through it sometime and you will feel our pain—endless pictures of penguins and slogans such as "Teamwork Makes the Dream Work."

The Antarctic cuties couldn't save morale or our bottom line and there was actually much relief when the news broke that a corporate cowboy, whose last acquisition was a gourmet cooking equipment manufacturer, had taken over the company. You could imagine our joy when he showed up at our printing plant to give a speech and immediately said, "Screw the penguins."

We were only ten minutes into the maverick's oddly motivational remarks when Josie showed me the pink notepad where she'd been keeping a foul-language tally. "So far," she had scribbled, "our new leader has said 'f--k' nine times, 'sh-t' twice, 'bullsh-t' three times, and 'I'm a biker' four times."

The biker bit might have been the biggest curse of all. I've always had a certain disdain for the maverick billionaire type who shows up on a motorcycle wearing jeans and cowboy boots, and I become even more irritated when people later exclaim, "He's so down-to-earth."

What else is he supposed to be? We're on f--king earth.

I figured the salty language was just another part of a stereotype we were supposed to eat up, but he wasn't really playing that game. He cut the ties to everyman right away. "If this deal fails," he said of his takeover, "I'm still going to be flying around in my private jet and living my lifestyle."

We'd already got an inkling of his raunchy persona and attitude when we all received new employee handbooks that he'd actually written himself. The rules against harassment in the workplace had been scaled down to such a degree that many employees mockingly whooped, "Harassment is back!"

At the meeting, a movie reviewer for one of the papers stood up to complain about no longer having the resources to cover a small foreign film festival in Miami. "It's not fair to our readers if—"

"Have you tried reviewing some porn?" the cowboy said, jutting out his bully belly. "Ask me something relevant."

I was getting a kick out of the guy. Our company was in such a shambles, I figured, what the heck, let's start over as if we're deep in the muck of Deadwood and there's a new sheriff in town.

Of course, after our new leader exited, our private jets weren't waiting. We all went back to our cubicles with mixed feelings. By late afternoon, many employees were doing imitations of the guy. A handful of ladies in an outlying office were actually organizing to report our new CEO to HR for his crude behavior.

He rewrote that employee handbook just in time.

Now I recall looking around at the meeting at some of the older women and thinking, *These are our moms. How can he talk like this?*

This woman, now before Gillian and me, is one of the moms. Trembling slightly, she thinks her prayers were answered.

"I want to work as much as anyone," she says. "But for me, this is the right thing."

I get the feeling we are all just one tremor away from joining hands in a prayer circle and dropping to our knees on the hard concrete of a parking garage, so I turn my wrist to a watch that isn't there and say, "Man, I didn't realize how late it's getting."

"Oh my, yes, I better get inside. Good to see you guys." Beverly scuffles off.

On the way to our cars Gillian and I argue over who's going to get to tell Artie about the guy who got fired in the bathroom.

"That was too much. I didn't think you guys even felt comfortable talking when you're lined up against the wall like that," she says, laughing.

"That's true," I say.

In Gillian's presence it is impossible for me to wallow. "I needed a push, and losing this job was it," she says, explaining her upbeat mood. "There are so many directions you can go."

It's as if she's been harboring a secret plan and being terminated is only the first step.

"I was already thinking of taking a class in museum management, but not to get involved with art," she says. Inspired by a visit to the house where Lincoln died, she's setting her sights on historical sites—two-hundred-year-old anecdotes, tours full of fifth graders, and starchy breeches carefully laid out over seventeenth-century furniture.

"I could see you getting into that," I say, trying to leech onto her ability to envision a bright future. I wish I could see myself doing something new so quickly. There is an excitement in her voice I want to mimic, but cannot.

"I'm going nowhere fast," I say.

Depending on how Gillian plucks and shapes her eyebrows every other weekend, her expressions either resemble those of a supermodel or an alien. She glares at me with a look that is the perfect mix of Gisele Bündchen and Prime Spock and says, "Come on, give yourself a little credit. You led that pizza charge out the door—the great escape. That's a start. That was out of character for you."

"But once I started it, I couldn't even keep up with everybody."

"Doesn't matter. You were the instigator."

At the sight of my dour expression, Gillian makes an abrupt switch to solemn. "Look at you. You've got time," she says. "You've got some severance."

I stop in my tracks and confess to her that during the seminar I was obsessing about the idea of going totally broke. I've decided that if I'm going to be destitute I'd rather do it abroad, in Italy, where I will sleep in a cobblestone alley beside a bakery and be awakened each morning by a dark-haired woman, hands covered in flour, the smell of lemon granita following her out the door, and her sweet voice simply saying, "Run along."

"I read that people in Berlin love being poor," Gillian says.

"Why?"

"They think it's sexy."

"I could see that, but I've always wanted to go to Italy anyway. Could you look up how to say 'run along' in Italian for me?" I ask.

"Sure," she says.

"Well, keep me posted on your progress," I say.

"Stay on toppity-top-top of it," she says, climbing into her car.

"Wait." I stop her. "Are you and the space guy going to be meeting at Chili's later or what?"

"Wanker."

for old times' sake, eh?

The energy in this closeted room off the kitchen is palpable. A main computer terminal is humming, and a laptop sits at my feet, teetering on a milk crate. My fingers are flying across the computer keys with the classical-piano virtuosity of all five of the 5 Browns. Every time I stretch my arms, sparks snap, crackle, and pop off the static-ridden flannel shirt I just took out of the dryer. I am kinetic, frenetic, and apathetic about everything but firing off the next résumé . . . or finishing the English muffin I just made without getting jelly on the computer keys.

I always start off strong. I've been rising early, putting on a show for Anna, so the last thing she sees before going off to work for nine hours is her husband intensely searching the job market. Any job opening that is compatible with my skills is getting emailed the one-page brochure selling myself. I am putting on the résumé blitz.

Until Anna walks out the door and then I fall into a heap. On top of a page inside one of the work resource packets Grace gave me it says, "Being unemployed is a full-time job."

No it's not. Unless watching King of Queens reruns, teaching the cats how to dust with their tails, and unraveling 250 feet of tinfoil to cover your windows for daytime naps is part of the job, too. There are days when the hours simply drift toward escape. And you gladly follow. I know for a fact that Artie is addicted to Snood. Having no job will do that to you. No place to go combined with a lack of discipline equals mornings such as this:

8:33 A.M.: Eat Apple Jacks and a small portion of leftover spaghetti.

9:12 A.M.: On ESPN the sportscasters are talking about their fantasy baseball leagues. Lord knows I have all kinds of fantasies, but not one of them involves baseball.

10:01 A.M.: Try to look up shiv in the dictionary. Can't find it but come across *shit*. And *shit-can, shitkicker, shitfaced*, and *shitlist*. I didn't even know shitlist was one word. And they have all the details: "shit·list (shit́list) *n*. vulgar slang. A number of persons who are strongly disapproved of." As in, "You're on my shitlist."

10:04 A.M.: Look up Amanda Peet on IMDB. She's five feet six. Anna has half an inch on her.

10:06 A.M.: Try a new font called GlooGun.

10:07 A.M.: Message Artie to notify him that the man who invented the Egg McMuffin just died.

10:21 A.M.: I know everyone has a shitlist in their head, but do you think some people actually have one buried in a drawer with their car title, last year's tax forms, and the suspended license they've had for three years? It would be great to be rummaging through someone's personal property and come across a sheet of college-ruled looseleaf with SHITLIST neatly printed across the top. "Hey, I just found Uncle Drew's shitlist. Yeah, all typed up and everything."

10:31 A.M.: Decide to exercise to try to get my energy level up. Lie down on weight bench.

11:06 A.M.: Call Gillian to see if she's looked up how to say "run along" in Italian yet. "No," she says in English.

11:34 A.M.: Contemplate Steak-umms.

11:51 A.M.: Look up market price of littlenecks.

Noon: I'm into making homemade panini sandwiches but basically what I do is make a regular sandwich and then press it down with my hands. I made one for Kristin yesterday but she screamed, "Your freaking fingerprints are all over it. This isn't a panini, it's a smush sandwich."

12:01 P.M.: Make a smush sandwich.

12:03–1:59 P.M.: Watch four HGTV *House Hunting* shows in a row. Every time prospective buyers walk into a kitchen they look at the island countertop and say, "This would be great for entertaining." Who are these people entertaining?

2:28 P.M.: Recall how, when I was suspended from school for three days in eighth grade, my dad came home at lunchtime and heard me and Joey Bocchino laughing and playing pool in the basement. "Oh no, you are not making a party out of this. This is no vacation," he shouted down the stairs. "Go rake up some leaves."

2:43 P.M.: Go out in the yard to rake up some leaves.

2:44 P.M.: No can do. The leaves are all still up in the trees. Sorry, Dad.

I start thinking about my dad but end up thinking more about Joey Boc-chino. I can't help going back to what Grace said as we rushed out the door. *"Did you have a best friend in fourth grade? Maybe they grew up and now operate the largest search engine development company in the Northeast and you can beg them for a bloody job. Ring 'em up. For old times' sake, eh?"*

I can't picture Bo in the tech industry but he must be out there some-where, doing something. I used to pick a particular day sometimes and wonder what people I haven't seen in thirty years are doing. I get an odd feel-ing knowing everybody is still out there, existing. Doug Twohill, the only guy on my second-grade soccer team who would pass to me, what's he up to on this particular Tuesday? Is he in the kitchen, listening to some corny hillbilly music and making French toast for four kids? I was in love with Bonnie Swan-son when I was eleven. Odds are she hasn't croaked. She's out there right this second, probably rustling through boxes at an old drive-in that morphs into a tri-county swap shop on weekdays. I see my older brother's friend Nick Santos waxing a semi-classic car, a Nova or Impala, under a blooming maple tree. I haven't seen him in thirty-eight years, but chances are he's out there, too, right? Skip Dekker, the older son of my Cub Scout den mother and who flashed me on their upstairs landing and tried to convince me I could earn a merit badge by flashing him in his room at the end of the hall. What's he got going on this afternoon?

All through elementary and junior high school, Bo and I were inseparable and then . . . Ordinarily, when I have these thoughts I quickly smush them down like a panini. Who has time for reconnecting? But even with Anna's daily orders I've obviously got a little idle time, don't I? One hundred and eight days to be exact. You can go decades without a best friend, but I think I could really use a best friend now, and I could use Grace as the excuse to make the call.

3:10 P.M.: Find the phone number to Bo's younger cousin Dave Parker, who used to hang around with us sometimes. I see he is still listed at the same Long Island address he grew up at in West Babylon.

"Yeah, I bought the house from my parents," he says. "Man, I didn't ex-pect to hear from you today. "

I explain that—believe it or not—there are eighty-six Joseph Bocchinos listed in the Suffolk County phone book.

"And not one of them is the one you're looking for," Parker says. "Actually, he's down in your neck of the woods. At least that's what we think."

"What do you mean? Where?"

"It's not all good. He ain't somebody you're gonna find on Facebook if that's what you were originally thinking. Everybody up here is pretty worried about him. He had a place with his wife in West Palm Beach."

"That's only a few miles from me."

"That's over, and the only information we really have is from her. They had split up, but after he was gone she hinted that he had a problem on some odd job he was working. He might have had a head injury of some kind. And he's not quite right. I guess that's the best way I can put it."

"OK," I say. "But . . ."

"You know he did talk about you when he and his ex-wife Linda first moved down there. You're a writer or something, right?"

"Something."

"He knew you were in the area. Said he was going to look you up, but you know how that goes."

"I know, I know. So even you haven't heard from him?"

"I saw his sister Amy on Sunday and still no word. It's been three and a half years."

"Jesus, I'm really sorry to hear all this."

"If you find him we'd sure appreciate a heads-up here, especially his mom. Mrs. Bocchino's a wreck about it."

"Yeah, but I don't know where I would begin to—"

"We'd love to have a set of eyes and ears down there. All we have to go on is Linda's version. I don't have it with me offhand but I could email you the address we had on her, and if you hold on a sec, I'll give you Amy's number right now. You remember Amy, right?"

"Not really. When was she born?"

"Hold on. I have to get . . ."

I don't want to be rude but maybe I don't need a best friend this bad. (*For old times' sake, eh?*) I really don't want to be anybody else's eyes and ears. As it is, I haven't been seeing too clearly myself and . . .

"Here it is. Yeah, we'd really appreciate all the help we can get. We'd all be indebted to you. As soon as we hang up, I'm going to tell his mom you're looking into it. Whoa, I almost forgot to ask. How are things with you?"

"Good."

"Good."

3:41 P.M.: Attempt to drink a third of a twenty-four-ounce can of a Budweiser-and-Clamato drink called Chelada that someone left at the house.

3:41:58 P.M.: Fail.

liberty for all

Andrew, who's home from school today, finds me sleeping on the weight bench in the backyard (it's become a habit now) and hands me a hand-written note from Alex, the girl next door.

I unfold the tangerine-colored stationery and it reads: "if you're still inter-ested in work (you know *i'm* not!) you can meet 'enterprising dude' behind panera bread company on congress ave. at 10:30 a.m. destroy this message after reading. just kidding—a."

"Does she mean today? It's nine . . . nine-twenty. Does she mean this morning?" I ask Andrew.

"I don't know," Andrew says. "She handed me the note and ran. She didn't have much clothes on."

If it's today, I'm glad I fell asleep before working out so I'm not all sweaty. OK. Calm down, I tell myself. It's just an interview behind a restaurant, prob-ably near a Dumpster. Put some pants on. Put some deodorant on. Those are the two most important things when it comes to making a good first impres-sion at a job interview. (I read that on msn.com.)

Rushing to catch the light on Congress, I nearly hit some goofball kid dressed in a Statue of Liberty costume and pointing a giant arrow to advertise Liberty Tax Service in the shopping center on the south side. I don't even slow down at any of the bogus stop signs in front of the grocery store and take the brunt of six speed bumps as I race down the side of Panera at exactly 10:29.

A stocky, dark-haired man wearing an old-school Tim Hardaway Miami Heat jersey and shorts that extend to the tops of his ankles is standing beside a well-worn van with REGISTERED LOCKSMITH stenciled in small letters over the front wheel well. "I like your sense of timing," the enterprising dude says, opening the side door of his van. "Alexandra said you'd either be very en-thusiastic or the biggest mope-ass I'd ever met."

"I should put her down as a reference for all my jobs," I say.

"You probably should have worn shorts," he says.

He turns and leans into the darkened interior of the van, his arms sweep-ing around like someone searching through a closet for his best suit.

"Here it is. This is the longest I've got," he says, bringing out a garment that even while covered in dry-cleaning plastic is unmistakably the aqua-green gown of Lady Liberty.

With the flash of a man who has to pick the lock of a stranded mother of two stuck on I-95 before becoming a hit-and-run statistic, he has the garment up and over my head in an instant. And this is no dress rehearsal.

"You might have seen Avillo out front doing his thing," he says.

"Yeah, I almost ran him over."

"That's his thing. He likes to make sure he catches everybody's attention. No matter what," he says. "I want you on the opposite corner."

He pulls out a foam crown that's a step up from those souvenir jobs and perches it on my head, but it's as ill fitting as Denis Leary's fire helmet.

He keeps saying, "Pull it down," but each time I try, it springs back up.

"Here, let me get it," he says, squishing it over my hair. "Can you flatten this nest of yours at all?"

I'm standing very still while he works on trying to get the crown to stick when it pops up and tumbles to the ground. He picks it up with one hand and punches the side of the van with the other.

"I'm not your beautician, man. You know your hair. Don't make me keep touching your hair if it's not going to happen. Are we wasting our time? Can you get this Brillo head to stay down or not?"

I start wiping my hands down the sides of my head and he calms down when he sees I'm trying. "Wait, wait, that's it," he says, tugging the crown down below my ears. "Those ears will be the stopper. Yeah, it's not going anywhere now."

"How does it look?" I ask.

"How does it look," he says, smiling and shaking his head.

He steps back, leers one more time, hands me the big arrow, and says, "OK, go get 'em."

"Is there a torch?"

"The arrow is your torch."

"Do I do anything special when I get out there?"

"Do anything special," he says, shaking his head in amusement again. "Watch Avillo to get some ideas. You'll be fine."

I double-check which corner he wants me on, then start toward the side of the building. "No, no," he says. "Take the gown off and carry it until you get on the corner. You're a grown-ass man. Don't be traveling in that thing."

I start to pull it up over my head and he says, "Careful, leave the crown on. You don't want to fuck with that again."

I move quickly, hoping to get out to Congress before the van leaves, but he's blasting by me and screeching down the highway before I'm halfway across the parking lot. I feel my legs strengthening. After all that career counseling and job fair nonsense it feels good to be actually involved in something real. I'm shaking off the atrophy of networking.

There's a slight wind on the corner so I get lost in the fold of the costume and am blinded for a few seconds, but then the outfit drops over me like a soft curtain and I get down to business.

I swing my arms a little like the sign is on a pendulum, but it hurts after, like, two minutes.

I'm trying not to stare, but my eyes keep darting over at Avillo. He's such a natural. His crown is cocked in a manner that says, "Not being disrespectful, just inhabiting the lady." Under the crown is a red bandana. The wires of his iPod intertwine with several chunky silver necklaces bouncing off his chest. The hem of the gown trickles over deep brown combat boots and his feet are in constant motion.

He does this spin thing with the arrow that looks like he's about to harpoon a whale and pop the raft of a dozen overzealous Greenpeacers at the same time. He rocks off the curb, playing chicken with cars that appear to be in on the game.

My feet are so flat, but I try to mimic the way he rocks on his heels and spins to address both sides of the street at the same time. I saw him in a crouch earlier that turned into an urban update of the Russian Cossack dance, incorporating a more violent kicking style that could perhaps also be used to fend off a crazed pit bull.

I do a set of side stretches like you would in an exercise class but keep the arrow pointed rigidly toward the Liberty Tax, barely visible next to the Dunkin' Donuts beside it.

I drop into a squatting position and immediately hear a shout from the other side of the street. Avillo is wagging the arrow upright like a giant finger of scorn. "No, no. Get your own thing going."

"My back hurts. I was just stretching it out," I yell back.

He points the arrow directly at me and leaps into traffic. The honks are sharp and his hips are swiveling, as if rhythm is foremost no matter what action he may be involved in—taking out the trash, pushing a cart down a grocery aisle, crossing traffic to attack a Statue of Liberty wannabe.

I swear it appears as if his hips and upper thighs are actually grazing up against the front and back quarter panels of the hunks of steel passing by at 45 mph. He's in a zone, prancing through his double yellow promenade as if it's a fifth-grade square dance.

A stoplight must have triggered up the boulevard because the traffic has suddenly dissipated and he's in the far lane. His head is down, the arrow up. I raise my arrow as if this is going to end in a jousting match, but he blurs right past into the market and Mobil Mart behind me.

I spin and get back on my mark, awkwardly shoving the arrow at the air and slightly bending at the knee. Grace should see me now. I'm drenched in sweat and I pull the crown up over my ears and wring it out like it's a headband that Roger Federer's been wearing since the third hour of a five-hour-and-twenty-minute match. I'm in the splash zone of my own sweat.

My head is down when I get a jab in my side. Avillo is standing to my left with a tallboy Monster energy drink that seems to effortlessly fit in with the rest of his ensemble. "Hey, have some self-respect, man," he says. "Don't copy me."

"I was told to get some ideas from you."

"Ideas don't mean stealing someone's whole personality, does it? That's not what Omar is talking about."

"No?"

"Steal my whole show. Steal my soul, why don't you."

"I got you. Sorry," I say.

"And don't point where I'm pointing," he says, backing into the traffic without even looking.

"What do you mean? I have to point at . . ."

"Point somewhere else."

Avillo is back in action before I can even get my crown back over my ears and an incessant honking starts up behind me. The passenger's-side window on Sal's Dodge Durango slides down just long enough for him to shout out, "Nice dress!" as he veers toward the Dunkin' Donuts.

I'm about to sneer at him when I'm suddenly blinded. For a second I think my sweaty crown has slid down again but the wet on my eyes is cold and frothy . . . and chocolate. I've been shaked. The whole front of my outfit is covered with a milk shake tossed from a passing car. The straw is stuck about midway down and I pluck it off and curse it to the ground.

"Happens!" Avillo yells.

I'm just getting my bearings when the enterprising dude strolls up behind me and hands me a bright red Slurpee. "Here, got to keep hydrated," he says.

He's parked a few rows back in the lot and he says, "Walk me back to the van."

I don't want to whine, but I mention Avillo's aversion to my style. "Yeah, nobody wants to be standing on one side of a street while a guy on the other side steals their personality," he says.

"Yeah, but he doesn't even want me to point the arrow the same direction as him so how can I—"

"It wouldn't kill ya to point the arrow somewhere else."

"Omar, don't you—"

"Don't call me that."

I am this close to 100 percent certain that Omar is what Avillo called him, but I can see it's no use pressing the point. I go silent and when we reach the van he seems to want me to peel off the costume.

"You screwing Alex?" he says, looking at me cross-eyed.

"No."

"I hadn't heard from her forever. I thought something must be up. That girl's a piece of work. I asked her once why she never knows what she's doing from one day to the next, and she told me she finds the future irritating."

"Sorry about the mess," I say.

"You got shaked, huh?" he says. "Happens."

I hand over the outfit as if I'm surrendering my livelihood once again. "You can throw out that crown. I'm not touching that thing," he says. "We'll get you a new one next time."

"Next time?"

He acts as if he hasn't heard me. He tilts his head, scratches his chin, and mumbles, "Ir-ri-tating."

"Next time?" I repeat.

"Yeah, you're a keeper. Most guys don't last twenty minutes out there. That was a good solid half day."

"Half day? Man, that went fast."

"Time flies when you have someone attacking you," he says, handing me a twenty, a ten, *and* a five.

The way I've got the entire family counting pennies lately it immediately makes me want to hide this cash, not just from the government, but from them. It may be the last wad of unaccounted play money I'll ever pocket. We used to have a Panera Bread near work and I could really go for one of their turkey artichoke sandwiches with Asiago-parmesan cheese, tomatoes, and caramelized onions on the homemade focaccia.

"I'd like to do some pressure cleaning, too," I say. "I like that keep-your-head-down kind of work."

"Maybe someday. What do you know about killing iguanas?"

"Only what I read in the papers."

He rummages around in the van to the point where only his legs are sticking out and then slings a bootleg movie at me. "*Hangover 2*. Won't even be in the theaters until July. You can return it next time you see me."

"Next time?"

build-a-bear?

It's six-thirty in the morning, still dark, when I pull into the parking lot of a Krispy Kreme that went out of business months ago.

"The signs have already been stripped away, but the green awnings are unmistakable," I told Gretchen, my former office manager, yesterday.

Gretchen had been emailing me that she still has a box full of "all my stuff."

Since I wasn't allowed to return to my desk for any possessions after being terminated, she gathered what I missed in the frantic desk sweeping and has been keeping it all in the trunk of her car.

Because the abandoned Krispy Kreme is directly off the interstate on

Gretchen's way to work, I thought it would be a good place to rendezvous, but now, in the pitch black, the location seems a bit seedy.

"Well, this is kind of nasty," Gretchen says as she gets out of her Suzuki. "People are going to think I'm a prostitute."

Police report: Unemployed Man Solicits Prostitute at Abandoned Krispy Kreme.

"This is South Florida; people expect you to be clandestine," I say.

I immediately go for the box so she can flee quickly, but I stop to ask her a question that's been gnawing at me.

"Hey," I say, "when you said Gillian and Artie would be fine but you worried about me—why?"

"The thing is . . . How should I put this?" she begins. "The thing is, you're your own special island."

The way she says it sounds like a school administrator labeling children she can't sum up as "special."

"I don't mean that," Gretchen says. "But you need to end up someplace safe."

Safe?

What does she see that I don't?

"You mean like managing a Build-A-Bear?"

"That's exactly what I don't mean," Gretchen says, getting in the Suzuki and driving off.

Back in my car I flick on the dome light and start rummaging through the box.

On top is an old, faded *Amélie* postcard I stole from the movie reviewer's desk when her position was eliminated. Amélie's bright eyes are still popping beside the words "She will change your life."

On the morning I was dismissed at work, I'd gotten a call from a publicist for figure skater Sasha Cohen. The PR lady not only wanted a listing but also said we could speak with the skater for eleven minutes. Normally we wouldn't be highlighting figure skaters in our publication, but then I had an idea that I thought might get the editor's attention and a byline for me. I thought, what if I do the entire Q&A acting as if I think I'm interviewing Sacha Baron Cohen? I know, it's stupid, but in the magazine business you can't just interview people anymore. Everything is supposed to be disorganized, bizarre, and hard to follow, which are all my strong points, so I never complained about how idiotic it was.

In the box there are notes for other half-baked story ideas, various trinkets, and a stack of fresh, unused pocket notebooks I am immediately grateful for. (I miss having a stock closet full of free supplies.) Folded in half is a plain 8½ × 11 sheet of white paper with "#63" written in blue Magic Marker.

When our office relocated from its previous building more than a year ago, I was designated #63 by the moving company, and the paper was tacked above my desk. I never took it down. I remember the big boss had visited our branch recently and said, "Hey, Jeffrey, I think you can take that down now."

Of course, once he said that, I was never going to remove it, but beyond that, I just liked thinking of myself as #63. In a way, I wish it remained above my now-empty desk so future employees might inquire, "What's with the 63?"

"Oh, 63. I remember him fondly. He was a decent sort."

The sky is taking on the glow of a child's nightlight as I drive around the back of the Krispy lot. Man, I remember not so many years ago when their stock was climbing and *The Wall Street Journal* was reporting on the decadent return of the mighty doughnut. I wonder if I could have made a killing by selling the stock short, or would it be long? Either way I probably would have lost everything. I spot a Dumpster the construction workers are still using to gut the place. I spill the unused notebooks onto my front seat, neatly fold #63 into my pocket, and hurl the box and the remainder of its contents into the trash bin.

there's no beyond

Hold up," Alex yells across the driveway as I'm getting in the car. "I've got your next assignment."

She stumbles over and hands me another piece of tangerine stationery. I unfold the paper and it's the address for some pizza place I've never heard of—Augie's.

"What about the signs?"

"I guess when he wants you for signs he'll want you for signs and when he wants you for pizza he wants you for pizza," Alex says.

"I wish he'd want me for pressure cleaning."

"I think you have to work up to that. Don't give back *Hangover 2* yet. I want to borrow it."

"Is his name Omar?"

"Who's Omar?"

"Why is this guy so mysterious?"

"This is South Florida; people would be disappointed if he wasn't," Alex says. "Either that or he wants to get back in my pants."

"Back?"

"Are you in a hurry?"

"Not really. I was just going to meet some people I used to work with for—"

"Hold on, don't go. I want to show you something. I'll be right back."

I'm sitting in the car for several minutes when Alex pokes her head out the side door of her house and holds up one finger. "One minute," she says, ducking back inside.

I'm zoning out when I hear a slap on the hood and spot Alex galloping by the windshield. She rips open the passenger's door and tumbles in with a bright red Caboodles carrying case.

She puts it on her lap and lifts the top. With several levels, it's set up like a tackle box, but instead of feathery lures and shiny hooks it's full of name badges from jobs she's held.

"See, I've done my share of work," she says, pushing the box between us so I can dig in.

"Carvel? I didn't even think we had a Carvel around here," I say.

"We don't. Anymore. I closed the place down. There are four or five places in here that don't exist anymore. Remember Linens 'n Things?" she says, holding up an "Alexandra Linens 'n Things Associate" name tag.

Chili's; Friendly's; Dollar General; CVS; Olive Garden; ACE; Mail Boxes, Etc.; Papa John's . . ."

She's saved the name badges from every job she's ever had. I can't believe it. There must be fifty or sixty of them. At her age, she must have changed jobs every other week.

"I should introduce you to my older brother. He keeps going from one job to another, too," I say.

"Don't do me any favors," she says. "Careful, some of the pins are open. You're going to stick yourself."

My hands are pawing and digging through the name tags as if they're a pile of jewels, a treasure chest of occupations. "You've had quite a life, young lady," I say.

"And you thought I was just a stoop sitter."

"Later today I'm meeting the coworkers who got fired with me for lunch," I say. "I'm going to have to tell them about this treasure chest."

"You want to bring me for show-and-tell?" she says.

"Oh, you worked at Claire's? Kristin always goes there."

"I still have a goldfish bowl full of hair scrunchies if she needs any. I was always snagging a handful on my way out. I filled my bra with them when I was in high school. My breasts were very scrunchy."

I have to admit that even before my job loss I contemplated shoplifting Mach 3 razor blades, the ones for which they charge the outrageous price of eighteen dollars for a four-blade pack. If you've never used them, they give the most magnificent silky-smooth shave. I don't mind when the rich have a nicer house, car, or boat than me, but I do not think I should have to live in a world where they can receive a better shave than me just because they're in a higher tax bracket. To me, swiping the blades would be like stealing from the rich and giving to my face.

"Look, I was going by Alexis back in 2006." She holds up a Target tag.

"Where haven't you worked?"

"I draw the line at Home Depot. Too much square footage for my feetsies to be hiking around."

I've been thinking about checking into several of these types of jobs so I'll have a fallback for benefits or if I have to go the two-job route but—and I'm embarrassed to say this—I'm not sure I could hack it. When you have the same job for over a decade, you just sort of end up on autopilot and rarely challenge yourself. I don't know if I could compete with the likes of Alex at this point.

Whoa, she's got a Macaroni Grill in here. I always marveled at how the servers there introduce themselves by writing their names upside down on the paper-covered table with a big crayon.

"Yeah, I don't know if you've ever tried writing your name upside down, reverse ass backwards, but it's not easy," Alex says. "There was another Alex at my location and she copped out by going with AL but I gave customers the full ALEXANDRA treatment."

"I would have liked to see that."

"If there were cute guys at the table I'd sometimes use lipstick instead of a crayon."

Alex goes quiet, her head down, holding several of the name tags for more than a fleeting moment. "I never should have worked at Bedding Barn," she mumbles, tossing it back into the pile. "That place was stupid. I hated being under that big red roof."

"Why do you save all these?" I ask.

"I like to reminisce," she says. "Reminiscing isn't just for old farts."

"Aren't most of the memories of you getting fired?"

"Seventy-thirty," she says without looking up, but I can sense she's hiding a grin.

"ACE is the place," I say, picking up one that says "Lexi."

"My Lexi phase," she says.

She pulls out an Old Navy tag, opens the pin, and jabs it into my sun visor. "That one always reminds me of this coworker who was from North or South Ossetia—a Russki. She had the body of a gymnast but wasn't a gymnast," Alex says. "Hairy forearms, but cute. Anyhow, when we cleaned up at the end of the night she liked to sneak off, put on outfits, and then pop out from behind a rack and go, 'Tuh-dahh!' Only she couldn't say 'tuh-dah.' It always fell flat like 'tah-duh' or a weak little 'tada' like 'Prada.' We'd crack up but then she got a complex about it and started questioning herself. She'd be all excited, her little wings spread, doing a ballerina curtsy but then she'd just burp out, 'tada?' It was so funny. Maybe you had to be there."

"No, I'm there."

"And her voice was kind of coarse and deep to begin with. I tried to help her, get her to practice saying 'Ahhh,' like when a doctor checks your throat, but it only got worse . . . 'Darhhh.' So funny, the funny little hairy-armed girl who couldn't say 'tuh-dah.'"

Alex plucks the Old Navy Alexandra out of the visor as if it has been up onstage and puts it back into the Caboodle.

"It is quite the collection," I say. "Definitely worth holding on to."

"You can have one if you want. For inspiration. Not that one," she says as I'm fingering Mattress Giant. "I like the little giant in the corner."

"Bed Bath and Beyond," I say.

"There's no beyond, trust me," Alex says. "Anyway, I just wanted you to see these so you don't feel like you have to stay put in any one thing."

"What kind of work is next for you?" I ask.

"Oh, I'm done."

"Done. You're twenty-three years old."

"Twenty-four."

the window unit

B elieve it or not, I've got a cellphone, and I've got seven minutes of time
left on it. So I'll call when I get out of jury duty," Artie said earlier in the
day. "Hey, at least I'll be getting paid."

I've got us a table outside a downtown restaurant near the courthouse.
This used to be our place when our offices were housed on the twelfth floor of
a nearby skyscraper along the river. The restaurant has these fun, canopied
swing chairs but I can't get mine to budge. I look around at the rest of the
customers and no one is swinging or rocking. When the server stops by, I ask
her what's up. "Oh," she says, "one of our customers swung out of a swing
chair and broke his collarbone. He sued, so—and I love saying this—we no
longer rock."

She smiles for a good ten seconds and then says, "It's sad, isn't it?"

"Saddest thing I ever heard."

I see Artie hustling across the street and Gillian is supposedly on her way.
Artie immediately alerts me that he's already been released from jury duty—
laid off from the criminal justice system.

"Oh, I've got to tell you about this guy who got fired in the bathroom. The
boss followed him right—"

"Gillian already told me. What else have you got?"

"I kicked a dolphin."

Gillian arrives and informs us that she has officially made the leap into
volunteer work—putting in half days at the local historical society along
the river.

"Jeffrey, you'll like this," she says. "There's one exhibit that can't be touched
by the bare hand, so they have these white gloves I'll have to put on."

"I did volunteer work at the zoo that time," Artie says.

"That was court-ordered community service," Gillian gently reminds him.
"That doesn't count."

"I dressed up as the Statue of Liberty and made thirty-five dollars," I say.
"Enough to buy lunch at Panera and cover whatever the bill is here. I'm just
doing it as sort of a lark right now because I've got some time."

"Oh yeah, how many weeks did you say?"

"I'm not doing weeks anymore. It's days now—a hundred and eight."

"That sounds like a lot," Artie says.

"It's really only a little over three months when you think about it, but I don't like to think about it."

"Then don't," Artie says.

"Jeffrey, you should talk to Eileen," Gillian says. "She used to have a second job dressing up as animals and objects for a promotional company. I remember she was a giant hot dog one time. She said: 'People treat hot dogs even worse than they treat people.'"

"I find that hard to believe," Artie says.

"You should call her though. Maybe it's the same company you worked for."

"I don't think so. I'm delivering pizzas tonight."

"Who are you working for?"

"I don't know."

Gillian excitedly mentions she applied for a "long shot" job at the Museum of Natural History in New York City to create and edit exhibit cards.

"That's something I never would have thought of applying for," I say.

"Well, start thinking," she says, picking up a fork and tapping it against my head. "We're going to have to crack you like an egg so everybody can see what's inside there."

Artie starts in on how, when he got the job at the company more than a decade ago, he was relieved to be able to buy a condo with central air-conditioning. "Before that all I ever had was the window unit," he says. "I don't ever want to go back to the window unit."

All three of us agree: No one wants to go back to the window unit. There is nothing worse than reverse when it comes to income.

One former coworker asked me excitedly, "Did you get enough severance to pay off your mortgage or, like, just enough for a Jet-Ski and a trailer?" I had to say the latter, and both would have to be bought used.

My severance is coming in a lump sum, but we were offered several choices on how to receive our final pay. Gillian says she's still contemplating an option that will entitle her to ten dollars a week for the rest of her life, the thinking being that she will stay in fantastic shape, living on grapefruit and acai berries on that island off the coast of Korea where people survive to 147, just so those corporate stiffs will have to keep paying her for all eternity.

"I will be collecting a check and they will all be dead," she says.

"You're funny," I tell Gillian.

"Only when I'm with you guys," she says, pushing back on the swing chair. "What's wrong with this thing?"

"I'm in no real hurry to get another full-time job," Artie announces. "My parents just bought me a new computer because I was complaining I couldn't afford to replace it. I'm trying to think about what else I can complain about."

His parents again.

I scan the other diners, dressed in business attire, periodically peering down at the BlackBerrys resting in their laps. For us, this is the opposite of the power lunch. "Hey, this is the lunch of the powerless," I say.

"Stop that. We have so much to offer," Gillian says.

"Speak for yourself," Artie replies.

"You guys have to drop that attitude. The self-deprecating stuff may charm other losers, but you've got to ditch it if you're going to thrive and get a fresh start somewhere. Like after I broke up with Neil, I started wearing lip gloss again. You're going to have to make yourself all fresh and shiny and put yourself out there to find a new job."

Artie leans back quietly for a second, then pops to the edge of the table and says, "We should have called him out into the middle of the parking lot."

"What?" I ask.

"When Mark stuck his goat head out the door and told everybody to come back inside. We should have called him out."

"That *was* nervy of him," Gillian agrees.

"Once you get someone in a parking lot all the rules change," Artie says, clenching his fists. "Parking lots have no rules."

Artie brings both hands up over the table and clasps them together. "Feel that," he says. "It's solid. A mallet. I just swing it back like this and *wallop!*" he says, knocking over an empty glass and sending a handful of crumpled napkins to the floor.

He is seething, and I'm a bit envious of how he can bring up such rage so quickly—one minute laughing and joking, the next clenching his teeth and ready to kill. I could use a little of that in me.

"Calm down," Gillian bemoans. "You're scaring the seagulls."

"That whole morning was surreal," I say. "Eileen tells me they now have desk drills once a week. She said, 'You know, like during the Cold War they used to have drills where schoolkids would get under their desks. Only now, instead of ducking under our desks, we have to see how many seconds it takes to throw all our photos, knickknacks, and holiday tequila into a box and run out the front door.' "

Artie laughs, but then starts to sulk about his loss of attractiveness to the opposite sex. As long as I've known him, he's spent all of his time trying to capture the love of a single woman—one Cassie Hayes of Hayes, Hayes & Hayes Real Estate in Boca Raton. After a year and a half of almost embarrassing persistence, he was finally making some serious headway. They went to a music fest in Chicago last April and the talk around the office was that they were already planning on moving in together. But Gillian told me on the phone earlier that the whole relationship has now unraveled, and Cassie may even already be seeing someone else.

"Joblessness does not appeal to the ladies," Artie claims.

"That's not true. It'll just make you seem more Bohemian," Gillian says. "That's sexy."

"Gillian met a guy at our career counseling seminar," I say.

"Is that bad—meeting over unemployment? Do you think it's like hooking up with someone in rehab?" she asks.

"Doomed," Artie declares.

"I bet—"

"I should have been an ass kisser," Artie says, cutting me off. "I thought people saw through it, but they don't. It works. It gets you more money, promotions, window seats. I can't believe I always thought ass kissing was a waste of time."

"That's what people like us think," I tell him. "That's why we never get anywhere."

"Here you guys go again." Gillian sighs. "It's just business. If we were the greatest ass kissers in the world we'd still be out of work. Sign o' the times, boys."

"I wish I really believed that," Artie says.

"Ahh, I'm stuffed." Gillian lazily leans back, shuffling her feet, desperately trying to get some motion going. "What's wrong with this thing? Does the other side swing?"

I really wish we could sway right now, rock through a sweet afternoon with our bellies full and the waitress bringing Artie and me new attitudes for dessert.

"I almost forgot," I say, reaching under the table and pulling up a brown paper bag. "Close your eyes."

Nobody closes their eyes but I rip the brown paper away anyway and they both shout out, "Excaliburs!" so loud all the power lunchers look up from their BlackBerrys.

"One for each of you," I say proudly.

"Way to follow through, Reiner," Artie says. "With all the chaos that day I'd forgotten all about them. You son of a bitch, you pulled it off."

"They look even better in sunlight," Gillian says, holding hers up. "The sword is glistening. I'm going to put it in the center of a cluster of candles at the end of my bathtub. Thank you."

"Was that just your acceptance speech?" Artie says.

"I believe it was." Gillian beams.

"Next time we should meet at a bar," Artie suggests.

"Ahhh, my tooth," I say, spitting out a piece of hard crust from the mahi-mahi sandwich. "I think I cracked it."

"Oooo, that's a piece of your tooth right there." Gillian flinches. "Check please!"

"I know exactly when my dental coverage ended," I mumble. "And it was two days ago."

something's gotta give

The door opens. I've got a hot pizza cradled in my arms and a six-pack of Diet Dr Pepper in my teeth. The woman's got a towel over her head, a tiny baby in her hands, something that looks like a canister of Carpet Fresh tucked tightly beneath her chin, and what appear to be heat-seeking missiles but are probably just toys of some kind clenched under each armpit. She's using every nook and cranny of her body to hold the things that hold her life together, and we've got, absolutely got, to do business. Something's gotta give.

This is, like, my ninth stop and they keep getting better and better. My seventh stop was to a woman sitting in an idling car outside Curves on Lucerne Avenue. I forget that people with cellphones can order pizzas from anywhere. You can be in line at the DMV and order up a pie and a dozen wings.

Omar? (I've decided to refer to the enterprising dude as Omar with a question mark because I'm tired of inquiring about his name) was sitting out-side Augie's when I showed up. "Seven an hour and the tips are yours," he said, backing up the Jeep Grand Cherokee he was driving this time. He was in a rush and quickly explained (only because I asked and held on to his side mirror) that he'd been subcontracted by several small pizza places that, due to rising costs, didn't want to insure their own drivers. "So you insure us?" I asked.

"What do you think?" he said, knocking my hand off the mirror.

Before I headed out for my first delivery, Augie gave me a smart speech about how I should get personal during the brief moment I have with each customer. "Especially if they invite you into their homes." Pet the pets, point out nice furniture. Let them think of the experience as more of a friend stop-ping by for a visit.

"Nice baby," I say to the woman before me.

"Come on in for a sec," she says, pointing the way with her head. I can't see her face but she has the sweetest voice. She hasn't really seen me, either, because if she looks up she'll lose her grip on the Carpet Fresh. But she knows who I am. She can see my midsection and the bright red blanket warmer I've got her next meal in.

I follow her across the hardwood floors to the big soft couch where she starts to lower the baby and everything comes tumbling down around us like someone just whacked the belly of a stork-shaped piñata.

"I've got to go upstairs and get the money," she says.

Due to my training I immediately say, "OK, I'll watch the baby," and be-fore I can take it back she is gone. She has complete faith in me. People do that at dinnertime. I stand there looking at the baby and tell myself it's no big deal to take responsibility of a two-month-old baby on your first day on the job as a pizza deliverer. I'm a friend stopping by for a visit. Besides, if I let her waste time fussing with the baby, the next pie is going to be late for sure (we have a twenty-four-minute limit). Then I notice there is no nice furniture, no furniture at all, actually, except for the couch centered on the high-gloss floor. Where am I going to put the pie?

I almost forget about the baby until it moves. I didn't expect that. It looks too new to be moving. The tiny hands grab the feet, transforming it into a spherical humanoid capable of wobbling and rolling in different directions. The Scotchgarded couch is perfect for these antics and she keeps pulling these cliff-hangers on me, rolling up to the edge and then tumbling back into the crater her father probably created by plopping down in the same spot after work day after day.

I think about picking her up, but I don't want to tip the pie. (That's another thing Augie was very clear about.)

The baby starts to whine a little but I can't get my priorities straight and for some idiotic reason I put both hands under the pie to keep it secure and stick my pinkie in her mouth, figuring I can lead her back to her father's ditch. That's all I am willing to give up from securing the pie: one little pinkie.

"Come on, girl, keep it level, baby," I say to her as she spits out my finger and starts screaming. I jump back, thinking I might have scorched her with the pizza bag.

"I'll be right there," the mother hollers down, as if it is nothing to hear her baby screech with pain while she's downstairs hanging out with the pizza man.

The baby is hanging its head over the edge now and it is kind of a big melon, so I know the weight of it will soon bring the rest of the cargo down onto the hard deck. On the other hand, the drop is only like a foot and a half. I start thinking pros and cons. Now, the kid and the pie probably weigh about the same, I think, considering that the pie has everything on it, and if the kid crashes she might end up with a little knot on her crown, but if this pie goes down from three or four feet it's all over. I gotta call the boss and . . .

The teeny-weeny hands are moving out front now into a diving position. What instinct. She is telling me, "I'm OK, don't worry about me, I know what to do." She probably does this all the time, I tell myself. Besides, if anything happens it's the woman upstairs with the towel over her head that'll be guilty. What's she gonna do, tell her husband, "It wasn't my fault. The pizza man was supposed to be watching her!"

I never expected it to come down to this. The baby or the pizza? A newborn or a $12.22 pie?

"I'm sorry, here you go," Mama says, slowly coming down the stairs like a bride whom everyone has been waiting on for hours. The towel is off her head now and barely covering her torso. I have a fetish for tan lines and hers are extraordinary but they are eclipsed by a hairdo that is extravagantly styled, all fuzzed out and fizzing. I *thought* I heard a blow dryer. The princess was putting 1,250 watts to her hair while I was standing her baby up against the couch, trying to use my legs as a fence, stuck between a 480-degree pie and a 98.6-degree ball of chubbery. If I wasn't such a good friend I'd be angry. Plus when she places that tip in my hand, that healthy tip, all is forgiven. I have my answer in several sheets of green folding commodity. I've made all the right moves.

"You're good with children. Do you babysit?" she says.

I laugh but she says, "Seriously, I'm new to the area. My husband, if he ever comes, is going to be at least three months. I just started at Tri-Tech and I asked people in the office there if they knew of a good babysitter and they just stared at me."

I don't want to just stare at her so I say, "I don't know. I haven't really thought about it. I—"

The baby starts to scream again so she hurriedly says, "Here, scribble your number on the pizza box. Maybe we can work something out."

I glance back to see if the squirmy imp's face is turning bright red yet from that one little slip-up, but she looks grand as the happy mother picks her up and holds her high over her head, about an inch from the ceiling fan. "Thanks, ma'am," I say, breaking into a trot. I'm definitely getting the hang of this. I may have found my niche. Screw pressure cleaning.

As I'm lifting up the hatchback of the car to throw the warmer bag in, I get a slight nudge right behind the knees like a sneaky uncle would do to make you buckle. But it's the nose of Omar?'s car—a white Prius this time.

"I love that you can sneak up on a pizza man," he says.

"That engine is quiet. I didn't hear a thing," I say. "Are you following me?"

"Just checking up. How are your times?"

"Eighteen minutes on each delivery, give or take."

"Augie seems pleased. What about you?"

"People are always glad to see me. I'm not used to that. And I like going into strangers' houses. Hey, do we do babysitting?"

"I don't know," Omar? says.

"That's what I said."

i'm glad nobody sent you

This is my seventh pass by the house tonight. The front window is giving off the blue light of a TV flickering deep inside. I hate to have to bother someone during one of her favorite shows. I keep doing a U-turn by the canal at the end of the street, dragonflies erratically diving in front of my head-lights with each cut of the wheel. On my fifth pass I noticed the lawn is im-maculate. The turf is thick and the edging is military straight. Not what I expected. On the sixth pass I noticed a child's motorized jeep on the side of the garage. No one mentioned children.

On my eighth pass, my nerves are no better than the day I was sent to interview that family of the helicopter crash victim. I stop just beyond the property line, my car now aimed toward the main road in case I need to make a quick getaway.

"No one ordered a pizza here." A sharp voice drifts across the lawn before I even reach the front path.

"No, no, I'm just here looking for Bo. Are you Linda?"

"Bo? Who are you? You know damn well he's not here! Who sent you?"

I am lost in the light of the bright lamppost but still heading toward the front door when there is a burst of noise, a loud rattling. The garage door is ris-ing and it barely reaches the three-foot mark when a woman limbos beneath it. She is wearing bright red leggings without shoes and a black dress, and is carry-ing one of those long poles that people use to pick fruit from high branches. She's pulling at the cord that snaps its jaws and I stop in my tracks at the thought of her plucking off one of my ears like a sweet clementine orange.

"I was just in the neighborhood so I thought I—"

"Don't! Don't even."

"OK, I knew he wouldn't be here but he was my friend."

She crosses the lawn directly in front of me and walks up the path to a small bench on the front porch. She sits down and quietly rests the fruit picker across her lap.

There's no place for me to sit so I walk up and stand over her, looking down into the intricate curls of her hair.

"You have a very nice home," I say.

"He said he never loved me," she says without looking up. "Why would you bother saying something like that? Even if it's true. Why? What kind of person does that? Yell, 'You're a freaking bitch' or an 'f-ing wench' or what-ever. But why say something like that?"

Her head is pointed away from me, so I move to the other side of the bench. A bright light on a motion sensor flashes on and she has to shield her eyes.

"Sorry."

"Go! Back to the other side!" she pleads. "Thank you. And could you take off that hat? It's distracting."

"Sure. Listen, I don't want to bother you."

"His family call you? Amy? That girl doesn't know life beyond her frilly bordered scrapbooks."

"No, I had called them. Bo and I were best friends up through junior high."

"What happened?"

"Huh?"

"What happened after that?"

"I don't know. I've been thinking about that myself."

"You must have a lot of time to think about things."

"I'm recently unemployed."

"Jesus, is this the kind of stuff you unemployed people are doing with your free time now—looking up your long-lost buddies?"

"Just me, I think."

"I'm not some hardass."

"I don't think you're a—"

"I worry about him, too. I'd like to know something . . . that he's all right. I mean, people do disappear down here. His family didn't even want us to move down here to begin with, but my parents are nearby and Joseph got a good job at BG Correctional. What's your name anyhow?"

"Jeffrey. Jeffrey Reiner."

"Bo never mentioned your name."

"Well, it's been a long time."

Linda crosses her legs and starts swatting dirt and mulch off the leggings covering the soles of her feet. "I was going to try and pluck a mango off the tree of the neighbors behind me," she says. "They go to bed early."

"Mom." A head pops up from under the garage door. "Are we getting pizza?"

"No, silly boy. You just ate."

"Can I go on the swing with you?"

"Mommy will be right in. Back inside."

She looks over her shoulder and waits a moment. "That's not his child. Though he treated him like he was, until he didn't. Guess he never loved him, either."

Through the bay window I spot the silhouette of the boy racing across the living room and up the stairs.

"At least he didn't feel the need to tell him," she says.

I walk around in front of her to see if she'll look at me. She won't, so I step back and stare off at the Norfolk pine she has on the corner of her lot.

"We were in a midnight choir together," I say. "Sixth grade. Christmas Eve. Our moms had gotten us identical blue double-breasted suit jackets. It's the only time I was ever in a choir."

"Listen, I don't have the time or the energy to get into any of this right now," she says, getting up. "I'll make a deal with you. Help me get the mango and I'll get you a contact that may be of some help. I don't know."

She picks up the pole and throws it over her shoulder like a fishing rod. I trail behind her along the side of the house. Her back lawn is drenched from the sprinkler system so she races across the wet grass and climbs up to the second rung on the backing of the high wooden fence. She's totally unsteady and using the pole in the manner of a tightrope walker to balance herself.

"Hand over the pole," I say. "I can reach it easily."

"No, you shouldn't have to steal fruit. Just grab my waist so I don't go over the side. Don't let me go over."

"I gather that has happened," I say, clutching her from behind. Her waist is small and firm and fits my hands perfectly. I wonder if Bo ever had that same thought every single day until one day he didn't, but suddenly she's in violent motion and I have to focus on holding her steady.

My vision is obscured by the small of her back so I can't see her in action but her narrow shoulders keep whipping back and forth and there are several thumps from the mangos landing in the soggy grass behind us.

"There," she says, turning and jumping down before I even have time to let go of her waist.

She wriggles free and scurries across the yard, gathering the fruit as she goes.

"Here's one for you," she says, walking toward the rear door of the house. "I'll just be a minute. I'll meet you back out front."

In exactly a minute she comes outside but seems more businesslike. "People call the gym Gold's, but it's not like the Gold's Gyms you see all over. A Francis Goldstein owns it. The son, Jeremy Goldstein, is the one who called me," she says, handing me the address to the gym. "He was worried about

Joseph but I was in no mood to hear about it at the time. Apparently he had worked at the gym for a short time after he left us. He was getting into fights with the customers, without reason. This Jeremy said he was acting odd and blaming it on an injury that he got at BG—a blow to the head. That was news to me."

"His family said something about that, too," I say.

Her face turns sour when I mention the family, so I start to thank her and she puts a small drawing of the gym's location in my hand. "It's in an industrial area so it's a little tricky," she says. "And wait a day or so to eat the mango. They're not quite ripe yet."

the sink trap

So you're the accident investigator now—Reiner PI?" Sal says, crawling under the sink.

"I have a little free time and I just feel like I'm the only one who will even look for him now," I say.

"Jesus, what did you cake on here to stop the leak? What is this, C-4?" Sal says.

"Mighty Putty," I say proudly. "I saw it advertised on a late-night commercial. They showed a monkey swinging from a two-hundred-ten-pound chandelier that had been attached to the ceiling with nothing but Mighty Putty."

"Oh yeah, I wish I'd invented this stuff," Sal says. "I'll get to the leak after the garbage disposal. Sorry it took me so long to get over here."

"What does it take to remove a dead-end sign?" I ask him. "Is it just a pole jabbed in the ground or what?"

"What you have," Sal says, sliding out from under the sink (he always likes to come out in the open when he describes something), "is a solid cast-iron pole imbedded in concrete. The concrete is poured in nice and neat but it seeps down and just turns into this big blob—a giant meatball of cement. That's what you'd be pulling up.

"That sign is really driving you crazy, huh?" he says, squirming back under the sink.

"Only on certain days."

"Just say the word and I'll make it disappear."

I hesitate to say the word because Sal does tend to do dramatic things on a whim. On the next corner down from my house a family put up one of those castle bounce houses for a birthday party but then never took it down. Weeks went by and Sal said to me, "You think I should shoot an arrow into that stupid bounce house?"

"Yes, definitely," I said.

The next night an arrow arched through the sky and pierced the bounce house. I guess those things have several points of inflation because it only deflated half of it. We were left with a lopsided puffy castle but it was enough of a disaster to force the people to discard it about two weeks later.

"No, that's OK. I can live with the sign," I say.

"So what are you doing about work?"

"I'm just sending out résumé after résumé every day. Waiting and waiting."

"You should do something completely new. Something that's never been done before."

"Everything's been done."

"Oh no, there's all kinds of things to do and discover out there."

I chuckle to myself hearing these words coming from a guy who rarely ventures beyond a ten-mile radius and spends damned near most of his time on his back in cramped spaces.

"I saw a documentary the other day about these three guys who went to this country called Kyrgyzstan," Sal says.

"Where's that?"

"I think it's in central Asia. Have you become one of those people who always have to know where everything is? Anyway, they found nine mountains there that had never been climbed, and I guess if you're the first to climb them you get to name the mountain or *pik*—Russian for mountain."

"Who lets them name the mountain?"

"I don't know. Generals, kings. That's the rule in Kyrgyzstan. It's on the books, I guess. So they started naming them after their girlfriends—Pik Ashley—and their dogs, Pik . . . I can't think of the name of the guy's dog; it'll come to me. And when they started to run out of names, one guy even named one after his cleaning lady, Pik Hilda."

"I'm not going to set off to be an explorer. That's not going to pay for Kristin's college."

"I'm just sayin', the world is still fresh. You don't have to have big aspira-tions like that but . . . I always wanted to captain a ferryboat, and look at me now."

"You can afford to be adventuresome, pension man."

"You must have some little dreams left."

Not really. I remember we were all sitting around work one day and we were fed up about something or other and thinking we'd all quit until one as-sociate said, "But what would we do?" And we just kind of sat there. It wasn't as if one of us was going to go off and become a soloist for the philharmonic or a syndicated cartoonist or a relief pitcher for the New York Mets.

What would we do?

"You know, next time this thing gets a trickle don't put this gunk on it," Sal lectures. "Just get one of those . . . like they use with the horses. One of those girdle-like things . . ."

"A bridle."

"No, no," Sal says, sliding out again. "Like the buggy horses in Central Park have to catch the crap. That crap-cradle-like thing."

"I've never seen something like that under a sink."

"Yeah, same premise, only smaller," Sal explains before ducking back under. "I wish I'd invented that."

"Sal, you are a godsend," Anna exclaims, strolling into the kitchen.

"You have the most beautiful calves," Sal says. "You don't have to be stuck with this guy, you know. You can use the work thing as an excuse to vamoose. Plenty of wives do."

"Honey, why don't you get down lower and watch what he's doing?" Anna nudges me.

"Yeah, learn something," Sal says, getting back to work.

I crouch down.

"Get out of here!" Sal barks. "No, no, I'm just kidding. There's no reason you can't pick this stuff up. You've just got some kind of damned mental block about it."

He's right. Years ago I had a neighbor who took us out on his boat and grew furious every time we docked because I was completely useless when it came to tying the boat up. Over the winter I got a book and became a master at everything from the single doucot knot to the double cut slantbanger.

Knots have really cool names. My neighbor was amazed. He was so proud of me. I remember him standing at the bow shaking his head and saying, "I did not know you had it in you."

Neither did I. I guess that's the point. I guess that's Sal's point.

"Ah, good thing I got this done today. I'm going to be tied up for the next few weeks," Sal says, crawling out of the cabinet. "Peggy bartered with our vet. I build a deck for him and he fixes our Goldie's hip."

"Sal, if there's anything I can do for you, just let me know. I mean it."

"We're going to hang, right?"

"Sure."

"And let me know about the dead-end sign."

"Don't worry about it. I'm all right. I've sort of accepted it as the family crest."

simply soda

asked for this.

No wonder Sal showed up to fix the sink yesterday. He called late last night to find out if I could give his younger stepbrother a ride. I was jumping out of my skin. "A ride? Oh yeah. I'm excellent at that."

"Bennie's a bit of a whack job," Sal said. "So this will repay me for every pipe I've ever snaked at your place. If I have to drive him to one more meeting, I'll kill him. So you're not only doing me a favor, you're saving a life."

Meeting as in Narcotics Anonymous and I'm already late picking him up. I don't like to beep the horn for anybody so I walk up to the door of Bennie's duplex and he's currently rummaging around for his keys. "I've only got the one door in my life, so I like to keep it locked," he says.

Bennie's a scruffy, scrappy-looking character. He's wearing those skinny girl jeans and sea green Converse sneakers. As soon as he climbs into the car, he burrows back in the seat and puts his knees against the glove compartment. He reminds me of one of the Oasis brothers, whichever one is more unruly and obstinate. I've always wanted to have that wiry British look. It's more than just the clothes and the shave. I guess you have to have a certain body type, too. That Green Day guy pulls it off. I think he's from Oakland. But you'd think he'd been breastfed in Liverpool by a harem of Clash groupies.

"How do you get that British look?" I ask.

"I don't know. The drugs?" Bennie says. "It just happens."

Bennie goes quiet quickly, but we've got a decent ride ahead of us so I try to make conversation.

"I was really disappointed when I first found out what meth labs really are," I say.

"I don't do meth," Bennie says.

"I wasn't saying that. I'm just talking about how when I first saw one of those CNN reports about the DEA raiding a string of meth labs in some small town, I didn't know a meth lab is just a hot plate and some Sudafed on a kitchen counter. The lab thing confuses people."

"I got you," Bennie mumbles.

"You pick up the real estate section in any town in West Virginia and it has like Ranch House, three/two with large family room, meth lab, screened-in patio . . . And it's very misleading," I say. "I mean, I show up to buy that place, I want to see a decent lab in the east wing of the house with stainless steel counters and Bunsen burners and stuff, not some clutter on the kitchen counter."

"Are you going to be driving me all the time?" Bennie asks. "I have to be there by seven-thirty."

"How often do you have to go?"

"Four times a week."

"Well, we'll see. I've been looking for some volunteer work. Looks good on my résumé."

Bennie reveals that he was arrested two Thursdays ago on buying and possession down by Dixie Highway in West Palm. I can see that he's avoiding something, straining not to tell me what he was possessing.

"Crack?" I ask. I know if I was a drug addict that's the one I'd be most embarrassed of.

"They found the soda can first," he says. "I'd put the Mountain Dew can in my sock."

"Mountain Dew?" I say.

"Diet Mountain Dew," he says.

I don't know what the heck he's talking about (I know more about meth labs), but he explains how you puncture holes in the can to do the crack and . . . Anyway, he had stuffed the can in his sock when the cop pulled him over.

"But they found residue and then they tested my saliva," he says. "What would you be doing tonight if you didn't have to drive me?"

"Watching my favorite TV show," I say.

"What's that?"

"*Bones.*"

"I used to have favorite TV shows," he says.

We pass a Miata pulled over on the side of the road. A tall guy is around the far side taking a leak, oblivious that the teeny car is providing zero camouflage.

"That looks liberating," Bennie says. "Someday I won't have to do all my pissing in a cup. Hey, have you ever gotten anything out of a dream sequence on a TV show? Entertainment, meaning, anything?"

"No."

"I don't know why they keep doing it."

"Can we go back to the soda can? Where'd you learn how to use the can? I'm trying to learn how to do things. I mean, if someone gives me drugs, I usually know what to do with them. I mean, it's easy to pop some pills or smoke something. I've never even done coke but if someone gave me some, I know I'd just have to stick it up my nose. But this whole can thing is puzzling."

"Believe me, it's not that complicated," he says.

We drive a little farther, and I feel like I should say something to try to help. You know, I say, there're a lot of prescription drugs that doctors will give you in a second if you're depressed or whatever. "I looked into that," he says. "They all list diarrhea as a possible side effect. I don't like diarrhea. You ever see that commercial where everybody is taking Paxil and they're all emboldened—going to their high school reunions, volunteering for dunk tank duty at charity events and whatnot? I don't want to be a guy dropping into a dunk tank and bursting with diarrhea."

"I hear you. How come there are never any good side effects like 'long-term use of this medicine could add six inches to your broad jump or lead to supervision and improved cornering skills while driving at high speeds.' Stuff like that."

"Cornering skills would be nice," he says.

"Maybe you could—"

"The meeting is about this stuff," he says abruptly. "I really don't want to have a meeting on the way to the meeting. I'm already going four times a week and . . ."

"Right, right. Do you know if the police, when they filed a report, listed the evidence as just 'soda can' or put down that it was Mountain Dew?" I say to change the subject.

"They put Mountain Dew."

"Diet Mountain Dew?" I ask.

"I don't know," he says, annoyed. "The report is in my folder here if you want to look at it."

As we pull into the parking lot he says, "This is the first time I've been to a meeting at this place. But they told me there's a Denny's just up the road if you want to wait for me."

"No, I'll just hang out in the car," I say.

He forgets the folder so I look through it and find the police report. Put dome light on and start searching for . . . there it is. I'll be damned.

"Diet Mountain Dew."

The driver's-side door suddenly opens. Bennie's back. "They kicked me out," he says. "It's just an all-women thing. No men are allowed at this one."

"Wow, I didn't know they did that," I say.

"Well, they do," he says, showing me a pamphlet that lists separate meetings for gays, African Americans, couples, teens, and Jews.

"A lot of segregation in the drug addiction world," I say.

"Yeah," he says.

There's another meeting he can attend at a Catholic church at 8 P.M. so I offer to drive him over there.

"They gave me a school flier back there. 'Too Good for Drugs' is the new slogan," he says, flicking the flier onto the floorboards.

"I guess that's a replacement for 'Just Say No,'" I say. "My son got one of those fliers."

"Kind of cocky—Too Good for Drugs," he huffs. "You too good for drugs?"

"I'm not too good for drugs," I say.

In fact, I used to fantasize about having a bad drug or alcohol problem myself, where I reached the point that my whole life was falling apart, visibly going to pieces. All my peers could say, without a doubt, "His life is shit." All my family and friends were estranged. Well, maybe the dog or the pizza delivery guy still cared about me. But that's it. I was violent, uncaring, selfish, incoherent, and carrying nothing in my back pocket but a suspended license. Does anyone know if they actually give you something that says SUSPENDED LICENSE on it, or is it just that the one you have is no good? Anyway, then I'd go into an expensive, extensive rehab program and then—and this was the good part—once I got out, all the pressure would be off. Nobody would expect a damn thing from me anymore. I could get a little stressless job, maybe caddy for a while, and get away with it. I could live on tips. I've always wanted someone to pass me in the street and say, "Hey, what are you doing with yourself these days?" And my reply is "I'm living on tips."

So my new job would be wholesomely carefree, but not nearly as whimsical as my new home life, where every little thing I did would become monumental. There'd be dozens of daily remarks from the in-laws. "He's doing so well." "His eyes are so clear." "He hasn't hit anyone in over a week."

And every year, probably around the holidays, people would ask, "How's Jeffrey doing?" and the answer would be "Great, he's been off the drugs for over a year now." And the following Christmas: "Great, he's been off the drugs for over two years now."

You can see how this works, can't you? Every year, as long as I stayed off the drugs, people would ask how I'm doing and the answer would always be . . .

"Great."

But I never took that route, what with drugs being so expensive and all, and my predicament now doesn't really lend itself to that formula, does it?

"Why don't you just come in this time?" Bennie says as I pull to the front of the church.

"Go in? No," I say. "I'm the driver. I have to stay with the car."

"This isn't a bank heist," he says.

"Let's just pretend it is so I don't have to go into an NA meeting, OK?" I say.

"OK," he says, grabbing my biceps and squeezing it forcefully. "I could thank you now, but someday you're going to need me and I'll be there for you. So do you want to put the thank-you on hold and have me owe you? Or do you just want the thank-you?"

"Can I think about it while you're in the meeting?"

"Sure thing," he says, getting out and skipping toward the meeting.

He's back. "There's absolutely no one in there," he says. "This one old woman was on her way out, and I asked her where the priest was, and she said he's playing racquetball."

I start to drive through the church lot and notice a building in the back all lit up, and sure enough, they have signs on the door for MEETING GOERS.

I pull up to the entranceway so he can get in quickly. As he gets out, he turns to me and says, "I used to play racquetball."

Park the car and start trying to reprogram my radio stations. I have no idea what I'm doing, but that's just as well.

Think about the Diet Mountain Dew can, and how embarrassing an incident like that would have been for me. Not because of being arrested, or confronted with my drug problem, but because I'm too cheap to buy brand names. Right there on the police report, in big bold generic letters, it would have said, "SIMPLY SODA (from COSTCO)."

Wonder about the crew in that meeting. Probably talking about all the things they used to do before the drugs took over their lives. "I used to have favorite TV shows, used to play racquetball, used to pee in private, used to sleep in a warm bed, used to have a good job, used to have a wife, used to have pride in myself . . . but at least I don't have diarrhea."

Get out of car and sit on the hood. Look up at the milky, phosphorescent parking lot lights and think about the future.

I used to do that.

the irregular

've been summoned to the state's Workforce Alliance Center but I can't find it. The name sounds like something out of *Battlestar Galactica* so I think my main mistake is I'm searching for a tall-pillared futuristic building made of crystal and magnesium alloy when I should be looking for something more akin to an abandoned Dairy Queen. Names will confuse you sometimes. In this case, I think it is meant to. "Workforce Alliance" sounds all socialist and worker-friendly, but it actually seems to be the way the state of Florida shakes you down over your unemployment claims. I'm pretty sure they're going to demand documentary evidence that I've been knocking down doors for another job. No proof, no more unemployment checks.

I pull over to call the center's information line for directions, but my phone is already vibrating. It's Gillian. "I've got news," she says excitedly.

"One second. I'm just pulling over. I've been summoned to the Workforce Alliance."

"Oh, they called me. I refused to go," Gillian says.

"You can refuse? Hold on. I'm pulling—"

"I've got an internship that I think is going to lead to a job."

"Frame Publishing? They called me for a reference on you."

"No, I didn't get that. I don't know what you said to those people. But remember when I applied for that Museum of Natural History position?"

Of course I do, but Gillian is talking furiously and losing me fast. If I'm getting this right, her long shot at the museum was a bust, but the people there put her in contact with an opportunity to work with the curator at the Hard Rock Hotel & Casino in Broward County.

"Wait, what's the connection?" I say, perplexed. "You apply at the Museum of Natural History and end up at the Hard Rock?"

"I'll get into the details later when we meet at that bar Artie's been talking about."

"OK. Good enough," I say, pulling up on a stretch of grass adjacent to a large outlet complex. "Have you ever seen this Alliance building?"

"It looks like a giant wind sock made of brick," Gillian says.

"OK, I see it. Thanks."

I make it as far as the parking lot before a woman with greasy blond hair approaches me for (1) A cigarette. (2) A ride. (3) "A little bit of some kind of cash."

I once had to pick up a friend at the county stockade and had to put up with similar inquiries, but I didn't expect it here, at the unemployment outpost next to the Shoe Carnival.

There are also several other small gatherings around cars, sort of an unemployed tailgating atmosphere. Only instead of hearing fragments of complaints about the coach or the running back, I pass by mutterings of "The state is ripping me off. I've got at least thirteen more weeks of checks coming."

I'm getting more nervous with every grumble. Years ago, in order to collect unemployment benefits, you'd have to come by an office like this one with proof that you'd been applying for at least three jobs a week. Due to everything being online now and the astronomical number of unemployed, it's mostly on the honor system, unless you're called in and someone says, "Do you have your log with you? No. Well, how soon can you get it here? We'll have someone follow you home to see if it actually exists. Have you been applying for at least four jobs per week? Are you by chance working off the books for a dubious businessman who remains nameless and appears out of nowhere behind the wheel of a variety of unregistered vehicles? Could you just turn to the last entry in the log, please?"

It shouldn't be a big burden to keep such a log, but everything that has to do with work seems like a burden to me now.

In the waiting area, a well-manicured woman is keeping several others titillated by her stories about food stamps. "I had no idea you could use them for sweets," she says. '"My neighbor came home with two boxes of Häagen-Dazs bars."

My anxiety about being singled out is quelled when a woman named Nelida dubs herself "our facilitator" and corrals about thirty-five of us into a horseshoe in the center of a large conference room. She passes out wristbands that we're all supposed to wear now so the public at large knows we're unemployed.

"You're tagging us," a woman up front says.

"You never know. You're in line at a coffee shop and a headhunter for Scripps spots your I-need-a-job wristband, and next thing you know you're back in business," she says.

Maybe it could also serve as a MedicAlert bracelet, you know, a message to the paramedic saying, "Do not revive. His family is probably better off without him."

She begins taking us back to the basics. "Now, your résumés should be one page and that doesn't mean just making the font smaller if it's two pages. You need to hone it down."

This is all becoming so repetitive. I don't mind going through the motions but all the assistance and resources available feel as if they are set up to motivate and enlighten everyone but me. Nothing seems realistic or helpful.

"I wish I had enough to fill one page," a guy around the first bend in the horseshoe says. "Can we make the font bigger?"

"No, that will make you look like a kindergartner," she says.

Everybody giggles like a bunch of kindergartners.

"Oh, we have some bad body language in here," she says.

All of us look at our neighbors. We are refugees at slumping camp; any second we could slide off our chairs and all land in a heap on the floor.

Nelida gets four of us to sit up straight and begins to rattle off the usual jargon—careers targeted for growth, skill sets, and something called SWOT, which stands for "strengths, weaknesses, opportunities, and threats."

We all sit up when she mentions threats, but then her voice lowers. "OK, we've got food coming in."

"Nice," the bigger-font guy says.

"Not for you people," she says. "We're going to have to cut this short. But . . . I don't know what to tell you. How's that? I don't know what to tell you."

It's an odd moment, as if we've caught Nelida at the instant she, too, is tired of going through the motions. Or maybe it's just a craving for Olive Garden breadsticks. Who knows? She doesn't even give us a signal to move out, but a handful of people take the lead and quietly shuffle toward the door.

I'm in hot pursuit, right behind the lady with the food-stamp-sweets neighbor. I'm making a clean getaway when I hear "You!"

It's never me. It's probably never you, either, right? But you turn anyway and standing right before a narrow stairway that winds down to the street is a broad-shouldered man in a blazing purple shirt. I put my head back down and start to make the turn when I feel the grip. His hand has reached out like one of those arcade claws and plucked me out of the mass exodus like a stuffed Stewie doll.

"Look at you," he says. "Back to my place."

I'm supposed to follow, but I think about making a run for it. Maybe this is how the state does it, sort of an unorthodox audit. They can't check everybody's log so they just snatch one suspect (we're *all* suspect) and put him through the ringer.

"Oh, you have that look," he says, peering over his shoulder without breaking stride.

What look? He's making me feel like I'm an assembly line reject. I'm the doughnut with no hole, the cracked egg. He stood there letting all those other jobless mugs go by, but mine stood out? *I'm the irregular?*

And what's with the "back to my place"? Who says that?

"You packin' any rage?" he says, turning again.

"No."

"Good. I don't need any of that up in here."

The purple shirt is shimmering and it grabs his body like a silk sheet each time he dodges left or right. I can see the contour of his muscles highlighted every three or four steps. He's a remarkable physical specimen.

"Watch your step," he says when we reach an alcove at the end of the hallway. "It's sunken."

A sunken office—this really is a place. There is only one computer terminal, but it is circled by a variety of well-kept desks. It looks like this could have been a storage room for extra office furniture, but he has made it his own, utilizing everything the place has to offer. Taped across two of the desks is a homemade computer banner that simply says CARL on it. Yeah, this place is all Carl.

"I don't have my log," I say.

"What's that?" he asks. "Make yourself at home. Spread out."

I grasp a chair and slide it toward where's he's setting up. "No, spread out. Let's utilize the space."

I back off toward an oval-topped desk. "Pull a drawer out," he says. "Like this. You can put your feet up on it."

He leans back and lays his feet atop an open filing cabinet drawer so I do the same.

"Don't do it just because I'm doing it," Carl insists. "I know you're not that type. So what brings you here?"

"I was told to come. The Alliance sent a—"

"Have you been getting God's guidance in all this?" he says.

I'm startled that a state facilitator is coming at me from this direction. I start to say that I'm not a particularly religious person, but he drops the spiritual search before I can answer. "What do your skills lead to?"

"I did listings for a paper but there're no jobs there. People tell me I should look into technical writing."

He jolts up, gives me a once-over, and says, "I assume that doesn't involve anything technical?"

"I'm not really—"

"No, no technical nonsense for you. What else?"

"I had some retail experience years ago so I went to apply at the new Kohl's—"

"Kohl's. No. That ain't your style. My wife shops there. Half the place is sandals. I sense something else inside of you. You got something going on. Thing is, every so often I take on an unemployed fellow like yourself as a project. Used to take on women—some problems. To the point!" he says, stiffening his back. "I call it my piloting program. It's not some state mentoring crap, so get that out of your head. I just call it pilot because I do the radio-controlled planes out at Okeheelee Park on the third Saturday of every month. Don't worry, I won't steer you into the wires and zap your ass."

Carl chuckles, opens a wide bottom drawer, and puts both feet in it as if it's a whirlpool footbath. "The pilot program takes a little extra effort, but I think it's worth it," he says. "Plus I'm on a diet. I have to keep my mind occupied when the breadsticks are callin'. Anyway, I've got to step it up. A job is like gold now. Who would have ever thought? During the time when everybody wore those hats—those fedoras."

"During the Depression?"

"The big depression, yeah. They be wearin' those hats all the time, even in the soup lines. I don't like to wear hats, but I'd like to have one to sail across the room once in a while. Where was I? A job is gold. But I don't want you thinking that way. You're only thinking about survival, aren't you? Don't let that happen," Carl says, slapping his hand down on the desk. "Something's going to fall on you. Something good. I can sense it. You feeling it?"

"I'm actually kind of numb."

" 'Cause you're running around like a little ninny—'I need a job. I need a job. I need a job.'

"Sorry, you don't deserve that. You know, I was watching that Histrionic Channel the other night, and they were commenting on some general— Pittan or Pattin, something like that—and they referred to his finest hour as crossing the westerly front at the Battle of the Bilge or some nonsense."

"I don't think I've ever had a finest hour."

"That's what I'm saying, you can't rush a man's finest hour. Time, time— give it to yourself."

"I actually have a little time because I have some severance."

"Oh, that's what I like to hear. Sev-er-ance. It rolls off the tongue, doesn't it? Yeah, something is going to fall on you. Just wait. You zig or zag the wrong way it's going to miss you. Stay pat. What's tucked up in your gut? You must have had some expectations when you were a squirt. Let it out. It's not all trapped for good."

In the past, I never really liked it when people thought I should be doing something different, something better. Some people thought my job was mundane. I didn't think of it that way. I've never had big dreams. I know I don't have any special talent. I kind of accept that. It might sound sad, but it's real basic to me. Work may be a hole you disappear in, but accepting the job gives you things in return—health insurance, food, a place to sleep. A place where you can *stop* dreaming.

"I came up with this little ditty in my head this morning on the ride in," Carl says. "This fully formed tune just popped in my head. My own personal hit. God knows how long it was trapped in there. I might have to book some studio time."

I laugh, but Carl stops me short. "I'm not the entertainment," he says.

He seems to want more from me. I gauge that, so far, I am a poor substitute for garlic buttered breadsticks, so I admit to him that I have had this daydream about being famous and having one of those odd overseas followings. You know, like David Hasselhoff being huge in Germany. I can already hear people in the business saying, "When Jeffrey Reiner performed in New York, people just stared at him. But in Armenia, he's all the rage. They've even named a creamy dessert after him."

"Hah, imagine having a creamy dessert named after you in a foreign land," Carl says. "Now we're talking. How 'bout the spiritual? What you got going?"

"I almost got on my knees in a parking garage the other day."

"That's a start. But don't be telling me what I want to hear. It's always easier to put it on than it is to pull it off. You understand what I'm saying?"

"I think so. I don't want to be a phony."

"Are you meeting new people?"

"I've actually gotten mixed up in searching for an old friend. This guy Bo I haven't seen since eighth grade."

"What are you going to do with him when you find him?"

"I don't know. See what he's doing."

"That's peculiar. But yeah, go find BoBo. Keep him in the mix. Boy, I'm glad I got ahold of you," Carl says. "I know your type. You wouldn't have stopped and reevaluated your life until twenty years from now and then you would have been a puddle of regrets—a sticky waffle-syrupy puddle of what the hell just happened? Lucky you had this forced upon you now. Damn lucky."

Carl starts to stand but his feet are stuck in the drawer so he sits back down. "Yeah, I'm going to be keeping an eye on you. I'm going to be checking up on you," he says, rattling both feet. "This one cabinet is a bear trap, I'm telling you. I know you're straight up. I don't say that to many people but sometimes it just takes one other person to know you're straight up and then there's no stopping you. Go. Go home and discuss all this with your lady. Not about a job. No, no—fulfillment and spiritual rejuvenation. That's what you discuss."

"OK."

"And don't forget to look for me out at Okeheelee. Bring the missus by. Just look in the sky for the Tiger MiG Seventeen with the red tail."

"OK, maybe we'll take a ride out there."

"And take off that stupid wristband."

My one leg is asleep from resting on the open drawer but I strain up and head for the door. It's a shame I'm limping because I'm actually feeling a bit empowered now. I can see the light. I finally have a mentor, who fits my style. Omar?'s giving me a little work here and there. I've cut my ties to the company and all the bullshit self-help and career counseling propaganda out there. Plus I still have a pile of days before me to provide the perfect incubation period while I evolve into something new and fresh and shiny. I actually feel a little indestructible, but you'd never know it by my spastic body language. I've got the Boggle hobble going and I'm only halfway to the door and contemplating how I'm going to hurl my frozen right leg up out of this sunken office when Carl blurts "Rodney Hindrick!"

"Excuse me?"

"Hindrick, my best friend in eighth grade. Wonder what that lard-ass is up to this afternoon?"

Carl picks up the phone receiver and then lets it slip from his grip. "You!" he says, pointing at me again and shaking his head.

"I'm still curious why you picked me." I say.

"Why question things now?" he replies.

on the back of a headrest

Oh shit, Anna has her glasses on. Don't get me wrong, I love her glasses— thin, timid black frames—but when she puts them on, it always means trouble. Her bountiful eyelashes batting above the rims would be a turn-on if I didn't know what was coming.

"Where have you been all afternoon?" she says. "Were you with Artie and Gillian again?"

"No, we just met that one time for lunch—to network. I was at the Workforce Alliance. Doesn't it sound intimidating?"

"How much did you spend on that networking lunch?"

"Artie treated. Well, his parents actually. They weren't there, but they told Artie to pick up the check on them."

"Look at this," she says, turning to the several forms and documents that are evenly spaced across the kitchen table like unwelcoming placemats. "This all came today. Your company kind of screwed us here," she says.

"Hey, I told you I put the 'my company' days behind me."

"I know. But look at this. It says here the severance pay was taken from a frozen pension fund so even though—"

"Wait, are these notices from the company or the government?"

"Both. The bottom line is it says the money—the two weeks' pay for every year you've been with the company—is being treated as if you made an early withdrawal on a 401(k). The tax is outrageous."

"How outrageous?"

"Thirty percent outrageous."

"Shit . . . shit, shit, shit," I say, pacing all the way to the end of the hallway leading to our bedrooms and back. "Shit, shit, shit."

"Shit is right," Anna says.

So, not only am I terminated but now the last check I may ever receive as an honest-to-goodness salaried worker with twenty vacation and five wellness days, the money that's supposed to carry us over while I'm unemployed, is now being taxed 30 percent? Shit. Shit. Shit.

"This changes everything," Anna says.

She turns over one of the sheets where she's been penciling calculations, and you know I'm not good at math, but when you put words like *weeks* next to familiar numbers like 19 and then cross off the 19 and put 13 in its place, I'm a genius. I'm fucked.

"Even with savings that's the best I can do," Anna says, picking up the pencil and double-underlining the unlucky number 13. "Maybe it's for the best."

"For the best. That's your aunt Rosie talking."

"Some people really need that nine-to-five. Too much freedom doesn't really agree with you."

"Freedom agrees with me."

"You don't understand what I'm saying."

"Elizabeth says I might have been a free spirit trapped in a mundane job," I say.

"Who's Elizabeth?" Anna says.

"The 1-800 mental health professional."

"When have you been talking to her?"

"Here and there. Usually when I take Alonzo for walks."

"Poor Alonzo," Anna says.

"Freedom agrees with me."

"I'm not talking about whatever kind of freedom you and 1-800-Elizabeth are discussing. You can talk about that with her. I'm just talking about you being a little lost by not having anything to do. And I think you're losing sight of certain goals. You're just going through the motions."

"That's all I can do at this point. You sound like Grace."

"Who's Grace?"

"The career coach. The one the company set me up with."

"Well, she's right. There's a lot more you could be doing."

"Like what? What should I be doing? I'm even doing volunteer work."

"That's going to look great on your résumé: 'Drove drug addict around four nights a week.' Have you even checked with that hospital administrator yet? Is it possible for you to focus on your job search instead of running around with people and doing whatever?"

"You're the one who told me I have to open up and get out there, make contacts. I'm putting myself out there."

"Way out there." She looks at me over the tops of her glasses. "Now you're getting started with tracking down this Bo person."

"I didn't mean to get involved with the whole Bennie thing. That just happened."

"It's weird."

"The family doesn't have anybody else to look for him. I thought I had some free time and could help."

"That's the problem again. Freedom doesn't agree with you."

"Stop saying that. Freedom agrees with me."

"You don't know how to use it properly."

"Freedom's not supposed to be proper. You don't map it out with graphs and charts and comparables."

"Well, it doesn't even matter now. Look at these papers. Free time is over."

"It's a lot easier to put it on than it is to pull it off."

"What?"

"I was just starting to . . . I was hitting my . . . Carl says something is going to fall on me."

"Who's Carl?"

"He wants to meet you and . . ."

I shut up. I don't want to say any of it out loud. I don't want those eyes of reason and reality peering up over the frames and giving me that suspect look.

"It's time to bear down. Just find work," Anna says.

"I am bearing . . . I don't know what else I can do. I've started doing stuff for the guy our neighbor knows and I'm sending résumés everywhere."

"You can't spend your days waiting for enterprising dude to call."

"He doesn't call. He relays a message."

"Where's the money from those jobs? Never mind. It's ridiculous."

"I've been planning to have a garage sale to make some extra money, too."

"But you haven't."

"You're not helping with my focus, with all the errands you keep coming up with for me," I tell Anna.

"What are you talking about?"

From the beginning, since my schedule was flexible, Anna has been loading me up with errands. First it was important things like picking up tax documents, but it quickly deteriorated to include my going by her friend Janet's place to pick up an Oklahoma quarter, the last one she needed to complete her fifty-state set. The worst was her asking me to bring a bag of stale bread to her at work so that she could feed the ducks by the lake behind her lab. I was so disgusted that on the drive over I ate half the bread, even though I knew I was only hurting the ducks.

"I ate half the bread that day," I say.

"What?"

"That day you made me bring the bread for the ducks you forgot on the counter. I was so irritated I ate half of it on the way."

"That's sick. I wasn't giving you a chore. I was asking a favor. Sor-ryyy to interfere with your freedom. No more wasting time. This is serious. Jeffrey, I'll help you. But no more searching for long-lost friends or . . . or anything other than getting work. Right?"

I look down at Anna's wrist. She's doodling, tilting the pencil down to shade in the shell of a turtle.

"Any kind of work," she says. "We don't have any other choice."

The lines are wispy and disconnected, comparable to those of real artists, but the results are cartoonish and childlike.

"Stop doodling," I say.

"What?"

"Stop it," I say, ripping the paper out from under the point of the pencil. "Let me see this."

I walk out to the living room and sit in the corner, my back against the wall. It's a spot where you can recline and see the whole of the first floor of our house. I flip the paper over and read some fine print regarding a 1099-R. The R must stand for retirement. I flip the page back over. *How many weeks? How many days?* The math has never been simpler, more elementary. I can do it in my head but I'm staring the numbers down as if it is the hardest equation ever placed before a mortal man with sixty-eight days of community college. Plus and minus are alien to me now and, for safety's sake, my mind is drifting elsewhere.

"Where are you?" Anna says, standing over me. "You're getting kind of flighty."

I stare off but she puts her fingers on my chin and turns my face up toward hers. "I know you've been on some kind of weird little odyssey but . . ."

"Huh?"

I turn toward the window.

"The world can't be your garden-variety gazing ball," Anna says.

I know that.

"I just feel so desperate."

"You should feel desperate."

"Why was dad saying 'shit' outside my bedroom door?" Kristin says, walking into the room.

"We're just dealing with something," Anna says. "Don't worry about it."

Anna picks up a quilt lying at the end of the couch, wraps it around her shoulders, and walks out toward the den. She always gets so cold, even on summer nights. The first time I realized it, we were in the yard of her parents' house. We'd only been together about nine weeks but things were getting serious and we were big on having what we called "future talks." On this night, she had goose bumps the size of M&Ms up and down her forearms from the cold. She claimed she had a thalassemia trait that made her constantly chilly. I kept rubbing her arms til the bumps subsided and then we sat on the fence, watching the sky turn gray.

Her folks had one of those hokey corral-style fences that you only see in the country, even though this was a gated community. We were making fun of the fence, and I guess that's what got us talking about the horses. She said, "I want our life to be wide open and full of horses." I immediately thought she wanted a horse farm because when I was a kid I always wanted a horse farm, too. Everybody does, right? It's the same as the emu or alpaca fantasy. But Anna made the point that we didn't have to necessarily have a horse farm per se, especially after we talked about the cost of the upkeep and considering how we whined about how much our asses hurt every time we rode at the Chapel Stables in Wellington. She said, "The main thing is that our lives together be wide open, even if other things might take the place of the horses." I wasn't sure exactly what she meant, and then the lamppost was flashing, signaling her parents had dinner ready, and I just wanted to kiss her. But now I wish I'd taken a few more seconds to ask her about us . . . in the future . . . and the things . . . that take the place of horses.

Agitated, I lure Alonzo up with some Sargentos and gingerly attach his leash. He's nowhere close to his old self, but when I force him up he has a way of slowly maneuvering along without the foot of his injured leg even touching the ground. We're sharing the string cheese and methodically pacing around out front—he for the exercise, me for a few seconds of respite.

I try to explain to him that even if he never has use of the leg again it's not the end of the world, even if it drops off. "Every town has a three-legged dog or two," I say as I guide him back and forth. "People write songs about three-legged dogs."

The leash gets wrapped around the mailbox and as I'm trying to unravel it I notice a glow coming from a car in Alex's driveway—her brother's old Acura. Looks like they might have left the dome light on; perhaps a door is ajar. I know that can kill the battery so I head to check it out, but within a few more feet I can see the glow of Alex's face slumped down in the backseat. I poke my head in and she and a friend are leaning against each other with a plastic bowl full of popcorn between them, watching a movie on the back of a headrest.

"*Avatar*. Epic," Alex says before I can decipher what film it is. "My brother only uses the screen for video games, but I like to watch epics on it. I like big, sprawling things brought down to the size of an ashtray. I saw *Benjamin Button* on this headrest. Snoozefest. We didn't wake up until the next morning. What else?"

Alex nudges her friend, who has white blond hair and is a bit tanorexic, and she ekes out, *"Australia."*

"The first movie we watched out here was *The Passion of the Christ*," Alex says. "You haven't seen *The Passion of the Christ* until you've seen it on the back of a headrest."

"OK," I say. "I just saw the dome light and—"

"Taylor's my brother's girlfriend."

"Hi, Taylor."

"Hey."

"You don't need to introduce yourself. I'll tell her everything she needs to know about you the second you're gone," Alex says, laughing. "It's Taylor's birthday and my brother passed out on her."

"Not before giving me this," Taylor says, holding her hand up.

Alex grabs her wrist, pulling it into the blue light of the Na'vi. "It's a semiprecious stone. Why do they even have semiprecious stones? Who are you going to impress with something that's semiprecious?" Alex says. "You want to join us? I can squish over."

"No. No thanks," I say, pushing off the side of the car and standing up straight.

"Hey," Alex says. "You didn't say 'happy birthday' to Taylor."

"Happy birthday, Taylor."

"What's with you?" Alex says. "You look like you had a mini-stroke or something. Is the left side of your face numb?"

"I'm just, it's the weeks. I mean, the days."

"You want to talk? I can pause this beast right in the middle of a cattle drive."

I do want to talk to her but I don't know why. I don't understand why I can talk to her but not Anna.

"No, you guys enjoy your epic."

I jerk on Alonzo's leash a little too harshly and head back toward the house, then abruptly go back to the car.

"If that guy has any more work for me, I could use it," I say, poking my head back in the window. "It's not just for a lark anymore and—"

"Say no more," she says nonchalantly, taking a handful of popcorn and shoveling it in her mouth as if she's got it all under control. A tiny Sigourney Weaver in a safari hat fills the screen on the headrest.

"I really appreciate it," I reply.

"Excuse me, I'm trying to watch this," Taylor huffs.

"Yeah, sorry. OK. Good night," I say, backing off.

"Good night for real this time?" Taylor moans.

"Good night for real."

Not thinking, I tug at Alonzo's leash and he lets out one of those alarming yelps. I want to think he's improving, but it's more likely that he's just learning to live with the pain. I let the leash go limp and allow him to slowly lead me up the front path, with nothing left to think about but where Alex is going to begin and end when she tells Taylor everything she needs to know about me.

circuit breaker

s that the microwave beeping? Is the shower running? It's two-thirty in the morning!

"This isn't Las Vegas!" is the first thing I yell after getting out of bed and rumbling down the hallway.

"I know that," Kristin says, turning down one of the three TVs that are also on.

"I can't have this. You guys can't be up all night. I can't afford to keep this place running twenty-four hours a day."

"I'll sleep all day tomorrow to make up for it," Kristin says.

The kitchen is the only room that's dark but there is an orange glow coming from the toaster oven. "Who's having fish sticks?" I mumble. "When your brother gets out of the shower we're having a meeting."

I'm starting to hate the sound of my own voice constantly nagging everybody to conserve, but the alternative is giving up. I can't stand the TVs, lights, and computers in the house going . . . going . . . going. And the water heater.

I ask Andrew how many showers he took today.

"This is tomorrow," he says.

"He takes a shower before he goes to the gym and then again when he comes back from the gym," Kristin says. "Oh, and he took one before he went to the beach the other day."

"Who does that?" I yelp in pain.

"He does," Kristin says, pointing to Andrew, who is wrapped in two towels.

"Do you have to use two towels?" I say. "I'm putting a moratorium on showers. We've got to conserve. I'm trying to save every cent I can. Cut back on everything I can. I don't even buy any clothes for myself."

"That's because new clothes look weird on you," Kristin says.

"That's beside the point. You know why *I'm* up at three in the morning? It's not to watch a movie I already saw four times or to take my third shower of the day or to eat fish sticks or to—"

One of the two laptops on the dining room table, both of which are plugged in, is making the sound of a buzz saw, signaling . . . something. "That's not mine," Andrew says.

Side by side on the coffee table are empty bags of Cool Ranch Doritos and Cheez Doodles. I slap at the Doodles bag and a cloud of orange dust bursts out over a pile of Kristin's magazines.

Kristin dives for the books before the dust can settle and says, "Dad!"

"Yeah, I'm right here. I'm standing here in the middle of the night because I don't know what to do. How am I going to keep feeding you guys?"

"Dad, don't do that baby bird thing with your mouth," Kristin says, turning away. "You look weird."

"The reason I'm up is because I can't sleep. I'm too worried to sleep. And you guys . . . I have to keep worrying about keeping a roof over our heads. This roof!" I say, pointing up.

Kristin and Andrew both look up as if the whole place could suddenly cave in.

"Do you realize it was my job keeping that roof up there? Me! Keeping that roof up there and now . . . Why do you have to keep the laptops plugged in constantly? The idea is you charge them up and plug them in when—"

"I don't like charging things up," Kristin says. "It's a pain."

"A pain, a pain," I say, walking over to the dining room and ripping the plugs from the wall sockets.

"We're just going to plug them back in," Kristin says. "You can't stop us from doing anything."

"That's it. I'm just throwing the circuit breakers."

I start striding down the hall and Kristin slithers up past me, knocking a framed vacation photo of our family white-water rafting to the ground, as she races to block the circuit box.

"Move. I'm not kidding. Move!" I'm shouting before I even reach her.

"What the hell is going on?" Anna says, running out of the bedroom.

"We're having a family meeting," Andrew says.

"Mom, he's nuts," Kristin says. "He's exaggerating everything. He went from giving us a little speech about saving power to throwing the circuit breakers. He says he's the roof—Mr. Roof. Mom's the roof, too."

"Damn straight I am," Anna says, shooting me a glance.

"I didn't say I was Mr. Roof."

"He put a moratorium on showers."

"You guys are the vampire generation," I say. "Not because of all the stupid movies and books. I just mean because you never sleep. This place has to shut down at some point in the day. I mean it."

"Dad, I don't need your power," Kristin says, flicking the hall light on and off, creating a disturbing strobe effect. "I don't care if I have to walk around with a cupcake with a candle in it to find the bathroom in the middle of the night. I really couldn't give a flying. I don't need any of this."

"Kristin thinks she's better than us," I say.

"That's his girlfriend talking—the slacker next door."

"What?" Anna says, snapping the electrical panel door shut with a gesture of finality that says no sense can be made of all this until the light of day, or even better, perhaps we can act as if none of this ever happened.

"Does this have anything to do with dad saying 'shit, shit, shit' outside my room?" Kristin says.

"That's exactly what this is about," I say. "We need to stop . . . everything around here. Everything."

"You need to sleep," Anna says to me as she waves Kristin and Andrew off. "Is that fish sticks I smell burning?"

"Dad," Andrew says, "am I ever going to be able to go to the dentist again?"

"I don't know. I don't know."

I hang the vacation photo back up in the hallway. I'm stiffly perched on the back of the raft, surrounded by class-3 rapids, an oar scraping at the air. I look so unnatural in the wild. I remember when Andrew first saw the photo he said, "Dad, you look like you're sitting on a toilet. It looks like they Photoshopped you onto the boat."

Anna goes right back to sleep, as if she is used to popping up and breaking up 3 A.M. fights in a college dorm or something. She snores but it's a very velvety snore and I try to latch onto it so I can drift off.

But I can't.

I keep seeing Andrew at the end of the hall, draped in terry cloth and the stop-action flashes of Kristin's homemade strobe light, tentatively watching us scuffle at the breaker box. Kristin and I have been snapping at each other for months for reasons I can't comprehend, but watching us then, Andrew had that look of someone coming to a realization of some kind. I hope this isn't all frightening him. While I was rehanging the photo frame, he quietly came up behind me and said, "Dad, we have to do something about this. I want to help."

"I know you do," I told him. "I know you do."

You know, even before I lost this job, I used to curse the fact that I don't think I'll be able to help my children monetarily much further down the road. Even beyond college, my parents were always there, especially early in our marriage when those little things went wrong between paychecks—the transmission goes in the second car, rent comes up short. My mom and dad were always there unconditionally with that extra four hundred dollars, or whatever, to see us through. Sometimes I made a point of paying it back, sometimes I didn't. I just . . . I just wish I could give my own children the comfort of knowing they can get in a jam with money and their parents will bail them out. The Mr. Roof thing is a joke really. I couldn't even afford to put a new roof on this house when I had a full-time job. We had to take out a second mortgage to put the new roof on in 2002, and that was with low-grade shingles.

When Kristin and Andrew both looked up at the ceiling earlier I know they weren't thinking about it suddenly crashing down. That's all me. The fear's all mine. They were just averting their eyes from their father's meltdown.

Years ago, Kristin had given me the same "you can't stop us" speech after she'd been grounded for something in junior high. We had taken all her hair and makeup supplies away, but she told me point-blank that she and a number of friends already had a locker set up at school stocked with hair gels and nail polish for that very reason. "Dad, you can't stop us. We prevail," she said. "We're like a virus."

The first night I came home with my walking papers I had calmed myself by drifting off to sleep while holding Anna's hand. She is still lying sound asleep, but I dig around, trying to find her right hand between the sheets and the blanket; it's nowhere to be found. I feel like I'm in the middle of a feverish dream, but I know I am wide awake. I'm peeling and scraping through the bedding, clutching for the tips of her fingers, but I cannot find her hand.

I toss and tumble, eventually dreaming of fish sticks swimming upstream. When I wake in the morning there are two neatly folded but faded Quiksilver T-shirts and three dollars and forty-two cents in change on my nightstand, along with a scribbled note. "Dad, some money for the utility bill—Andrew. P.S. and some clothes."

Now we're talking, I'm mumbling to myself until I get to the kitchen and find another note from Anna saying she's taking a wellness day from work to go visit with her mom, who's been dealing with some kind of severe kidney infection. All I can envision is her fluffing up her mom's pillows every couple of hours while turning the spare bedroom into a scientific command center, covering the walls with maps and charts and photos. *OK, Mom, if you need anything, holler. I'll just be in the other room strategizing on how to extract my husband from our lives with a minimum of collateral damage. And let me know if you want a liverwurst sandwich.*

unemployment talking

Y ou really called yourself Mr. Roof?" 1-800-Elizabeth says.

"I think so, I don't know. I had to fall asleep counting fish sticks. Do spouses leave when the other loses a job? Is that a regular thing?"

"I guess we'd have to look up statistics on that. Are you sure you don't want me to search for a counselor in your area?"

"I think she's setting up a command center at her mom's."

"A command center?"

"Yes, and I envision her doing one of those crazed scientific equations on a long blackboard, eraser dust flying, the chalk down to a nub in her fingers, but frenetically tap, tap, tapping away like someone trying to figure out the proximity of the next comet in 2018, only she's trying to pinpoint how expendable I am in 2011 and—"

"Slow down. I lost you at comet."

"I can't slow down. Everybody's leaving me notes now. Like they can't even look at me."

"That's the unemployment talking."

"The what talking?"

"The unemployment. There's going to be stress and strain on the family and the marriage, but that's to be expected and—"

"A guy waiting at the unemployment office told me he's been out of work for so long he doesn't even want to work anymore. That's kind of how I feel."

"But you haven't been out of work that long. When you first called you said nothing would be OK until you found a job."

"All the career counseling and self-help books and job fairs and networking crap—it's all monotonous and repetitive. There's too much emphasis on working. They act like nobody can exist without having a great job. There are other things I'm doing. Important things."

"Maybe you can balance things out. One day you intensely work on the job search and the next day you spend on your other concerns. Or split each day into work time, family time, and time for personal growth. You'd be amazed at how much you can get done in a single day. I mean *amazed*."

Toward the end of last night's argument Anna actually said she was amazed by how little I can get done in a single day.

"We have patient confidentiality, right?"

"I'm only . . ."

"I don't want to work. There, I said it."

"Well, I don't know what your financial status is, but—"

"Severance can be stretched. If you just sit still and don't do anything, if you just lie there waiting for something to fall on top of you, it can . . . She thinks freedom doesn't agree with me. Who wants to hear that, especially since people are always fighting—dying even—for it all over the world."

"Freedom doesn't agree with you?"

"Is that the unemployment talking from her end? She's using one of those upper math scientific calculators to evaluate freedom on a per-person basis. You know those greater-than and lesser-than symbols? When she looks at me it's as if there's always a lesser-than symbol pointed directly at me like a giant arrowhead."

"I think for lesser, the point would be aimed in the other direction, aimed away from you."

"You know how when someone is told they have a certain disease and they're in shock and then the doctor says, 'Don't worry, it's perfectly treatable and there's no reason you shouldn't lead a perfectly normal life'?"

"Sure."

"That's how I feel about my job being terminated. I'm in shock and all the counselors and seminars are set up to convince me that all I have to do is find another decent job and there's no reason I shouldn't be able to have a perfectly normal life. But you and I know good and well that nobody—doctors or whatever—should be promising anybody in the world a perfectly normal life."

"Wait, can you hold on? I've got a box of Sour Patch Kids on my desk and the entire thing just spilled . . . Just a sec, I have to wrangle them back into the box."

"My son always gets those at the movies."

"You have a son. How old is he?"

"Fourteen. He's trying to help out. He gave me some of the T-shirts he's tired of. Originally my wife gave me the option of living off the grid, in some kind of alternative situation. I mean, I really don't want llamas poking their heads in my windows, but if that's still an alternative . . . If I can get her to start thinking like that again—to go to a place where she can find a good job while I eternally try to find something to do—maybe that's the answer. But I just tried her cellphone and she's not even answering. Who takes a wellness day when everything is turning to shit?"

"My hands are all sticky. I should probably pass you off to another . . ."

"No, that's OK. I'm good for now. Just wanted to run a few things by you. You've been helpful. I'll call back."

emergency flashers on

hate when someone forces me to shut down my lawn mower. They'll be walking their dog and frantically waving their hands for your attention like Sal's wife, Peggy, is doing right now, and then it's about something totally senseless or annoying.

"Hey," I say, cutting the throttle.

"What are you doing? What's with all the squiggles?"

Annoying.

"It's whimsical mowing," I say. "It's better for the grass."

"You look like a kindergartner with his first box of crayons out there."

"OK," I say, starting the mower back up and making a dragon tail loop under the olive tree.

I think it was in *Lawn Digest* or *Turf Builders Review* that I first read about whimsical mowing, but at the time I had the kid down the street mowing the yard, so I never got to try it. The theory is that the up-and-down, back-and-forth method of mowing isn't good for the grass. Better to mix it up, zigzag into the middle of the lawn, and trace the curves of Salma Hayek or the rear spoiler of a 1970 Road Runner Superbird. Whatever. The first mower move I made was a receiving pattern over the middle from my JV football team. I never got to play, but I had Coach Hammerson's "24 Fake z-motion 37 sweep route" memorized just in case I was ever called on.

I also like to do teepees and then add etchings of wild buffalo. And eagle wings are easy. Native Americans never let their artwork get too complicated. It's as if they knew some artistically limited schmo would one day try to find release in duplicating their drawings on a canvas of overgrown floratam sod. Along the easement, I already made a greater-than or less-than symbol, depending on which side you stand on. I think Elizabeth was right about the direction of the point, but I'm not going on either side of it until I'm positive.

The Native American stuff is my favorite, so right now I'm doing a pony kicking up dust on the open tra—

Damn.

I hate when I run out of gas right in the middle of mowing. The engine just lets out. Two coughs and then nothing.

I go around the side of the house to the shed. The gas jug is empty, but I can't leave the yard half done, especially since I'm trying to get it spruced up for the garage sale. I grab the can, hop in the car, and back out of the driveway. I drive up behind a Volvo sedan that's also turning at the corner, but quickly realize the car's not turning. The emergency flashers are on.

I could just pull around, but I decide to tap on the window to see if there's anything I can do to help. The driver's head is down on the steering wheel. When she looks up and opens the window, I can see she's very upset. "What?" she says.

"I saw your emergency flashers. You want me to help you push the car to the side or something?"

"Oh, no, no," she says. "I've got an emergency, but it has nothing to do with the car. It's just, just . . ."

"Hey, aren't you the woman with the Corvette?"

"I can't drive that thing anymore. It's too corny." She puts her head back down but then pops right up and starts muttering something about a flight being canceled and her father being in the hospital and her ex-husband ruining her credit and there's no food in the house and . . . and she got up to the corner here and just folded—put it in park, hit the flashers, and dropped her head onto the wheel.

UNTIL IT HAPPENS TO YOU

"Well, at least you made it this far," I say. "A lot of people I know wouldn't have even gotten out of bed. You got dressed, pulled out of the driveway, made it to the corner. Maybe that's enough for today. You want me to back up so you can turn around and go home?"

"I'm just going to sit here," she says. "I'm not sure what I want to do yet."

"OK," I say.

Get back in my car. For a second, I think perhaps I've also exceeded my own expectations today. I, too, made it to the corner, and maybe that's enough. Sometimes God has a strange way of getting his soldiers some rest.

Decide to just sit here behind the frozen Volvo. I'm not sure what I want to do yet.

Put emergency flashers on.

Still not sure what I want to do.

Dawns on me that the woman had mentioned she had no food in the house this morning.

I hop out of the car, walk back to my garage, retrieve a Lunchable from the outside refrigerator, and tap on the woman's window again.

"I thought you might be hungry."

"Oh, that's sweet. What is that?"

"Lunchable. Turkey or chicken . . . or ham or . . . some kind of meat."

"I'll have that tiny Baby Ruth," she says, tapping on the little plastic Lunchable window with her burgundy fingernails.

"Sure. Do you want me to sit with you?"

"If you want."

I go around to the passenger's side and she clicks the lock to let me in.

I pluck out the candy for her and then peel back the covering over the cheese and crackers. She starts going on about some kind of storm in Indiana that is affecting all the flights in and out of South Florida. "I hate when something happening in Indiana affects our lives," I say. "That should never happen."

She really seems distraught and full of gibberish. I want to console her, but the main thing stuck in my mind is that I wish she had the Corvette. I've never gotten to sit in a Corvette.

"Leena, right?"

"Lyla."

"My wife, Anna, says she talked to you a couple of times."

"Oh, the colorful woman, yes."

"You're a hospital administrator."

"For the moment. That's a whole other mess. Helion—that Ohio health-care monster—just took over our operations. We don't know where that leaves us."

"I hate when something happens in Ohio that affects our lives. That should never happen."

"Tell me about it," Lyla says.

"I bet the hospital always needs people to write press releases, huh? That's the kind of work I do."

"You write press releases?"

"That's the kind of thing I might do, yeah. Would you like to see some examples of my work? If you have a minute I'll go get a couple."

"I'm not going anywhere."

I run back inside and quickly paper-clip a couple of listing pages. I try to put something she might like up top (Wine tasting 7 P.M. at Total Wine, 2333 Linton Blvd., Delray Beach. For more information call . . .) along with a couple of religious briefs and my résumé. Inspired by Elizabeth's guidelines, this is supposed to be the part of the day where I don't have to search for a job, but I'm making an exception.

"I like that this candy bar is chilly," Lyla says as I climb back in the car.

She puts on a pair of dainty ruby-red-framed eyeglasses and looks over my work. After she turns each page, she takes these little squirrel nibbles out of the Baby Ruth, as if she wants the meager confection to last forever.

I'm not really hungry, but while waiting I nervously start building some Lunchable stacks, placing the cheese and meat on top of the crackers.

"That's GlooGun font," I say.

"Huh?"

"On my résumé, that's the font I used. Stands out."

"Yeah, that stands out all right. Well, the surgeons always have us spitting out some crap," Lyla says. "They like to brag about everything they do, even if it involves colons."

"I've written about colons before," I say. (True. Colon Screening and Colon Hydrotherapy 2–6 P.M. at Montgomery Health Center, 222 Ridgewood Drive, Margate. For more info . . .)

"To be honest, it's hard to find somebody who can string two sentences together," Lyla says, crumpling up the Baby Ruth wrapper and flicking it toward the backseat.

Truth be told, I'm OK at writing when I stick to the model for the listings, but beyond that I can get a bit incoherent and cumbersome. She doesn't need to know that right up front.

"We're always going through people so, yes, I'll keep you in mind. I know right off that within the next two weeks we're going to have to put something out about Helion taking over operations . . . You're getting crumbs all over."

"Sorry."

Another car pulls up behind mine. I'm watching in the mirror as the driver gets out to check my car. It's that guy I think is a chef or a baker because there's always powdery white stuff on his hands and shoes when he strolls his little girl up and down the block after dinner.

I wonder if he is about to fall into this trap with us, to start thinking about the weight of his own life and that maybe there's good reason to just shut down. Even if he didn't have any valid reasons, I could probably come up with some for him. I'm good like that. But then we'd have three cars in a row on a dead-end street, all with their emergency flashers on and no mechanical problems whatsoever. What would we be saying to the schoolkids who will soon be flocking to the bus stop only about fifteen yards from where we now idle? What kind of example would we be setting?

Would they have pity and say, "Well, at least they made it to the corner"? Or would they have no mercy, see us as weak, and perhaps slash our tires for kicks?

The guy walks back to his own car, climbs in, backs up, and drives around us.

Phew! He'll never know how close he came to having his entire life come to a screeching halt.

Out of the corner of my eye I see my mower sitting idle in the center of the lawn, dead behind a galloping three-legged pony. I'm sitting perfectly still so as not to quake the Lunchable stacks resting on my knees like edible sand castles. I vigilantly watch Lyla licking the tips of her fingers before she slips my résumé into a valise between the Volvo's front seats.

"OK, so I guess we'll be in touch," I say. "I've got a garage sale coming up if you want to stop by then or whatever."

"Fine," she says, handing me her business card. "It's been nice meeting with you."

self-induced coma

You've got a real glow about you!" Artie shouts across the bar.

"I took a meeting this morning," I say. "I'm on a roll."

I swore I wouldn't do this—go to a bar in the daytime. I've always been a night drinker. I'd been going back and forth about meeting Artie and Gillian today—more back than forth when I thought of Anna—but now that I've got some chores and networking done early, I shouldn't feel guilty at all. Though I do.

Artie claims this place is a networking bonanza during weekdays anyway. "A real mixer of opportunity" is how he put it.

The place is packed and it's only noon.

"How many weeks?" Artie says, shouldering me. "I mean days!"

"It's not even about days anymore," I say as he pulls me toward the bar. "Do they even serve food here?"

"Hell no, empty bellies all around. This place is for drinking."

I'm barely up on a stool when a guy wearing a sweater vest pushes me aside to have the bartender cash his unemployment check.

"They cash unemployment checks here?" I say to Artie. "I don't know about this."

"What's to know?" Artie says. "Did you get direct deposit for your unemployment check? I didn't. I hate that direct deposit shit. I wish I'd never started it. If I ever get another job I'm not signing up for it. I want to get a check, cash it on my lunch break every other Friday, and then buy a twelve-pack. That was the routine when I was nineteen or twenty. I miss that."

"Doesn't sound like a bad routine," I say.

"Oh, you want to talk about a routine. When my friends and I first got jobs in high school I would cash my check on Fridays and then go straight to the woods near the Billy Blake's shopping center. There was this old washing machine and I'd fill it with beer and have it all ready. I'd sit around getting a buzz on from smoking menthols and just wait for everybody else to get off work. It was great to see that first face come through the brush. A bunch of branches would peel back and there'd be—"

"Yo, don't you live in my building?" A slight guy slides up to Artie. "You outta work, too?"

"Yeah, I think I've seen you around."

"I'm on the seventh floor with my parents. Well, see you around," the guy says, ducking back around the side of the bar.

"This is quite.the mixer of opportunity," I mumble.

"My parents are going to help me lease a new car," Artie says. "What am I going to do? I need one and they offered."

"My brother-in-law took Anna and me on a mini-vacation with them right after we were terminated. Everything was comped."

"You pitiful bastard."

Gillian comes striding up to the bar, kisses me on the cheek, whispers in my ear, "Is there a back door?" and exits straight out the rear entrance.

Oh, great.

"Shots!" Artie yells to the bartender.

"Artie, settle this one for us," a redheaded guy with a friend in tow says as he squeezes between our stools. "We need you to tell us whose life is worse."

"I'm sort of a mediator around here," Artie says with a wink at me.

I do need a shot.

"OK, who's going first?" Artie says.

"I was in the hospital," Red says. "I should go first."

"Shoot."

"My wife wanted to stay overnight at the hospital with me, and I thought that was nice and all, so she got all set up with one of those foldout sleep chairs."

"Go on."

"Middle of the night, I get shaken awake, and I think it's one of those people who take blood. But my wife is pulling at me and saying, 'Get the hell up. I can't sleep on that thing.' I tell her to just go home, but she insists on staying and wants the bed."

"Your hospital bed?" the slobbery guy says, as if even he hadn't grasped the severity of the situation the first time he'd heard his buddy's story.

"Gary Zimmer," Artie blurts and slugs me in the arm. "That was the first face I'd see coming into the woods. Gary Zimmer. Man."

"Anyway, I got tubes sticking out and everything else, and she drags me onto this chair," the guy continues. "I could barely move, and she just overpowered me. All my hoses were crimped. My intravenous tube broke. I woke up in a puddle of intravenous."

"You woke up in a puddle of intravenous? You win," Artie says, swiveling his stool back to the bar and tugging at my arm. "Hey, you're spacing out on me. What are you thinking about?"

"The only real friend I ever had is out there somewhere, kicking the hell out of people for no reason," I say. "I wonder what that means?"

"You had a real friend? When?"

"First grade . . ."

"Oh shit."

"Through seventh grade."

I try to explain to Artie how I kind of stumbled into this manhunt for Bo, but all he does is push another shot over and say, "Drink. Drink up."

I stand up to go to the restroom and immediately have to clutch the back of my stool, the too-early-in-the-day alcohol already making me woozy. There's a short line outside the men's room and I think, *I don't fit in with unemployed people.* I mean, I fit in with them when we're all bumping into each other at a job fair or being tutored on how to become Me, Inc. But not here, not like this.

A song starts up on the Muzak (what kind of bar has Muzak?). It's an orchestra, but I recognize the Beatles tune. "And now my life has changed in oh so many ways, my independence seems to vanish in the haze . . ."

"Whoa, is that you?" the guy in front of me in line says, getting about two inches from my nose. "Is that coming out of you?"

"What?"

"The Beatles tune?"

"No, that's the Muzak."

"No, the words."

"Sorry, I'm drinking too much too early."

"No, no. It was awesome. Wild good. Do it again."

Luckily the bathroom line suddenly makes a leap and urinating becomes much more important than my singing.

When I get back to the bar, Red is in my seat, one arm over Artie's shoulder, going on about putting himself into a self-induced coma. "I got the idea when I was in the hospital. They do it under certain circumstances," he says. "I read about it in the *Herald*. And it's cheap. Check out this scenario: You lose your job, and instead of getting all panicked, you simply sign up for unemployment, send out a stack of résumés, and then go into a self-induced coma for six months or so. The checks will be piling up, and you won't have to worry about utilities or anything. You could even let your car insurance lapse."

"What about your cellphone?" Artie asks.

"Yeah, I'm stuck in the thirty-six-month contract. You cash my unemployment checks and pay that for me? That's where you come in."

"Sure, I can cash your checks," Artie says. "How do you eat while you're in this coma?"

"Oh, it's like an intravenous setup, but the food bag is huge. It's the size of a forty-pound bag of Eukanuba large-breed adult maintenance."

"Where's your wife in all this?" I ask.

"She left about a week after I stopped working. Anyway, I don't have to worry about chow. But Artie might want to come by and jiggle my tubes once in a while in case they get crimped."

"I don't know if I want to come by and jiggle your tubes," Artie says.

"OK, but can you check my email periodically to see if anyone gets back to me on those résumés?"

"I guess so," Artie says.

"Only wake me if something looks really promising."

"Got it," Artie says.

Red heads for the door as if he's going to put his plan in action, and why not? Any plan of action would be a plus at this point.

"We should make a pact," Artie says the second I get back to the bar. "When we get our next unemployment checks we cash them at the bank, pick up a twelve-pack, and drink in the woods."

"I've got a patch of woods at the end of my block," I say. "I bet my neighbor Sal would go for that, too."

"Beautiful. Deal," he says, shaking my hand. "See, you got real friends right here. You don't have to go back to the sixth grade."

"It's just that this guy has been through some kind of bad accident, serious brain damage maybe," I say. "And nobody else seems to be trying to help him."

"Well, maybe that's just the project you need," Artie says. "I've been considering my own project. I'm thinking about going full-time at getting Cassie back. I've got the time. That could be my job. You know how they always say you need to work at a relationship. I'm ready to go to work."

"Did you guys really break up because you lost your job?"

"No, I guess I just like to use that as an excuse. Man, we were so close to moving in together. But, to be honest, there was a lot more going on than just me being jobless when it fell apart. There's even this guy who works for the family's real estate business in South America. Her sister, Marti, told me they were always on the phone and it's not all business."

"That doesn't sound good."

"Marti is just trying to piss me off. I know that now. She doesn't think I'm good enough for her little sister. She wants me to think there's some Don Juan in Chile or somewhere just to make me crazy. She gets off on shit like that."

Artie sounds a bit in denial, especially since I've heard the rumor that he'd gone kind of bonkers and was wielding a knife and stabbing at the kitchen cabinets when Cassie came to his apartment to break it off. Sometimes there are things you just can't come back from.

"You don't think you're beyond the point of getting back together?" I ask. "You don't think it's too late?"

"Too late? You're chasing brain-dead fourth graders."

"I just mean after the knife incident and all."

"It was a butter knife . . . over the phone."

"Oh, I had heard she was in your apartment when that happened. That you might have scared her off completely."

"You heard. Where are you getting your information? Rumor mongerer."

"Sorry."

"Cassie is so complicated," Artie says, lowering his head. "She was always weighing everything in our relationship. I wish she was more like me. I wish her heart was a slob like mine."

I look at the neon lizard clock over the bar and it's almost two o'clock. I promised myself I'd only stay for two drinks and I don't know how many we've had now.

"I have no time for self-pity or the shallows of loneliness but am passionate about both, so I make the time," Artie says, tilting his head back to do another shot.

"You're getting heavy," I say. "It's too early in the day for that kind of talk."

"I really miss it," he says. "Not the work, but the people. I just miss being around people. I'm not so good, that way. I miss Erika in sales . . . our lunch date every Friday. I bet I couldn't even get her to eat lunch on a Tuesday now. If I disappeared right this second, no one would even care."

"What about your wealthy parents?"

"I mean people that matter. People who will have sex with you."

"Oh, those people."

"You ever think about leaving life?"

"That's a nice way of putting it. No, but I think I'm going to have to get out of here. Listen, I'm going to have to get a ride home from somebody."

"Marty—he never drinks. Let's go find him."

After a big search that involves about eleven steps, Artie comes up behind Marty's wheelchair and spins him around.

"Artie, it's my birthday." Marty grins.

"Happy birthday. Can you give my buddy a ride home? He's just up near Belvedere and Ninety-five. I'll take a ride with you."

"Road trip. Sure."

On the way to Marty's van the guy from the bathroom line rushes us. "Artie, you know this dude. He sings the Beatles like a goddamned master singer!"

"Give it up or we don't get in the van," Artie says.

"Give it up," Marty says.

"Help me if you can, I'm feeling down . . . And I do appreciate you being round . . ."

"Shit, I've drunk thirteen Yuenglings and seven shots of Early Times, but that's stunning," Artie says.

"It just happened when I was in the bathroom line." I shrug. "Very organic."

"Nothing organic happens with you," Artie says. "Who knows about this?"

"Just you guys. Can we get in the van now?"

The whole back of the van is empty except for these wood planks on the sides with seat belt straps bolted to the wall and metal floor. "You have to crisscross the straps over your chest," Marty says.

"Bolero-style," Artie says, buckling in.

I'm getting kind of faint and I'm in and out a little, but every time I open my eyes Marty is still staring at the dashboard.

"Let's go!" I finally hear Artie yell.

"Artie, I can't do it," Marty says. "There's all these levers and shit. I can't drive this contraption."

"What the hell are you talking about? It's your van. You've had it for seven years. Have you been drinking?"

"It's my birthday." Marty turns around, grinning.

"Christ," Artie says. "Let me do it."

Artie stands in the place of the wheelchair, braces one arm on the dashboard, and starts flicking switches and pushing buttons. It's impressive, like when some action star jumps into a helicopter and you go, "I didn't know he could fly a helicopter. This guy can do anything."

"I can't do this," Artie yells. "This is like trying to fly a pinball machine."

"The flippers are over there," Marty says, cackling.

"Fuck! Marty, can you talk me through it?"

"I can talk to you. But I can't talk you through it."

The van is spinning and I'm not sure if it's due to Artie pulling levers or the four shots of Gentleman Jim taking me for a ride.

"Artie, forget it. I'm just going to take a nap here. I'm good," I say.

"You want me to unstrap you?"

"No, this is fine. I feel very secure."

Marty is already nodding off; his long arms are limp at his sides.

"OK. I'll sit with you until you fall asleep," Artie says.

"Artie, I like that your heart is a slob," I say.

"Thanks. And it's OK if you find your friend and he's brainless. Friends don't need brains."

That's a good point. Bo and I were brainless when we were seven years old, brainless when we were nine, definitely brainless when we were twelve. So what's the difference if he's brainless when I find him now? Friends don't need brains.

It gets very quiet, peaceful.

"Hey, you still awake?" Artie says.

"Yeah."

"I know it's sad I have to say this about myself, but at this point, who else will? Here goes: I'm not only talented, but I'm a nice guy and a hard worker, too. So what is wrong with me?"

"Sign o' the times."

"You guys keep saying that but what about Drew Hinden? That fucker's fifty-seven years old and the company kept him. Because he's good. He's the best at what he does. He's better than me. You think he's better than me? Are you listening to me? You think it's because he's taller than me?"

"Stop it. That's just the unemployment talking."

My thinking is currently hazy but, in a way, I still believe that the best will win out. I've learned that from Kristin. When her teachers told her there were only two bioengineering scholarships granted at the University of Florida and thousands were going to apply, she simply responded, "Then I'll be one of the two." When she thought about being a physical therapist she was told there were going to be a massive amount of PT graduates in the next several years and few open positions. "But they'll hire me because I'll be the best," she said. Where does that attitude come from?

"Do you or do you not think I'm good?" Artie says.

"You're great. You're the best. Hey, you really think I have something with the Beatles stuff? I mean, you're a music guy."

"That's par for the course that you don't even know what to do with a newfound gift."

"Come on."

"Well, it's not like you're doing a cover version. It's a different beast."

"Maybe I'll book some studio time. That's what Carl would do."

"Who? Keep a lid on it. Let me stew on how we should proceed."

Marty gently rolls past me until the front wheels of his chair butt up against the van's back doors.

"Artie, are we on a hill?"

"Hey," Artie says. "Give me the end of that song, when he starts pleading."

"Please, please help me-eee . . ."

"That was weak."

"Anna thinks I'm at another job fair."

Big fat raindrops start plopping on the windshield several seconds and several inches apart. We've been in a drought lately. We need a real downpour. This rain seems so insincere, as if nothing is going to come of it.

"Come on, pour," I mumble.

"I wonder what Gary Zimmer is doing right this second," Artie says. "I wonder if he's gainfully employed. Hey, do you want me to wake you at any certain time?"

"No, no," I say, drifting off. "Only wake me if something looks really promising."

sexy bones

Dad, you reek," Kristin says. "The guy in the wheelchair said he couldn't even wake you up."

"Marty called you? How'd he even get your number?"

"Your friend—*some friend*—Artie gave it to him."

"It's not Artie's fault. I told him I'd be fine."

"What kind of bar is that? It doesn't even have a name outside."

"A lot of businesspeople. Networking-type people. I guess no name is trendy now. Thanks for coming so quickly. Here's some gas money."

"I don't want your money. I just want to get home. I have to be at work by five-fifteen."

"Can we just make one quick stop while we're up in this area? It's on the way," I say, digging around in my wallet for the directions Linda had given me. "My head's killing me. Can you look at this map?"

"*On the way?* This isn't on the way to anywhere."

Kristin's cheeks blow up and she huffs. She does that a lot with me now, releases these little huffs and puffs of toleration that seem to say, "Well, he's my dad. I'll work with what I've got." That's her nature, working with what she's got. And she's good at it.

She has one shoe on and one shoe off, a bare foot on the gas pedal. When I asked her about it another time she said, "It just makes driving seem more organic." I like the way she's turned into this . . . this person.

I give her so little guidance, and I don't know if that helps or hurts in the long run. My parents were the same way. I knew they cared about me and loved me, but they always played the role of observer more than participant. All they seemed to do was watch me grow up, watch me live. I'm not sure if it was only because by the time they got to the second child the whole act was getting old, or because having experienced my older brother's attitude, they realized that no matter what they did it could all go to hell in an instant. I don't even have that excuse. For the past several years, all I've done is watch my children live. Is that wrong?

"Dad, what are you staring at?"

"I'm watching you live."

"Lordy, go back to sleep. I'll wake you when we get there."

"It's just up the road."

She lurches, toes pressing hard on the gas to bolt through a yellow light but then changes her mind at the last second and jams on the brakes as the light turns red above us.

"Good choice," I say.

A car full of teenage girls pulls up beside us and they are laughing their heads off. For some reason, every time I see a group of young girls together lately, they are laughing their heads off. I don't see that with guys. The young males of the species seem glum and solemn while the girls are giggling and falling on the floor in hysterics. It must be glorious to be young and pretty in America.

"Teenage girls have too much fun," I say.

"Oh yes, it's a nonstop funhouse," Kristin says, pulling into the industrial area. "I'll wait out here."

"You sure?"

"Oh, I'm sure. And, Dad, for the record, I don't know what you're doing, but I'm not your partner in any of this. I'm just your driver."

"Got it."

My eyes play tricks on me as I pull open the heavy metal door, like I'm in an air duct of some kind, but then it opens up into a black-walled lounge area.

"Welcome to Gold's. You've got the whole place to yourself today," says a young girl sitting on a stool behind a large presidential-style desk.

Something tells me that no matter what day or time I enter this gym, I will always have the place to myself. There's a dank smell to the thin carpeting but as my eyes adjust to the dim lighting the equipment appears to be all up-to-date.

"State-of-the-art," the girl says. Her skin is orange and her neck has a bit of a wrestler's daunting flair at its base, but she has a delicate smile.

"I'm actually just looking for Jeremy. Jeremy Goldstein," I say.

"You hear that," she says, cupping her ear and tilting her head.

I can hear an odd clanking in the distance that sounds more akin to a blacksmith fitting a workhorse with a new set of shoes than the thrust of exercise equipment.

"Yes, I hear it."

"That's Jeremy."

I follow the noise and Jeremy is on the far side of a dried-up juice bar that looks like it hasn't seen pulp in a decade. There is an old-school, rusted-out barbell set on the gym floor, and he's standing before a mirror wearing nothing but a towel that he keeps readjusting around his hips.

I feel awkward sneaking up on him but he spots me in the mirror. "Look at how low I've got this towel and you still can't see my sexy bones," he says without turning around. "Look, I can't go any lower."

He twists the towel and drops it down his torso an obscene inch. "Still nothing. Man!"

He turns around, disgusted. "I've got the abs. Obviously. I'm cut," he says, slamming his stomach. "But you know it's not about that anymore. Do you think it's hereditary? My pelvic bones are genetically recessed or some shit? I can't recall ever seeing my dad's. But he wasn't ripped like this."

I see what he's talking about. I have noticed that guys in movies and magazines have to have towels or jeans low enough to show the pelvic bones as if it's the new erogenous zone.

"Matt McConaughey started it in *EDtv*. That's how far back it goes," Jeremy says. "It's been getting bigger and bigger every year but now that's all that matters. You don't have those bones jutting out like Ryan Reynolds, the ladies just walk away."

"I think I can see them poking up a little bit there," I say.

"Where?"

"Right there," I say, pointing at a slight protrusion.

"That's just the way I'm standing at this angle. Look," he says, putting his weight on his other foot. "Gone."

"But it still looks like—"

"No. You stare at anything long enough it'll start to appear. Trust me, I know. Am I in your way here? You trying to get to these dumbbells?"

"No, as a matter of fact I just came to see you about Joseph Bocchino."

"Well, hallelujah. It's about freaking time. I was beginning to wonder if anybody out there gave a damn about Bo. What kind of shit is his family? I told them he wasn't right in the head. He needs medical attention or something. And that ex-wife of his, one second she's a sweetheart and the next she sounds like she'd bury you alive for calling her after nine o'clock on a weeknight."

"So you know where Bo is?"

"Not now. Damn. Not now I don't! Why'd you people wait all this time?"

I explain to him that I'm only a friend and I've only been on this quest for a week or so and . . .

"You know about him clobbering people, right? I lost four clients here because of his outbursts. And the auto-body place six bays down had trouble with him, too. The roach coach still won't stop out front here because of him. All we have nearby is an Arby's now. Try eating that every day of your life and come up with enough combinations to keep it interesting. You know, someone needs to put a leash on him and walk him to a clinic. I tried, but I'm not family. He wouldn't accept my help."

It's so out of character for Bo. I remember one time when this kid Nick Vasilatos stabbed our basketball and everybody started ganging up on him. It was a mob scene and Bo came running from the far end of the court at full speed. Vasilatos was on the ground, people were kicking him, and he went completely pale at the sight of Bo charging at him. I turned and my leg was winding up when I felt someone grab my leg from behind. Boom!—the grip of Bo on my calf muscle. "Not right," he said, looking me in the eye. "Not right."

"Why do you think he's acting like that? Did something provoke him?"

"Provoke? No, he'd start to act a little loopy and then lash out. Something happened at that correctional facility he was working at. I know it. I told him he should sue them. He suffered some kind of head injury there and if anybody in his family gave a good goddamn they'd have gotten him to a hospital.

"This is my theory," Jeremy says. "The guy was acting like an asshole with his wife and maybe his family to begin with. But, you know, normal asshole stuff. And then when the head injury happened those close to him didn't even notice the change; it was just par for the course."

"I guess you never know what exactly could have—"

"Or he'd already become so estranged from those close to him that there was nobody close enough to realize there's a dent in this fucking guy's head and he's acting incredibly strange. Lucinda and I bounce these ideas around when we're slow. Lucinda!" he shouts toward the front. "What were some of the other Bo theories we were coming up with?"

"He made the mistake of acting strange before the injury, hence the injury goes unattended!" Lucinda shouts back.

"I gave him that one already. Anyway," he says, turning back to me, "I'm telling you, if he had a happy marriage there would have been a trauma hawk on his front lawn the first time he came home with a bad headache. You don't want to take a traumatic blow to the head the exact moment nobody in the world cares about you. That's what I'm saying. Is that simple enough for you? Sorry, I don't mean to talk to you like you're a simpleton."

"That's OK," I say. And all I can think about is going out to buy a helmet that I better start wearing 24/7 from this point on.

"You're all right. Listen, if you are his friend—and you must be a good one because you're the first person that's come calling—then just take the time to see this through."

"I don't know where to go from here."

"After I had to let him go I hooked him up with the church right up the road here—St. Vincent's. Father Richter comes in here all the time. He's got the sexy bones going, that son of a gun. What a waste. Anyway, he talked to Bo for hours and eventually got him set up to help a hermit nun who lives way out in Belle Glade. Goat farm, I think. Father was in recently and said he was no longer helping the hermit, but that would be a good place to start."

"This is a Catholic church? There are Catholic hermits?"

"Yeah, I guess. I don't question what Catholics do. I thought Father was crazy for even having Bo alone with her but he seemed confident that Bo might find some peace out there and she could handle him. She was a World War Two pilot or some shit."

"Do you have a phone for her?"

"Hermits don't have phones, buddy. I have an address, though. Lucinda up front will give it to you. Lucinda!" he yells.

"Yeah!"

"Give this guy the address to the Hermitage."

"Okaaay."

"It's way out there. Two lanes. Keep your headlights on the whole way. Honey, the pole classes are at four-fifteen," Jeremy says, looking over my shoulder.

"Dad, I've got to get going." I hear Kristin behind me.

"Oh, this is my daughter," I say as I turn around.

"Pleased to meet you," Jeremy says, saluting her.

Kristin salutes back, pivots military-style, and says, "I'm going to count to ten. Ten, nine . . ." as she marches toward the exit.

"OK, I better get going," I say to Jeremy. "Thanks for your help."

"Keep me abreast. Don't let Bo down."

"I'm trying not to. He saved me plenty of times. Even from myself."

Jeremy turns back to the mirror but raises his voice again as I'm making my way past the front desk. "If you do find him I've only got one word for you . . .

"Duck!"

tires for life

This is an oasis.

Not because it's the only meditation garden at a car dealership in the entire state and there's a concierge at my disposal and a spread that goes way beyond the usual coffee and doughnuts—oversize bagels, strawberry cream cheese, melon slices, crunchy carrots and dip, premade bacon, egg-and-cheese wraps—and I'm sitting in a massage chair set to "soft wave," but also because I am taking advantage of the Tires and Batteries for Life guarantee that came with my Toyota.

I've got to at least show Anna that I can stretch every cent we do have. How much is money on my mind at this point? Like a pudding skin on my brain, it is the first thing my thought process comes in contact with. There is no getting around it, no avoiding it.

My mind instead leaps to the fact that we will soon be completely broke. This morning my eyeglasses flipped out of my pocket and I stepped right on top of them—squash. A year ago the first words out of my mouth would have been "Ahh, my freaking glasses! What a pain, it's going to take ten days to have a new pair made and . . ." Today: "I will never see the world in focus again."

There will be no replacing . . . anything. Having to replace any essential these days is disastrous. A family meeting must be called, accounts must be checked, and sacrifices must be made. We have one of most everything left— one dishwasher, one bicycle, one automobile, one prescription for high blood pressure, one Vizio TV, one cat—and they all have to last for the next thirty years.

And don't tell me there are always free kittens. I've been down that road—shots $112.00, flea treatment $36.00, spaying $150.00, Fancy Feasts four for $2.23 . . . Nothing is free, especially free kittens.

But this tire plan at the Earl Hindell dealership in North Palm Beach is as close as I'm ever going to get. All I've had to do is come to this dealer for my regular oil changes. It usually runs about ten bucks more than a ten-minute place, but have you checked out the price of tires recently? Even at Costco you can't find a single P175/65R14 81T for less than $190. Plus this place is also a Lexus dealer, hence the snacks and furniture upgrade. The meditation garden even has a koi pond and a kanyi altar. Couples have been married in this garden, have exchanged nuptials while only fifty-five feet away their Toyota Tacoma's universal joints were being replaced and lubed.

"Mr. Reiner! Jeffrey Reiner!" the service rep shouts out.

"Sorry, I was meditating," I say.

The rep's name tag reads TANIK and she's exotically attractive, Sudanese/Belgian would be my guess. She has a clipboard in her hand and quickly lays an update on me. "The techs are finishing up on your oil change now and you were right about the front tires. Both are going to have to be replaced."

Yes!

"I just want to give you a rundown of the charges," she says, tilting the clipboard up for me to view. "Of course they'll have to do an alignment."

I hadn't thought of that, but yes, of course.

"And then the tires will be—"

"I have the Tires for Life plan."

"I know. But the wear is uneven so the tires aren't free, but they're prorated. We guaranteed new tires when total wear is at two/thirty-two of an inch."

"What does that even mean? Nobody brought up two/thirty-two when I signed up for the program. I . . . What am I doing?" I say aloud, stopping myself abruptly.

It hit me. The hotline.

Near the service check-in, off on a small concrete island is a red hotline phone with a small sign that says. "Problem? Pick up this phone and talk directly to me—Earl Hindell."

I've never seen anyone go near the hotline but I always wanted to pick it up just to see if someone would actually come on the other end. A receptionist who would say, "Oh, Mr. Hindell is currently in a meeting about the new Scions but your call is important to us." Or just a prerecording: "Earl, here.

Sorry I missed you but you can fill out a customer satisfaction card when you check out."

I start for the island. "Sir, I can have my direct supervisor discuss it with you," Tanik says.

"No, that's OK," I say. "I'll take it up with Earl."

I'm probably jumping the gun, maybe I could work it out with a Bryan or a Tim at midlevel but my eye is focused laserlike on the red line. There is nothing left on my horizon but that phone. I could hit it with a burp from twenty yards out.

I am a man who has lived forty-six years with inherent hesitation but there is none of that now. Riding a dolphin might not have been worth taking a stand over but this certainly is.

"Earl Hindell, can I help you?"

"Yes, yes you can. My name is Jeffrey Reiner. Tanik is my service adviser today and she just informed me I'm going to be charged for new tires even though I have the Tires for Life plan."

"OK, let's see if we can't work this out," Earl says pleasantly. But after I get two sentences into the 2/32 details he clears his throat as if he's about to take me to school.

"Oh," he says. "It's obvious you're tires were underinflated."

"That can't be," I say. "There's a light that goes on and beeps when the tires in my car are underinflated and I always fill them up immediately."

"That only goes off when the tires are grossly underinflated," he says.

The use of the word *grossly* isn't lost on me, and a small riot is breaking out in my brain. "What!? So this must happen all the time to customers."

"This is actually very rare."

"How often are you supposed to check your inflation?"

"We recommend every two weeks."

"So this is rare. So I'm the anomaly. Everybody else is running around checking their tires every fourteen days but me. The whole busy, crazy world out there is keeping a sharp eye on their tires. They're Twittering in one hand and gauging tire pressure with the other ["hey everybody, my tire pressure was a perfect 35 lbs. today." How many characters is that?]. Where are they filling these underinflated tires up? Because I passed two hundred gas stations on the way here and not one had someone kneeling down putting in air. Half of them don't even have the hoses attached."

"By the way, you should have been given a free pressure gauge when you signed up for the program," Earl says.

"Well, I wasn't. Are you telling me I'm the only one with this problem?"

"Now we're doing a three-sixty. Going back to the same thing," Earl says.

"I go out of my way to come here. I have recommended this place to people. Now I can't recommend it. Now I have to warn people. Why are you doing this to me? Since the deadly recalls, Toyota should want to cater to the customer's every whim."

"You have to understand we can't be handing out free tires to people who aren't maintaining their tires."

"This is just me? Everybody else is getting free tires. I'm the rare case?"

"Well, here we go again. We're doing a three-sixty."

"You're doing a three-sixty because this is the second time you said three-sixty. We're locked in this together. I'm staying on this hotline for . . . the rest of my life. At some point my car is going up on the lift for free tires, maybe a year from now, maybe two years."

"You won't be putting any wear on the tires if you stay on the phone," Earl says.

"Oh, I bet you've got an excuse for that, too. If I claimed I never drove my car you'd say, 'Oh, that's why the odd wear—the tires had been sitting in one place too long.'"

"Well, that's true."

"I'm sitting down on the ground now. I hope you know that. The cord on this phone isn't even made for sitting. It's too short and I have to crane my neck but I'm in this for the long haul. I've got no place to be. You've probably got a Scion meeting in ten minutes but you might want to order out for lunch because—"

"Why don't we just go inside and you can calm down." I hear a voice behind me that sounds very much like Earl, only more alive.

Earl is taller than me, steely-eyed with a big, gray swept-up Mark Twain hairdo.

"I don't want to talk to you if you're not on the hotline," I say. "I just want my tires for free. You can't be messing with people like this—guaranteeing a product for life. You know what that means these days? Maybe when you first started selling this plan back in 2006 or whatever . . ."

"2004."

"Maybe then you could pull something like this, but not now. You can't be doing this to people. To be guaranteed something for life, you know what that does to a man like me?"

"The prorating isn't a bad deal," Earl says. "If you want to sit. Come sit in—"

"Oh, don't try to drag me into the meditation garden. It's stupid anyway. The rock garden is all wrong—it's all pebbles. And the smell of antifreeze constantly wafts over from the garage. Who do you think you're fooling with that Zen-Lexus bull? Everybody that's gotten married in there has been divorced in eight months."

"Is there someone we can call?" Earl says.

I'm up and pacing now and I think it's making him nervous. Tanik has joined us and other customers are starting to stare. "Gather 'round," I say. "You all should hear this."

"Mr. Reiner, you're bleeding. Your tooth is—"

"I know, I know. A piece cracked off but it doesn't hurt. There's no pain. If it doesn't hurt it's OK. You don't have to go to the dentist."

"Tanik," Earl says, "does Mr. Reiner have a home phone number on there?"

Tanik hands him the entire clipboard and he walks over to the hotline. He somehow goes through the switchboard and is trying to . . .

"Oh, don't use the hotline to call my wife. That's just not—"

"Mrs. Reiner, Earl Hindell. Yes Hindell Toyota and Lexus. I have your husband on the line," he says, taking the phone from his ear and holding the receiver out to me.

"Honey, don't say anything. You're on the hotline. No. No it doesn't make sense. They want to prorate the tires instead of giving them to me for free. Come on, don't you get all rational on me. They put out strawberry cream cheese for the Lexus people here. They can afford to give me tires."

"Tanik, why don't you get Mr. Reiner a raspberry apple Snapple from the buffet? Do you like raspberry, Jeffrey?"

"No! Anna, did you hear that? They're talking to me like a little kid that has to be pacified. I'm going. I'm going. This call never happened," I say, and hang up.

"Earl, just answer me this," I say, steadying myself. "Why do you have the hotline if it's not to make customers like me happy? I mean, why even have it?"

"That's a good question."

air ball

Why did you have them call me?" Anna says.

"I didn't tell them to call you. It was fucking Hindell's idea."

"I don't need to be getting these crazy calls at work. This manic act of yours isn't helping us at all."

"I'm not manic. I'm intense. You said I need to—"

"You're manic. Or you wouldn't be causing a scene at a Toyota dealer."

"Somebody needed to shake that place up."

"Listen to yourself."

"I needed to take a stand."

"Somebody answer the door," Kristin yells from the TV room. "Somebody's at the door."

"I don't have time for any of this," Anna says, heading for the front door.

"If your initial calculations weren't so far off I wouldn't feel so much immediate pressure," I say.

"Stop right there. I just came by the house to get some fruit and my other shoes. We got the government contract and we're starting tonight. So you're in charge of dinner."

"No problem," I say, following her.

I open the door and it's Kyle, the boy from down the street who used to mow our lawn. He's carrying a sawed-off rolling pin in one hand and a gaudily stitched pillowcase in the other. "Is Andrew here?" he says.

"No," I say. "What are you up to?"

"We were supposed to meet here."

Anna is trying to rush out the front door but can't help asking about the rolling pin. "For the iguanas," Kyle says, raising it over his head.

"What?"

"You know. Bag 'em and tag 'em," he says, holding up his grandmother's pillowcase. "We've been getting twenty-five dollars apiece. Well, thirty-five, but then we have to give the guy who drops us off in Manalapan ten dollars from each kill."

"Each kill! You've got Andrew involved with this?" Anna says.

"He got me started. Said I could make more than with the lawns. Everybody's been cutting back on their lawn service but they seem to have money to kill the iguanas that are crapping in their pools."

"Stop using the word *kill*," I say, trying to calm things down.

"Execute," Kyle says.

Anna turns away from Kyle, looks directly at me, and says, "You find our son and find out exactly what the hell is going on. I have to get to work. You hear me—*Exactly what is going on.*"

"On my way home I saw him at the basketball court. Shooting by himself," Kristin says, coming up behind me as Anna is pulling out of the driveway. "An iguana-killing loner."

"Can I go with you?" Kyle says.

"No."

"Tell him we're losing our window," he says.

"What?"

"The easiest kills are at dusk."

From a distance I see Andrew picking his spots on the court, his back to the hoop. He's turning blindly, practicing a quick release. When he sees me he throws the ball the length of the court and I heave an air ball up at the rim. As I wait by the foul line for him to chase it down I can see that he has much more control of his limbs than he did even six months ago.

"Kyle came by," I say.

"OK."

"With the rolling pin."

"Oh, I don't know what his rush is. We still have time," he says, looking at the height of the sun in the sky. "You want to play some H-O-R-S-E?"

"Not really. What is going on? How did you get involved with this?"

"Alex gave me a note but—"

"Alex?"

"Yeah, for you. But you weren't around so I met with the guy."

"Omar?? Why?"

"To help out. To make some extra money," he says, pulling a roll of bills out and handing it to me.

"My God, how many iguanas have you killed?"

"Dad, it's just an extermination process," he says, stepping around me for a lay-up. "The state set up the guidelines."

"I know. I read the paper." After several homeowners and municipalities complained that the dragonlike iguanas that grow up to eight feet were destroying rare plant life and crapping in resort hotel pools, the state declared the nonnative creatures a nuisance and it's been open season ever since.

"There's a whole set of rules we have to go by," Kyle says. "You can only bludgeon them once in the head or it's considered cruelty."

"I don't want to hear the state's iguana-killing rules. You're the boy that used to stop your aunt from crushing snails on the back patio."

"This is humane. People were running the iguanas over with their cars, maiming them with crossbows."

"You were so vigilant with Alonzo. How can you be this way with another living creature? Some people have them as pets."

"That day Alonzo got hurt. That was part of this. I might as well tell you that now."

"What?"

"Kyle and I had him in the woods trying to see if he could help us search out the iguanas. Like a hunting dog."

"A hunting dog? He's not in the hunting/sporting group. Don't you ever watch the Eukanuba dog shows on Animal Planet? He's a working/herding dog."

"What's the difference?"

"The difference is he doesn't have it in his genetics to hunt lizards. Jesus, what did you get him into?"

"I'm sorry."

"Well, he's tough. He's getting used to the idea of only having three legs now. I've got him thinking somebody might write a song about him. But, come on, why are you doing this? For this?" I say, holding up the money.

"Dad, don't flatten out the bills. I like when they roll up like that."

Andrew tosses me the ball and takes the money back. I toss up a shot but it clunks off the rim. I grab the rebound and quickly shoot again, but this time I totally miss the hoop *and* the backboard. I used to have such a sweet jump shot. It's been a while, but it has never failed me before.

"This has to stop," I say.

"But you're trying new things. You jump at anything that comes along."

"That's because I've been doing old things for so long. I have to try new things. You need to be more choosy."

"I'm just trying to help."

"Massacring iguanas is not helping. That's scaring the living shit out of me."

"You gotta do what you gotta do."

"Who's that talking?"

"You."

the lobster bisque

More iced tea?" the waitress asks. "Refill?"

"No, no thank you. I'm good."

I spent the entire morning putting fliers under windshield wipers near the Bingorama up near I-95. There is nothing worse than parking lot heat in Florida. Plus Omar? was extremely nitpicky, monitoring the whole job and constantly reprimanding me for manhandling the wipers.

When I went off on him about the iguanas all he said was "I thought we discussed this already and everything was cool."

"We never discussed it and it's not," I said.

"OK, cool. I need to know that."

I didn't even mention Omar?'s involvement to Anna because she's all about accountability and I will surely be held accountable. Ordinarily I would take immediate responsibility, but I need a little space between incidents right now. You can understand that. If everything is copacetic the rest of this week, I've got it penciled in to tell her next Thursday.

Anyway, the wiper work was grueling. Apparently the last guy Omar? had putting fliers on car windshields snapped the wiper blades off a Saturn Vue and it not only cost Omar? eighty-four dollars for new blades and mechanisms, but his entire operation was banned from the shopping center near the dog track, which is constantly packed and a favorite target for gentlemen's club fliers.

Omar? was obsessed and, grabbing at my fingers, showing me how to lightly pinch the blade. "Only rubber. Only rubber. Don't touch the metal."

I kept telling him I have a delicate touch but he insisted on making the task of putting yellow bagel shop fliers on windshields totally unbearable.

"Dad?"

"Kristin?"

"What are you doing here? You're eating the lobster bisque," she says, looking down. "What the hell?"

"What are *you* doing here?"

"I work here," she says, pointing at the Lantana Ale House logo on her peach-colored polo shirt. "I told you last week after the boutique cut my hours. I can't believe this."

"I know. What are the odds we'd run into each other here?"

"Did you shut the air off in the house this morning?"

"I just put the thermostat up to ninety-one to try and conserve during the day so—"

"Look at my hair. I was sweating in the shower. I can't believe you've got us all pinching pennies and you're sitting here eating lobster bisque. Mom working overtime and making her lunch every morning—cottage cheese, saltines, and a nectarine. I'm unplugging my laptop every forty-five minutes and using generic body lotion while you're eating lobster bisque for lunch."

"Mom loves nectarines."

"You don't get it."

"It's not like that. I had to work in a parking lot all morning. I was just going to get an iced tea and cool down but the waitress—"

"Server."

"The server charmed me into getting the soup."

"Chelsea!" Kristin yells across the dining room.

"Hey, Kristin. I appreciate you coming in early!" Chelsea shouts back. "I have to take Riley to the vet this afternoon. Thanks."

"No problem. My last class was at twelve-thirty anyway. Can you come here for a sec?"

"Sure."

"Did you charm this guy into a bowl of lobster bisque?"

"Huh?"

"And just for the record, are you not the least charming person that works here?"

"Honey, I couldn't charm a starving man trapped in a dungeon into a bowl of soup. You either want it or you don't."

"Thank you. This is my dad, by the way."

"Nice to meet you."

"Has Mom factored this into the equation?" Kristin says, nudging the soup bowl.

"There is an equation, isn't there?"

"Move," Kristin says. "This is my serving area. Move to a table by the aquarium on the other side. *Throwing circuit breakers.* And you've got Andrew bashing iguanas to help pay the bills while you're cooling down in restaurants . . . that I work at. I cannot believe you. What have you become?"

"Sit down for a minute. Let's talk about this. I'll tell you what I've become."

"My shift is starting. Move. Now!"

"Are you still going to want the cracked conch?" Chelsea asks.

dinner with alex

strolled down and pounded on Sal and Peggy's door for a quarter stick of butter but no one answered. As I'm walking back, I'm dreading having to go to the grocery store. Maybe I can use lard.

Alex's brother Troy is out front working on his car. He gives me a nod that I would ordinarily take as meaning absolutely nothing, but in this case I decide it's very clearly trying to convey "If you ever need anything—like a quarter stick of butter—I'm your man."

He holds up his greasy hands expecting me to say, "Oh, don't worry about it." But I don't.

He heads into the house and quickly returns with a whole stick.

"I don't need this much," I tell him.

"I'm not measuring butter," he says.

Anna is pulling another one of her government shifts and Kristin left me a sarcastic note in her big loopy penmanship: "went to my friend kimmie's to take a shower. be back in a week . . . or two."

It's just Andrew and me for dinner and Andrew already said, "You're not going to make any of those smush sandwiches, are you?" so I'm making macaroni and cheese to go with . . . something. For some reason, no matter the meal, I always center on the side dish first.

I'm trying to find the strainer when there's an incessant knocking at the door. It's machine-gun-style—rat-tat-tat.

"Troy told me you're cooking. What's going on? You need me to help?" Alex says excitedly.

"No, no, I'm fine."

"What are you making?"

"Just some mac and cheese so far."

"Oh, you gotta double-cheese it," she says, pushing past me into the kitchen. "Do you have more than one box?"

"I think so," I say, scouring the cabinet.

"Get me the cheese packet out of the second box. Same amount of noodles. Double the cheese."

"But then I've got a box of macaroni and cheese left without the cheese."

"Yeah, some poor soul ends up with nothing but wet, soggy noodles on a Sunday afternoon, but we can't worry about that now."

She breaks the seal on the second cheese bag to prove her point and then props herself up on the island counter as if her work is done.

"I like this counter. Nice granite," she says.

"It's great for entertaining."

Andrew walks in and takes an entire two-liter bottle of Mountain Dew out of the refrigerator and tucks it under his arm like a football.

"Hi, Andy," Alex says.

"Hey," he says, heading back to his bedroom.

"By the way, no more passing Omar?'s notes to Andrew. OK?"

"Yes, siree. I heard about the iguana thing. Where's the rest of your crew?"

"Anna's lab has a government contract that they have to work nights on, and Kristin went across town to take a shower."

"How's the search for your friend going?"

"Not so good."

"The friends that don't want to be found are the keepers. You know that."

"I do now."

It seems oddly relaxing having Alex sitting up on the kitchen counter, rubbing her knees together like some sort of anorexic Jiminy Cricket and espousing her flimsy wisdom.

"Don't you just hate waiting for water to boil?" she says.

"I'm getting used to waiting for everything now."

"Sometimes I don't have the patience for boiling. You ever eat the powdered cheese right out of the packet?"

"No," I say, moving the packets to the other side of the counter.

"How is your job search going?"

"A counselor told me I need to manage my expectations."

"What a thing to manage."

"Anna says I need to 'double my efforts.'"

"Oh God, I could double a lot of things, but not my efforts. You know, you should come up with your own five businesses, be your own enterprising dude."

"It may come to that."

"Or don't work. People like to act like everything is about work."

"That's a nice thought, but I have to work."

"Do you?"

I keep my mouth shut, but I know I can be honest with Alex and tell her that I hate the thought of ever working again, especially now because I'm sure once you get a job the whole mind-set will be "You're lucky to have a job." The bosses can treat you like crap, wages will be eternally frozen, benefits nonexistent, and, in case I didn't mention, don't you dare complain because "you're lucky you have a job."

"Is mac and cheese your specialty?" Alex says.

"No, it's smush sandwiches." Andrew pipes in from the hallway, as if he's been listening to every word.

The thought of that stifles me. Alex, with her exaggerated features and animated gestures, is almost like a cartoon character to me now, but I don't know how Andrew sees her. I don't want to be a man standing in the center of his family's kitchen, complaining about his wife to another woman. I best keep the talk to food.

"Actually, frozen ravioli is my specialty," I say. "You know how once the boiling water gets roiling they start to break up? That never happens when I watch over the ravioli. I really tend to it. I have a very delicate touch with the frozen ravioli. I've never lost one. Never. Isn't that true?" I shout out to Andrew.

"True. They always explode on Mom. She sucks at it."

"Anna's a great cook," I proclaim.

"I'm sure she is," Alex says. "Hey, did you ever write about food for that paper of yours—restaurant reviews and stuff?"

"Other people did. Artie did. Every time I tried to get involved they just said 'come up with something really original and we'll see.'"

"It's hard for some people to be original."

"Right, but they were doing a special food issue, so at the story meeting I brought up the idea of inventing the 'chew kiss.'"

"The chew kiss?"

"Yeah, you know how food is supposed to be all sensuous and whatnot? Anyway so the idea was that when a couple is chewing something really warm and delectable they kiss while still chewing. The lips are moving around anyway. I don't mean like they open their mouths and mix up the food. Nothing gross, just a light kiss while still chewing. I suggested we describe how to do it and then include a few romantic recipes."

"And you were going to do the describing?"

"Yes."

"Mmmm, what did the people you work with think of the idea?"

"Like everything in America today, some people thought it was awesome and the rest thought it was lame and corny. It never went anywhere, but I don't think I got enough credit for the idea. I mean, the kiss hasn't changed in centuries. French kissing is the last innovation I can think of and here I was coming up with a new one."

"Whoa, you're boiling over."

The pot is all white foam and the water starts splashing onto the burner so I rush it to the sink and clumsily dump the noodles into the strainer, losing half of them down the drain. There goes my perfect record.

"That's OK, higher cheese-to-noodle ratio," Alex says. "Here, we have to put the packets in simultaneously. Go."

She starts stirring up the noodles and it does look to be the lushest macaroni and cheese I've ever seen.

"It was supposed to just be the side dish but—"

"But you got distracted. Trust me, this is going to be filling."

Andrew comes in to get a plate, looks at Alex propped on the counter with a bowl in her hand and me eating standing up, and does an about-face, taking his food out by the TV.

"Don't you find it ironic that while you're searching for your long-lost friend, half your family is abandoning you?" Alex laughs.

"I don't know enough about irony to say," I say.

Without moving off the countertop, Alex leans over and plucks a bigger spoon out of the utensil drawer.

"How'd you even know where the utensils were?" I ask. "When I'm in a strange kitchen I have to open six drawers to find anything."

"I wander around your house when no one's home," she says with a smirk.

Andrew has the TV blasting and Alex is wolfing down the mac and cheese, scraping at the bottom of the bowl. She ends up sucking on the big spoon like it's a cheese lollipop and then jumps up and says, "What's for dessert?"

"I didn't plan anything."

"We just need something to warm up," she says, opening the snack cabinet. "Anything. Even old cookies will do if you warm 'em up for ten seconds."

She zaps a plate of stale Chips Ahoy chocolate-chip cookies and holds the platter over her head on the tips of her fingers to go out and serve Andrew.

The TV goes mute and Alex says, "Dessert, sir. Careful, they're hot."

I can hear Andrew mumble, "Thank you," and then the TV roars again. Alex puts the plate under my nose and I take two.

"Chew kiss," she says with her mouth stuffed.

I laugh at her puffy cheeks as if she's hoarding chocolate chips for the winter. "Come on, it's been centuries since somebody tried something new."

"You're exaggerating your chewing."

"I exaggerate everything."

She goes perfectly still, which I know is not easy for her. Her eyes close and only her lips are in motion, gently rolling. I don't want to mock her. Since I've known her, this is the first time I can tell for sure that she is serious about something.

"I can't," I say.

Her eyes open and she's trembling a little.

"No biggie. I can find someone else to experiment on," she says, jumping off the counter. "I'm going to need a to-go bag, for the rest of these cookies, please."

Peggy made a dish

The sun is just touching the tops of the distant trees when I make a dash for it.

"Whoa, where you sailing off to?" Alex says as I'm cutting across the driveway.

"The woods."

"What woods?"

"At the end of the block. We're going to drink in the woods."

"Who's going to . . . Can I come?"

"I don't know. It's a small woods."

"I won't take up much room. Wait right here," she says, running back toward her house. "I've got to grab my cigarettes."

"Meet me down there!" I shout back.

"You better be there!"

Artie sticks his head out of the brush while I'm still several yards away, then disappears back into the thicket like a chunky, skittish rabbit or, better yet, a sinister hobbit.

"This is perfect." Artie pokes his head back out. "Check out the area I cleared in here."

"This *is* an ideal drinking spot." I marvel.

"I'm tellin' ya." Artie grins. He's decked out in camouflage shorts and a They Might Be Giants T-shirt, a cigarette hanging out of his mouth.

"Menthol?" I ask.

"You know it." He hands me a Yuengling from an ice-filled backpack. "I told you I'd set us all up. Hey, I ran into Cassie last night. She—"

"Make room for Daddy," a hairy arm says crashing through the foliage. "Take this, take this."

Sal is thrusting a Saran-wrapped casserole dish into my face and dragging what looks like an old washtub across the dirt.

"What is that?" Artie asks.

"What is this?" I exclaim, holding up the casserole.

"Peggy made a dish—five-layer taco dip. She thought we were going to a block party."

"It smells good," Artie says.

"And this is the closest thing I could find to an old washing machine. It's a 1954 ice-cream churner," Sal brags, turning it over and dumping Artie's beer and ice in, as well as another twelve-pack of Dos Equis.

"Artie, what were you saying about Cassie?" I ask, but Artie glances Sal's way and acts as if it's too personal now.

"I was reduced to wanting to ask my mom for money the other day," I say.

"What's wrong with that?" Artie says with a shrug.

"It just seems wrong. I even considered asking my uncle and then I thought about how you become one of those guys that people are leery of when they hear from you. They see your number on the caller ID and it's 'Don't pick up. He's going to want to borrow money.' I don't want to become one of those people."

"You don't want to become so many people I'm surprised you're able to exist at all," Artie says. "Everybody else is being pigeonholed as some kind of people; why not you?"

Alex comes clomping into the clearing wearing clown-size work boots, her orange and yellow flannel pajama pants sloppily tucked in. "I know you!" she shouts, pointing at Sal. "You're the guy who shot the arrow into the bounce house. That was awesome. Oh, and you buffed everybody's car that time."

"It was a new toy. I had gotten this car buffer for Father's Day," Sal explains. "I was just having some fun."

"In the middle of the night," Alex says.

"More early morning. Four-ish."

"He went up and down the block in the middle of the night and buffed and shined every car sitting in a driveway. The next morning was a crisp bright day and every hood up and down the block was gleaming."

"That was before you moved here." Sal nudges me. "I owe you a buff."

"Lordy, this is awful," Alex cries out, spilling her beer out into the dirt. "I've got a bottle of Gosling's Black Seal in my dresser drawer. I'll be right back."

"We need a lookout," Artie says. "I'm shimmying up this tree."

The tree is only about five and a half feet tall but once he reaches the top, Artie claims he can see the interstate and a Red Roof Inn "with a blue roof."

"You see the dead-end sign?"

"Can't miss it. Man, I can see your whole future from up here."

"Did anyone see that street magician on TV last night?" Sal asks.

"Criss Angel?"

"I don't know—one of those guys. He was going on about all his accomplishments—surviving in a block of ice, squatting in a crate above London—shit like that. But then he alleges the reason he does what he does is to challenge people—to wake their asses up."

"Wake *our* asses up?" I yelp. "I don't know about you, but my ass is up. I'm crawling out of bed every morning, doing the best I can. It certainly hasn't reached the point where I'm looking to a street magician for inspiration. My ass is up."

"Hey, here comes that girl," Artie announces. "She's drinking out of the bottle already. And she's got a bag with her. Looks like—"

"Some scoops for your dip there," Alex says, handing over the bag.

"Excellent," Sal says.

"Dip!" Artie yells, sliding down the tree.

"I'll take a slurp of that Gosling's." Sal reaches for the bottle of rum.

"Man, it's like God made this dip," Artie blurts with four of the five layers hanging off his beard.

"Don't say that," Sal insists. "Peggy doesn't like anybody else getting credit for her dip."

"God already gets too much credit for things," I say.

"He's been living off the same accomplishments like . . . forever," Artie adds.

"God is coasting." Alex raises the bottle of Gosling's. "Hey, I'm toasting here," she says.

"Yeah, yeah, God is coasting," we chorus, raising our drinks.

I flinch a little, knowing I'm the biggest coaster of all right now—drinking in the middle of the woods, waiting for something to fall on top of me.

"Cassie looked amazing," Artie says.

"Whoa, I thought you didn't want to talk about it in front—"

"I'm comfortable with these people now," Artie claims. "I ran into Cassie outside of the dry-cleaning place in that plaza where Salvo's Vinyl is. She was in a big hurry. Off on a trip, but she wouldn't say where. She had that incredible look about her but she acted like I was just a guy, like a thousand other guys."

"But you're one in a million. She must know that," I point out.

"One in a million isn't what it used to be. Too many people. To stand out now you have to be one in, like, five hundred million or one in a billion even," Artie says. "The Chinese used to be out of it, but now all those Chinese guys are getting into it."

"He's right," Alex says. "All those China boys are getting cars now."

"It's like looking for a job. There's just too many people out there and they all look good and have cars and college degrees," I say.

"Cassie's smart, so if there are a few billion people in the world, she's thinking there's at least eighty people out there better than me, right?"

"Did you try the old 'You only live once, let's just give it one more shot' bit with her?" Sal asks.

"Of course," Artie says, dropping his head into his hands. "But, you know, some people just don't care about only living once."

Sensing he might start weeping, Alex places her hand on Artie's shoulder. She leans in and forcefully puts the tip of the Gosling's against Artie's lips like she's trying to force-feed a bottle to an infant that won't stop crying. Artie guzzles with abandon, and when Alex pulls the bottle away he keeps his head tilted back and begins howling at the moon like a jilted madman.

"Quiet. You hear that?" Sal says.

"What?" I say.

"I think it's an iguana . . . I heard, I heard." He laughs, slapping me on the back. "Hey, the boy is right. There's good money in it. What the heck."

"Did you see they found that fourteen-foot Burmese python in the canal in Wellington and killed it?" Alex mentions.

"That I understand," Artie says. "The thing's Burmesean. It doesn't belong in Wellington. But iguanas, come on. They're just transients like the rest of us. Why not club us all? Club us all!"

"Artie, you going to be all right?" I ask.

"Sure, sure, I'll be my old self in a minute."

"Let's not talk about this stuff while we're in a dark woods," I say.

"Oh, I keep having this dream about the Chinese." Alex changes the subject. "I guess they finally get around to taking us over and they're going door to door and they storm into my house shouting, 'In the street! In the street!' That's all they say. And everybody is filing into the street and into these white, oblong vans that take us to a factory where they make all the little carnival toys, like those . . ."

"Monkeys on a stick?" Artie says.

"Yeah, stuff like that. At first I was scared but then it was kind of fun. I liked making carnival toys."

"That's the only way we're going to make it," Sal rants. "I know free-trade people don't like to hear it, but for the next ten years we have to say, sorry, we'll make our own carnival toys and everything else—wiper blades, Blu-Rays, oscillating fans, you name it. We gotta just make it across town and put you people to work."

"I would work in a sweatshop," Artie says. "They make it sound so horrible with that name—*sweatshop*. But it's mostly just sewing, right?"

"Hey, you OK over there?" Sal catches me staring off into our finite wilderness.

"I'm good. My ass is up," I say. "How 'bout you, Alex?"

"My ass is up."

"Yo, that could be our catchphrase," Artie decides.

"This is really uncharted territory. We're deep in the forest," Alex declares, rotating around. "It's like we're in the VIP room in a forest."

"It's just a woods," Sal says.

"It can be a forest. Why you gotta be that way?" I ask. "Let her have her forest."

"OK," Sal replies.

"Can I ask you something?" Artie says to me before buckling over and putting his head between his knees.

He raises his hand to signal he's OK, gasps a couple of times, and belches, "Scoop, wrong pipe. I wanted to ask you why you and that friend Bo lost contact after eighth grade."

"I don't know. In high school he went on to football and drugs and . . ."

"What about you?"

"I went on to football and drugs, too, but I wasn't good enough at either one to keep up. Plus, his musical tastes were becoming more sophisticated. He was getting into John Mayall."

"No shit," Sal says, sighing.

"Hey, tell me something about this guy I don't know," Alex says, nodding my way as she passes the Gosling's to Artie. "What's he like to work with?"

Artie looks me over, ponders the question, and looks me over again. "I don't know what he's like to work with."

It's kind of true. A lot of times you stop judging or even paying attention to the caliber of work your fellow employees are doing. The day becomes more about wry comments, funny faces, and how far you can throw things.

"Yo, wait," Artie says. "Has he ever sung the Beatles for you?"

"No!" Alex shouts.

"Absolutely not," I protest.

"He does this thing. It's really different. It's . . . like the Beatles being sung by a guy with his legs hanging out of a freight train heading toward the Great Divide. That's how I'm going to put it if I ever write a review."

"Oh now you have to," Alex insists, punching me and waving a lit cigarette in my face.

"I can only do it with the early stuff."

"I don't give a damn. It's all ancient to me."

"OK. Here goes. 'Here I stand head in hand . . . Turn my face to the wall . . .'"

"Man alive, where is that coming from?" Sal says. "That's spooky. How long you been able to do this?"

"About a week and a half now," I say.

"Something is gone, man. You don't pick up something like that without losing something else," Sal says. "Something major."

Alex butts in. "Stop it. You're scaring him. You're drunk."

"You're drunk," Sal says.

"I wish *I* was drunk," Artie mutters.

"That's it. We meet back here first thing in the morning when everyone is sober," Alex says.

"Yeah, we better call it a night," Sal says. "I've got a shitload of Norwegians to ferry over to the bunker first thing in the morning."

"Into the street! Into the street!" Alex raises the bottle. "Hey, I'm doing a toast here."

"Into the street!" Sal raises a fist.

"To uncharted territory!" Artie howls.

"And to good friends, loyal neighbors, and a young lady who doesn't take up very much room in the woods," I fervently add with a nod to Alex.

"Let's hit it," Sal says.

"I'm going to stay here and finish the dip," Artie spouts. "Hey, Reiner, don't forget Gillian wants us to go to that street painting festival."

"It's a date!" I shout back. "Oh, and be careful out here alone. Don't fall in the ravine."

"What ravine? . . . Hey!"

I push through the brush and back out under the streetlights. Our houses look so far away.

"Maybe I lost the ability to find gainful employment. Maybe that's the major thing I've lost," I tell Sal.

"No, no, that's not it," Sal says. "You'll know when you know."

"You know I hate you. You . . . you . . . man with a pension. You I'll-know-when-I-know person."

"You're drunk."

"I hope so."

"That Beatles thing is impressive. I once had a Tracy Morgan imitation come out of my mouth, but I could never get it back. Story of my life."

"You're drunk."

"I hope so."

"Can I tell you something for real?" I say. "You're a great guy and all, but can I tell you something for real?"

"Shoot."

"Your chili sucks."

it's just lunch

Anna is going to be shocked. The octopi are going to leap right off her scrubs and splash into the petri dishes at her lab station.

Omar?'s got me working as a courier for a pediatric center in West Palm Beach and my first stop after the lunch hour is Langley Medical Lab, better known as Anna's place! And, for once, I'm not wearing a funny hat. I had to pull out a clean pair of khakis and a crisp collared shirt for this one. "Class it up," Omar? said.

This is my chance to make a great first impression on Anna, if that makes any sense. All the flaws that have been rising up since the job loss will be erased by the sight of me making a punctual first-class delivery. I'm not even using my own car. I'm in a bright red Ford Focus with a big white cross on the roof. I've got instructions for all my stops and for Anna's it simply says, "Pull up to the back service entrance. Press buzzer." This is going to be great.

A static-ridden hello comes over the intercom box above the buzzer. The voice is so garbled it could be Anna for all I know, but I don't want to give myself away yet.

"Merrick Pediatrics. Drop-off," I say, reading off my instruction card.

There's no reply. The door just clicks open to the back stockroom. I used to come up here and use the massive shredder machine in the corner. The shredder at my old job would choke if you tried to put three sheets of paper through it at once, but you could throw a human head in this behemoth and it would shred it into slaw instantly.

There's an employee break room to the left, but if I stroll through there I'm sure to be spotted by one of her coworkers who might let out a big "Look who it is" and the jig will be up, so I slip up the hallway by the billing office and cut back around to where I can pop out right at Anna's lab station.

I see Anna's coworker Renee on the other side and put a finger to my lips.

"What are you doing here?" Renee says, ignoring my signal.

I leap in, but Anna's nowhere in sight.

"Your wife went to lunch."

"Lunch? It's almost two-thirty."

"She said she had a big breakfast."

"Is she in her car?"

"I don't think so. She left her cellphone here, though. Probably hasn't gone too far. What have you been up to?"

Renee is a character. She recently got married on a trapeze in Las Vegas. I'd ordinarily like to pepper her with questions—How exactly did they do the vows? Did the groom swing from the opposite side? Did the minister have to double up on the bar with one of them to meet in the middle? Was there a net?—but I'm too disappointed about Anna's absence.

"Nothing," I say.

"Tell Anna to hurry up if you see her. I'm getting backed up here."

"OK," I say, heading toward the stockroom. Luckily nobody has to buzz me out.

I walk along the canal and see Anna's car but it's all locked up. I start up the Focus and circle around the back of the building to the front exit. You have to go one way and then make a U-turn to get back to the highway and I'm stopped at the first legal turnaround when Anna comes racing past in the passenger's seat of a dark blue BMW. I don't even glimpse the driver. I only see Anna's profile leaning forward as if she is changing the radio station or turning up the AC.

I try to turn back to the lab building but traffic is pouring in and I'm getting anxious. Gas. Brake. Gas. Brake. Gas. Brake. As soon as I get an opening I floor it, but by the time I reach the back door I see Anna slipping in the service entrance and the BMW is heading straight at me.

He's a toothy, Dudley-looking guy with sandy-colored hair. Something weird around his neck, like an ascot.

I screech around the rear lot and am right on his ass by the time he reaches the first intersection, so I pull up alongside him.

It's not an ascot. It's just his necktie thrown over his shoulder, the way businessmen are known to do when they go out for midday soup. I hope Anna took note of that. What kind of person still has his tie thrown over his shoulder long after the soup is gone?

He speeds off the second the light changes and gets in the far lane to the interstate ramp. I jerk the car over and trail him up the ramp going south. He has absolutely no regard for the speed limit and I don't know if the Focus can do more than the 84 mph it's clocking now. Did he drive this recklessly when Anna was in the car?

A dozen exits have flashed by, but I've still got him in my sights. He's the type that gets up behind people, hits his brights, and then rips around them before they have time to move out of his way.

A voice comes over the Nextel I was issued. "Courier Three."

Damn.

"Courier Three, pick up. This is Monica."

It's just lunch. I can already hear people telling me that. Gillian saying, "It's just lunch. We've gone to lunch. People go to lunch."

People don't drive this far just for lunch.

"Courier Three. I need your location. We've got an add-on. Can you handle? Copy."

I met Monica this morning. She had a tube of Pringles tilted up as she tried to get the crumbs out of the bottom and a curling iron plugged in at her desk. She screamed at me like I was a peon when I almost touched it. "You wanna burn yourself? Stay away from my desk." If anybody should cut me a break right now it's Monica, but I can't even respond.

"Courier Three. Where are you? Add-on in the box. Courier Three."

Let Courier Two fucking get it.

I don't know why I can so easily comprehend Anna losing interest in me, but I could never fathom her taking an interest in someone else. She's not built that way. *She's not built that way,* and I can't help wondering how she *is* built.

"Jeremy." A raspy voice comes over the radio. "Jeremy? Talk to me, man."

"This is Jeffrey," I say into the radio. "Are you trying to reach *me?*"

"Yeah, Jeffrey. What the F."

"Who are you?"

"I work for your employer."

"Omar?"

"Where are you? Merrick's people say you never even dropped at Langley Lab."

Crap. I was so worked up about surprising Anna that I forgot to bring the specimens in. "I was there; they just didn't know I was the courier. They thought I was just there to see my wife. How'd you get on this radio?"

"We're on the channel. That's all you need to know. That blood gonna curdle on you. Whoa, you just crossed the county line. What are you doing to us?"

"How do you know where I am?"

"All the fleet has GPS, dumbass. I gotta get back to you. I didn't know you crossed county lines."

"What, I'm just crossed over from Palm into Broward County. It's not like I'm crossing the border into Mexico or something. I'm in purs—"

"Out."

The BMW lurches across three lanes, but I'm able to whip right behind it. This Focus handles remarkably well, and by the time I get to the exit there is only one car between us.

At the light on Commercial Boulevard West, the BMW's window comes down and he flicks out a small piece of cellophane.

Fucking litterer.

I bet Anna does not know that about him. I bet she knows everything about this guy except that he's a fucking litterer.

When I hear couples use the expression *cheating,* it always sounds so sixth grade to me. It never seems to have severe connotations attached. "Oh, Doug is cheating on Meg." "Oh really. Wanna go by the mall after school?" But in the time it takes a yellow caution light to go to red, all I can think of when it comes to cheating is fucking and sucking and my wife being bent over hotel sinks at lunchtime.

It's just lunch.

Dudley slathering chocolate cream cheese over her chest in the parking lot of Einstein's Bagels.

It's just lunch.

Maybe he threw his tie over his shoulder going down on Anna behind the Applebee's.

It's just lunch.

I'm nauseous. As traffic slows to a crawl I open my door and vomit onto the road.

I don't consider it littering.

"You're still over the line." The raspy voice returns on the radio. "Talk to me."

I bet Mr. BMW fantasizes that he's getting a blow job from Amanda Peet. That's all she is to him—an Amanda Peet look-alike. For the record, Amanda Peet didn't even exist on film when I first met Anna, so don't even try to turn it around and pin the same rap on me.

I don't recall pulling in, but I'm parked directly in front of Ameron's

Dermatology. A dermatologist. Everybody knows they're all scumbags. Why wouldn't Anna know that?

He opens the trunk of the BMW, takes out an odd-shaped case, and passes directly in front of my car.

He's got a lope.

Shit, I know women go for that.

Who knows what he's up to? Who knows what Anna's up to? Companies have that Take Your Daughter to Work Day, but they never have, like, a Take Your Husband to Work Day so you can see exactly what the hell your spouse is up to. All we get is little stop-bys and meet-and-greets at holidays that reveal nothing of what is truly going on behind the scenes. People who work get into all kinds of things. They can't be trusted.

"Got to get back over that line if nothing else." The voice comes back on the radio.

"Could you please tell my employer I'm following a guy that might be screwing my wife?"

"Might? Is he or isn't he?"

"Is."

The scumbag dermatologist litterer holds the door open for two women coming out of the building and, if I hadn't already thrown up, I would now. As he's heading through the door, both women turn back to check him out. They are giggling and whispering to each other as they pass by my car window.

All I can envision is me stuttering, *"Do you . . . Do you . . . Do you want a divorce?"*

"All right."

In haste, I had even forgotten to pack the specimens in the cooler so the blood in the thick glass tubes is openly sitting in the sun on the backseat, curdling.

The radio crackles, goes quiet, crackles again . . .

"OK." I hear Omar?'s distinct voice grumble. "But fill up the car's gas tank before you bring it back in."

When I get home I collapse into a chair right inside our front door. Kristin is on the other side of the living room stretched across the couch with a wet washcloth over her eyes.

"Can you leave the room?" she says. "I can feel your vibe from here. It's bad.

"Go," she says, blindly waving her hands. "Take it into another room. Oh, a Mrs. Bocchino called."

"Did you know?" I say. "That your mother is seeing some other guy."

"What?" Kristin says, jumping up as if it's the first exciting news she's gotten in months. She slaps the washcloth over the top of her head, rolls onto the floor, and crab-walks across the tile until she's right in front of my chair.

"I'm listening," she says.

I tell Kristin the whole lunch scenario. She appears disturbed but says nothing.

"I was hoping you were going to say, 'It's just lunch.'"

"You threw up in moving traffic?" she says.

When I get to the part about the dermatology center she stops me short.

"Sandy hair? Chiclet teeth? Pumpkin butt? Kind of a goon?"

"Yes!"

"Remember when Mom took me to work with her that day and we both went for the microdermabrasion? We kept having you touch our cheeks to feel how smooth they were?"

"Yeah, was that him?"

"Could be. He's not a dermatologist, though. He's their marketing person. He's trained with the dermabrasion machine so he can go around to local businesses and give free treatments and solicit clients."

My heart sinks a little. I'd much rather say "my wife left me for a dermatologist" than "my wife left me for some toothy marketing guy." But that's just how my mind works.

"Oh wait, he's on her Farm Town page on Facebook."

"What?"

"He's on there as a neighbor. He plows her fields sometimes."

"You're not funny."

"No, I'm trying to think of his name. It's familiar," she says, crab-walking across the room. She sits on the end of the couch and flips open her laptop.

"If it is happening, it's not about sex. Mom doesn't like sex that much. She told me," she says, waiting for the site to come up. "I don't like it that much, either. I mean . . . I like other stuff more. That's all. Here, is that him?"

I'm too stunned to speak as she points at an illustrated figure with a caricature head. "You create your own image. But that's the guy, right?"

"Yeah, I mean he's an avatar, but that's him. Wait, his name is Andrew! She's going behind my back on some fantasy farm with a man with the same name as our son? Are you sure that's not our Andrew?"

"I thought that at first, too, but here's Andrew. He's going by Drew."

"Yeah, that looks like Andrew. It's a nice farm."

"I know. I like the windmill and the bridge over the river. Are you going to throw up again?"

"He looked like a Bradley," I say, getting up. I start pacing back and forth in front of Kristin. When I mentioned earlier that my wedding reception anecdote didn't really illustrate how Anna's actions weren't always honorable and righteous, I never imagined something like this would pop up as a better example. That this would be my punch in the face.

"Don't say anything to Mom," I say.

"I'll say anything I want," Kristin says. "People want to know, I tell."

"I don't even want to know."

"I'm not taking sides. You're on your own."

"Has she been saying bad things about me?"

"I don't think she went for that whole band of merry men drinking in the woods bit you pulled."

"I needed a night like that. That was fun."

"When was the last time you had fun *with* Mom?"

"Do you think there's even a government contract?"

"Oh boy. Maybe I will be on your side."

"That whole plan of hers—miniaturizing our lives. She wasn't talking about us. She was just talking about me. Sure, send me off to live on the head of a pin while she stays here getting dermabrased by that goon all night long. I don't need a llama poking its head in my window to know what time it is."

"Dad, I don't want to hear this."

"That's why she's been pushing me to get a job, isn't it? That's just her way, isn't it? Showing her concern and maturity by wanting me to have stable employment before she checks me off her list."

"She wants you to find a job because you need a job."

"Do I?"

"Leave me alone. Call Elizabeth."

"She sleeps so well."

"What?"

"Mom. She sleeps so well. Always dozes right off. How could she be doing this to me and sleeping so well?"

"Are you kidding? You ever see what she takes before going to bed—two valerian roots, melatonin with theanine, Benadryl, and then a shot of Nyquil. That's after the two wine spritzers when she first gets home. And it has nothing to do with you losing your job. She's been doing that for months."

Months? I feel as if I hadn't stopped working I would have been completely oblivious to all of this going on around me. It's like I'm Encino Man, readjusting to the world. I don't know if everybody is losing sight of me or I'm losing sight of them.

"Are we a family anymore or just sharing a house?" I say.

"I don't need parents, if that's what you mean. I just need my room."

Kristin's palms are flat on the floor, her almond eyes glaring at me between her towering knees.

"When I fell in love with your mother it was right up the road here, on Sunrise Avenue," I say. "Mom was driving. There was a homeless guy in the turn lane and she was emptying change out of the car's cup holder to give him. She had her hand out and he had his out but the light changed and people started beeping so she had to take off."

"That's nice."

"But when we got to the light she made a dangerous U-turn and drove all the way back around to give the homeless guy the money. I used to tell everybody that story—the homeless turnaround story. Mom said she wouldn't have turned around if I wasn't in the car with her."

"I don't know those people."

"Who?"

"Those people you and Mom were. By the way, this might be a good time to tell you that I may not go to State for school. I might stay here, and if I do, James and I are probably going to get a place together near the community college."

"James. Who is that? I've never even met him."

"You know I don't bring my personal business around here."

"Is this because of me? Because of the money for college and—"

"Have I ever done anything because of you?"

"What's happening to us? You're totally detouring off the course you've been on for the last three years. Mom is . . . I can't even say it and Andrew, killing innocent creatures, suddenly has the heart of a serial killer."

"Dad, we're all devolving. It's not only you. You're just the catalyst."

"*James?*"

last hurrah

Maybe it was only lunch," Gillian says. "We have lunch."

"Let's just keep moving," I say as we sidestep another work of art.

"That's Cubist," Gillian informs Artie as we hover over the street version of an original work by Lyonel Feininger.

A reed-thin, shirtless artist is feverishly rubbing a sliver of mauve chalk in a few bare crevices, putting on the finishing touches.

"I wish someone would put the finishing touches on me," Artie says.

"You see how the painting allows for multiple points of view all at once," Gillian explains.

"Blurry," Artie says.

"That's because you've had too many of those slushy Asphalt Bangers," I reply.

Artie had informed us as soon as he arrived at the street painting festival that he wasn't really "into it artistically," but the whole scene really is fascinating. Traffic on main street has been shut down and local artists and students have been laboring since dawn. Using pastel chalks, they have re-created dozens of Renaissance and other classic works from one end of the street to the other.

I must have written about this festival for the past six years, and I had always wanted to attend, but it would always pour by the weekend, washing away all those blacktop Monets before I could get there. Since we have the luxury of unemployment this year, Gillian insisted we come on Thursday, the first day of the event.

"I don't know how you can care so much about music and so little about art," I had said to Artie earlier. He just shrugged. "That's OK. I like the street fair food and that bar, Igot's."

So far, he's run back and forth to Igot's about three times to get another rum-loaded theme drink.

The pastel chalk replica of Feininger's work is called *Vogel Wolke.*

"Bird Cloud," the artist says, looking up at us. "That's the translation."

"Beautiful work," Gillian says.

It is beautiful work, but Gillian is wearing a tiny, checkered skirt and every time she crouches over the art my eyes divert from the Cubist angles and cling to the non-Cubist curve of her thighs like I'm some kind of pervert. Or maybe my eye can wander as easily as Anna's.

"Anybody want an arepa?" Artie says, heading toward a vendor's cart up on the sidewalk.

"No, but I wouldn't mind sitting down somewhere and getting something to eat," Gillian says.

We head toward a café called Pelican Pete's, pausing briefly to admire a half-finished copy of Alesso Baldovinetti's *Portrait of a Lady in Yellow.* The woman working on the piece is standing above it. Overheated, she wipes at her own face. Streaks of yellow instantly adorn both cheeks like gentle war paint.

As we stand outside the café waiting for the server to clear a table for us, Gillian says, "OK, I've brought one unbelievable story with me from my first day at the Hard Rock," and opens her purse as if the story is going to pop out and tell itself.

"Wait, I still don't get it. What's the connection?" I say. "You apply at the Museum of Natural History and end up at the Hard Rock?"

"King Tut, Prince, what's the difference?" Artie says.

"It's a little crazy, and it's only an internship, but the great thing is there's an actual opening for an assistant curator, and the Natural History lady says I'd have an excellent chance at it. She knows the Hard Rock curator."

"They probably met at a convention," I say. "Everybody meets at conventions."

"Who did you ever meet at a convention?" Artie asks.

The server, an elderly woman wearing a green apron and a cockeyed artist's beret as if she's forgotten it's atop her head, leads us to a table just inside the doorway by the front windows while Gillian continues to gush about the new internship.

"I'll be responsible for Twittering all the exhibits and writing the little cards for displays—'Cowboy hat worn by Richie Sambora during acoustic version of "Wanted Dead or Alive" at the MTV Music Awards. April 12, 1992.'"

"Sounds like big fun. I'm jealous," I say.

"Schlock work," Artie says. "They care more about Lady Gaga's panties than they do about Muddy Waters's guitar."

"Oh Artie," Gillian says, swatting him with the menu. "Do you want to hear my story or not? OK, it was only about four in the afternoon but this frat guy, this giant blockheaded guy, is blazing drunk and you know how we have all the outfits and stuff in glass cases around the hotel."

"Of course."

"Oh look, a catfish Reuben," Gillian says, sticking her menu under my nose. I glance up but my eyes glaze over the fish slapped with sauerkraut and slide down to the freckles dotting Gillian's chest.

"Where was I?" Gillian says. "So, out of nowhere the frat guy smashes a case with a pub glass and pulls out the Big Suit—the one David Bryne wore in *Stop Making Sense*. And in a flash he puts on the jacket and starts racing through the casino."

"Are you kidding?"

"You know I'm not."

"Were you right there?"

"He nearly knocked me over. And the suit—it's tight on him. The thing is tailored for a small building and it's snug on him."

"A giant buffoon racing through a casino in the *Stop Making Sense* suit. That's classic," Artie says.

"When you think about it, it's surprising stuff like that doesn't happen all the time," I say. "Everybody at the Hard Rock is always loaded. After seven Jager bombs, it must be tempting to look over your shoulder and there's James Brown's cape screaming at you to put it on."

"No doubt," Artie says.

"You guys should come by one afternoon when I'm working," Gillian says. "You can't break into the cases but I can probably let you mess with stuff before it goes on exhibit."

"Really?"

"I'll let you wear Sid Vicious's shoes. Oh, and we just got a box in marked 'Peter Cetera Wardrobe: 1979–1981.' You know you want to be there when I open that up."

"You know I'm out of here Monday," Artie says. "I'm going to meet Cassie in South America."

"What? Did you know about this?" I turn to Gillian.

" 'Meeting' is a stretch," Gillian says.

"What? What am I missing? What's Cassie doing in South America?"

"She's working real estate with her brother. They were in Honduras, but now moved to a town—a village—near the equator, Tacombre," Artie says.

"The equator. Man. Does she know you're coming?"

"I'll just be in the neighborhood and jump out at her one afternoon," Artie says.

"Imagine you're at the equator. You've basically left all civilization behind and, out of nowhere, Artie jumps out at you."

"It gets worse. Everybody is saying she got married," Gillian says.

"People are married and then they're not," Artie says with a shrug.

"Is it that guy her sister Marti was telling you about?"

Artie doesn't respond.

"It's an awfully long way to go to . . . Are your parents paying for this trip?"

"Not all of it."

"You're going to be so out of touch with everything. Aren't you going to feel like you've completely left the planet?"

"I left the planet a long time ago," he says in a tone that is strangely frightening.

"So this is our last hurrah?" I halfheartedly try to lighten things up.

"Basically."

I'm stunned that Artie could make such a major decision so quickly. I know he has no wife or kids to consider, but I would still think he'd dwell on it before taking off.

"So what have you got for us?" Gillian asks me pointedly.

After my frantic phone call to Elizabeth detailing Anna's plans to curtail my sense of freedom, then extract me from her life, I had also made one to Gillian, and I'm not sure what I said. Afterward, I just hoped I was so mumbly and scattered she might have let it go as a drunk call.

"I gave someone a ride the other day," I say, hoping she's going to let me off the hook. I really need this get-together just to be a distraction.

"That's cool," Artie says. "Hey, Miss Hard Rock, did you know Jeffrey sings Beatles songs better than the Beatles?"

"Just the early stuff," I say.

"Give her a taste," Artie says.

"Don't you dare." Gillian glares at me. "That's sacrilege to even say something like that. Just stop it. Don't ever mention such a thing in my presence again."

I'm not sure if Gillian is disturbed about me not opening up and spilling my guts about my personal situation, or if she's really a stickler for leaving legendary material untouched.

"I'm not claiming—"

"Stop! You don't mess with something like that. It's ludicrous to go around saying you sing Beatles songs better than the Beatles."

The server stops by and Artie asks for an Asphalt Banger.

"Sorry." She laughs. "I think it's Igot's that has those."

"I'm outta here," Artie says.

Artie springs up and out into the street, leaving Gillian and me to fumble for cash and math to make sure we leave the proper tip.

It's starting to get overcast as Gillian and I stand over a painting called *Hope II* by Gustav Klimt. "Klimt used real gold and silver leaf in his paints, platinum even," the artist informs us. "That way, even if people didn't like the art it would still be a highly valuable piece of work. Of course, this is only chalk."

"That's OK, I like the art," Gillian says.

We catch up to Artie at the edge of a massive portrait of a rabbit just as he's asking a kneeling artist, "Is that your pet?"

"That's Dürer's *Hare*," Gillian tells Artie with a nudge.

Artie looks as if he's insulted, saunters up several yards, and stops where an artist getting a late start is just finishing applying a base—a square of deep purple. For the first time all day, Artie halts in awe and gazes into the block of purple as if he might enter it and disappear into the gravel.

"Look at the way the landscape becomes one with the hems of their dresses," Gillian says, pulling me in the other direction, toward Edgar Degas's *Four Dancers*. "Oh. Look . . . Is that? Yes it is, it's Mark."

Sure as hell, up near the Bob's Lemonade stand is our old boss Mark, fondling a skinny reporter's notebook and looking totally lost.

"I guess there's no writers left, so he actually has to do some work himself." Gillian snickers. "Uh-oh."

"What?"

"It's Artie."

"Oh shit," I say, already moving.

Artie is headed directly for Mark, and I am not exaggerating when I say his footwork could only be described as the motion of a madman. His knees are rising too high; his arms are windmilling as if they just broke off the spindle.

"Artie! Artie!" Gillian is yelling but I know he's in a zone. He's going wide now along the edge of the crowd, like a wolf gearing up for a wilding. His neck cranes. I speed up just in time to catch a glimpse of his hands clasping together. Oh no, not the mallet.

I am stepping between Rembrandt's *Night Watch* and something very Flemish influenced and leaping over Monet's *Water Lilies*, Gillian's sandals slapping the ground directly behind me.

"The mallet. Jeffrey, the mallet!" Gillian is screeching.

"I know, I know . . ."

I'm close enough to grab him by both his shoulders but . . .

"Oh my fucking God!"

I stop short, Gillian screaming in my ear as she slams into my back. Mark is down and Artie is doing a weird, limbs-akimbo dance over the body. I grab him. "What the hell . . ."

"It was me or him! Me or him!"

"What are you talking about? You fucking blindsided him. Jesus."

"I had to use the mallet. I had to use it."

Mark is laid out across Biagio d'Antonio's *The Betrothal of Jason and Medea*, covering his head with both hands like he's still under attack.

Gillian pokes her foot at his torso. "Don't kick him," I say.

"I'm just seeing if he's alive. If the CSI people put a chalk outline around him it'll look like—"

"Stop," I say.

"At least *he* has medical," Artie says.

Both Artie and Gillian seem so cold to the whole scene. "I'd say I didn't think Artie had it in him, but we know he did," Gillian says. "I think we all have it in us."

"Hey, I'm like your brainless buddy Bo," Artie says. "Only I had a reason. And I'm about to leave the country."

"Just please get him out of here," I say to Gillian. Artie is sitting in a heap, huffing and puffing. "Take him down the street."

"I want a corn dog," Artie says.

"Mark, Mark," I say, lifting him to his feet. He throws an arm around my shoulder and I half drag him to a table in Pelican Pete's.

I don't really want to be around him myself, but I bend down as he holds his head in his hands. It's starting to drizzle outside, a wet wind whipping up. A tall girl with her hair bound back by a bright blue bandana is frantically trying to duct-tape a tarp down over her work. For a second I think she is more deserving of my help and start to get up. "Was that Artie?" Mark says through his hands.

"If you're not sure, then no, that wasn't Artie," I say.

"He came out of nowhere. What the hell did he hit me with?"

"The mallet."

"Man."

"Look," I say. "I know it was inexcusable and all, but Artie's having a hard time and he's been drinking nonstop since we got here and I hope—"

"Oh, don't worry, I'm not going to make a big deal of it," Mark says, waving me off with the hand that isn't cradling his head. "Last thing I want to do is press charges against a guy I just laid off."

"That's decent of you," I say.

The rain is coming down harder. The bandanaed girl outside the doorway has given up on the tape and is lying on the tarp now, her arms and legs spread like she's about to make an angel on the asphalt.

"Can I tell you something?" Mark asks.

"Sure."

"Can you sit down?" He kicks out the chair beside him.

I perch on the edge of the chair. "Maybe I didn't say what I wanted to say that morning you all got let go. Maybe I didn't say, 'Jeffrey, I wish this weren't happening' or 'Jeffrey, it has been nothing less than an honor and a privilege to have worked with you' or 'Jeffrey, I am sorry.' Maybe words failed me that morning. Ahh, my head is pounding . . ."

"I'll see if I can get you some ice."

"No, no, wait. Words failed me that morning or maybe, just maybe, I'm human, and thought even the most heartfelt apology or praise would prove insufficient—would sound lame."

It sounds like a prepared speech, but it's something. "Still, I'm glad you said it," I say. "As soon as I get home I'm going to take you off my shitlist, if that makes you feel any better."

"It does. Thanks."

Gillian walks in the door. When she sees me with Mark, she stops abruptly and steps back outside.

"I gotta go," I say to Mark.

"Right, take care."

I join Gillian under the awning out front. It's pouring now. The bridge of Gillian's perfect nose is covered with dew. The street is taking on a sparkly sheen and the water flowing toward the sewer grates is tinted with pastels. The angel girl lying atop the tarp has her tongue out, lapping up the rain.

"Artie calm down?" I ask.

"I took him over to where they let the kids draw on the road. It's all under cover over there," Gillian says. "He was helping some seven-year-olds copy Thomas the Train off a lunchbox. No remorse."

Gillian glances at a painting near our feet, which is sheltered from the storm by the restaurant's archway. "I'm really starting to love Monet's haystacks," she says.

"Me too."

"Not bad for a last hurrah, huh?"

"Not bad at all."

In a way, I'm envious of the rage Artie unleashed so effortlessly. I know that if you let your anger get the best of you, before you know it, you're head-butting fashion designers at cocktail parties. But I just wish I had a little more passion, a little more fury in my bones to unleash on the world.

"Yeah, a little fury always helps," Gillian says.

Part of me thinks that when I find Bo, I can take a little of the fight out of him and put it back in me. Then we'll both be better off. But everything seems so harsh. The whole world seems so harsh right now. I want something soft in my life.

"Kristin told me she doesn't need parents. She just needs her room," I say.

"Didn't we all feel that way at her age?" Gillian replies.

"I guess. But coming from her, there just seems to be something mean about it. Maybe I'm a little sensitive right now. You want to do something to-night?" I say, as if I could.

Gillian must have noticed me leering at her thighs and her freckles and the dew on her perfect nose (they *always* notice, even when you're certain they hadn't), because she says, "Why, so you can try to hump my leg while your wife is hunkered down in her command center planning her escape from you?"

I'm chastened to silence, until she says, "Sorry. Can I change that to 'I'm busy'?"

"Please."

"I'm busy."

"I miss you sitting on my desk."

"It was a good hiding spot," she admits. "And comfortable. Thanks for always keeping it clear for me."

"Is it my looks?" I say. "Because I'm just going through an awkward phase right now."

"Stop it. Oh, I just remembered. All this Italian art, how could I forget? I've got it somewhere," Gillian says, digging around inside her purse. "Here it is."

She hands me a Chick-fil-A coupon. Scribbled in the white space along the edge are the words . . .

"It's the translation for run along," Gillian says.

"Oh, man." I hand the scrap of paper back to her. "Could I trouble you to say it like a sweet but harried bakery worker sweeping the cobblestone walkway in front of her shop on a soft morning in Umbria?"

"Corrono lungo . . ."

going to the country

Your car stinks. Can we stop for breakfast? You said if I came we could stop for breakfast," Alex says.

"I know, I know. But there's nothing out here. When Goldstein said it was way out there, he really meant it."

"Are you sure she accepts visitors? It doesn't seem like a very hermit thing to do."

"When I called the church, the secretary said she doesn't accept visitors, but she won't turn anyone away. Whatever that means."

"I understand that."

"Don't stick your feet out the window."

"Yes, sir." Alex moves her feet to the dashboard.

I don't mind the drive. It really is beautiful out here. I'm amazed at how quickly the terrain changes once you head west of town in South Florida. Cattle and farmland, sugarcane and cornfields.

"They always talk about how farmwork is so hard—up at dawn and all that—but I've yet to see anybody working on a farm," Alex says, gazing out the window. "And I'm not just talking about now. I mean, I must have driven past a thousand farms since I was a kid, and I've yet to see one goddamn farmer out plowing the fields. Everything is bullshit. You know that."

"I know that."

"Especially the notion that farmers work hard."

"Agreed."

Except maybe on the Facebook farm, where scumbag litterer farmers are always plowing someone else's wife's fields.

"Oh, sheep," Alex says, pressing her face against the window. "Look, they've just been sheared. I bet that's the best time for the sheep—the time between shears. They know they're free and clear for a while, like life between dentist visits."

A car passes with a license plate that reads YYYYYY. "That's the first vanity plate I've ever liked. Why? Why? Why? Why? Why? Why?" Alex says. "You think that's what they intended?"

"Life is one giant question mark. I know that."

She turns up the radio and a peppy voice is singing over and over, "Where did you get that blank expression on your face?"

"This song reminds me of you," she says, lowering the window. "Aww, look at the baby mare. And that calf. I like anything babies."

I'm getting the full Alexandra here, and just now thinking what a peaceful pilgrimage this would have been past the beet farms and cornfields if I'd gone it alone. I much prefer her in small doses.

She noticed.

"Why did you invite me to come along anyway? I usually have to force myself into your situations."

"I'm beginning to wonder that myself. I think maybe because you remind me of my daughter, only you like me."

There's a man-made hill at the end of one of the farms and several kids on four-wheelers are rising up over its peak, half of them hanging on by a thread.

"That looks like fun," I say.

"Not as fun as riding shotgun with an unemployed man heading west in search of a hermit."

"Get your feet back in."

"You know, I shouldn't even say 'unemployed man'. I don't think of you that way anymore. Your life's not about work anymore, is it?"

"No, I guess not."

"You're turning into an adventure story, aren't you?"

I keep glancing out over the fields myself, as if I'm going to spot Anna's windmill or that bridge over the river.

A huge billboard on the horizon reads: "Drive the speed limit or PAY THE PRICE!"

"Let me drive," Alex demands. "I don't like being threatened like that. There's no reason to threaten us. 'Pay the price.' Fuck them."

"You really want to drive, we can switch at the waffle place. It says it's only two more miles."

I reach over to change the radio station but Alex slaps my hand. "That's Faith and Tim, asshole."

Just before the restaurant there is an ominous graveyard that covers several acres. No one lives out here, but the cemetery is oddly huge.

"I read somewhere that when you're buried with fake breasts, they're the only things that will remain intact. So if they dig up your coffin after two hundred years, all that will be in there is a set of silicone breasts. In a thousand years, there'll be nothing left of me," Alex says. "Real breasts are fleeting."

My tires crunch on the gravel in front of Norrie's Waffles, where the only other vehicle is an army transporter.

"I think there's a base out here somewhere," I say.

"Whoa-ee, there must be a whole platoon in there."

As we head for a booth she stops and pats a bulky soldier sitting at the head of a banquet table on the back. "Morning," he says.

"Morning to you," she says, looking over her shoulder as she strolls to the booth.

She slides in and whispers, "When people wear faux camouflage, I think it's stupid, but when it's real, it's cool."

Right after the food arrives, a little girl comes by the table, stares at Alex, and says, "You look like Kim Possible."

"I am Kim Possible," Alex claims. "But I'm on a secret mission, so don't tell anybody."

"I won't," the little girl promises.

"And don't tell anybody that I eat like a pig. What?" Alex says, looking at me shaking my head.

"You've got all this pent-up energy you could put to use," I say. "And so much personality. It's hard to imagine you're wasting so much time hanging around your house all day. You're so—"

"Oh, I'm full of life. I just don't have a life. Yet," she says. "Don't try to rush me out into the world. We have to get you back on track first."

"That's the thing. I need tracks to run on. You could go anywhere you want. You could even fly if you wanted to."

"You know, I still have all those plastic pin-on wings they used to give kids when they flew. They're somewhere in that box with all my name tags. Do they still do that? Or have plastic pin-on wings gone the way of in-flight meals?"

"Alex, can you be serious for one second? You'd be good at—"

"At what? You saw all those other badges—service and retail. What am I going to strive to do, manage?"

"I think you'd be a great mana—"

"Putting on some phony act to creep up the ladder doesn't interest me. I'm sorry," she says, fidgeting with the clunky silverware. "Putting my energy toward something like that doesn't appeal to me at all. There's nothing romantic or intriguing or enthralling or mysterious about it. Please, don't wish that on me."

I don't. I really don't. But where does a person like Alex go to apply for romance, intrigue, and mystery? I just know it's not the front steps of her parents' house. I'd like to will her off that stoop and down the road, faster and faster until she builds enough speed to lift off. But that would just be one more thing for me to fail at.

The server brings us a caddy full of syrups, from blackberry to boysenberry. Alex grabs one in each hand and starts mixing and matching. "Berrypalooza. I love getting all sticky," she says. "So are you going to confront your wife about McDermy?"

"No."

"Maybe it *was* just lunch. Hey, is this just breakfast?"

"Stop."

"The sooner you confront her the—"

"I really don't want to know yet," I say.

"Therapists have a name for that," Alex says.

"Yeah, it's called 'I really don't want to know yet.'"

Alex goes solemn while she's eating. Nothing but a crunch here, a slurp of a milk shake there, a scratch of her nails on the table as she nervously fiddles with the napkin dispenser.

"My new favorite sound is the sound of you eating," I say.

"Stop," she says.

The small house is fenced by rows of evergreens. The path to its front door meanders through gardens packed with horse manure. Alex is tiptoeing. "This is like a shire," she whispers.

"People call it a jungle," Sister Meredith says as she steps out, wearing a plain brown habit.

She does not ask us what we're doing here. She simply starts pointing out the sycamore tree, the bald cypress, the miniature roses.

"We weren't sure if you accepted visitors," Alex says.

"There's an old Russian proverb: 'There's no lock on the door of a hermitage,'" she says.

"I came to talk to you about Joseph Bocchino," I say.

"Ahh, Bo," she says. "Come inside."

The church secretary had told me that Sister Meredith rises each morning at five-thirty and spends every second of the day praying for the poor, the disabled, the homeless, orphans, sexually abused children. "You name it," she said. "Her sole duty is to pray."

So I want to make this visit brief. The idea of Alex and me holding up a prayer for a sexually abused child freaks me out.

"You have a TV!" Alex says.

"If there is an earthquake somewhere, I need to know about it," she says, leading us into a small room off the kitchen. The second bedroom in her home has been turned into a chapel where the Blessed Sacrament sits beneath a whirring ceiling fan. Resting on a small table is a copy of a book titled *A Woman Wrapped in Silence*, and seashells are scattered about. "I love the sea; nature is so close to God," she says. "I call my hermitage Star of the Sea, though there isn't so much as a lake nearby."

I don't know how to talk to a hermit.

"He called me Hermie," Sister Meredith says.

"Excuse me?"

"Bo, he liked to call me Hermie. He was only around for a few weeks. He slept at the rectory in town and helped me during the day. Those cabbage palms along the drive, those were planted with his hands."

"How did he seem?"

"He seemed like someone who needed to help other people before he would let anyone help him. I think—"

"Were you really a World War Two pilot?" Alex interrupts as if she's bored with my line of questioning.

"No, no dear. I attended the Knotting School of Aviation in Coral Gables and after I graduated, at nineteen, I was asked to teach navy cadets how to fly. That was during World War Two. I've always loved very exciting, dangerous things."

"Why'd you stop? How did you end up here?"

"The flight school closed down. There was no big plan," she says. "I sometimes wonder, if the business hadn't folded what direction my life would have taken. I really can't explain what led me here. But I did feel as though I was led."

Alex takes out her Bic lighter and starts torching up several candles by the window. "I like that you don't have those generic church candles," she says. "What is this one? Is this black raspberry vanilla?"

"Yes. Yes, it is."

"Did Bo get into any fights here?" I ask.

"No. Father Richter had some reservations about something like that, but I never saw any of it. Something was wrong, though. Mentally there was an alienness to him that I can't quite explain."

"He was like an alien?" Alex says excitedly.

"No, I'm sorry. I don't talk to people much. When you only talk to God your vocabulary starts to suffer. The word *alienated* is what I meant, I think. He seemed disconnected and maybe disabled somehow. We prayed about it."

"Mmmm, this is different," Alex says, her nose almost touching the flame of a squat brown candle. "What is this?"

"Amaretto biscotti," the sister says.

"Do you know where Bo went from here?" I say.

"I really am at a loss. I even filed a missing-persons report because it was so abrupt. It's around here somewhere," she says, digging beneath a pile of prayer requests. "One thing. Afterward, people at the rectory said he had mentioned Homestead. Some work down there."

"Homestead, that's the dregs," Alex sighs. "We got lost coming back from South Beach one night and ended up there. It's the end of the line for people on the run who don't have enough gas money to get to Key West."

I excuse myself to use the bathroom. When I come back out, Alex and Sister Meredith are both down on their knees, digging around the base of a withered fan palm.

The sister holds her hands up as if she would embrace me before sending me down the highway if not for her grimy palms. "I will pray for your friend," she says, putting her hands together.

"Oh, we can get him dirty," Alex says. She wipes her hands down my back.

We head toward the car and Alex leans in and says, "I'm staying."

"What?"

"You didn't think I was going to go help you hunt down some alien in that Homestead hellhole, did you?"

"Stop messing with me."

I look back at the sister and she is nodding and giving me what amounts to a holy shrug.

"You're kidding?" I say to Alex.

"Nope. I want to disappear for a while, like your friend. Don't tell anybody what happened to me."

"I can't."

I can.

In the rearview mirror I watch Alex stick up one filthy hand, wave, and then disappear behind the cabbage palms.

news at 11

I am flying down the Beeline Highway, already seventeen miles gone from Hermitville. For the return trip I'm all tunnel vision, my eyes straight ahead, ignoring the acres of farmland, the produce stands, the pickup trucks idling at the crossroads. The sun is leaving, darkness creeping across the horizon, and all I can think about is turning the tables, giving Anna an ultimatum: "*You, you take three weeks—twenty-one solid days—to figure out where you stand. Figure out what YOU want to do.*"

The steering wheel suddenly feels like I'm holding a jackhammer. I glare at my hands vibrating into a blur and I immediately think this is it, some kind of royal meltdown—*I should have seen a counselor face-to-face.* The bottom drops out and I am raised off my seat, like a trick of gravity on one of those death-fall rides, and then everything is moving in slo-mo. The car is careening out of control, but gently. I am tilting and it's as if the lean of my body weight has the power to steer and direct the nose of the car off the pavement. There is a crunch of gravel, the smell of dirt, and I am still.

I force my hands up to the door handle, leap out, and run several yards up the road's embankment before tumbling onto the ground, as if I expect the car to explode.

I'm shielding my eyes when a robotic voice with a sweet cadence says, "Too bad you didn't flip. I could have been the first on the scene."

A tall woman, both picturesque and statuesque, is standing over me. She is dressed elegantly and has the most flawless, roundest kneecaps I've ever seen up close.

"I'm just kidding," she says. "You OK? A double blowout. Wow."

I look around her and both tires on the right side of the car are blown. One is shredded, the rim bare on the ground.

"You were zooming. Lucky it wasn't worse."

"Those tires are brand-new," I say, standing up. "They're prorated but they're brand-new."

I'm still a little dazed, but when I look around I expect to see several other cars or a patrolman approaching. The shoulder on both sides is empty.

"Where did you come from?" I ask the woman.

"Oh, I'm stationed right over there at the moment," she says, pointing across the road to a small stepstool and a medium-size Igloo cooler. "I'm just waiting for my crew to get back to do a spot shot. I've got a couple of vitamin waters in the cooler. Let's cross over."

She seems to realize I'm still disoriented and puts her hand flat on the small of my back, carefully guiding the way to the other side.

"Dragonfruit OK?" she says, handing me a water.

"Yes, yes. Thank you."

"You going to call Triple-A or something?"

"Yes, yes," I say, getting out my wallet to look up the number.

She reaches into the cooler again, pulls out a tiny brush, and starts sweeping her eyelashes up, up, up. "Trying to keep myself alive in the heat out here."

"You look fresh, very fresh," I say.

"It's my job to be fresh," she says, walking over to a big duffel bag lying in the weeds. She reaches in, takes out a microphone, and starts unwinding the cord.

"It's obvious you're some kind of newsperson," I say. "But what are you doing out here?"

"Oh sorry, I didn't think you were quite with it yet," she says. "I'm Adele Winn, WPEC-Twelve."

"Twelve. That's the station with the weekend weather guy who's too tan."

"Too much time off during the week." She smiles. It's totally dark now but her blazing white teeth are like a bright beacon, and seem to provide enough light for me to see the AAA number.

"That attorney whose body showed up in the canal a few weeks ago— that was right behind us."

"I guess I was fortunate," I say.

"My crew went into town to get a new charger for the overhead power pack. They should be here any minute."

The AAA call center keeps picking up but then the line goes dead. Twice they call me back but no voice is on the line.

"The incident with the lawyer happened two weeks ago, but every time the police release some new information they want me to come stand out here. You know how that works," she says. "We're always standing somewhere long after the action is over."

"What's the new information?"

"The lawyer wasn't behind the driver's wheel. He was in the trunk. And a former state prosecutor, Laura Werder, might have been behind the wheel."

Traffic has completely subsided, the moon is nowhere to be found, and the darkness is now thick and black and daunting.

"It can get a little spooky, but I actually prefer standing out in the middle of nowhere when I have to do a report. When I'm in front of the courthouse or something all the men look like they want to eat me up like a giant Cadbury egg," she says. "What do you do? Are you with the sugar company up the road?"

"No, I was in Belle Glade visiting a hermit nun."

"That could be an interesting story."

"My friend says I've become an adventure story."

"Really. We're always looking for adventurous human interest stories."

"It's only because I'm currently unemployed and have been—"

"Oh, unemployment is so five minutes ago. Hold out your hands," she says, squirting a blob of insect repellent into my palms. "Put it on your forearms. Now. Trust me.

"Jeeze, where are those guys?" she says, looking west up the highway. "I don't want to hear one more sad-sack unemployment saga, no offense."

"None taken."

"Here they come," she says, reaching into the cooler and taking out a soft blue scarf trimmed with tiny white seahorses and affixing it around her neck. "I always keep it chilled. That's one of my secrets. Take it to your grave."

"You ever do any consumer pieces?" I ask. "You wouldn't believe this tire situation at Hindell Toyota. That Hindell's a tyrant. People need to know about it. I had the Tires for—"

"Listen, you've been a great time killer but here come my guys. I'm going to need you to go back on the other side of the road now. I can't have you in the shot."

"Oh sure," I say. "Nice meeting you."

"I'll send Toby over with one of my cards before I finish up just in case anything pops up on your radar or you have any news tips in your area. You never know. Citizens are my allies."

"Great," I say.

"Shoo," she says.

The mosquitoes attack the back of my neck at about the halfway mark across the highway, so I take refuge in the car, turn the air on, and listen to a CD Anna had left between the seats—Sugarloaf. No, Sugarland.

It's nine-thirty and the AAA dispatcher says they're still thirty to forty minutes out. As the music plays I keep hearing Anna's voice in my head saying, "We're a good match."

Early in our marriage there was such a natural effortlessness to our days. We rented a small town house just off Las Olas Boulevard in Fort Lauderdale and on the weekends we walked everywhere. We'd buy breakfast sandwiches and then eat them at an eclectic furniture shop beside the bakery. Anna had become friendly with the owner, a diminutive man named Angelo, so we had free rein to lounge in the furniture he'd put outside under the store's awnings. I can still see her kicked back in a big puffy recliner as we lazily planned the rest of the weekend. Sometimes she'd have her eyes closed and be off in a daydream so I would hesitate to disturb her.

"I want you to disturb me," she'd say without even opening her eyes.

I can't imagine anyone else saying that to me . . . ever. *That was my ever-lasting taste of euphoria, Anna, spending those drowsy mornings with you, camped out among all those soft furnishings.* There is this strange mix of anger and longing rising up inside me and I almost want to use those words in a letter to Anna, remind her of those moments now and make her ache for those mornings, too.

Before Anna, when I got involved with other women, I was always fighting to get over that hurdle of intimacy. And I don't mean to get into someone's pants, though I'm always happy to get into someone's pants. I mean getting to that point with someone where you feel an ineffable sense of comfort—a place where you don't feel as if you always have to be proving yourself. I know I reached that with Anna early on but now it is fleeting. Honestly, I don't know if we are beyond repair, but I think I'm coming to the realization that it is unfair to her for me to keep chasing that innocence. It's really no different from my admitting I can't be the carefree guy I'd like to be because I'm too busy having to kiss everybody's ass. With all of life's complications now, I shouldn't be surprised that a level of comfort can only be reached in spurts. I am tired and annoyed of being such a disappointment to Anna and having to prove myself every day but anything short of that and I'd be getting off easy, wouldn't I?

How do I prove myself now? How?

An extremely bright light is on the Channel 12 lady. The landscape surrounding her is so blacked out it appears as if she's bathed in the light of an alien spaceship that is about to beam her up. She puts on a serious face, talks for about thirty-five seconds, and then winces or laughs or shakes the mic in frustration before repeating the thirty-five seconds with her serious news expression back in position. It is an act of repetition I could watch for hours.

The Sugarland singer has a forceful voice that is only wasted on about half the material. In a song titled "Stay" she is begging, but she brings a certain admirable strength to the art of begging.

Adele Winn removes the powder blue scarf as if it is an expensive string of pearls and gently places it back in the cooler. She never looks back in my direction but, as promised, Toby the cameraman taps on my window and hands me one of her business cards.

When the tow truck arrives the driver tells me he can use the doughnut for one wheel but he'll have to replace the other. I hand him a credit card that might still be good and he simply says, "This is going to take a while."

I get out of the car and watch him work, just as I would with Sal. He's wearing clunky southwestern jewelry that rattles with every pump of the jack as the rear of the car rises up.

To kill my own time I move out of sight, pick up a pointy stick, and begin tracing in the dirt at my feet. In one loopy swoop, I attempt to write JEFFREY upside down, reverse ass backwards.

Try it again.

And again.

And again.

Alex is right. It is not easy.

jackity jack-off

t's almost 1 A.M. and every single light is on in the house. Before I even round the corner of our block, I can see the whole of its 2,036 square feet glowing. The front door is wide open. Jesus, I know the AC is going full blast. What the hell are Kristin and Andrew doing now?

"Don't close that door," Anna says the second I bound into the living room.

She has her back to me and is spilling fish food into the large tank in the corner. The cichlids are getting huge and I can hear their lips pursing and snapping as they rise up above the waterline.

"But the air is on," I say, turning to push the door shut—

"Do not close that door!" She turns, throwing the container of fish food directly at my face.

She's drunk.

"I want all the energy out of this place," she says.

"What is going on?"

She is wearing tight black shorts, gladiator sandals, and an off-the-shoulder loose-fitting T-shirt, the type women used to wear over spandex back in the eighties. Only there is no spandex beneath it.

"Why are you dressed like this? Where'd you get those sandals?"

"Jack. Jack-of-all-trades. What's your five this week, Jack?" she says, reaching her arm deep into the fish tank to right an Easter Island head that has toppled over. "Don't you have a pizza to deliver, Jack? Jack-of-all-trades. Jackity, Jack, Jack."

"What the hell's your prob—"

She's not righting the statue. It's rising almost in slow motion but once the head's brow reaches the surface I barely have enough time to raise my forearm and deflect its impact into a small lamp by the dining room that immediately shatters.

"Why are you attacking me?" I say, slipping on fish food flakes that have now settled on the tile like sawdust.

"I'm not on the attack, Jack. I'm playing defense."

"No, you're putting me on the defensive." Is she trying to provoke me so I'll be the one who walks out? That's such an old trick that Anna would have dismissed it—erased it right out of the equation—the second it entered her mind.

"I'm opening every goddamn window. How do you like that, Jack? All the energy is going to escape," she says tumbling toward the den, throwing a window wide open, and then grasping for the TV remote.

"Stop with the 'Jack' already."

She's pointing the remote at the TV and manically jabbing at the on button. "What the hell is wrong with this thing?" she says, dropping it on the floor and sliding on her knees to the base of the TV, squinting for the power button. "Where the hell's the on button?"

"Bingo," she says as the television blinks on, the volume all the way up.

She giant-steps back to the window and starts waving her hands, directing the cold air out. "Go, go. Escape."

"Stop it," I say as she bumps into a rocker and then kicks it out of the way, sending it hurtling onto its side to put an obstacle between us.

She spins off, puts her arms out, and shoves as if she's pushing me away but I'm still clear across the room.

"Get away from me," she says, reeling into the kitchen and poking at all the buttons on the dishwasher—which I'm certain is empty—until one of the cycles kicks in and then she turns on the sink faucet and extends her arms to fling open the kitchen window.

"That's enough!" I yell.

"Where have you been? On one of your jaunts? Driving Bennie and the Jets to another meeting? Off with your merry men in the woods? Dining alone at Carrabba's? I'm sure you weren't out looking for employment."

"I told you I had to go out to Belle Glade. Two tires blew on the way back and there was no signal so I couldn't call."

"Triple-A called here when they couldn't reach you. You could have been dead for all I knew. Coulda had a dead Jack on our hands," she says, opening the refrigerator door and leaving it ajar. She ricochets off the walls of the hallway until she falls through the open bathroom door. "I know you could have called at some point."

"I didn't think you'd care."

"What?" she says, plugging Kristin's blow dryer in, putting it on high turbo, and resting it on the toothbrush rack. "Don't touch that."

"I thought you'd be asleep."

"Are you screwing that high school musical girl next door?" she says.

"She's twenty-five, and no." I instantly realize I should have reversed that response, but why should I even care? I want to shoot back, "Are you fucking that Farm Town freak?" but I stop myself just in time because I don't want to be on the end of one of those cruel confessions where the woman is so wasted she gets really graphic to teach the man a lesson. "*Yes, I'm fucking him. And I love wrapping my legs tightly around his ears while he laps at my pussy and I like swirling my tongue around the tip of his big bronze cock and I like when he forces me to do things I would never do with you. I love performing the rusty trombone on command and . . .*"

Anna's up on the edge of the tub now, struggling with the latch of the small bathroom window. A gold strap leading from the bottom of her left sandal to the top of her calf catches on the spigot and I try to reach for her body as she falls backward but I'm too late. I cringe, but the luck of a drunk kicks in and the contours of the tub gently scoop her up.

She takes in a swift breath, springs to her feet as if she's possessed, hurdles over the wall of the bathtub, and makes direct contact this time, shoving me aside as she heads back up the hallway. Alonzo is sidestepping her and trying to stay out front—not easy on three legs—until he tangles up her two very good ones. She stops short at the rafting photo on the wall, says, "You do look like you're sitting on a toilet," and then feels her way to the thermostat, slashing it down to fifty degrees.

She streaks to the end of the hall, stops abruptly in front of our bedroom door, and turns to stare me down.

A bright light that we put up to highlight a painting that has long since been removed is directly over her head. After the tub slide her hair is a tangled mess, there is a streak of dark red lipstick on her forearm from wiping at her mouth, and her left breast is innocently dangling outside the lopsided T-shirt.

"Jackity Jack-off," she mutters.

"I know how you sleep," I say.

"Fig you, Jack. Nobody knows how I sleep."

"I know. And why don't we stop ignoring the four-hundred-pound gorilla in the room?"

"What?"

"Andrew."

"Don't you drag him into this. That whole slaying of those weaselly dragons thing was your fault, getting him mixed up . . ."

"Not that Andr—"

I want to say so much to Anna. I have to say so much to her. But I know this is futile. This isn't the time to retract vows and exchange ultimatums. Not now, not when she's in such a drunken state. But I never know what to say when I can't say everything I truly want to say.

"One of your . . . your left breast . . . it's out."

"Is that all you have to say to me?" she says, looking down at her one rogue breast before stepping into the bedroom and out of sight.

I stop, cut the air-conditioning off completely, and follow her into our room. The ceiling fan is on the highest speed, whirling like a helicopter rotor, and the floor is covered with piles of sorted laundry.

"I already started the washer," she says. "I think I'll wash my clean clothes, too. Anything you want me to wash, dear? Dear Jack."

"Please, stop calling me Jack. I don't deserve any of this."

She drops to her knees at the base of the closet. In the time it takes me to maneuver around a dark load, she has transformed one of those rubber exercise bands into a slingshot, and a watermelon-colored Croc is bouncing off my shoulder.

"Don't act like you don't deserve that!" she says, twirling the rubber band overhead until it nicks the ceiling fan, hard, propelling her backward.

This time it's a soft landing into the bright load, but there's an odd screech followed by a spunky plea, "Get off me honeybell. Pretty pleeze." I look down at Anna flopped on top of the laundry and for a second it appears as if she has two heads until I recognize the second one belongs to Peggy.

"Oh my, I must have nodded out," she says, squirming out from under Anna.

Peggy is all stripes and polka dots, blending into the bright load perfectly. Anna is wide-eyed but not budging from the pile so I offer my hand to Peggy, who is wearing one stiletto-heeled shoe. She teeters up unsteadily, tries to slip the other shoe on, but flops back into the pile.

Anna begrudgingly rises, pulling Peggy up with her. "Thank you, baby," Peggy says.

"I'm sorry you got all dressed up and we never made it out," Anna tells her.

"I'm sorry I drank all your rum," Peggy says.

Anna sits on the edge of the bed and Peggy leans over and kisses her on the cheek. "You have the softest skin. Doesn't she have the most beautiful skin?" Peggy says, turning to me.

"Yes, she does. You want me to walk you out?"

"Oooo, a nipple," Peggy says. "Anna, you naughty girl."

"It's not for arousal. I'm keeping it out in protest."

"You go, girl."

I try to lead Peggy toward the bedroom door but she pokes me in the stomach and then playfully slaps at me. "I know you. You're the bad guy in all this," she says. "You can't hang around my husband anymore. Swinging from trees and gangbanging that neighborhood girl. Shame on you boys.

"OK, drag me away," she says, putting her forearm under my nose.

"It's eight-hundred-pound gorilla," Anna mumbles.

"What?" I say.

"You don't even know the weight of your own clichés."

I grasp Peggy's wrist but her legs go out from under her again. As I pull her back up she licks the side of my face.

"Anna, I just licked your husband's face," she says, giggling.

I lead Peggy up the hall. As she tick-tocks along on the one shoe she says, "I tried to drag Anna to Shooters for Ladies Night but she's so anal about her wine spritzers having to be measured just so and it has to be in her tumbler with the abyssinian cats on it and blah, blah, blah so we ended up drinking here. Oh, who left the hair dryer on?'" she says as I whisk her past the bathroom. "That's a fire hazard."

She's putting all of her weight on me now and as she talks into my face I am struck by the strong scent of Mexican food mixed with dirty laundry. "We put it all on you tonight," she says. "Next time we'll take it out on the other guy."

"What other guy?" I say.

"Oh," she says, sinking. "Call Sal with the wheel barrel. Tell him Mommy has to come home in the wheel barrel again."

"Wheelbarrow?" I say. *"Again?"*

"Are you kicking me out?" She grabs at an empty wine box on the kitchen counter. "We couldn't break this bad boy down to put it in the recycling bin. They use that industrial glue on the bottom. They should know wine drinkers aren't that strong. Sal will be able to do it. He's a beer drinker. He's big and strong. I'll watch him tear it down and then let him have a go at me."

We're inching toward the front door when she pinches my forearm hard and breaks away to the side door. I see it coming the second she touches the doorknob and I almost feel the electricity squirming through her body as she goes stiff and her eyes roll back.

"Zappo," she says as she falls back to the floor. "That was interesting."

While on the ground she puts one of the old flip-flops by the door onto her unstilettoed foot and then reaches up, grabs both my cheeks, squishes my face in, and says, "How come we don't have block parties like we used to? I love a good block party. Oh, when's your garage sale? I need plates."

I guide her back toward the living room and the wine box whacks against the screen door as we stumble out onto the front walkway. She puts her extra shoe in her teeth and wraps her hands around my neck from behind as if I'm supposed to hoist her up and give her a piggyback ride home. I'm trying to fight her off when Kristin comes ripping around the corner and freezes both of us in her headlights.

She jumps out of the car with a sense of urgency and simply says, "Dad, I'll take it from here."

"Kristin, you have the most beautiful skin, just like your mother," Peggy says, draping herself around Kristin's shoulders.

"You sure?" I say to Kristin.

"I've got you Mrs. Rogers. Dad, just take this empty wine box off our hands," Kristin says.

"Over my dead body," Peggy says.

I can't tell who's dragging whom as they trek off but I head back into the house to check on Anna, flicking off light switches as I go.

In the bedroom a tall tumbler with melting ice rests on Anna's nightstand beside a plastic shot cup adorned with a bright green residue. Anna is lying on her side, sound asleep, one beautiful breast still righteously hanging out.

pineapple shoots

As I'm sweeping up a trail of fish food and glass I hear the ding of the timer for the toaster oven, which I'm certain was cooking absolutely nothing. I switch off all the aquarium lights, unplug the hair dryer, and pull open the dishwasher door to automatically stop whatever cycle it's in the middle of. The clothes washer is empty of clothes but full of water so I decide to let it run through its paces.

I walk out into the den to shut off the television but I am mesmerized by the sight of a man on the screen who goes by the name of El Chapo. He is alone in the center of an arena, sitting atop a dancing horse and singing while a lone trumpet chirps in the distance. Between refrains of the serenade, as the palomino high-steps, he tips his red Mexican palm hat to the ladies in the audience, who feign heartache and wave kerchiefs of blue and gold.

I'm suddenly starving so I leave El Chapo prancing and go into the kitchen to dig out a box of mac and cheese. While I'm heating it up I go to check on Andrew. He too is sound asleep, lying atop his bedspread fully clothed, headphones covering his ears.

I take my food out to the backyard and as soon as I drop down into a plastic Adirondack chair I notice I missed two open windows, but fuck it. I aim the chair away from the house toward the Akebono cherry tree that once a year sheds the most precious white-pink petals. The lawn is blanketed in a soft glow. I close my eyes and mechanically breathe in and out, as if I'm going to have to instruct myself to do it for the rest of my life. OK, in. Now, out. In, out, in, out.

When I open my eyes, I focus on the tips of the cornstalks peeking over the top of Mrs. Dupont's fence. I remember when we were all laughing about her idea for an urban garden that would include not only the usual basil and tomatoes but also four rows of Wocken golden corn, and she said, "You'll see."

I see. I see.

For a second, I think how great it would be to pull a Sal and do a midnight harvest. Mrs. Dupont wakes up and the fields are cleared and the corn is husked and piled on her doorstep. But I'm . . .

"I thought I'd find you hiding out here." Kristin comes up behind me, tossing Peggy's lone stiletto across the patio. "She insisted I take it as a gift for helping her home. What are you thinking about?"

"That I'm too tired to harvest."

"Hey, have you checked on your pineapple shoots lately?" Kristin says, trudging across the lawn. "Weren't they in this area?"

"I forgot about them," I say. Mrs. Dupont had told me that whenever we had a pineapple we should cut off the top, plant it, and in fourteen weeks a new one would sprout to the surface. "I think it was more toward the mulchy area. No, a little closer to the fence. Does your mom even know I've been trying to grow pineapples? I'm doing things she doesn't even know about. Doesn't she know that?"

"And she's doing things you don't know about," Kristin says, sitting down Indian-style on the grass beside me. "I will resume the pineapple search at first light."

"You look tired, too."

"Smell my hair," she says, butting my knees with the crown of her head. "It smells of crustacean. The sous chef threw a crab cake the size of a snowball at me tonight."

"It's a night for throwing things," I say.

"Look at that shoe. I could never wear shoes like that," Kristin says. "Mrs. Rogers can. Mom can. I feel like a big goof when I try a pair on. How come I can't get all sexed up and look hot? Sorry, I'll ask somebody else."

"I thought your mom's head was going to explode tonight and I was going to be covered with McDermy condoms, chocolate cream cheese, and Jimmy Buffett's blood."

"Are you drunk, too?"

"What do you think would come out of my head if it exploded?"

"Something stale and mildewy that you should have let go of a long time ago. You know, I know it's quiet out here and the yard looks pretty, but this might not be the best time for you to do your heavy thinking," Kristin says. "What time were you born? They say people think most clearly around the hour they were born."

"Who says that, Aunt Rosie?"

"No, Dr. Abigail Heizer, a seventeenth-century physiologist."

"Maybe I can get Peggy to talk to Mom and see what's really going on in her head."

"She's drunk."

"Not tonight. Another day."

"I don't think Mrs. Rogers will be your champion in this."

"Mom was like she wanted to kill me tonight."

"She was busting on me earlier, before the liquor even kicked in. That's why I volunteered to work late tonight."

"So it's not even me."

"Sorry. I know you don't want to hear it, but I'd bet whatever she's worked up into a frenzy about has nothing to do with any of us."

"So it's about—"

"Listen, I don't know exactly what the heck transpired here tonight, but I'm going to turn the AC back on whether you like it or not."

"Of course, of course," I say. "And don't walk barefoot in the living room. I'm not sure I got all the glass."

"What is that you're eating?" Kristin says, pushing off my knees to stand up.

"Wet noodles."

omar?'s ladder

think the rusty trombone is only something gay guys excel at," Avillo says.

"Really? I don't really have much of a sexual imagination," I say. "I was just grasping for stuff. I should have prepared better."

"No, the other bits were right on. Basic, generic images that would pop into the average man's head. It's to be expected. You're just livin' the soft-porn life."

"Really? Is that what I'm livin'?"

"You just don't know any better."

"I know, all it takes to get me excited is a pointy bra."

"Oh, but that thing from the first time—the sour cream and chives."

"You mean the chocolate cream cheese?"

"Yeah, that was a keeper. You were just off base on the trombone thing. Next time go with the Danza Slap."

Omar? has called a meeting. At Checkers. And he's over an hour late.

He sent Avillo by the house to get me first thing this morning. "He said that cartoon girl is incommunicado, so I should come by," Avillo said when he knocked at the door.

Three other guys and a small, stout woman have been summoned here as well, but they seem determined on keeping to themselves. Avillo spent the first ten minutes calling me "Douchie," but then he came around. The sun is brutal, so the two of us have been jumping from one red umbrellaed table to the next each time the shade slips away from us. We talked about all of his problems before we got to mine, so don't go thinking I started spilling my guts to the first person I came in contact with today. Anna was up and gone before my eyes even opened. I looked around for a note or something, but nothing. "No words left. She's out of words. Oh brother," Avillo said, shaking his head.

"Why is Omar? calling this meeting again?" I ask Avillo.

"Something about restructuring his operation."

"How do you restructure something that has no structure to begin with?"

"With pure genius."

Omar? finally pulls up in a brown Volvo sedan and begins scolding us before he even gets out of the car. "Didn't you all buy nothing? I told you they don't want me gathering my meetings here unless it benefits their establishment, too."

"I didn't know that," the stout woman says.

"I know you knew that, Janice," Omar? says, pointing at her. "You of all people."

Omar? pulls a twenty out of his wallet and tells me to get a half dozen drinks. "Strawberry lemonades, whatever. And use the drive-through. Service at the walk-up is crap. Drive-through gets preferential."

"I don't have a car with me," I say. "Avillo picked me up."

"Take the Volvo. Keys are in it," he says. "And go through the right side. The left is always slower than shit for some reason."

I order and the line inches along. I can see from here that Omar? has everyone circled up under one red umbrella. Avillo's stuck in a sun gap. I can see the sweat beginning to seep through the back of his shirt.

Omar? is exuding a ton of body language. One second he appears angry and the next he's flexing clownishly and grinning widely.

The line is taking forever, but Omar? never even glances in my direction. He hands out blue pieces of about five-by-seven-inch cardboard. Some kind of parking permits maybe. Avillo peeks at the back of the card but by the look of his expression there's nothing on the other side.

The car directly in front of me finally moves but when I pull forward my view of the meeting is obscured.

I'm almost up to the window when Janice pops her head around the corner of the building and says, "Omar? wants you to get some of those fireass fries too."

"But I already ordered at the speaker."

"Work it out," she says.

The clerk rattles her head at my fries request, slides the window back shut, and disappears. The clock is ticking but when she eventually returns she doesn't even charge me for the fries.

As I park the car I see my fellow employees have already dispersed and Omar? is sitting alone under the red umbrella, rubbing his elbows on the table. "Concrete is like a pumice," he says, taking the cardboard tray of drinks out of my hands. "Keeps the elbows nice and smooth. I hate the way people let their elbows get all nasty.

"Sit down," he says, but he walks away with the tray, stopping at a nearby table of women wearing Sir Speedy uniforms, giving them each a raspberry lemonade.

"Enjoy. Not you," he says, turning back to me. "I don't want you enjoying anything."

"Don't say that."

"I'm just messin'.'"

I'm just sensitive. What if everything that goes around *does* come around and I'm getting my due? I can't see what I've ever done to deserve this downfall, but you know those people who always have you shaking your head and going, "Do they even see themselves?" Maybe I'm one of those people. I can see me not being able to see myself.

"Bridge tending," Omar? says.

"That sounds serious. You'd have to know what you're doing."

"That's why I saved it for my best guy."

I have always been a big believer that if you show up for any kind of job, no matter what it is, and keep your head down and just work you can move up the ladder, even Omar?'s ladder. Even if you let blood curdle across county lines.

"There's probably all sorts of levers and controls," I say.

"You can handle it."

"I almost drove a handicap van once."

"There you go."

"I don't know."

"The only other thing I have is unloading an assistant principal's stash."

"What do you mean?"

"This AP from Cleaver Middle School is always confiscating students' iPods and cellphones. If they want them back the parents have to come in to claim them and only about half do, so twice a year she lays a pile of electronics on me and I gift her back thirty-four percent of what we make in profit."

"I wouldn't feel right pushing kids' confiscated iPods."

"That or bridge-tending or we can talk again when I shuffle things up again in a few months."

A few months: I can't even begin to imagine what kind of shape I'll be in several months from now.

"I was doing some deep thinking and staring into my wife's fish tanks last night," I say.

"That's nice."

"No, I was studying the fish that suck the algae off the sides of the tanks."

"Plecostomus. I got a pair in my tank. Rachel and Audrey."

"I know they get big, depending on the size of the tank. I've seen them at real aquariums. And I was thinking, what if we raised some big ones to clean pools?"

"People don't want those ugly things in their pools. But . . ." Omar? says in a tone befitting a genius who is able to evaluate all scenarios of need within milliseconds.

"But?"

"All these pools at foreclosed homes are so green they're becoming health hazards. I bet we could sell the banks on some cheap fish labor. They have no scruples."

"We'd have to breed some."

"We could start with Rachel and Audrey. I don't know what sex either of them ugly motherfuckers is, but maybe we'd get lucky. Ahh, but I can't take on a sixth thing. I know a man can do five things well, but six?"

"Maybe I could start my own five and this could be my first thing."

"I can't have all my people going out and starting their own five," he says. "But you are my best. I don't want to keep you down. These are extraordinary times. I'm trying to convince myself, but I'm not there yet. Wait, I do have some troughs I could loan you for breeding, and a percentage of course."

"Of course."

"Look at those Sir Speedy ladies sipping on those raspberry lemonades," Omar? says. "Ain't that a beautiful sight?"

It is.

"Anyone ever call you a jack-of-all-trades?" I say.

"No, that some 1950s shit. That's just wrong. She shouldn't be messing with you like that."

"Who told—"

"Av filled me in, and I'm telling you right now that idea of turnin' it on her, giving her an ultimatum, giving her a certain amount of weeks to figure it all out, you better think that stratagem through."

"What do you mean?"

"How you going to survive those weeks? What if she takes three weeks? That's three more weeks of those visions of yours. Her mouth here, that toothy farmer's face there . . . Long afternoons of them discussing the situation while she lays flat on her belly and he lazily slides in and out of her from behind until she's begging for the Cincinnati Bow Tie or—"

"All right. Enough. It's a bad plan. I know, I know. I just want to have a plan. It's important that I have a plan now. Everybody else has a plan. Even Artie has a plan."

"Artie?"

"All my former coworkers—the ones that got fired with me—are moving on."

"We your coworkers now, Droopy."

"I know, I know."

"OK, you get started on researching how to breed those fish. I'm going to see if the ladies want any of these fireass fries."

"Hey, am I going to get one of those blue cards, the parking passes?"

"Blue cards? What you talking about?" he says, walking away. "But I am still going to need you for the bridge next Thursday."

sign of affection

t's for you," Kristin says, putting the phone receiver down on the counter before walking out the kitchen door. Would it have killed her to hand it to me?

"Mr. Reiner?"

"Yes."

"This is Meryl Atkins, interim director of Brighton Gardens Assisted Living. We've had an incident involving your mother and she is fine but she has injured one of our workers—a volunteer actually—which makes this a bit more complicated and there are liability issues and the woman is quite hysterical and—"

"Wait, wait, slow down," I say.

"It's fine if your mother only bites you boys, but if she's going to go outside those boundaries we're going to have to—"

"Please, slow down. She bit someone?"

"Yes, right at the back of the shoulder. One of the other workers held a mirror up for her to see it, but it was one of those reversible cosmetic mirrors that magnify a bit, so it appeared worse than it actually is. I've tried to calm her down. She's in my office right now and she's asking about our attorneys and insurance and hinting toward litigation and, as far as your mother is concerned, I believe we're going to have to take some immediate action and—"

"No, no, don't take action."

I don't know what the action might be—putting Mom up into a higher level of care and observation that goes up in thousand-dollar degrees. *Kicking her out?* God no, no immediate action. I can't take anything else immediate at the moment. I just can't.

"I can be there in an hour," I say.

"I don't think this can wait that—"

"Forty-nine minutes. I'll talk to the woman. I'll make this right. I'm on my way."

When was the last time I made something right? I question myself as I speed into the parking lot and pull into the spot nearest the door, marked EMPLOYEE OF THE MONTH. I've no time to spare.

I'm taking giant steps and my fingers angrily pry at the gap between the automatic doors at the entrance because they refuse to respond to my sense of urgency.

I'm used to going straight up to my mom's room on the third floor so I'm a little disoriented about where the offices are located. Plus, today's theme is Arabian Nights. All the old ladies are wearing silky seen-better-days scarves partially covering their faces, which makes them look much more like bandits about to hold up a bingo hall than a harem of ladies vying for the affections of a Persian king.

"Mr. Reiner," Mrs. Atkins says, finding me. "I'm not sure what you can do or say. The woman, Lisa Stephani, is a nurse at Martin General and she's been volunteering twice a week for over three years now. She's really been great. We're lucky to have her donating her time. She's very valuable. If we have to choose we can't—"

"Is she still in your office? Can I just go see her?"

Mrs. Atkins leads me through a narrow hallway to the left of the lobby. I have no idea what I'm going to say beyond pleading.

The woman isn't what I expected. She's petite with a shaggy haircut and wearing soft blue scrubs highlighted by a bright Pink Panther embroidered over the pocket. My first thought, which I hope she is not reading on my face, is that she would be a hard person to sink teeth into. There's no fleshy meat on her bones to latch on to and make a real go of it. Her face is still alarmingly red and flush from the incident, but she seems more pissed than hysterical.

"I'm Maureen Reiner's son. I'm so sorry about what happened."

She doesn't respond to my greeting.

"My husband's on the way," she says.

Ugh.

"I don't know who you think I am," she says. "But I don't volunteer here for society points because my husband is a partner in the biggest law firm in the county or something. I don't volunteer for a plaque at a spring luncheon sometime down the road. I'm not that kind of volunteer."

"I didn't assume you—"

"I lost my own mom four years ago."

"I'm sorry to—"

"I don't want sorry. I'm just trying to let you know why I'm here. I like being around people that remind me of my mom, that's all."

"Does my mom remind you of your mom?"

"No."

"OK, but . . . ," I say, stalling and stuttering. All right, I can't go with her identifying with my mom. What else? What else is there? I've got to make a connection.

"What really got me is that this isn't the first time," she says. "The staff here told me she makes a habit of this."

"It's only a habit with family, my brother and me," I say. "We're used to it."

I walk toward her to reveal some of the pockmarks and small scars on my arms. Perhaps we can bond over both being victims of an elderly woman with a few odd—albeit dangerous—eccentricities.

"You should wear long sleeves" is all she says.

"It's actually a sign of affection—the biting—I think," I say. "She must like you."

"My husband will be here any minute," she says in a tone that reminds me of when my mom used to say, "Wait until your father gets home." Her husband might be a big softy, a physical therapist or something with a soothing voice that will explain to her how we all have to share the burden and go easy on each other when it comes to a usually loving mother's violent attack. Maybe he'll say, "This will be something to learn from and laugh about down the road." But I don't think so.

"I would have appreciated a warning," she says.

I immediately picture my Mom's giant Oreo cookie replaced with a yellow

BEWARE, RESIDENT BITES sign, including an illustration of an old woman show-ing her teeth in black silhouette.

"Your mother was wearing these gold slippers that curl up at the toes for the Arabian thing," she says.

"All her slippers do that now."

"I was complimenting her on the slippers and then she ducked around behind me. This facility has an obligation to warn caretakers, especially when there's a history. That's very negligent. That's going to mean a lot in court. Human bites are the worst bites, you know."

"I like your scrubs."

"What?"

"The Pink Panther."

"Oh, thank you. I have this in black, too. The Pink Panther really stands out. I'm a little too much Pink Panther on some days."

"Not today," I say.

"My ringtone is the Pink Panther theme," she says. Her red face seems more of a blush now.

"That's cool," I say. "My wife's scrubs—"

"Your wife is in medical?"

"Yes, a lab. She had wanted to be a pediatric nurse but got sidetracked."

"I'm in pediatrics!" she says. "That's why I was saying I come here to get my fill of old people. Some workers here complain about having to be around old people all day, but being around two-day-old people can drive you pretty crazy, too."

"I could imagine," I say. "What I was going to mention is that my wife's scrubs always seem too busy to me—so much stuff going on in the designs—but I like when you only have the panther over the pocket like that. Stands out more."

"But of course now it's ruined," she says, extending her left hand to reach around and feel the material on the back of her shoulder. "Ahh, this whole thing is so aggravating."

Shit, I'm losing her. I'm losing her. I strategically move in closer, lean over her shoulder, and say, "I think it's more indents than holes in the cloth."

"I don't think that's possible," she says. "She broke the skin."

"Are you sure?"

"I saw blood in the mirror. I had them put gauze on it."

"Maybe it was just really red and irritated. Inflamed."

"You know, you shouldn't be too hard on your wife with her busy scrubs. Sometimes all of us in pediatrics will pick a day and wear crazy identical scrubs, especially around the holidays. We had this one with all these tiny Tasmanian Devils erratically stringing Christmas lights. It was totally outrageous and an eyesore when we were all side by side, huddled up by the nurses' station."

"I could imagine," I say just as the Pink Panther theme breaks in.

"That's my husband," she says, looking at the phone.

"Oh, all right," I say, backing off.

"I'm going to tell him not to bother coming. He's in the middle of a big job anyway. He shouldn't be wasting his time with this."

"Oh, I'll wait outside the office so you can talk," I say, exiting.

Phew.

"We're good," Mrs. Atkins says to the woman as she whisks out of the office.

"Oh sure, see you Thursday."

"Great, Lisa. You know we love you around here."

"Thanks for being so understanding," I say.

"No problem," she says, zipping off.

As soon as she's out of earshot, Mrs. Atkins says, "You must be good with people. I wasn't getting anywhere with her."

Today's lesson: I can be good with people. When I'm extremely desperate.

"I tried a lot of different angles," I say.

I start to rush off in hopes that I haven't been ticketed for being in the employee parking spot yet. A real cop couldn't actually give you a ticket for that, could they? There can't be any actual law on the books that stops us from parking in Employee of the Months spots, could there?

"Where you running off to?" Mrs. Atkins says. "Don't you want to visit with your mom?"

The thought freezes me. Maybe I should. Maybe I should bound up three flights of stairs, throw open her door, and ask her a series of burning questions I've carried with me most of my life: Mom, why do Lawrence and I act as if we were born on distant planets, even though we grew up in bunk beds in the same room? Why didn't Dad leave me with enough wise sayings to at least get me through *the first major setback of my life? Why did you continue to make me tuna fish sandwiches when I was already getting a lethal dose of mercury on a weekly basis? Why can't I seem to firmly connect with my wife when we're going on nearly twenty years of marriage? Why didn't I go to school to become an optometrist? Why didn't our centuries of family lineage provide me with a special talent? Or at least a knack for accounting? Why do I so naturally choose security and stability over risk and far-fetched dreams? Why didn't I ever even have dreams? Tell me that, at least. Are we not dreamers? Mom, why does your only remaining act of motherly affection have to be expressed with your incisors upon my hairy forearms? Why . . .*

"Mr. Reiner," Mrs. Atkins repeats. "Are you going to visit your mom?"

"No."

string of things

A nna is avoiding me. I mean, I can tell she's been here. But she's like a domestic ninja. Moisture in the shower, the nearly imperceptible smell of Clinique products, wine levels down, tangerine rinds on the kitchen counter, Magic Markers lined up in perfect rows near the telephone—but no actual sightings of Anna. Since the night she and Peggy spent getting trashed and trashing me, she's twice stayed at her mom's and has supposedly been working that government contract nonstop.

I'm scheduled to pick up Bennie in about four minutes, but I keep lingering in our bedroom, trying to find some clue as to what her next move may be. I half expect to discover a countdown calendar with days x-ed out like a prisoner jonesing for the next parole hearing. Maybe she has a secret stash of money hidden at the bottom of the hatbox filled with our wedding photos. I've heard of spouses hoarding cash so they can make a clean break with their pockets flush. I can't help wondering about how indifferently Anna behaved when I first brought home the news of my job loss. I thought she was being a rock, but perhaps there was a sense of relief. She needed something to happen to disrupt our lives, a stick in the spokes. She didn't want to be the stick. God forbid. No, it would be me jamming the wheel, sending us all reeling off in different directions.

I've shuffled through her drawers a dozen times, but so far the only thing I've found worth mentioning is a tube of KY warming gel. Unopened. I don't know if that's good or bad.

Bennie is waiting out in front of his duplex and starts singing, " 'My ride's here . . . My ride's here.' You know that song?"

"No," I say. "How's the rest of it go?"

"The Houston sky was changeless, we galloped through bluebonnets . . . I was . . . You were—MmMmmm . . . I don't know—My ride's here, My ride's here . . ."

"Easy on the dashboard," I say, trying to get him to stop drumming.

"I think I'm starting to get that high-on-life feeling," he says. "It's not bad. I had a girl that used to drive me nuts with her natural highness—a real grinagog with serotonin oozing out the ears, but slutty, too. We got along OK for a while."

I sense that Bennie gets along with a lot of people for a while. I got a real kick out of him for a few weeks there, but he's become kind of a burden. And I don't mean the chore of driving him to the meetings. I just mean the weight of his circumstances. I hate seeing how far you have to rise up once you bottom out. The struggle back almost doesn't seem worth it. Best to stop short a few rungs from the bottom, I keep tutoring myself.

"Sal says you need some contacts down in Homestead," Bennie says.

"You have friends down there?"

"It's the only place I have friends. What a coincidence, huh?"

"It's a small world."

"No, just a mysterious one."

"True."

"The whole town is like a safe house to me. If my people haven't run across your guy yet, then they will make it their top priority just to keep their reputations intact. Nobody gets by them. Even if he's changed his name and spends ninety-four percent of his time underwater spearing tarpon, they'll know where to throw a net and scoop him up out of the deep. Even if he vaporized they'll know where the stain is and have a picture of it for you to frame. Even if he's hiding out, recovering from a sex change in the mother-in-law suite at

Dr. Rafael's, they'll know how to put you two together. If all else fails, there's only one Winn Dixie in town, so soon enough everybody shows up for some form of sustenance. If you want to voyage down there one day next week, I'd be up for it. We could pack a cooler."

"You allowed to cross over the county line?"

"I could go to Switzerland if I wanted to as long as I make it to a registered meeting. I have an app on my iPhone that lists meetings by the hour no matter where I am."

He hunches forward, fiddles with his phone, and then says, "If I was in Tehran right now we would make a left at the next intersection and then a right on Forty-first Avenue. One-forty-eight Forty-first. Second floor."

"You smell something funny?" I say. "I smell something funny. What is that?"

"I only use deodorant under one armpit, just to keep it real," he says. "Maybe it's that."

"No, it's not body odor. I don't know. Never mind. It's probably just me."

Bennie keeps shuffling his feet and restlessly twisting and turning in his seat. I realize I have never seen him still.

"How do you sleep at night?" I ask.

"I used to sleep."

"I think my wife might have a drinking problem and she has to take like four or five things to knock herself out at night."

"A knockout cocktail. No matter what my mix I always have to have Benadryl in the number two or three slot. Everybody has their own concoction. The Joker had his. The Gloved One had his—guess that worked a little too well. But whatever. You need something you can count on at beddy-bye time. When you can sleep, that's something. That's royal," Bennie says with a sense of wonder, as if the natural occurrence of true sleep is some long-gone fantasy from his childhood.

While I'm waiting for Bennie to come out of his meeting, I ponder calling Anna. I doubt she'll answer, but I know I could race home and go online to see where her phone is located. If the cellphone locater map doesn't show the lab in Boynton, then I'll know. But that's not how I want to find out—a Cingular blip on my laptop.

I get out of the car and walk up the road toward a small public skate park. There's a group of four skaters using the half-pipe. I want to sit up close to be near the action, but I also need to make a call. I start moving backward across the adjacent empty baseball field to see how far I have to be to hear my phone over the clacking of the boards. I round the bases and end up settling in the dugout, which is quite cozy. There is no safer place to be than a vacant dugout.

"Elizabeth, please."

"She's not available. My name is Scott. Can I help you?"

"I usually call at this time on Thursdays because I know Elizabeth is there."

"Well, it's Thursday, but she's not in."

"She said this would happen one day."

"I can help you."

"I don't think so. There's some things that are happening and I'm afraid they're going to keep happening."

"What's happening?" he says in a tone that would be more fitting for two friends meeting at happy hour than a counseling session.

"That's the thing," I say. "I don't want to get into that with someone who doesn't know everything else. Do you have a chart there with notes from my conversations with Elizabeth? Is that on the computer?"

"We don't keep charts. What are you saying, there's a series of things happening you need to discuss?"

"It's just . . . There's always a series of things leading to other things, right?"

"I don't quite understand."

Neither do I. How would it sound? Trying to explain everything? *Yes—I've got some standouts here—kicking a dolphin, breaking down at the meditation garden of a car dealer, tailgating my wife's possible lover thirty-eight miles up the interstate, visiting hermits, chauffeuring drug addicts.* Odd things infiltrate all our lives all the time, but you lump my odd things together and it sounds like an over-the-top storyline for one of those lame David E. Kelley shows. A lot happened before and between those incidents. I did a lot of average stuff. I ate lots of cereal. I drank in the woods. I went to a library grand opening. I watched baseballs fly through the sky like shooting stars. I made a hundred ham and cheese finger-pressed panini sandwiches. In the first two weeks of my unemployment, I spent one entire afternoon shooting hoops with Andrew. Swish. I guess what I'm trying to say is, if I'm going to lay out a string of things leading up to this moment, I want the swishes in there, too, not just the weird shit.

"I don't want to be typecast," I say.

"What?" Scott says.

"How 'bout I just tell you that Elizabeth and I talked about all kinds of things, normal things, like, *Extreme Makeover*—"

"I hate that show."

"And snorkeling, and hiking the Appalachian Trail, and Lincoln's melancholia, but just lately, just in the last two weeks or so, after weeks and weeks of normalcy . . . a few odd things have happened . . . nothing major."

"If it's nothing major, you fluff it off," Scott says. "If you realize midafternoon that you've had your underwear on backward all day you shrug it off, like, 'I'm not going to bother turning it back around now.' You let it ride."

"I don't want to play down the incidents," I say. "I—"

"Come on, you got me going now. You gotta give me a little."

I don't know, perhaps I need to tell Scott everything and let him decide what's major and what's not. But it's just too much at once, isn't it?

I try to spoon-feed Scott—little peach Gerber servings—and he doesn't act as if anything is alarming him.

"No, a lifetime guarantee is a lifetime guarantee," he says. "But you might want to get that tooth looked at. Hey, what's that clanking noise?"

"Skateboarders. I'm in a dugout but I guess you can still hear them in the distance."

"A dugout. Where are you in the rotation? Are you coming up to bat soon?"

"I don't think so."

"So, she really said, 'You don't even know the weight of your own clichés.' That's how she put it?"

"Pretty much."

"You know, I think it's nine-hundred-pound gorilla. I think she was wrong, too."

"Now you tell me."

"And you never should have gotten hung up on weeks to begin with. Most weeks have yesterday and tomorrow in them. You start worrying about those two, you're a goner. That's for sure."

"You know, I've been realizing lately that everything is kind of set in fourth grade or so. No matter where you go from that point, you're always surrounded by the same group of bullies, nerds, and know-it-alls. But nobody ever told me that I would always be confused. Shouldn't they have just gotten that over with in fourth grade, too? Why didn't someone tell me that I would always be confused?"

"My sister just told me in June," Scott says. "Better late than never."

We go back and forth and Scott smacks his lips each time I reveal something slightly disturbing.

"Your own child? Your own flesh and blood is murdering the iguanas?"

"You believe in karma?" I ask.

"What goes around comes around? Definitely."

"Shit. I did help steal a coin collection once. And me and this kid, Brian Myers—it was his uncle's collection—spent it at an arcade. I never told anybody about this. Took the guy years of collecting and scavenging at trade shows for rare coins, and we just Donkey Konged it all in one afternoon. Lots of silver dimes with the lady's face on them instead of the guy's. Maybe I'm paying for that now. Maybe I should."

"Nah, everybody's got a stolen coin collection indiscretion in their past."

"Really."

"I wouldn't worry if I were you. I sense you're keeping a few juicy tidbits from ol' Scottie, but the details I'm getting don't make me see this as a major crisis. Nothing major."

"Nothing major, right?" I say. "Nothing major."

I keep repeating the phrase. But I don't know what my next move is. I don't know what's going to "happen" next.

"It's not like you're on the bus to nutsville," Scott says out of the silence I've left on the line.

Nutsville. That sounds like a term that would be on the No-Say list a counselor would have on his desk. Go past the Fs (freakazoid) and just past the Ms (mental case) and there would be Nutsville, several exits before Whack-town.

"Are you guys regular psychologists or LCSWs?" I ask out of curiosity.

"What's an LCSW?"

"Licensed Clinical Social Wor—"

"No, no. We're mostly just a referral service. We set you up with counselors and psychologists in your area. What's your zip?"

"But Elizabeth . . . She's a mental health professional."

"I think she's a buyer for a department store during the day. She's worried about her job there, so she's been doing this nights and weekends as a fallback until—"

"But she's always talking as if—"

"People like to talk."

"That's true."

"Well, I better get going," I say. "My ride's here. Tell Elizabeth I said hi."

"Will do."

rachel & audrey

Y ou've been here before?" the principal's assistant asked me during our brief phone conversation.

"Of course."

"So you know how most of the visitor parking is on the northeast side?"

"Of course."

I can't believe I've never even been to Andrew's school before. He always deters me from parent/teacher nights, and the private Christian school holds very few athletic events. Which way would be northeast?

I'm extremely nervous. The administrator's assistant simply said they needed to see one of Andrew's parents as soon as possible. "How 'bout now?" I said, not wanting to leave room for my mind to do any undue racing. Already I was jumping to the scenario that something on campus showed up dead. Even if it was only a possum clobbered by a janitor with a garbage can lid, fingers would probably point at Andrew first. "That Reiner boy is in the killing business."

Andrew is already waiting outside the principal's office, slouched on a worn, pale yellow couch. His eyes aren't giving up anything and the principal calls us in directly.

"I assume you remember these," he says, placing a document in front of each of us. It's the pledges to the Lord we had to sign to get into the school, along with our commitments to attend the church regularly. Our signatures are boldly written on both of them. Andrew's penmanship has more flair.

"We had our midyear evaluations this morning and, well, you know the father."

"Sure. Father Daughtry."

"Donahue."

"Daughtry's that bald singer," Andrew tells me.

"Yeah, I get that mixed up." I laugh nervously. "Because they're both bald."

"Father will be surprised to hear that," the principal says, coming around to the front of the desk, moving the pledges aside and clasping his hands together.

"He's not bald, is he?" I mutter at Andrew.

For a second, the way the principal is pressing his hands together, I think we might pray this off, but he's just working up into his posture of reprimand.

"Some parochial schools, some Catholic schools, take these pledges lightly," he says. "But we're a Christian school growing Christian leaders for the future."

"I didn't even know there was a difference between Christian and Catholic," I say and Andrew immediately looks at me as if he should do all the talking.

But he doesn't say anything.

Last year, the public school in our district was graded an F by the state and there was even talk of the possibility that the high school would be closed down by the time Andrew reached his senior year, so Anna and I figured out a way to budget this in. We looked at a secular private school, but it would have cost about as much as a year at Harvard. When it came to the pledges, I thought it *was* a technicality, the real deal closer being the contract for the $312 monthly tuition payments.

The office lady who signed us up may have even winked when she said attending mass was mandatory.

But this principal looks as if he hasn't so much as blinked since the day he was baptized. I start mustering up some excuse about how things have been tough at home or whatever and we just haven't had time to squeeze church into the mix, but I don't want to saddle Andrew with some dysfunctional-family scenario and create the impression that I will soon be sending bad checks to cover the tuition.

"So, what can we do to make this right?" I say, clapping my hands together.

"I've already had Melanie draw up two new pledges and I want you to use this pen," he says, holding up a fancy pen with a white pearl finish.

He hands it to Andrew as if it is the pen of our savior, but Andrew just turns it upside down and gazes at it like it's one of those old pens where a red-haired starlet's clothes disappear when you flip it over.

"Is this one of those astronaut pens?" he asks.

"Melanie, we're ready now," the principal says, pressing the intercom.

Melanie whisks right in. She is the woman who winked at us when we signed the last pledge, but she doesn't even make eye contact this time.

"Nice pen," I remark, handing it back to the principal.

"Be sure to stop by after mass Sunday and say hi. Make yourselves noticeable," he advises. "Prepare for a little face time with Father Donahue."

"Definitely," I reply.

"Andrew?" the principal addresses him.

"Yes, definitely." Andrew nods.

"You want to get out of here for the afternoon?" I ask Andrew the second we exit the office.

"What for? Oh, I know. We could say I have a dentist appointment."

We find Melanie again and she gets the sign-out sheet and tells us she wishes she was taking off for the afternoon. "I could use a spa day," she says.

"Put 'dentist' in that box there," Andrew says, guiding me through the sign-out.

As we drive off, I see the Christian leaders quote emblazoned on the school sign out front. Why am I not paying attention to these things? How could I be so oblivious when I'm sending my son here eight hours a day? Is this the type of school that turns out those fundamentalist Christian right-wing types?

"Should I be apologizing for sending you to this school?" I say.

"It's not all bad," Andrew says. "They work God into every subject, though, even geometry. All the word problems involve God, but you get used to it. I think of God as a sort of a crazy uncle now who keeps showing up in the oddest situations."

"Like in the obtuse angles of a newly constructed warehouse?"

"Exactly. You think I'll ever really go to the dentist again?"

"I doubt it. Are you hungry?"

"Not really."

"Do you mind making a stop with me?"

"No, whatever you want. You broke me out."

When we reach the row of duplexes I ask Andrew if he wants to wait in the car but he says, "No, not in this neighborhood."

"We're looking for one-oh-nine-D," I say, leading the way.

Andrew is always a step behind because he leaves the laces of his Converse sneakers untied so he has to keep stepping around them so as not to fall on his face. It's artful and ridiculous at the same time.

When we find 109D Andrew goes to knock on the door but I stop him. "Nobody lives here," I say. "We're supposed to just go into the back porch. It should be open."

It is. The patio is set up like a cute little Florida room and on top of a white, wrought-iron dinette table is a small basin, the type a person might use for a footbath, but this one has fish in it.

"The smaller ones must be Audrey and Rachel," I say. "But what are those big ones?"

"Those are catfish, but who are Audrey and Rachel?" Andrew asks.

I leave the fish on the table and look out across a slab of concrete and, beside a dilapidated shed, I can see the troughs poking out from under an old tarp.

Andrew helps me uncover one of the troughs and, just my luck, it's extremely clean.

"It smells good," Andrew says.

"Omar?'s sister-in-law used them to make big batches of flan for a catering company," I say. "But we need to fill them with mud. I read online that they'll only mate in mud. Where are we going to get mud from?"

"Dad, water and dirt."

"Right, right."

I find a sawed-off shovel and Andrew goes around the side of the duplex to hook up an old, gnarly hose that was wrapped around the poles of a rusty swing set.

Mud *is* easy to make.

"OK," I say. "Let's get the fish."

I briefly explain to Andrew the whole plan of breeding the plecostomus to clean pools at foreclosed homes. I figure we need at least fifteen to start and, according to my research, a pair can give birth to up to four thousand babies every twelve weeks.

"But how do you mate a Rachel and an Audrey?" Andrew says.

"Don't be fooled by their names," I say, maneuvering around the basin. "That's not our problem. The problem is those catfish. Here, you take one side and I'll take the other and then when we get out to the trough we'll just tip in the plecostomus and keep the catfish in the basin. Wait, do you want to tie your shoelaces first?"

"Why?"

We take it real slow, but even tipping the basin slightly puts the cumbersome catfish on the edge, blocking off Rachel and Audrey. With each attempt we're losing water from the basin and neither of us wants to touch the fish, so we decide to go with plan B. We'll dump all the fish in and then quickly scoop the catfish back up with the basin.

"Go!"

The mud immediately kicks up as the catfish dart to the bottom then straight back up to the surface.

Dunking the basin back in like a soup ladle, Andrew attempts to scoop one catfish but instead pulls up in a herky-jerky motion and clobbers both the catfish and me with the basin. Both catfish retreat to the bottom but the mud is swirling so it's a tail here, a fin there, and then we lose sight of the pair altogether.

"The heck with it. I'm just going to scoop my arms in along the bottom, like this," Andrew says, imitating a baby-in-the-cradle pickup.

Better him than me.

"Here goes."

He plunges, his shoulders dipping below the surface, and shoots back up in a flash, but he freaks . . . and shrieks at the sight of both catfish in his arms slapping up at his chin. The fish with the longest whiskers shimmies up his shoulder and Andrew flails his arms and jumps back as if he's being attacked by bees, sending both fish to the turf.

I scurry to pick one up but it's like trying to capture Jell-O. Out of the corner of my eye I see Andrew wielding the shovel and I yell, "No! No!"

"I'm not going to kill it," he says, scraping the edge of the shovel along the ground like a pooper scooper, trying to get an angle on the fish. He crouches forward and the second he gets it onto the shovel he flips it toward the trough. The fish twists in the air like that cow in *Twister*, but we both can tell he's way off target and headed for the bushes, a good five feet past the trough. We simultaneously reach out and dive forward, the trough slamming us both in the stomach, knocking the wind out of us.

We buckle and fold, landing flat on our backs on the lawn.

One catfish is deep in the bushes but the other one is lying right between us. Its belly is breathing hard, but it doesn't appear to be in a state of panic—no wild flapping like you might expect.

"Is this Rachel?" Andrew says.

"No, Rachel and Audrey are the plecostomus."

"Oh."

"I thought you were used to handling wildlife."

"Not like that." Andrew laughs. "Iguanas are docile."

"That shriek you let out. I'm glad you acted like such a wuss. I was beginning to wonder if—"

"It was the whiskers that freaked me."

"You ready to give it another try?"

"Let's just wait another sec," Andrew says, his chest still heaving.

The catfish seems to be breathing very methodically now, as if he or she has reached some sort of amphibious Zen mode. I can see those deep black eyes calmly sizing up the situation: *One of these guys put me in the water before; they can certainly do it again.* I've got so many people annoyingly trying to guide me and teach me things, but the catfish is content to teach by example. I am proud to learn composure in the face of dire circumstances from an innocent, landlocked fish caught up in a scheme to have plecostomus suck the algae from the pools of bankrupt couples who threw their keys in the middle of the living room and headed for Tucson to make a fresh start. Very proud.

"Yeah, let's wait another sec," I say.

"Dad, remember when grandpa used to say, 'Not in a million years did I think I would be doing this today,' only he'd be referring to something like eating shrimp scampi or going into the hospital to have his gall bladder removed. Well . . ."

"Not in a million years did I think I would be doing this today," we both say in unison.

"Dad, I'm glad you lost your job."

"Me too."

a note

finally got a note from Anna this morning, but all it says is "don't forget—my brother's tonight. i'll be home by 7."

I was supposed to go to Homestead with Bennie and then deliver pizzas later on this evening, but all I've been able to do is stare at the note and stew about how far things have deteriorated. Anna is rarely home and when she is, she creeps into bed beside me.

For several days now, when she gets up in the morning I've feigned sleep. I don't want to get in her way. I don't want the awkwardness of stepping around each other in the hallway. I don't want to see this whole situation on her face. But I can feel the weight of us as she plods around the house—doors opening and closing, sink going on and off, hangers scraping back and forth in the closet. If a relationship is disintegrating, shouldn't it get lighter? Maybe when things still feel so heavy it's because there's still so much to work through. I remember reading about a couple who had been married for fifty-five years. Someone asked how they were able to do it and the old woman charmingly said, "We managed to never fall out of love with each other at the same time. We took turns so there would always be one of us to fight for our marriage."

I catch glimpses of Anna's colorful scrubs as her hips graze the end of the bed or she steps into the bathroom with her back to me. To my eyes, the colors don't fit her anymore. It's like covering an old card table with a new, brightly striped tablecloth for a holiday gathering, strictly camouflage. She ties her hair back, I hear the jangle of keys being picked up off the kitchen counter, and she is gone.

It's ten minutes til seven now and I'm anxiously waiting for her to come through the door. Maybe she's got a plan. She'll tell me straight out, "I never loved you." Wouldn't that be brave?

I know before Anna met me she had one other serious relationship, with a radiologist by the name of Mike Legere. It ended badly and it was always so much ancient history, but now I remembered an incident I had intentionally blocked out. Several years ago I was in the bathroom at a party and overheard Anna talking wise to some new acquaintance right outside the window. They were laughing about relationships and Anna said, "Oh, I've been there. I had that type of super-good-looking guy with a prestige job, but he turned out to be a jerk. Trust me, just find a decent guy who'll treat you right."

Imagining that she thought of me as a compromise, a kind of consolation prize, really irked me at the time, but I tried to brush it off, as if I'd just noticed my underwear was backward but the day was almost over. I even got a chuckle out of the fact that I had fooled her into thinking I was a decent sort. Of course, fooling somebody into thinking you're "super-good-looking" with a high-paying job is much harder.

Afterward, I walked over to where she was gabbing. She introduced me to her new friend. The look the young woman gave me was like "This is what she wants me to settle for. No thanks." Anyway, you can see why I'd erased the whole episode from my mind until now. It makes me angry, and I guess what I want to say is that maybe Anna's the one who's truly devolving, especially if she's reverting back to the great-looking-guy-with-great-job mentality.

"Dad, you need to come look at Alonzo," Andrew says, coming up behind me as I'm staring out the front window, watching for Anna's car.

"Not now," I say.

"Please."

I follow him into the kitchen and we both kneel down beside him.

"His eyes are yellow and I looked real close where the vet was touching and clumps of fur have dropped out and the skin around it is gray," Andrew says.

I squint but I'm not sure I'm seeing what he's seeing.

"I think it could be infected. Something internal. I think we did the wrong thing. I don't think he's getting better. He was trying but I don't think he is," Andrew says, his voice trembling.

"Maybe I can get some pills for possible infections," I say. "Maybe the clinic will just give them to us if I explain our situation."

"What is our situation?"

The house phone rings and I can see by the caller ID that it's Brighton Gardens but not my mom's phone.

"Don't pick that up," I tell Andrew.

I ignore the call but ten seconds later my cellphone starts vibrating against my thigh.

I ignore that, too, then immediately listen to the voice mail. It's the voice of Meryl Atkins again, but this time it sounds much more shrill and demanding: "Mr. Reiner, this is the fourth call I've made today. I also tried your brother Lawrence but got no response. Someone needs to call us back immediately. I'm leaving for the day but you can reach me on my cellphone. There's been another incident with your mother and it's already gone above me so we can't deal with it on this level. In these situations the first order of business is to see if a relative can take the resident. Can either you or your brother take your mother in? That is my main question. Please respond."

Oh, Mom. Oh, Alonzo. I can't deal with all this alone.

The door flings open with an unmistakable rush. "Are you ready?" Anna says, whisking past me. "I just have to change real quick. Have you got everything?"

"I haven't got anything," I say, trailing her back to the bedroom. She quickly kicks off her shoes and hurriedly pulls the top of her scrubs up over her head, tossing it toward the hamper . . . and missing. I stare at her bare back as her arm strains around to unhook her bra. I can't help but imagine this is a scene McDermy enjoys three times a week, lazily lying in a businessman's bed at the Courtyard Marriott on Glades Road as she races into the room, hastily peeling off her clothes—*"I've only got forty-three minutes before the next batch of specimens have to be processed."* He smirks, props a pillow, sits upright, clasps his hands behind his head, and lecherously watches as her feet flip off the clogs, her fingers undo the soft knot of the scrub bottoms, and her long legs step out to straddle him atop the king-size bed.

"We should probably talk before we go," I say.

"We can talk on the way," she says, dropping a turquoise sundress splattered with red poinciana blooms over her head and allowing it to parachute down her body until it delicately billows over her breasts and bunches up at her thighs. "Can you get the snowglobes? I promised we'd bring the snowglobes."

"Snowglobes?" I say, walking back to the living room and waiting on the couch as if this is a first date, but I know it is a last date. What are the proper manners and etiquette of a last date?

She must be deliberately putting on this rush act to keep this from coming to a head, but why? I am doing the same, but that's my MO—forever postponing the inevitable—not hers.

Don't laugh, but when I was younger I used to think that if anyone and I mean *anyone*—man or woman—took the time to get to really know me they would fall in love with me. I don't think that anymore. I know Anna is a rarity. I know I need to fight for her. I need to be the one who stays strong while she takes her turn at falling out of love. I was going to go by her mom's the other night and take a stand, make my passionate plea, but I wanted to be able to hold something up, something tangible that I could point to and say, "This is why, this is why we should be . . ."

She's flitting around the kitchen, tapping her nails on the counter. "What am I forgetting?" she mumbles to herself. "I should bring my own wine. And those gift cards I wanted to show Hania."

She calls my name and, seeing me on the couch, hands me her purse and keys and says, "Hold these while I get the other stuff. Don't you want to put those snowglobes in a little bag or something?"

"No," I say.

I bet she will use the term *involved*—"I'm involved with someone else." It's such a clean, tactical term. People find it so easy to say, "I'm no longer involved with him," or "Oh, no, I'm not involved with her anymore," or "Didn't I tell you, I'm involved with someone else now." Involvement is so impersonal.

Anna waits until I'm in the car, then makes a frantic entrance into the passenger's seat. She's pulling at the hem of the dress, fiddling with the clasp of her left earring, tilting the mirror toward her face and pursing her lips. "Oh God, we're running late," she says. "You should probably take Congress this time of day."

This time of day. It's after seven. She's deliberately putting up this spastic wall of rush between us. There are so many things in life I am in a rush for, but getting to her brother's to sit on a white couch and drink wine spritzers would never be one of them. Worst of all, there seems to be an underlying cheer to Anna's behavior, as if she has an exciting announcement to make to everyone in the world but me.

She crosses her legs and smoothes the flowers across her thighs. She never crosses her legs in the car. What is that all about?

"Oh, I wanted to stop and get them something for the new house. No, forget it. There's no time. Let's go."

What is she saying, no time?

I'm determined to cut through this false race of hers, but the second the ignition clicks on she says, "Sugarland. Yes! You were listening to this? Oh, quiet. I love this song."

the unnecessary man

He's not riding the dolphin, he's hijacking it," Michael says, buckling over in laughter. "That's not going to make the final cut. That's for sure."

I've got to get out of here. The second I saw this new house of my brother and sister-in-law's, fully lit from top to bottom, built from obsolete pay phone money, I wanted to run. Their cavernous golf course house is bad enough. In that place, when wineglasses clink together there is an echo. I could not live in a house with a winey echo.

Michael has finished up the rough cut of the infomercial based on our trip to Disney's Discovery Cove and he wants us to see every frame before the "final edit." He insisted Anna bring the snowglobes because he wants to film one more scene of us shaking them over the credits.

"I don't need your faces. Only your hands shaking the snowglobes," he says. "But let's have drinks first to loosen up."

"I don't think I have to loosen up to shake a snowglobe," I say.

"Sure you do."

"You guys haven't even seen the wet bar yet," Hania says.

"Wait til you see the garbage can," Michael says. "Come on, it's only two flights up. We'll take the elevator."

"How many floors does this place have?" I say.

"Four!" Michael yells, as if he's just whacked a golf ball two hundred yards down the acre of hallway we have to tread across.

"The place is really beautiful. It must be great to be near the water like this," Anna says. "The views."

Turns out only three people can fit in the elevator so I trudge up the stairs. *Four floors?* Come on, who needs four floors? I check if it's about the view, because I've got no problem how high someone goes for a view, but the water is completely visible from the third-floor landing.

By the time I reach the wet bar everyone is already circled around the garbage can with a lid that opens by a motion sensor.

Michael is down on his knees churning out all the minute details— punctuating each feature with a howl of "Hands-free! Hands-free!"

When he gets to the part about how the liner ring conceals the trash bag,

Anna and Hania slip off to sit on a couch shaped like a giant Dove soap bar near the windows.

"Hands-free. Hands-free. The sensor is water resistant and this is fingerprint-resistant stainless steel. And it has battery-life energy saving. We're all green with this new house. All green. And hands-free."

"How can a battery-operated garbage can be considered green?" I ask.

"You could say that about anything," he says with a chuckle.

"They have those step ones that are hands-free," I say.

"Well this is foot-free, too," he says. "Hands-free *and* foot-free."

"What kind of batteries does it use?"

"Ds. Four Ds."

"Hell. Those are the big boys. Disaster in a landfill."

"Look," he says, "not that I'll ever need it. But here, on the back, that's a manual close button."

I walk away.

He follows.

"I think I'm loose enough to shake the snowglobes now," I say.

"Nonsense. Let me pour you a drink, " Michael says. "Relax. I heard you had a problem with your tire warranty."

"Oh, bringing that up certainly isn't going to help," Anna says.

"Help what?" I say.

"Listen," Michael says, leaning in. "I've got a guy who can get you some KJ/9814X440/15s for only two hundred and seventy-eight dollars apiece."

"I might want to get his number," I say in hopes Michael might have to go off looking for the guy's card or something, but of course it's right on his gold BlackBerry (he sent it out to be "dipped") and he puts it on speaker so a robot voice can dictate the number I need to get $278 tires.

I hate to be like this, to have this attitude. I know it's Anna's brother and all, and she enjoys Hania's company and so do I, but even without our current underlying drama, I get really antsy after about forty-five minutes of this kind of socializing. The last time we visited at their other house, Anna was perturbed, cornered me afterward, and said, "If we were some place *you* wanted to be, we wouldn't be leaving so quickly."

"There's no such place," I said.

Another time I was sitting by their pool, off by myself, while Michael and a few of his golfing buddies were talking investments. This one triangle-faced guy wearing a madras blouse was extremely boisterous, going on at length about cutting himself into a deal with a biotech firm that had recently sprouted up in the northern part of the county. "I'm going to make so much goddamned money off this deal I'll be able to . . ." And then he pointed across the patio to me and said, "Buy and sell that guy's whole family."

"To who?" I immediately shot back, but he was already in the thick of merger talk, so I never found out.

We sit on the couch for a few minutes. I inquire about how they decided on four floors and Hania, bless her soul, explains that if they only had three, the house wouldn't have come with an elevator.

"Oh," I say. "That's good enough for me."

"But it's really not, is it?" Anna says as if she's trying to provoke me.

"Well, I do think a fourth floor is completely unnecessary," I say.

"Maybe you're unnecessary," Anna says sharply.

It's an awkward moment with that special kind of silence that could make even a monk cringe, but those are sort of in style now, aren't they? What with those wince-inducing comedy shows and whatnot, awkward is the new suave as far as I can tell so I try to laugh it off.

But no one else does.

Hania nervously gets up and says, "I think we need some snacks. Come on, Michael, let's go raid the kitchen for these guys."

"You go, hon."

"*Michael.*"

"Right, right. Let's dig up some goodies," Michael says, forcing himself up off the couch.

When the in-laws disappear into the kitchen, I stare off into the game room and Anna rattles my arm. "What now? What are you thinking now?"

"The horses. I was thinking about the horses."

"What horses?"

"Remember you talked about the idea of having horses—the spirit of it. But you said other things could replace the horses. What did you mean?"

"I don't know what you're talking about, but stop it. This is what we're doing instead of horses."

"Do you plan on drinking a lot?"

"That wasn't a night I'm proud of, but I've put it out of my mind. You put it out of yours."

"My mother may be coming to live with us and Alonzo may be dying and you're not paying any—"

"What are you talking about? Are you just saying anything now?"

"Do you have a hidden stash?"

"Hidden stash?"

"I have to talk to you. I'm reduced to doing it in the time it takes your brother and sister-in-law to take an elevator to get snacks, and that's all you're giving me? How am I supposed to—"

"You've had all the time in the world to talk to me. You've been avoiding it. I know you."

"Since when did you start crossing your legs in the car?"

"Whenever I'm not driving."

"When aren't you driving?"

"Just stop it," Anna says as Michael and Hania return with two tubes of Pringles—honey mustard and fat-free crunchy dill.

After a little more four-floor talk, the conversation turns to cave diving, which makes me feel very claustrophobic so I head toward the balcony. I did once read a great book about cave diving called *Shibumi*. I highly recommend it, even though the only thing I recall vividly is that there is a cool assassin in it who kills people with a credit card or a comb. I think if I could go back in time, not a big leap, but maybe like nine minutes, I would have liked to kill Michael with a credit card somewhere between "hands" and "free." But all our credit cards are expired or have been cut up and discarded at this point. That wouldn't be half as cool—to kill somebody with an expired credit card. I guess that would make it premeditated, too, because the jury would certainly question why one would carry an expired credit card if not to kill someone.

I pick the snowglobe up off the bar and I'm approaching the sliding glass doors when I feel Michael's hand on my arm, turning me around. "You're going to be fine," he says, shouldering me. "You're totally employable. You're predictable and reliable and don't have any big ambitions for yourself. You have a talent for blending in, like a clueless chameleon. Hell, you're practically invisible, a middle manager's dream."

"Thanks," I say. "I'm just going to get some air if that's all right with you."

"Sure, sure," he says.

Predictably, Michael's next move is for the dill Pringles atop the table to my left. The second he attempts to cross over I extend my leg, launching him into clumsy flight. A splash of Merlot stains the air, he grunts, Hania and Anna crane their necks, slo-mo startled expressions rippling on both their faces like a take from the Zapruder film. As Michael's arms reach out to break the fall, the garbage can is flapping like one hand clapping and I am outside, peering back through the glass. I watch his right shoulder bounce off a snow-white hassock and his left knee slam the cocktail table.

"Fuck!"

I take the steps down the balcony's spiral staircase at a pretty rapid clip. By the third spiral I'm getting dizzy. I only had a glass and a half of red wine but I feel as if I drank a bottle of Ouzo. All I can hear in my head is the incessant pounding of "Down the road . . . Down the road."

In the driveway, it takes me a minute to get my bearings, but soon I'm speed walking toward town.

My cellphone is dead. At the first traffic light, a cleaning crew is standing outside a brightly lit Chase bank. I approach the shortest guy with the cleanest jumpsuit and pop the question. Without even the slightest hesitation he reaches into his stain-free pocket and flips out his cell. I call Kristin for a ride. "What now?" she says, just for me.

When she arrives, Kristin doesn't ask any questions about what happened. She just says, "Where to?" I had assumed I was going home but, when she gives me the option, I instinctively grab onto it. "Just go straight here," I say.

About ten minutes later, straight takes us to a dead-end row of economy motels. I get out. Well, I eventually get out. Kristin has to lean over to show me how to finesse the door handle again, and when that doesn't work, I have to climb through the back window. But I get out, gaze up at one of the signs, and say, "Tell Mom I'll be at the Judy."

Kristin gives me a look that is equivalent to the finger and peels out of the parking lot. Watching the dirt fly up reminds me of that song "Car Wheels on a Gravel Road," and for a second I feel very alt-country. But then I have to go knocking on all the cracked windows at the Judy to wake up the clerk, who lives behind the office. The sign taped to the door actually reads: KNOCK WINDOWS AFTR TEN PM.

I can hear rustling and shuffling and then see an amber lantern gliding past the windows of the shabby rear quarters toward the attached office.

When the door behind the front desk opens I expect the man to be heavy-lidded and rumpled, but he is adorned in colorful sheaths of night clothing and seems delicate, flowerish.

"He who comes at the height of evening," he says, looking me in the eye before resting the lantern on the counter.

He doesn't seem at all annoyed by my presence and he immediately has a calming effect over me. His hair is so wiry it's as if he had a hair transplant in which the doctors only used pubic hair plugs, but it seems more unearthly than off-putting.

His hand slowly dips toward mine like a spoon approaching hot soup. "One room?" he says.

"Yes, yes," I say, loosely shaking his hand.

He takes my information and then quietly begins tapping at his keyboard. There is a stray postcard lying on the counter beside a small bell. The photo appears to be of the Judy in its heyday. In the small print on the back it reads: "The Judy is named after the owner's 28-foot sport-fishing boat, which was named after his first wife, who was named after . . ."

"Last owner. Everything is changed now," he says, gingerly plucking the card from my hand and placing it below the counter. "I'll just be another moment."

There's a side door opening to a small courtyard. I walk back outside. It is a beautiful night, there is no denying that, and I hold the snowglobe up to the moon and give it a little shake.

"Mr. Reiner?"

"Yes," I say, stepping back inside.

"Will you be receiving mail?"

"I hadn't really thought about it."

"Well, you let me know. My name is Raja if you need anything at all."

I peer over his head and there is a small portrait of a Swami Raja that looks like him in sort of a caricature way.

"Are you a swami?" I ask.

"I'm not an official swami . . . yet," he says. "The portrait is a bit premature."

He goes into a short speech of how his spiritual name, Raja, simply refers to becoming "something higher and better than you were before." True swamis, he points out, renounce all attachments to the worldly life.

"Being a swami is something I'm not striving for completely," he says. "Possibly."

"OK," I say.

"Two-oh-three-B," he says, sliding a brass key across the counter. "There's assigned seating at the pool."

"Of course."

"Yoga is at nine-thirty."

punch and fluff

Luckily, it's ten-thirty when I awake. The room is dank and smothering. I splash some water in my face and head outdoors. There is a canopy of trees in a small area near the office. Two men are sitting at a picnic table beneath them. It appears they have claimed the spot as theirs, in the way that people who have nothing else can do. I head in the other direction.

I wrench my way through a row of sea grape brush and the moment I step into a small clearing something clamps down on my left ankle. I look down and Raja is sitting in the dirt, his hand the perfect trap.

In his colorful drapings last night, Raja seemed almost mystical to me, but this morning his outfit is drab, his worn sandals paper-thin, and he is centered among dingy motel towels strewn about for his yoga class.

"Sorry I missed your class."

"You're right on time," he says. "Take your place."

"I think I'll pass," I say. "I'm extremely stiff this morning. I've no flexibility. You'd have to boil me like uncooked spaghetti before I could even get into the simplest position."

"There is only one position," he says. "And you are already in it."

That sounds so heavy that it sinks me to the ground. I drag one of the towels under my butt.

"Be still," he says. "Look around."

Several rusting posts that look like they were once topped with hibachis or gas grills, back when the Judy was in her prime, surround us.

"In here. Only look in here," Raja says, reaching out and placing his hand on my chest.

"Oh, OK," I say.

He's sitting in a way that makes his feet seem detached from his body. I can only manage to settle into a basic Indian-style, but he doesn't seem to care. I'm uncomfortable and keeping one eye out for fire ants, but I'm thinking if I can stick it out, maybe I can inch closer to some kind of enlightenment.

"Everybody kept encouraging me to put myself out there. 'You want to make it in these economic times you really have to put yourself out there,'" I say. "But nobody mentions that once you put yourself out there it's awfully hard to get yourself back."

"Silence," Raja says.

"Can I just run one thing by you? There is a difference between not knowing what the hell to do and lacking ambition, isn't there? You must have a universal take on that."

"Extend your arms. Put your wings out."

"My wife's aunt Rosie says, 'Everything happens for a reason,' but in a remarkably short time, I've become a firm believer that absolutely nothing happens for a reason. Can you give me one reason why I—"

"This is not the time or the place."

"We're in a barbecue pit sitting on motel towels. Why can't we—"

"It will all go away. Breathe."

"How is breathing and jutting my elbows out like this going to make it all go away?"

"Talk later."

I'm disappointed. I know he's only a semi-swami but I thought this would include some kind of soul searching. I'm trying to obey the master and just be still but . . .

"My arms hurt."

"I think you have a misunderstanding of how to reach tranquility through yoga," Raja says.

"I'm sorry," I say. "Are we giving up on that now, because I'd really like to talk?"

He seems annoyed, breaks out of his pose, and says, "You've been brainwashed. Start there."

OK, this is more like it. I expect him to take me back to day one and notch off my misconceptions, beginning with "if you just work hard, boy, you'll have everything you'll ever want in this world," but he takes a deep breath and blurts, "Robitussin is useless. You know that?"

"No."

"They just released information that it does nothing for coughs. Absolutely nothing. How do we just find that out now, after all this time?"

"I don't know."

"Everything is bogus. You have to start from there," he says. "Did you see that revelation about fingerprints not being all that accurate? How only a few points have to match up, but they're really not that sure half the time? Squads of people dusting for prints all these years. Men sentenced to death. A joke.

"Mouthwash is a ruse. They say you get the same results from whistling or telling someone an anecdote that uses seventy-five words or more. *Bears hibernating?* It did always sound too good to be true, didn't it? That's because it is."

That last one stings. I always liked thinking about bears hibernating. "Sure they take long naps but they don't actually zonk out for months on end," he says. "That's crazy talk."

"I think I better take a walk," I say, struggling up.

"Yes, walk it off. Do not stop walking until you can no longer see the finish line."

But I'm finished. Raja has me so disoriented, I decide I want to hibernate, but when I get back to 203B, there's a young woman sitting outside in one of the aluminum chairs set up between rooms. Her blond-streaked hair is matted down with a wide headband and she's wearing an aerobic sports top and sparkly clean sneakers.

"Hi," she says, looking up from a crossword book in her lap.

"Morning." I nod at her before turning the key in the door.

"Any chance you know what a half man, half horse is called?" she says.

"Centaur," I say.

"C-E—yes, thank you."

"I like your sneakers."

"Just out of the box." She smiles, and goes back to the puzzle.

I take two steps in, flick the light on, throw the brass key on a small plastic table by the door, and turn to—

"Whoa," I say.

The young woman has walked in directly behind me.

"Oh, I'm sorry I startled you," she says. "I'm here to clean the room."

"That's not necessary."

"Has to be done," she says, heading toward the bathroom.

"Really," I say. "You don't have to . . ."

"You can help if you want," she says, briskly brushing past me as she comes out of the bathroom. "You're not a bathroom slob; that's a good sign."

"I got in late. I haven't really had a chance to mess anything up," I say.

She leans over the bed and strips off the sheets in one swift motion. "In the cabinet behind you," she says.

"What?"

"You said you wanted to help. The linens are in the cabinet behind you, below the TV."

"Oh, OK."

"I don't like to push a cart around. I keep all the supplies hidden around the rooms. There's some sanitary wipes under the ice bucket if you need any later. So what brings you to the Judy?"

"I tripped my brother-in-law."

"He probably deserved it."

"I don't know."

I really don't.

"Bethany," she says, extending her free hand across the bed.

"Jeffrey," I say.

"I didn't think you were one of those businessmen we've been getting lately. I guess companies are slashing their travel expenses so we get these uptight guys coming here now expecting the Courtyard Marriott. Yogi is going to put up a sign that says, 'No Wi-Fi.' That ought to scare them off."

"Yogi? You talking about Raja?"

"Yeah, I saw he had you assuming the position this morning. He snags somebody every few days or so. Did he start in about Robitussin? He's basically batshit, but he's been fair with me. I do the rooms here every other day and he lets me keep a room for myself at the other place he runs up the road—the Beachcomber. It's not as seedy, if you want to move over there. The little refrigerators actually work."

"This is fine," I say.

The light blue sheet billows up with a snap and the corners land directly in place.

"Tuck if the edges will reach," she says. "These sheets are supposed to be queens but sometimes they won't reach."

They won't.

She turns over the pillows and punches them before fluffing. "The ol' punch and fluff," she says. "Some people just like their pillows fluffed but I like to pummel them a little first. Really brings 'em back to life."

She unfurls the bedspread, which is embroidered with pheasants. "You OK with the pheasants? It's reversible if you just want brown."

"I'm OK with the pheasants."

She pats the spread down with one hand and pulls a spray cleaner out from inside the bed rail with the other to spritz the nightstand. "Is this you in this thing?" she says, holding up the snowglobe. "You look goofy in there. Hey, I can't help but notice, do you have any clothes?"

"I really didn't expect to be here. I sort of—"

"I also do marketing and promotions for the Pompano Blazers. You know, the arena football team. You a fan?"

"I am now."

"Anyway, in my trunk I've got some T-shirts I was rubber banding to toss into the crowd. I could give you a few to hold you over."

"I might actually take you up on that."

"I clean the pool, too. I'll get them when I go to my car for my pH tester. I'll be out there in about forty-five."

"Great. Is it really assigned seating by the pool?"

"I told you Yogi is batshit. Sit wherever you want."

The second she leaves, it becomes clear that I'm really not OK with the pheasants. I turn the spread over, then lie down on my stomach and stretch out. It's soft and very cool, and the best way I can think of to spend the next forty-five minutes.

I keep seeing Michael in that awkward flight toward the hassock, oddly serene in the moment before gravity and pain assert themselves. And then it's me in flight, my turn to be weightless and serene, as I wait patiently for the crash.

"There you be," Bethany says from across the pool.

I start to head toward her but she says, "No, no, stay where you are. I want to practice my tossing."

She lets go of the long pole attached to the vacuum that she's been navigating along the pool bottom and picks up three bundled shirts.

"Wave your arms. Look excited," she yells at me.

I halfheartedly flail my arms.

"No, really. I'm supposed to work the crowd up into a frenzy before we let any free shirts fly."

My cool is forever trapped in a snowglobe back in the room and I can't look any stupider than I did in the barbecue pit this morning, so I start giving it everything I've got, jumping and yelling and throwing my arms over my head as if I've been stranded on a desert island for eighteen years and have finally spotted a search-and-rescue plane on the horizon.

Bethany lets one rip that goes hurling about twenty feet over my head and up over the roof of a weathered cabana. "Sorry," she yells. "I was going for the rafters."

"No problem," I say, racing around the back of the shed. I take off the rubber band. Not bad. One hundred percent cotton. Extra large. Lots of lightning bolts.

As soon as I come back from behind the shed Bethany is twirling around like a shot-putter with another bundled T-shirt tucked under her chin. "I'll do this one lefty but you're still going to have to leap for it."

She heaves it and it lands right on the roof of the cabana this time.

"Think quick," she says.

I don't think quick. The line drive she releases slams me in the chest and bounces to my feet.

"You OK?" Bethany says, hustling around to my side of the pool.

"Yeah, yeah, I'm just lucky it was only a T-shirt."

"I used to play softball, fast pitch. I couldn't resist. Hey, you were very enthusiastic out there, jumping up and down and all."

"Thanks, not a lot of people have been praising my enthusiasm lately."

I gather up my bounty and sit down in a lounge chair while Bethany chases down the pole that has drifted to the far end of the pool.

"My wife is having an affair," I say.

"What?"

I raise my voice. "I think my wife is having an affair."

"Oh, my brother is doing that. He said it's not easy."

She drags the pole over to where I'm sitting. "I didn't want to yell this but my brother asked me to let him use my room at the Beachcomber a couple of times."

"What'd you tell him?"

"I'm used to changing sheets, right? I said I didn't give a crap, as long as he didn't let the woman use hairspray in the place. It's the worst. It settles everywhere."

"I don't really get the affair thing," I say. "Is it really like on TV where all these people do is meet in hotels and have sex and then go back to their lives? I mean, I like sex as much as the next person, but if I was really infatuated with someone I'd want to go ice-skating with them, too."

"Well, maybe they do that, too. I don't know," Bethany says. "Do you want me to call my brother and ask him?"

"I guess maybe I understand the traveling affair," I say, "where, like, two people hook up at a convention in the Windy City and have a whirlwind affair that includes shows and dining and maybe some window-shopping."

"I'm going to call him," Bethany says, pulling out her cellphone.

"No, no."

"No bother, he likes to hear from his sister. He's always saying I never call. I'll just see if they ever do anything else, like go for frozen yogurt or something."

"I don't think I really want to know."

"Nonsense," she says, turning her back to me as she waits for her brother to pick up.

I expect Bethany to blab away before working up to the question, but she gets right to the point. "He says they went together when he got her car detailed for her birthday," she says, turning back to me. "Hold on . . . And there was a Wendy's nearby. Do you want me to ask him anything else?"

"Eat in or takeout?"

"Eat in or takeout?" she says into the receiver. "Hello? Hello? He's gone. I'll call him back."

"No, I don't need to know. It's not going to make a difference."

"You don't want to go by anything he says anyway," Bethany says. "I love him and all but he's one of those guys who drinks himself into a stupor and then pops Viagra to get it up. I had a boyfriend like that once and there's nothing worse than a drunken penis that won't quit."

"This guy with my wife is in the medical field. I bet he has access to fistfuls of Viagra."

"I wouldn't worry about that. I don't know who these guys think they are going to have sex with for thirty-six hours straight. After twenty-five minutes it's like 'Keep that thing away from me.'"

"Do all women feel that way?"

"The general consensus is that there are a lot of things a woman would like to have at her disposal for thirty-six hours straight . . . but that thing is not one of them."

"I just wish everything was different," I say, slouching back in the lounge chair.

"I know what you mean," Bethany says. "Every year I vow to make everything different. I've got to get out of that motel room. Mostly because I want to get a big dog. Yogi said I could get a little dog, but I want a big dog with a big head."

"Like one of those mastodons?"

"I think that's a hairy elephant. You mean a mastiff."

"Yeah, a mastiff with a big, slobbering head."

"I like when people take turns being smart."

"Huh?"

"Like how you know what a centaur is and I know what a mastodon is?"

"Yeah, right. You know, this morning I thought I was going to squeeze some wisdom out of Raja because he's into yoga and meditating and he's a premature swami and whatnot, but you're much more . . ."

"My mom was a kindergarten teacher so I know how to talk to people like you. That's all." She grins.

"What's your story?" I ask.

"Hey, I don't give my story away like free T-shirts," she says. "You have to earn it. Buy me a Corona sometime."

I gaze around the pool and the assigned chairs are starting to fill up with a hodgepodge of disenfranchised but interesting-looking characters. I suddenly want to know everybody's story but I don't want to buy everyone a drink.

"OK. Been fun. Gotta run," Bethany says, hopping up and retracting the pole like a collapsible umbrella. "If you're still here tomorrow . . ."

"I won't be."

"I was going to say I could drop by some tickets for a game."

"I appreciate the thought."

I'm watching her clean, white sneakers, which are emblazoned with the same razor-edged lightning bolts as the shirts, as she turns and breaks into a trot. Her feet stop short. "Hey," she says.

I shield my eyes against the sun so I can look up at her, but it's too blinding. My eyes focus back on the sneakers, which are softly running in place now.

"Hey, what?" I say.

"To be honest, I don't think there's any such thing as things being different," she says.

"Go Blazers," I say.

"Rah, rah," she says, the spotless sneakers breaking into a sprint.

vagabond brain

'm still here.

From where I'm currently sitting, in a tightly strapped, sun-cracked lounge chair, I have a view of both Federal Highway and the CLEAN ROOMS AND AFFORDABLE RATES sign, but not much else. It's been three . . . no, four days now. I've mostly just been sitting around reading moldy, used paperbacks I pick up at the Bookworm next door—none of them particularly good, but remarkably similar. I like when things are only slightly different. I really miss that.

My uncle Randall once told me, "Sometimes your family loses sight of you, even if you pay sixty-four percent of the bills," and now that I don't even have that going for me, I'm not sure where I'm at in the big scheme of things.

Until I called Kristin to pick me up this morning—she's supposed to be on her way—I hadn't heard from any member of my family. Not one had tried to contact me since I've been here, if that tells you anything. I did finally succumb to calls from Meryl Atkins at Brighton Gardens, and she informed me that the Brighton board of trustees will meet the fifteenth of next month to decide the fate of my mother. It all sounded so official but, to be honest, I'm glad this has gotten tangled up in bureaucracy. The slight reprieve gives me a little more time to try to figure out what to do "about her situation."

Other than that, the only other contact I've had with the outside world is seventeen text messages from Omar? By the tone of the texts he's pissed that I skipped out on him right in the middle of our new endeavor. I was supposed to fill more mud troughs for the Pterygoplichthys foreclosed-pool-cleaning fish. Could be a gold mine, but my fervor keeps wavering . . . on everything.

"You're not even your own person anymore," Anna shouted at me a week ago yesterday. "You're morphing into this amalgamation of everyone you meet."

I do keep thinking other people can help me, even strangers. Is that so bad? The other night, I started walking toward the Beachcomber to claim those free tickets. Bethany had never stopped back. I even went to ask Raja why, but he hit me with a cryptic "Every other day."

"But it is two days after the other day," I said.

"She wasn't supposed to be here that day," he said.

"But . . ."

"I will not argue with a man like you," he said, retreating to his back rooms.

They were just free tickets to a lame sporting event, but for some reason I can't explain, the offer so freely made by a stranger gave me hope. And I thought Bethany would be the last person to betray my hope. From meeting to abandonment in record time.

Everything happens faster now. No one tells you that in any of the career seminars. What else? Oh, people say it's difficult to make money these days but it's much more difficult to not make money. The main reason I'm leaving today—aside from desperately needing to face down Anna once and for all—is monetary. I swore I would not waste more than one unemployment check ($218) holing up like a refugee at the Judy.

I want so badly to come out the other side of this. There have been rare moments in the past week in which I began to feel anxious, in the good way. I walked near the water earlier and the azure blue surf is always so flat and calm here in Florida but it was actually a little rough out there today and it made me recall the late summers up north when my parents would take Bo and me to Jones Beach and the gray water would suck us up, submerging our small bodies beneath the tumultuous waves. For several seconds you felt as if you were going to die as the crashing of the waves turned to silence, your head smacked bottom, the gravelly sand scraped across your back as you were churned up into oblivion. There was no equilibrium. The moment was airless; flashes of light, salt in the brain and spinning and spinning before being spit back out at shore. That was the beauty of it. Once you were on your feet again, glancing back to the maroon umbrella that marked your parents, there was this huge lift of exhilaration, and all you wanted to do was get back out there. That's what I'm holding on for. I want to stop spinning and step out of this into some form of exhilaration but each time I . . .

"Dad . . . Dad! Are you getting up?"

"Hey, petunia," I say, seeing Kristin hovering over me.

"Don't call me that. Come on, get up!"

"I'm up. I'm up. My ass is up."

"Have you got everything?"

"Yeah, thanks for coming to get me. Yeah, this is everything."

Kristin looks at the sundries I picked up at the CVS next door spilling out of my small bag and just shakes her head.

As we head toward the car, I'm lagging behind a little and she keeps glancing back.

"I'm still here," I say.

"Dad, do you have to wear that arena football T-shirt?"

"Yes, honey. I guess I do."

D oing some reading?" Kristin asks, eyeing the paperback in my lap as she backs the car up.

"Not really. I forgot to throw this one in the pool. Thanks again for picking me up."

"I would have brought you some clothes if you needed clothes," she says.

"I know. I wasn't thinking about clothes."

"You shoulda been."

There's a soft, mellow song on the car radio and I lean over to turn up the volume. I like playing quiet songs very loud.

"It's from hostessing," Kristin says.

"Huh?"

"When you were following me to the car and I turned around to see if you were still there. At work, I always have to say 'follow me' and I'm always worried I'm going to lose someone in the party, so I keep turning around."

"That's understandable."

"Two weeks ago I actually lost a party of four. 'Lewandowski—party of four.' They were right behind me past the kitchen, past the restrooms—still there. Did a double-check as we passed the billiard tables—still there—but then when I got to the table and turned to put the menus down—poof! They were gone. Never saw them again."

"Strange."

I watch Kristin's skinny legs working the gas and clutch, her bony fingers jamming the shift into third gear. Her movements are so vibrant, so fluid and in the moment.

She flips a visor down and a CD falls in her lap. "I want you to hear this band," she says, slipping the disk into her stereo. "Instead of a drummer they have a tap dancer. Listen, listen closely."

When I was sitting by the pool of the Judy waiting for Kristin to pick me up, my mind kept wandering. Not in a bad way, more in a meandering, daydreaming manner.

"I'm sorry," I say to Kristin, reaching over to turn the music up. "I'm having trouble concentrating. My mind keeps wandering, drifting."

"Hah, your mind is a vagabond."

"Yeah, I don't think it would be far-fetched for my obituary to one day read, 'He was a drifter who lived in one place all his life.'"

"I like that," Kristin says. "We've got this older lady at work, Myanta, and all she does is refill iced teas most of the time—'More tea? Refill? Refill?' She's like thirty-three and she's been doing it since she was my age. Can you believe that?"

"I guess if she likes it."

"She does. She loves it. Some of the staff makes fun of her. This one guy, Francis, does an imitation of her as an eighty-year-old woman hobbling around from table to table going, 'Refill? Refill?' It's pretty funny—the crotchety old voice he makes and stuff."

"Does she get upset?"

"He doesn't do it in front of her. But people are always pestering her with 'Don't you want to do something else with your life? You're going to be here forever.' But Myanta only smiles and says, 'I've always wanted to be someplace forever.'"

"That's kind of profound."

"Yeah, I thought so, too. I bet she's got a great backstory. I want to get all the details but we're always so busy."

"You're being nice to me."

"What?"

"You seem nicer today. I mean, I know you're always nice to other people. I see how joyful and entertaining you are with other people, especially kids, but you've been pretty short with me lately . . ."

"I'm just going easy on you today," she says with a grin. "I'm treating this like it's the pickup of a hospital patient or something. You're fragile, I think. Before I picked you up, I thought about packing the car with Styrofoam peanuts."

"Yeah, maybe the Judy was like my rehab center."

"You have to bottom out. It's the American way."

"Maybe I'll be all better now. Be my old self."

"Not sure we want that, either. Since you lost your job you've been a little more interesting."

"Are you getting anything out of this?" I say.

"What?"

"Me being your father."

"Oh boy, don't get all heavy on me. I just ate a Sonic burger for lunch."

"You know how you always hear people saying, 'My daddy always said this or my daddy said that . . .' All those nuggets of wisdom fathers pass down. Do I ever say anything like that?"

"If you ask me, the whole 'my father always said' bit is kind of corny. It's just because some dads repeat crap over and over and bore their kids to death," Kristin says. "They recall, like, four things their father said because he repeated stuff ad nauseam. I think it will be a credit to you if I never remember a word that you said."

"Thanks."

"Oh look," she says as she downshifts. "They're having that house tented. I love when they do that. Remember when I was little and we had the termites and had to have the house tented and stay at that hotel. I was mad at you because you told me our house was being used as a circus for the night so I was PO'd that we couldn't stay. And then you tried to calm me down by telling us it wasn't really a safe circus for kids—kind of a deadly circus. Then I couldn't sleep because I couldn't stop thinking about a deadly circus taking place in our house. There, there's something I'll remember you by."

I crane my neck, staring back at the red-and-blue-stripe tarped house and my mind wanders to the thought of having myself tented. A total fumigation to rid myself of all the anxiety, angst, and fear that has invaded my body over the past couple of months.

"Dad, Dad. Vagabond brain!"

"You know Mom called me unnecessary."

"Was she drinking wine spritzers? It was probably the wine spritzers talking."

"Does Mom ever cross her legs when she's driving with you?"

"No, that sounds like a new one. She's got a lot of new tricks lately."

"What do you mean?"

"I think when someone highly organized goes off the deep end it's a whole different animal. With someone like you, it's just goofy, but with Mom it seems demented somehow. Scarier."

"What aren't you telling me?"

"Nothing you want to know. Oh, by the way, I can't believe you tripped Uncle Michael."

"You want a piece of this Twix?" I say, holding up a stick of the candy bar I'd bought while I was waiting.

"No thanks. You trying to bribe me?"

I want Kristin to drive slower. She's a fairly cautious driver, and it has nothing to do with my apprehension about the high rate of traffic fatalities. I just want to stretch this interaction, pillage every insight she might have. She has always been smarter than the rest of us, and I guess that's why she loses her patience with me so easily. I put my head down, focusing on the dozen frayed bracelets sliding up and down her freckled forearm with every shift into a higher gear. I felt so righteous when I was claiming my family had lost sight of me, but I am the one losing sight of them, aren't I? I hope she's not noticing that I'm beginning to cry.

"No! Don't wipe it," she shouts in time to stop me from rubbing at a piece of Twix that has landed on the front of my shirt.

"You wipe it you'll smear it all over. Just pop your shirt. Like this," she says while pinching the front of her shirt out and then letting it snap back.

I pop my shirt and watch the Twix shrapnel sail up over the dashboard.

"That's OK. The car will smell like chocolate next time I run the heater," she says.

"How come you don't seem worried?" I ask. "How come my losing my job doesn't seem to get to you?"

"I don't know. I guess because you've never let us down before. Andrew is probably too young to remember, but I remember when they cut hours from your job when we were little and you started working that side job at the mail-order place."

"I thought you were embarrassed by that."

"Are you kidding? You used to bring home all the free samples of cereals and shampoos and those sticky things you throw at the wall. Those were excellent."

"Is Mom home?"

"Well, that is one of the reasons I've been nice to you," she says, reaching to the backseat and coming up with . . .

"Not another printout."

"The printout of printouts. It supposedly covers everything until she gets back. She said you had your breather at the Rudy and now it's her turn."

"The Judy."

"Whatever."

Printed on thick blue stock paper, it's a three-page manifesto that covers everything from an admonition to buy only the twelve-pack of Kirkland paper towels at Costco to the location of the extra-large skillet in the Rubbermaid cabinet in the garage, in case we want to make stir-fry.

"We all got copies, with slight variations here and there," Kristin says. "Andrew has to feed the fish, but Mom's going to come by every sixth day to change the tanks' filters. She doesn't want anyone else doing that."

"Are you going to make stir-fry?" I ask Kristin.

"I haven't stirred anything since I made chocolate milk every day after school in sixth grade," she says.

"Where is she going to be staying?"

"She wouldn't say, only that it's not her mom's. She didn't want you pestering her mom."

"Is that what I am now, a pest?"

"You can be."

I look down at page three where it states—listen to me, *where it states*—that she will continue to pay the mortgage, the utilities, and my life insurance online.

"Would you rather have me or my life insurance?" I ask Kristin.

"Stop it."

"She is demented. It's not me."

"I wouldn't go that far. But yeah, she's demented. But that makes her more interesting. Her hair is getting wilder, too. You should see it."

"You sure you can't eat the rest of this Twix? I feel nauseous."

"Do not throw up in this car."

It's not that kind of nauseous, really. It's an empty nausea.

"People come back," Kristin says. "My friend Olivia went psycho on me in seventh grade and we didn't talk for four years, but then she just changed back to her old self and we're good friends again."

"I always wondered what happened to Olivia."

"Oh, the permit for the garage sale came yesterday," Kristin says. "It's only good for that one Saturday. Are you still going to do it?"

"I guess. I paid nine dollars for that fucking permit. Sorry, you don't deserve that."

She reaches over, turns the radio up even louder, and keeps pushing her hair behind her ears but it won't stay.

"You cut your hair. It's short."

"About five weeks ago. Boy, you really have been in a walking coma."

"It's self-induced."

"Hey, how come you keep shaking your head up and down and . . . around? Do you even realize you're doing that?"

"No. What do you mean?"

"Your head is shaking up and down and it's not like yes and it's not like no. It's like weirdo," she says, putting her hand on my shoulder and keeping it there as she speeds up.

"Maybe I'm just anxious, in a good way. When am I going to get to meet this James you were talking about?"

"When you get your shit together."

I lean back and stare out the window. Nothing at all is catching my attention. It is a blur of trees, parked cars, and whitewashed strip shopping centers, but without an immediate confrontation with Anna looming and Kristin's hand still on my shoulder, I feel oddly relaxed. I find it oddly comforting knowing that the drum solo I'm listening to is actually tap dancing.

"I can see you leering at me over there," Kristin says. "I know what you want. I'll say it if you want me to."

"Okayyy, 'you're necessary.'"

ain't no marshmallows in that rocky road

'm running late, trying to make it over to the fish troughs before it gets too hot, when I remember I have to force Alonzo out for a therapeutic walk. I'm dreading the smell of the cheese required to lure him out of the den this early in the morning. But when I turn the corner, he is already camped out by the front door. At the sight of the leash he achingly rises and points his nose toward the door, sniffing for fresh air. We are only a few steps down the walkway when Kyle passes by on his bicycle and shouts, "Hey, looks like Zo is finally getting better."

Huh?

I gaze down and, lo and behold, his bad leg is touching the ground; he's daintily applying pressure to it for the first time. He's limping, adding a ticktock to his gait, but his head is up, determined and assured. I have been present for the first steps of both my children, but that pales in comparison to the odd exhilaration I feel at the sight of Zo healing right before my eyes.

I bend down, grab Alonzo's face in my hands, the way Alex would, and look into his eyes. They are crystal clear, a striking brown surrounded by pure white. "Alonzo, you're back," I say aloud.

Man, I had resigned myself to the idea that he would be a handicapped hound from here on out, maimed for good, doomed to long days of sitting at the front window, eyelids half open, longingly watching the world go by.

But now it seems that won't be his fate. "Will it, boy?" I say, patting at the sides of his thick coat. Perhaps I'm kidding myself but I think the vet was wrong. Alonzo is digging down deep, determined to come out the other side of this on his own. I desperately want to believe that. Maybe he's driven by the irritating thought of having some twangy hillbilly three-legged-dog song written about him. More likely it's the sheer force of his desire to once again escape from the yard and romp down the block, jumping in and out of the neighbors' sprinklers and dropping a load in Ms. Henderson's bed of azaleas. Who knows what keeps us going.

On the drive to the duplex, all I can think of is Alonzo gamely hopping back up the front steps into the house. He was back on just the three good legs and panting with fatigue and crazy thirsty, but he lapped deliriously from his bowl in the kitchen as if warm tap water with flecks of soggy dog food floating in it had never tasted so good. Watching his enthusiasm, I felt a shadow lift.

I park out front and walk around to the back. This abandoned property has already taken on that familiar tang of ambivalence any workplace accumulates over time. I'm bound to it by obligation, but it's also a place of pride. These fish need me.

"How could you abandon me like that?" Omar? says, coming up behind me as I'm trying to add more mud to the second plecostomus trough. "You don't even answer my texts."

"I'm sorry. It wasn't planned. It all happened spontaneously," I say.

"You haven't got a spontaneous bone in your body."

"Do so."

"Don't."

"Do."

"OK, you got a little fight in you, that's good. Just checking."

"It was only some personal stuff."

"Then you take a personal day. My people take personal days. I'm not running some half-ass operation. A man can take a personal day."

"It looks like I never had enough mud in here." I pour another bucket of dirt into the trough. "It's as if it all disintegrated."

Omar? stares down into the trough, dips his hand in, and starts stirring the water up. "You have to make it thicker. This water's too thin."

"Hey, I may have a news contact to kick this off once we have enough fish to start the business."

"Who?"

"Adele Winn. Channel Twelve."

"Winnie. Man, I seen her outside the courthouse once and my tongue started moving around in my mouth, like I wanted to eat her up."

"She gets that a lot."

"My mouth was closed so nobody could see my tongue darting around it but I was still kind of ashamed. Here, look at me right now."

I stand back and stare into his face.

"I'm doing it right now, but you'd never know, right? My tongue is whip-pin' and dartin' all over, but as far as the naked eye can tell, nothin', right?"

"She gave me her card in case I come upon anything newsworthy."

"Yeah, fish cleaning pools. That's a story. I can see it."

"Why'd you leave the catfish? They were a pain in the ass. We don't need the catfish."

"The catfish show the little fish how big they can get," Omar? says. "Fish grow by their surroundings—size of the tank, size of the fish across the room. I thought you did research. Man, how do you even exist without me?"

"I don't know that I do," I say.

Omar? turns away from me and starts baby talking to Audrey and Rachel.

I go to the other side of the yard where the ground is softer and I can dig up a bucket of dirt with less sweat. After a few minutes, Omar? walks over and says, "Can I see Winnie's card, there?"

"No."

"OK, later," he says, then strolls off along the side of the house.

"I'm having a garage sale Saturday if you want to swing by," I shout after him.

He just gives me a look like, "Yeah, right."

"Well, tell Avillo if you see him."

"Ah, I almost forgot. I had to have Av take the bridge. Fucked it up. I may have to pay for a fifty-four-foot mast of a mad Hatteras. That's on you. You and your disappearing act. You owe me big-time."

Topping off another bucket, I laugh at the thought of owing someone like Omar? big-time. For some reason I like being in debt to such an enterprising dude.

I spill two more buckets of dirt evenly across the top of the trough, but it's still not getting murky enough, so I begin shoveling straight from the ground until the water has the consistency of a thick, frosty milk shake. This doesn't feel like work. This feels like I'm one of those guys in the movies—a contem-plative soul—tending to his pigeons on a rooftop in the Bronx. I wonder if Omar? really meant it, that I have a little fight in me.

The water is totally still. I hope I haven't buried everybody alive. I wipe the sweat from my eyes and stand over the tank in vigil, waiting for a ripple or a trickle of bubbles rising up from the muck.

"Oh Audrey. Oh Rachel. Give me a sign."

No sign.

On the way home I pick up a Slurpee and take a detour.

"No sir. No shorts. Not in here. Not now. Not ever," the woman at the front desk of the Workforce Alliance Center is shouting.

"But . . ."

"Outside! Outside! No shorts in here."

The woman, dressed in an orange pantsuit, is coming straight at me now so I back toward the front doors and stick one leg outside to send the message that I'll gladly leave but . . .

"I'm sorry about the shorts. I was just in the neighborhood and decided to stop in," I say.

"This isn't a thought-I'd-drop-by kind of place. You're letting the air out. Please close the door. Go home and plan to come next time. You know the dress code."

"But I just wanted to speak to Carl for a minute."

"Oh, you're one of Carl's. Isn't that a surprise?"

"Can you tell him I'd like to see him if he's not busy."

"Carl, *busy*?" She snickers. "I'll give him the message. Go . . . Go outside. Wait by the Shoe Carnival."

I don't want to stand by the Shoe Carnival. I walk over to my car and keep my eyes fixed on the front doors. I guess I should have changed, but I'm trying not to make a big deal about everything, and I thought it would be fun to stop in and see Carl.

"Look at you. You know better than coming by here in shorty pants," Carl says, spotting me before I spot him.

"I know, I know," I say. "But . . ."

"Don't worry about it. Look at you. Man, my eyes adore you. You look bold and beautiful. You look bioluminescent. I know this is some kind of good-news day. You look like a new man."

I gasp as Carl jumps up on the hood of the car and the chassis drops to the point where I can't even see the tops of my front tires.

"You have the glaze of somebody who just went to a franchise seminar at the Doubletree. You didn't sign up for a Quiznos, did you? The meat will get in your pores, you know. No stopping it. You'll smell like meat all the time. Your wife—your lover—will smell like meat all the time."

"At the moment, my wife is staying so far away from me she can't smell me at all."

"Troubles with the missus? Ain't no marshmallows in that rocky road. You don't have to tell ol' Carl. I feel it."

"And I'm not getting a franchise. But I brought you a Slurpee."

"Look at that. What'd you do, a mix? I smell the Cherry Coke. Is that the green of the Dew? I can't touch it. My triglycerides are under daily watch but it is beautiful."

"I'm having a garage sale this weekend if you want to swing by."

"You know I swing, but I don't know if that's my thing—you out selling your wares. But it's a possibility. *Possibility.*"

"How come you never checked up on me?" I say. "I thought you were going to keep an eye on me."

"I don't call people in to this place. That's other people's doings. But I'm with you on a need-to-need basis. You know that. You didn't take a job, did you?"

"No, that wouldn't feel right for some reason. That's what I wanted to talk to you about."

"The thing is, you can't accept anything until you're ready, but you can't give up entirely," he says. "Sometimes the only way to find peace is to give up, but that's not you. Fine line, fine line."

Carl pops off the hood and starts circling me. "Yes, something's changed. You're not the sad sack of yesteryear anymore, but it's going to take more. You need a sense of grandeur about you to make it these days. I'm trying to instill this in all my prototypes. Or is it protégés?

"I like 'prototype.' "

"Anyway, you gotta pomp it up. Get self-exalted, create a state of splendor for yourself. Otherwise how on earth do you keep going? I'm not just talking about unemployment, but everything coming down on us. Fake your grandeur if you have to. I got it. You gotta get a swagger going.

"Like this," he says, strutting around the side of the car. "Oh boy, I gotta go. The new meds have me peeing every ten minutes. I have to go on runpee .com every time I go to the movies. It's crazy. I better get inside. But you know what I'm leaving you with: Gotta incorporate a new purposeful stride into your bag of tricks."

"I don't know—a new walk? That sounds like a hell of a lot of work."

"You!" he says leaving the Slurpee on the hood of the car and rushing off. "Let it come natural then. It'll come."

homestead unincorporated

There's a lightness to the air.

I'm along the riverfront near the courthouse. Bennie has an appointment. That's what he keeps saying, anyway. "It's not a hearing. I don't have to line up with all the other animals. It's just an appointment with a magistrate or some shit and then we'll be on the road to Homestead."

I agreed to wait and I'm glad I did. I'll take any excuse I can get to be able to loiter around the waterfront. The day is quiet and fat fragments of clouds are passing overhead like a slow-moving herd of manatee. I only walk a few yards when I'm cut off by two women who ask me to take a photo of them in front of a passing yacht. They are sisters, both dressed in cranberry with matching hats that read, PSSST . . . as if they are always about to tell the world a giant secret.

"Quick, quick," one sister says, handing me the camera. "I've got it on the fireworks setting. So keep it on that."

"Why, are you going to explode?" I ask, catching the cranberry sisters giggling, the brims of their PSSST . . . hats colliding and all their secrets revealing themselves in one instant.

I love people. You wouldn't know it by looking at me, but I really do.

The second I'm free of the sisters, a foreign couple approaches me to snap a picture of them before the ship is out of sight. I'm on a roll and I eagerly jump at the chance to do something for somebody . . . anybody.

"We're from Holland," the woman says in a stern voice.

That's great. I quickly reach for the digital camera as the man puts his arm around the woman's waist, pulling her tightly to fit in the frame. As I peer through the viewfinder, I'm thinking how this is something I've always wanted to do, but nobody has ever asked me before. Now that I'm unemployed, maybe my approachability is at an all-time high. My free time will be full of social encounters loaded with smiles and no pressure. I squeeze off a shot and send the couple on their merry way.

But they don't leave. They walk to the left of me in a spot of shade to see how the photo came out. "You can't take photo for shet," the fair-haired woman says nastily.

Why couldn't my approachability have been at an all-time high ten years ago, when tourists wouldn't see my crappy handiwork until they got to the Fotomat back home in Wichita or Bangkok or wherever?

I head off in the opposite direction and stop near a waterfront bar called Shooters. The lunchtime crowd is mostly made up of boaters, many having food served to them on their thirty-one-foot sport boats. We are surrounded by gluttonous wealth here in South Florida, but I can go weeks, months, years without feeling any jealousy whatsoever. We have what we have, right? But then there are days, and today is one of them, that there's no denying it. I wish I had money, too. I walk the length of a short dock jutting out into the water and ask a guy sitting on the nose of a forty-foot Windsor and eating a plate of coconut shrimp where he got the money.

"What?"

"What do you do for a living, to afford a boat like this?"

"Citrus," he says, turning to his wife. "Honey, the sauce for the shrimp is more sour than sweet. Catch that waitress and see if she has something more sweet than sour."

When he turns back he seems surprised that I'm still standing there. "Citrus," I say to remind him where we left off.

"I have a company that exports citrus to Canada. I don't grow it. I just ship it. I can get you a card," he says, going to wipe his fingers before realizing he doesn't have a napkin. "Honey we need napkins, too. Lots of napkins."

I wander off while he's distracted, but that makes sense, doesn't it? People in Canada need citrus and someone needs to get rich supplying it.

I stroll two boats down and just blurt, "Where'd you get the money?" to a guy standing on the bow of his boat with his hands on his hips in sort of a Superman pose.

"Mostly in the damaged-boxes business," he says directly. "Say you're a company that makes computer monitors and you have a hundred and fifty in boxes that got all wet, so you can't sell them retail."

"OK," I say.

"Then I find, like, an office that needs a hundred and fifty monitors but doesn't give a crap if the boxes are all wet. They just want a good price. I put the two together and take a commission."

"That's it?" I ask.

"You'd be surprised how many damaged boxes there are out there."

"Is it always computer stuff?" I ask.

"No, it can be foot massagers," he says. "We're going to have a commercial during the Super Bowl this year—big things happening! How 'bout you? What are you into?"

"Just walking around," I say.

Bennie is probably looking for me about now, so I pick up the pace and I'm heading back by the water taxi stand when a matronly woman standing in my path lets out the most majestic laugh I've ever heard. It is so melodious and powerful, like a laugh being played by a full orchestra. It is a laugh so mighty I can see it brimming over and flowing down her rounded shoulders like lava. I wish I knew what brought her to this laugh. If I could, I'd go back in her life and follow every step she took, even if it involved swinging off a frayed rope into an icy New Hampshire lake a hundred times in one day or obsessively sketching fruit bowls on dark afternoons and messing up the sublime curve of the peach every time. I'd stay the course, even if it meant marrying a sailor and losing him to war and then marrying an aluminum-siding salesman and losing him to a lithe, blond woman named Gloria. I'd keep going, even if it involved spending the last ten years working in the mobile Spay Shuttle, going from town to town neutering cats in Walmart parking lots. I'd hang in for the long haul just to be at the point where I could stand by a river on a soft autumn day and emit a laugh such as hers.

"Let's do it," Bennie says, busting through the moment. "Let's make the pilgrimage."

"Can we stop calling it that?" I ask.

"You can. I'm not. Oh, I've decided this was a 'court appearance,' not an appointment. Bennie made an 'appearance.' That's how you can put it if anybody asks," he says, taking off the long black raincoat he wore for his "appearance."

He unbuckles a red and black studded belt that looks like it came from the discount table at Hot Topic, cinches it up another notch, like a corset around his tiny hips, and says, "There, that's better."

"Much better."

"In the time it takes to get from here to the car, tell me one thing about Bo," he says. "One thing that makes this search worthwhile."

"In our neighborhood all the streets were named after generals. I lived on Custer. Bo lived on Lee."

"Something else."

"Well," I say as we trudge back toward the parking garage. "One time in second grade. I guess I was . . . How old would you be in second grade?"

"How the hell would I know?"

"Anyway, I was attacked by a German shepherd in our neighborhood. The thing dragged me to the ground and was chomping away."

"So Bo saved you?"

"No, he ran home. But later all the neighborhood moms were studying me for wounds. The beast mainly got me in the butt, but I wasn't saying it out loud because I didn't want everybody looking at my butt. This whole thing had moved into Mrs. Doyle's kitchen at this point, and other kids were starting to file in, too. Then Mr. Doyle lifts me off the ground and props me atop a chair and it's like I'm standing up on a pedestal and then whoosh. Down come my pants. 'Just as I thought,' Mr. Doyle says real serious. But everybody else is snickering and laughing 'cause I've just been pantsed on a pedestal in Brian Doyle's kitchen."

"Man."

"And then, out of nowhere, Bo appears from the gallery, grabs the elastic waistband, and pulls my pants up with one hand and waves the crowd off with the other. 'Go home, you pervians.' I think that's what he said."

"Yeah," Bennie says. "Everybody needs somebody who will pull their pants up in a desperate situation like that. A de-pantser. I'm surprised you weren't searching for him sooner."

"I know, right."

I know that that ineffable sense of comfort I no longer have with Anna can still be reached with Bo. I just know it. He is the only one left that I never had to prove myself to. Bo will not judge me.

"Pervians," Bennie says, rolling the word around in his mouth. "How great is that?"

thank you

The gateway to Homestead is marked by a shiny new sign with raised lettering and finely painted birds perching on the *t* and the *d* but the welcome is very misleading.

"Left. Left. No, one more block, then left. Everybody hangs out at the place with the tortillas on the canopy," Bennie says. "Everybody."

"Where is everybody?" I say, putting the car in park.

"That's the place," he says. He points to a small shuttered building with a faded blue awning. "I don't know. Maybe it's too early. I don't know if I've ever really been to Homestead in the daytime."

"Jesus."

"No, no. I know where we can go. Witter's is open twenty-four/seven."

We drive up about six more blocks and enter a small café that specializes in cereal. The walls are lined with dispensers loaded with everything from Cap'n Crunch to Special K. There are two guys in the corner who appear as if they might team up to kill somebody someday but just haven't agreed on who yet, and a woman in a full-bodied apron busting with frilly bows.

"Bo, a big husky guy?" she says, throwing her shoulders back.

"Yeah, yeah."

"A bit of a goner. Always has that kooky look on his face?"

"Probably. Yeah."

"Happy-go-lucky Bo."

"Aaa . . . Do you know any other Bos?"

"That's the only one I'm aware of, and I'm aware of everything," she says.

"She is," Bennie concurs.

"Bennie, why haven't you given Mama a hug yet?"

"Hey, baby," Bennie says, wrapping his arms around her. "Long time no see."

She and Bennie talk about a couple of acquaintances who recently overdosed, a drift-fishing captain by the name of Scopes, and the Miami Hurricanes losing their legendary stadium, then she looks back at me and says, "That's got to be your man. In an hour or so he should be at the Kava bar. A lotta people go there to chill around three or so. It closed about four months ago but people still hang on the back deck. Only the *K* and the *V* are left in the sign but you'll spot it easy enough. You know, right, Bennie?" she says, hugging him again.

"Gritty, can I get a couple of fistfuls of Lucky Charms for the road?" Bennie says.

"Dig in."

I wait in the car and when Bennie comes out, every pocket, both hands, and his mouth are stuffed with Charms. The cereal starts trickling down between the seats and under the dashboard but all I can say about that is "Which way?"

"Two lefts and a funky right," he says through a mouthful of sugar.

When we pull up at the K-V, Bennie says, "I'm going to run across the street to Koffeeoke to see if Angelina is there. She's a goddess. I'll meet you in the back in a minute. Order me a Budtini."

The front door is locked, so I hack my way through the brush in an overgrown alleyway. The deck backs up to a dried-out canal and a stretch of railroad tracks. Not a soul in sight. I turn back to the building, press my fingers against the back door, and say, "Hello," as it creaks open.

I step inside and immediately both my arms are twisted behind my back.

"Don't move, don't you dare fucking move," a voice whispers so close to my ear that it tickles. Then a speaker box is in my left ear. "He's alone. I repeat, target is alone."

"All right, Moran out," I hear as I'm spun around and come face-to-face with a Kevlar man, the type of faceless SWAT guy you usually see scaling down the side of a building, only this one has a face like a raptor with a mustache.

I start to mutter my case but there are instantly four more SWATters and the first order of duty is to contain me. "No, let's talk before that," I say, seeing the last guy reaching for one of those garbage-bag-like ties they use to cuff people now. They act like the shiny metal ones are only for special occasions.

"Face to the wall," he says.

"No, no, at least use the real cuffs," I say.

"What?"

"I'm not a tall white kitchen bag. Come on."

Moran has that glint in his eye like he would have gone Blackwater two years ago if not for a passport snafu. Now he's stuck in this shithole town and everyone is going to pay for it. Especially me.

"Officer Moran, give him the real ones," an officer with the dog says.

"All right," Moran says.

"Thanks," I say.

They pull me over to an area of the Kava Bar that has been stripped of all its fixtures and push me down onto a metal folding chair near a pile of pink insulation that appears to have recently been ripped out of the walls.

"Can I talk now?" I ask.

"No," Moran says, but he does not say it in that tough-guy manner. He says it with a hint of disappointment, like he already knows I'm a dud. They probably even have a Wrong Place Wrong Time acronym for a situation such as this. *"Just a WPWT, Lieutenant." "Roger, cut him loose."*

"Are you going to cut me loose?" I ask but get no response.

A female officer comes in, finds the commanding officer, says, "The car's clean," and steps back outside.

Several of the SWAT guys huddle in the corner and now I'm beginning to worry about what I'm going to say. What is my story going to be? If I start telling my Bo tale, they're sure to ask for his full name and I don't know what could pop up on the radar on Joseph Bocchino. And Bennie? God, I've got to keep him out of this. Best just to stick with me. I'm the whole story.

"I just heard the Kava was a cool place to check out," I say, raising my voice.

One dark-haired officer breaks out of the huddle, glances at me, and then returns to the group.

The female officer comes back in, takes off her sunglasses, and says, "Oh, they broke out the shinies for you."

"I requested them," I say.

"You'll be OK. You're not him," she says, walking over to the huddle.

That's reassuring.

"I know I shouldn't have touched the door," I say, raising my voice again, but this time no one even glances in my direction.

Why aren't they questioning me? Everybody is questioning every little thing I've been doing lately except the people who just handcuffed me and threw me in the type of uncomfortable metal chair that is built for only one thing: interrogation.

When the questions do come, best to keep my answers brief, I tell myself. And portray a sense of confidence, but not cockiness. I never used to have much respect for actors. You know, they're just memorizing lines and whatnot. But I'm telling you, there are so many ways to say things. I want to say things the right way.

The huddle breaks and everyone files out the back door except for two of the officers—Moran and the guy who had the dog. But he doesn't have the dog anymore. I always have high hopes for the cops in the canine units. I think perhaps they got into law enforcement not because they're power-hungry control freaks who want to rule over the little people, but simply because they like dogs. Maybe this guy was just holding the dog for the real dog lover who just left the scene.

The officers stand over me and begin bickering about paperwork. "We've been watching this place for eight months. We have to fill out something," Moran says.

"What if we go with the tourist pass. Last month, the mayor gave us that whole shtick about giving tourists a pass."

"How do we sell the tourist thing?"

"It took me almost two hours to get here," I say. "I'm a tourist."

They turn away, like I'm annoying them, and then a train roars behind the building and begins to pass directly by the open door. The officers walk to the front of the building to hear themselves. I watch as the light flickers through the panels of the open-air freight cars.

What am I doing, handcuffed, sitting in a metal chair, staring through the open door of a vacant building, watching a train head north? I think this is enough to dampen my enthusiasm for finding Bo. But, to be honest, once I heard Gritty's goner line about the "happy-go-lucky Bo," my quest took a hit. I was much more driven when I imagined him ranting and raving—indignant, passionate, righteous—and striking out at everybody in sight, reeling and pointing at the cracks in our society, lambasting politicians and corporate executives and outrageous windstorm insurance rates. We'd ride out the night full of rage and whiskey, little boys from the land of generals, to the end of the tracks. *Salud.*

But now I picture Bo's hand slowly rising at the sight of me, offering a gentle giant's handshake, a vegetarian-dinosaur handshake. No fire in his manner, just a dimness in his eyes from an unfortunate blow to the head. And what will I say to Mrs. Bocchino? "*Your son's a madman, just not the kind I expected. Just not the kind I need right now.*"

I can't save him any more than he can save me. I've never taken to closure anyway. Even at my father's wake everyone kept nudging me to go up to the open casket—"You need closure. You need to see him dead." Why? Why would I ever want to see my father dead? Why would I want the images of his lifeless jowls and mortician hairdo to be the ingredients of nightmares for years to come? No, I purposely left my glasses home so at most he was a fuzzy apparition as I stayed in the back of the room playing his Louie and Ella CDs on an old boom box. Closure? No thanks. I prefer an open-ended world. A world where Bo isn't pinned down by reality like a dead moth in a collection book, but a fuzzy phantom, still wavering with possibilities.

The train is still rumbling when Moran ducks down behind the metal chair, undoes the cuffs, and then, along with the other officer, walks out the back door without a word.

I stand up, shake it off, and step out along the tracks, the tough breeze from the blaring train pulling at my hair and my clothes as if it's going to suck me up in its draft. But I know I'm going home. I don't think I need anyone else's strength to keep going.

When I reach the front of the building I immediately spot Bennie, peering like a sniper from behind a three-foot-high hedge across the street. He pops up and hustles across the dusty road, the ominous raincoat flapping away. He looks like a cross between Doc Holliday and Billie Joe Armstrong. Before he gets within ten yards he starts apologizing. "Nothing I could do. What could I do? You know, what could I do? There must have been nine cop cars, man. I couldn't show my face in there. Nothing I could do. You know that."

"I know that," I say. "It's all right."

"Yeah, you definitely look all right. You didn't sell me out, did you?"

"No."

"Of course not. Of course not. You wouldn't do that. Man, don't you love this town? Aren't you glad you didn't take the 'Thank you'?"

"we're using it now"

The front yard has become a Caribbean street market, with frothy smoothies flowing and legal secretaries—who have traveled from as far as five blocks over—rustling through our personal possessions. I'm standing out here, naked to the world, trying to make pennies on the dime. My wares, my intimates on full display.

"I take," a rotund woman with a stilted accent says holding up a set of four "The Outer Banks" glasses.

"Two seventy-five," I say.

"No, I take. I have no money."

"I have no money," I say.

She holds her purse upside down in some sort of show of destitution. I don't know how to respond.

Turn my pockets inside out?

I don't want to get into a poor-off with her. She'd be pulling out her bank statement with a list of overdrafts and I'd be snapping my unemployment check stubs in her face. Where would it end?

"No money. You should give me as gift," she says.

"A gift? No gift," I say.

"I take."

"No!"

"Need money for car insurance payment. These I need free."

"My son needs to go to the dentist," I say, pointing at my mouth and clenching my teeth.

"Don't show me your teeth."

"Hey, hey. Dad, don't show her your teeth," Kristin says, stepping in front of me. "How 'bout buy two glasses and get two free?"

"I . . ."

"And we'll fill the third glass with a Berry Berry Splash smoothie," Kristin says, closing the deal.

"Pretty girl knows how to talk to people," the woman says, glaring in my direction. She reaches into a tiny satchel on her hip where she keeps her money a safe distance from the empty, decoy purse.

I don't want to give you the impression that so far this has been a messy, unrewarding garage sale with me having to show my teeth to every other person. Truth is, we've been slamming since daybreak and, at last count, have made about $404. I promised to take the kids to Red Lobster if we hit the $450 mark to make up for all that solo dining I did.

My solar-powered camping TV and musical-frog lawn ornaments went before the sun even came up. Neighbors have been coming and going, and there's been a steady line in the driveway where Andrew has been selling smoothies made in the Turbo II SuperSmoothie maker we have never previously used.

"We're using it now," he keeps shouting at me as a running joke every time I pass. (I hope the smoothies rub off on him. I sometimes think if all serial killers just had more smoothies in their lives, there'd be a lot fewer shallow graves dotting the hillsides of the Midwest.)

Cars are haphazardly parked up and down the street, on easements, and across sidewalks. In between racing in and out of the house, I've been cordially accepting condolences from neighbors who think they know what's been going on in my life better than I do. And maybe they do.

"A dermatologist. Ain't that a kick in the ass," Irish-faced Patrick said after he paid me thirty-five dollars for the eighteen-foot aluminum ladder a painter left on the side of my house six years ago.

I didn't correct him, just handed him back a five in exchange for the two twenties.

Peggy simply put a dour expression on her face and rubbed my back in a small circular motion for a moment before walking away with a three-volume set of *Cooking with Gas and Propane*.

The backrub and the sale felt equally good.

You know how if you run out of candy on Halloween you start giving out fistfuls of Apple Jacks or leftover New Year's Eve tooters, anything you can find? That's kind of how I've been keeping the garage sale freshly stocked. I'm sure if Anna were here she'd be standing cross-armed in her watchtower at the front door saying, "Where are you going with that?" with each pass, but unfortunately she's not. Kristin informed her about the garage sale, and up until the eleventh hour we kept expecting to get a detailed printout of what was off-limits, but her only response was in a last-minute text message: "go for it."

And that we are.

I uncover my father's war medals buried deep in the linen closet. After he'd died, I stuffed them back there for safekeeping with the promise to myself that I'd build a display box for them. I discussed it with my brothers and even detailed how I was going to use the silk map of European escape routes my dad carried in his navigator's satchel as a background to rest the medals on. Alas, I never carried through on any of it. I'm bad like that. I shove the medals back in and run outside with a Presto mini-burger maker I had promised a customer I was sure I had "back in the stockroom." "It looks brand-new," he says ecstatically and I'm thrilled when he hands me four dollars for something that has been lying in the closet next to our beach towels for six years. That's just one more example of the kind of action we're seeing out here.

"Hey, I just met your mentor," Mrs. Dupont says, stepping in front of me to rummage through a box of musical instrument instructional tapes. "He's a little touchy-feely. But I liked it."

What?

I look across the yard and there is Carl, decked out in an iridescent tracksuit and spit-shined black dress shoes, sticking out his big mitt, introducing himself to Sal.

"*Garage sale*. You call this a garage sale. This is an extravaganza," he says, widening his long arms to the point where he seems to be literally embracing my entire universe. "I get it. Play it down, play it all down and then let it erupt. You're upping your game. No doubt, no doubt."

"I didn't really expect you to—"

"How could I not? I gotta keep a closer eye on my pupils. I might add the home visit to my repertoire. Lay a bill on the state for a little bit of weekend wage. Why not?"

A tall woman steps between us. She's holding a hand-carved elephant head bookend and demands to know if the matching end still exists.

"Go, go, tend to your clientele. Let ol' Carl acclimate to these surroundings. Maybe I'll get the MiG Seventeen out and astound these fine folk people with a few soft landings in your neighbor's pool. Yeah, Sully-style. Go, we'll catch up on the backside. Whoa," he says, spinning around. "Don't tempt me with those smoothies."

I almost hate to leave Carl unsupervised, but "OK," I say.

"Go, go. Nothing worse than a bookend without a mate, whole other side falls down. That's right, that's right," he shouts after me as I head off to hunt up the other elephant head. "Whole other side falls down."

"Dad, I'm one step ahead of you. I know where the other elephant is," Kristin says, already digging through a pile at the edge of the lawn.

"Great, great," I say.

"What's with these?" Mrs. Dupont asks, poking me from behind. "Who plays the piano . . . and the banjo . . . and the clarinet and the . . . viola?"

"Nobody, I was just into the tapes for a while," I say. "I was burned-out on other music and I liked hearing only single notes. On the tapes the instructor says, like, 'OK, now try playing an A' and then he plucks a single note on the banjo or whatever. I was into that for a while."

"Thaaat's interesting," she says, delicately placing the box back down next to the olive tree and backing away.

I spot our postman in the middle of the road, trying to navigate through the tangle of parked cars. I walk out to the street so he doesn't have to bother. "You have time for a smoothie?" I say, trying to be cordial.

"Not today," he says, handing me two pieces of mail. One is a 20-percent-off coupon to Bed Bath & Beyond and the other is from my company. (Did it again. *The company*.) I stand at the edge of the yard and peel it open. Right on top is a check for seventeen thousand dollars and the letter attached claims that I did not respond to inquiries about rolling over the money from my 401(k), so the company was required by law to mail the total amount of the account. I guess I screwed up here again somehow and am going to get slammed with another tax bill, but man, what I could do with seventeen grand. My first instinct is to hide it from everyone—including my family—so I do. I slip it under my waistband and walk back across the yard as if I didn't just shove a check for seventeen thousand dollars down my underwear. Now it's definite. Even if we don't hit $450, we're still going to Red Lobster tonight.

I squat to reorganize some dishware, and Shane, the kid from down the street who used to mow my lawn after Kyle stopped, starts walking in my direction.

He was upset when I told him that I was going to go back to maintaining the yard myself. He got all solemn and said, "So this financial crisis is finally hitting me. My dad said this would happen."

"Why are these trolls all bald?" he asks, holding up a handful of the pygmies who look like they just went through chemo.

"You'd have to ask Kristin," I say.

Kristin seems to have all the answers today. I like when we all team up on something like an up-at-dawn garage sale. I figure whichever parent is in front of Kristin and Andrew at a given moment is going to get a decent chance, so I've fallen into this pattern of clumsily trying to stay in front of them, to the point where they're tripping over me every single day.

"Hey, Shane," I say, catching him before he gets away. "Remember when you came around before the holidays with that catalog to raise money for school and I bought that macadamia peanut brittle?"

"Yeah."

"I paid at the time but I never got it. Do you know what happened to it?"

"I ate it."

"Oh."

"Why? That was like a year ago. Has that been bothering you this whole time? Is that why you stopped having me mow your yard?"

"No, no. I've just had more time to remember stuff lately. Reflect. And I just thought of that. Don't worry about it."

There's this almost-brand-new cooler with no lid remaining, so I decide to take one more stab at finding the top of it in our back closet. No lid, but I get giddy when I find an old Splash Radio for shower use still in the box. I grab it and race back down the hallway.

"What are you doing here?"

Anna is standing in the middle of the living room barefoot, her hair tied back, and wearing the yellow rubber gloves, a denim skirt, and a neon halter top.

"I've been here for about twenty minutes—changing the filters."

"Right, right."

Funny how she's about keeping her fish habitat pristine, and all I've been doing is shoveling mud into mine. I'll have to figure out if that means anything when there's nothing left to sell.

"I had to park around the corner," Anna says. "That's quite a scene you've got going out there."

"Yeah, we're doing well. I . . . I better get back out there," I say, holding up the stupid Splash Radio.

"Don't forget to keep at least one spoon," she says, turning back to the fish tanks.

I fly back out the front door and a young girl I don't recognize is standing in my path holding a silver and blue balloon emblazoned with "Congratulations."

"We're having a graduation party—at the end of the block," she says politely. "My mom told me to ask you if it's OK to put this on the sign on the corner so people will know which road to turn down."

"Sure, sure," I say.

I start to walk backward and bump into the Corvette lady. "There you are," she says.

She doesn't mention anything about Anna or having work for me (thank God), but she wants to know all about the pencil sketches of city landscapes that are lying on the edge of the flower box. "Did someone already buy those?" she asks.

"No, no," I say.

She picks them up and says, "I love the way you can peer in the windows. Look, you can see the silhouette of a woman in a shower and the spray of water is so detailed. OK, I'll buy all of them."

"No, no," I say stiffly. "Take them. As a gift."

"Really? Well . . . all right," she says, pulling them to her chest and tucking the bulk of the pile under her chin.

She runs into Carl at the edge of the lawn and is so engrossed with pointing out things in the sketches to him that she leaves her car parked cockeyed on the easement and begins wandering down the block. I watch zombielike as she cuts across her own yard, Carl still at her side, his hand gently guiding the small of her back up the driveway and into her house.

What is Anna doing here? Why now? And she seems so indifferent again. We're clearing out the house and she's acting as if it's not even her home anymore. Except for the fish, of course.

"We're using it now!" Andrew shouts over the shrill of the smoothie maker.

I love him, but that line is getting kind of old and we're down to the nitty-gritty now. I need to condense what we have left into one pile and put it all into the shady corner of the yard.

"Dad, did you know Mom's here?" Kristin says, quietly coming up behind me.

"Yeah, yeah, we were just talking."

"Really? You OK?"

"Yeah, yeah. I guess we need to start wrapping this up, huh?"

"Dad, I want you to meet someone," she says, stepping aside and revealing a tall boy with curly blond hair. "This is James."

"James? Yes, nice to meet you, young man."

James puts out his hand. I grasp it and hold on a little too long.

"OK, James is going to help me clean up," Kristin says, pulling him away.

It's odd seeing Kristin attaching herself to that boy and drifting away but I do not feel disturbed or uneasy about it. Instead of always holding on to things, I've always been able to let go. I'm trying to find out why that is, as if it is a fault. But maybe the answer is simple. Maybe because it's the right thing to do.

I try to block everything else out and concentrate on bringing this garage sale to a close. I read the other day that when the economy collapsed in the 1880s the last thing to go was the piano, the possession that symbolized a tight family, one that had achieved a certain amount of respectability and status in the community. In our case, it's the air hockey table.

A family that was eyeing it earlier is now back with a gigantic cream-colored Ford Expedition and I feel a sale coming on. The slippery aqua blue table has been the centerpiece of this annual event. (Yes, with every purchase I've been saying, "Have a great day. See you next year.") Earlier, Kristin tried to use it as a display table and load it with knickknacks, but I put a halt to that straightaway. "It's an air hockey table. You have to respect that. Don't give people the idea it just sits around being used as a table," I told her.

"Or to put extra piles of laundry on near the washing machine, like we've been doing for the past three years," she said, a little too loudly.

Not that the table didn't have its day . . . or two.

"Ready to take her away," I say to the guy who's wearing a checkered sweater on perhaps the warmest day we've had all year.

"The electric scorekeeper still work?"

"Oh yeah. Everything works. Two extra pucks there."

"I guess the air is free," he says. "You're not going to charge me extra for the air?"

I give up a hardee-har-har in the name of getting this hockey table the hell off my lawn and, thankfully, the checkered man forgoes all haggling, pays the fifteen-dollar price scribbled on the special red discount dot sticker I'd put on our "high-end" items, and before I know it Sal is helping the buyer hoist it into the Expedition.

After they drive off, Sal walks to the corner and stands before the dead-end sign for a minute as if he's sizing it up, calculating the circumference of the hole needed, the strength of the tow line, the acceptable level of noise that can be generated at 4 A.M. and how many total man hours will be involved, including discarding of materials.

Jesus, Anna is leaning outside the front door talking to Carl. I tuck back around the bushes by the front patio to hear what the heck is transpiring, ready to intervene, but all I pick up is Carl boisterously saying to Anna, "Look at you. You're standing right before me as still as a tree but you're in flight—no landing in sight—I can see it in your eyes. Bedazzling. Bedazzling to behold." Anna peers right through him for a moment that stretches almost to the breaking point before she quietly says, "Well, nice meeting you," and disappears back into the house.

"I just sold the smoothie maker!" Andrew shouts at me. "Still had half a Tangerine Banana Dream in it."

"Glorious," I say. "We're headed for the finish line now."

I watch from a distance as Kristin and Shane discuss the loss of the trolls' locks. James is at her side and Kristin is all animated, snipping her fingers in the air like scissors and rapidly shutting and opening her eyes, probably weaving a tale about how she snuck up on the trolls while they were napping and cut all their hair off to build a nest for a hummingbird or something. I can only see the back of Shane's head teetering, shoulders jiggling. I'm sure he is laughing, mesmerized by this teenage girl's silly flight of fancy created on his behalf.

Sal walks over and hands me a cold can of beer. I don't want to drink it but I like the wet coolness of the can and I roll it across my forehead.

"There's no such thing as *Lawn Digest*," he says, popping his can open.

"If you say so."

Sal starts going on about how unlevel my front patio is—"When you laid the stones you didn't use sand, did you?"—but I'm paying little attention. My focus is still on Kristin, who is now entertaining Shane and James with her Olympic high-dive imitation. It's a staple around our house and so convincing that relatives often expect her to dive straight through the floor.

She kicks off her flip-flops, twirls her hair up into a knot, and closes her eyes. It's a first for Shane so he steps back to give Kristin space. She takes two bold strides to the edge of the board, extends her arms out, rotates her head to unkink her neck, gets up on her toes, and lightly springs, abruptly freezing and taking a tiny step back. The highlight is the hesitation. Her eyes close again, her lips purse. The tension mounts as she shakes her arms at her side to fend off the jitters. It took so much just to get to this point. The weight is upon her, the trials and tribulations: the 4 A.M. practices, the steep climb through so many levels of competition, the gulps of stale water from a series of indoor pools, the overbearing coach, the doubts, the reaching back to wring out so many fistfuls of wet hair.

"When I first retired I got into unloading stuff on eBay . . . for about fifteen minutes," Sal says, leaning up against the tree creating this shade. "I couldn't get into the packing. All that tape."

"I can imagine," I say, clutching my hands behind the back of my head and lying down flat. I can imagine a time when Kristin would tell me animated stories . . . I can imagine the cheesy biscuits at the Red Lobster . . . I can imagine Sal's garage lined with brown, open-mouthed boxes and the never-ending screech of the tape dispenser.

"I could be a pretty good best friend, you know," Sal says. "I'm not afraid to touch another man's waistband if the circumstances warrant it."

"I know," I say. "I'm beginning to realize what I've got right here on this block."

"Oh, Peggy would love this Coca-Cola polar bear lava lamp," Sal says.

"Hey," I say jolting up. "I want you to have it . . . as a gift. I've been giving some stuff away as gifts."

"A gift? Really," he says.

"I've still got the box to it in the garage."

"Nice try," Sal says, tossing the lamp back on the pile. "I don't want any of your old, useless shit."

Kristin is approaching the climax of her performance. She's stepping back, putting her hands tightly to her sides, eyes straight ahead, seeing nothing but the sinuous moves of the double twisting somersault and half gainer that will follow her springing leap off the board.

I tilt my head in the cradle of my hands to get a better angle on her, and there's Anna, standing in the window behind Kristin. Her face is as focused as Kristin's imaginary diver, only instead of gazing inward, Anna appears to be watching something she wants to etch deeply in memory.

I follow the slant of her gaze toward Kristin, but the angle is wrong. She's staring past Kristin, right at me.

Kristin's chin is up now, back arched, self-doubt in remission; the spring is forceful, her form flawless as she soars upward before slicing straight through a bed of mulch.

not in a million years

I am full.

I am pacing around in front of the house. I meant to walk inside and get Alonzo when we returned from Red Lobster but I ended up trailing off. Now I am a man taking the dog for a walk without the dog. The night has turned cool, our front door is open, and through the screen I can hear Anna laughing with the kids. They talked her into coming to Red Lobster with us. And it was normal. It was so normal because I continued to avoid that gap between the four-hundred and nine-hundred-pound gorillas, to keep my distance from the inevitable. It was normal until Anna asked for the check. She never does that. Did she simply want to speed things up? Or did she tell McDermy she'd certainly be back by 9 P.M.? Kristin and Andrew acted as if this is how it is now, and if this is how it is, they can deal with it—especially at Red

Lobster. They seem to be constantly monitoring my status. They're like a nurse popping in every few hours: "How you doing? Everything OK?"

I like that.

While we were waiting for a table and Anna was distracted, Kristin gently punched me in the arm and said, "You're going to be all right, big fella." Maybe because it is so early in her life, she doesn't realize how late it is in mine. Or maybe she knows something. After all, she *is* smarter than the rest of us. I'm telling you, I don't care if getting back in the flow requires being pulled behind a horse across a craggy desert landscape with the low cacti ripping the flesh from my back and completely decimating one of my favorite hand-me-up T-shirts. As long as it's my children dragging me back into life, I'm definitely OK with it. Plus, I can blame them if everything goes to shit.

I keep telling myself this happens, this all happens to so many decent people every day. Why not me? We are a family in transition. I have to deal with it.

"Hey, you forgot your dog," Anna says, tugging at the back of my shirt.

Her hair is down. Kristin was right. It looks wild.

She steps back, puts her toes out, and runs the soles of her bare feet across the tips of the grass.

"You look beautiful," I say.

"Thank you," she replies, sitting down and leaning back on her hands.

I collapse to the lawn in a heap, a safe distance to her left.

"I should be angry that you stole my move."

"What?"

"The tripping. You didn't think I'd forgotten about that, did you?'"

"I am really sor—"

"Hania still thinks it was an accident, even though you left without saying a word. Michael said even if it was on purpose he understands. He said he can't imagine what it must be like to not have everything you ever wanted."

"Jesus, that's what he said?"

"I thought you'd like that."

"Everything I ever wanted—like a motion-detecting garbage can?"

"I can understand how he gets to you. God knows I want to kill him myself sometimes, but he's my brother, the kids' uncle."

"I know, and I'm sorry I stole your move. I've got to come up with some moves of my own."

She smiles, then looks away.

"I'm thinking of staying the night to spend some more time with Andrew and Kristin. Did you meet James?"

"Yeah, he seemed like a nice guy."

"I'll just nest on the couch."

"You can have the bedroom. I'll sleep out there."

"No, no. It'll be fine."

"OK. Nest away," I say, looking across the lawn. Our view is obscured by the Corvette still parked cockeyed at the edge of the property.

"I've never sat in a Corvette," I say.

"I thought you ate a Lunchable in that thing."

"No, that was her other car. The Volvo."

"How 'bout now?" Anna says.

"I don't even know if it's open."

"Let's see," she says, springing up.

"No."

"Yes."

She gets to the driver's door first, flips it open for me to climb in, and then closes the door with the curtsy of a sexy valet.

I watch her float by the windshield and then glide into the passenger's seat. "It's all leather, isn't it?" she says, stretching out.

I'm gripping the steering wheel and fiddling with knobs like I'm in a Chevy showroom the day the new models come out.

She drops the glove box. "Peeking into someone's glove compartment is the opposite of opening up someone's medicine cabinet. Boring," she says, fluttering the pages of the owner's manual.

I tilt the seat back and look up through the tinted moonroof.

"Oh, let me try that. Is the lever on the side like normal cars?"

Her seat flops down and she laughs.

"Where are you staying?" I ask.

"I'm not staying with anyone."

"Then why won't you tell me?"

"Because I know how you are."

What does she mean by that? I still don't know *how* she is. I've never gotten a fix on her. Maybe that's why I love her so damned much.

She swivels and turns on her side as if she's lying on a custom-tufted mattress beside me and says, "When I was looking at you that day we stopped to pump gas on the way to Orlando, I was worried. But now I think you'll be OK."

"I guess OK would be a step up."

"You'll make it. With or without me," she says, moving in closer, stretching her right leg out and settling her knee against my crotch. "It's not because you lost your job."

"I know. It was as if you had your exit mapped out and I suddenly announced I had cancer. You wanted to wait until I was in remission."

"I want you to do well."

"Kristin thinks we're more interesting people now," I say.

"Maybe she's right," she says, effortlessly rolling her body on top of mine.

I don't know what is happening. This is going to be mechanical and awkward. My arousal is without question, but I wonder if she's suddenly going to have to break out that tube of KY warming gel to make this work for her. Is this the chore she was saving it for?

But then she is peeling up the flap of her skirt and I am easily sliding into her.

"It feels so good to be inside you," I say. "I need to be inside you."

But two fingers touch my lips to stop the words. Her elbow is propped on the dash and she is slowly rising up—leaving me—and then sliding back down—returning. *"You will make it with . . . or without me."* The touch and go is something I can accept, something I can live with. I want her to know that. Her fingers are pressing firmly on the top of the seat and I can see her wedding band is missing but she is still wearing the diamond engagement ring. The significance of that, I do not know.

I want her to feel my presence so strongly in this moment that she will hunger for it later. I desperately want to be at the helm of a J784 Skit-Kat earthmover, masterfully sending her writhing into ecstasy, but I am frozen. All I can do is accept her.

My eyes close. I'm not sure of her motive but the motion is as pure and natural as anything I've ever known. I am constricted in the seat but my face is buried in neon and the sense of participating *and* enjoying something without all the forced effort is not lost on me. Is that what her body is aiming for? Is that what her body is lying for? *"Because I know how you are."*

Her breath is heavy and sweet now, the rhythm harder and harder. I can no longer sense anything calculated or analyzed. I put my hands on her hips trying to guide her, trying to slow her down, but I cannot control her. She is in charge of this and it feels too good to fight.

I can't believe it's my first time in a Corvette and I'm having sex. Not in a million years did I . . .

Her body sighs and I feel her weight settling for an instant before she gracefully slips off me and immediately ties her hair back as if she only had it down for my pleasure. "Be careful now. Don't make a mess of this poor woman's seats," she says.

"What are you doing?" I say.

"Don't you mean what are *we* doing?"

"I have no idea what I'm doing. You know that. You have a fix on me. I don't have a fix on you. "

"I just feel sexier now that we're not together," she says.

"So it's official that we're not together? Because I didn't know."

"Life's a slow process for you."

"What does that mean?"

"You and your meaning. Do you want to do it again?"

"Some other time or now? I'd like to have something to look forward to, but if this is my last shot . . . I mean, it's hard to explain what I'm feeling. I don't know what's going on."

"This is going on," she says.

loser takes all!

Dad, Dad, are you awake?"

I shoot up and Kristin is standing in the dark in the middle of the bedroom. I look at the clock.

"It's after midnight. What is it?"

"That man who bought the air hockey table is at the door. Something about a cockatiel?"

"What?"

"He's got the air hockey table on our front walkway."

"You didn't let him in the house, did you?"

"No way, he was weird from the get-go. When he bought the table he went to shake my hand but he didn't shake. His hand didn't move. It was like he wanted me to do all the work."

The guy is framed in the front door wearing these goggle tortoise-framed glasses and a brightly striped sweater. Before I'm even halfway down the hallway he's started on me.

"Buddy, buddy, sorry to wake you. The table is just a no-go. Our cockatiel . . . the clacking of the puck . . . she just went ballistic. Spastic, feathers everywhere. My wife's in the car. She could tell you. It's a no-go. If I could just get the fifteen dollars and I'll put it on the side of the house for you."

"You came back here at midnight to get a refund from a garage sale?" I say.

"Did your kids even know you were getting rid of it?" he says, as if I might have sold it out from under my air-hockey-fanatic family.

"We don't want that thing," Kristin says, poking her head over my shoulder.

"You probably can't even play, but the thing is I genuinely love to play. My boys and I play at Boomers all the time," the guy says. "It's just the bird and . . ."

"What do you mean I can't play?" I say, opening the door and stepping outside.

"Yeah, Dad," Kristin says.

"No, I meant you probably don't 'enjoy' playing."

"Listen, how 'bout this," I say. "We play a game right now. Whoever loses takes the table."

"I don't even have the legs on it. I took them off to slide it in the truck."

"We'll play on our bellies."

"I . . ."

"Or keep the table. Just take it and put it out for trash on Monday. That's what you should've done."

"The pickup for big items is different in our neighborhood. It's a week from Monday," he says. "Otherwise I probably wouldn't have—"

"Driven your sixty-four-thousand-dollar Expedition over here to knock on my door at midnight for fifteen bucks. Come on, my ass is up. Let's just do this."

"I'll get the legs," he says.

He has no idea who he's up against. I mean, if it was any other kind of competition—even a teeth-brushing contest—my skills would be in doubt, but air hockey just happens to be the one thing I've mastered. It's all about defending the goal. Scoring is haphazard and ricochet-induced, but as long as you place full concentration on covering the goal you can't lose. I can't lose. I play no offense, only defense. He'll end up scoring on himself, just watch.

"Dad, he's got his wife with him now. She just got out of the car," Kristin says. "You know what that means. He's going to have *his woman* at his side."

"Is Mom still nesting on the couch?"

"I'm on it."

I grab a patio table to stand on while I unscrew the cover on the porch light to give us more visibility. There is such a rumble that the fixture shakes, two screws jump off by themselves, and I topple off the table.

"What the F is going down!?"

I look up and I see Alex, hanging out the side of a huge, idling monster-style truck. She's banging her hand on the door, slapping the metal. "What the . . . what the . . . what the hell is going down? What? What?"

She can't hear a word I'm saying so I walk over to the truck and she's all wired up. "What am *I* doing? What are you doing in this monster truck?"

She laughs and turns to the driver. "He thinks this is a monster truck."

"This is a tinker toy," the driver, a big pie-faced boy, leans over and says. "My cousin Gerard, he's got a monster truck."

"Oh yeah," Alex says, slapping the side of the truck again. "You should see his cousin Gerard's truck."

"You're a little wired up," I say.

"We're going frog giggin' out west. I'm just stopping by the house to say hi to the folks and grab a midnight snack, Jack."

"What happened with the sister?" I ask.

"Gainer happened. You know I like brutes."

"I'm not a brute, sir," Gainer leans over and tells me.

"I got a little numb at the hermitage, but luckily the army base was just down the road."

"So you're . . ."

"I'm livin' in a barracks!" she says, slapping the side of the truck again.

"She's not staying in a barracks, sir," Gainer says as if to ease my concern. "We have resident housing on the base."

"You don't seem like the frog-giggin' type," I say to Alex.

"Don't typecast me, bumblebee. Whuch you got going on here?"

I don't want to get into the whole story, so I narrow it down to the basics.

"I was just trying to get more light 'cause I challenged this guy to an air hockey game."

"What guy? Hey, we got light to spare. Gainer, hit the toppers."

"You got it," Gainer says, and instantly my entire house and the next three streets to the north are aglow.

"Let me get the right angle."

The truck lurches back, Gainer takes aim, and bingo, stadium lighting.

Alex jumps out of the truck onto the hood and Anna is coming out the front door, shielding her eyes.

"I know, I know. Kristin filled me in," she says before I can even begin. "He looks like that guy, the original host of *The Daily Show*. What's his name?"

"OK," the guy says.

"OK," I say.

He hunches over the table in a wrestler-type crouch and keeps shifting his weight back and forth from heel to heel as if he's about to pounce on his prey.

I try to play along and get in sort of an Elvis Presley "Suspicious Minds" karate crouch but my hand is limply holding the paddle directly in front of the eight-inch goal slot.

"Have your woman drop the puck," I direct.

"Maura," he says, giving his wife the go-ahead.

He's all over it. He's greased lightning. His hands are moving with the blur of a Benihana chef. Whap! Whap! Whap!

Block.

Block.

Block.

He just scored on himself.

"Wahooo . . . take that, sweater man!" Alex yells.

"Take that you Carson Daly–looking midnight door knocker," I shout.

"No, it was Craig Kilborn I was thinking of," Anna leans in and whispers in my ear.

"Oh yeah, I hear what you're saying. I can do that," I yell, as if Anna has just given me a coaching tip.

Whap! Whap! Whap! Whap!

He just scored on himself.

Twice.

It'll take him about seven more minutes to figure out what I'm doing, but by then it will be too late.

He's sweating profusely.

The puck flies off the table and as I'm coming around the side of the table to retrieve it, I sense a swagger entering my repertoire. It's a little too swishy—and Robert Downeyish perhaps—but feels perfectly natural. I suddenly hear music blasting in my head and, man, that saxophone don't sound so stupid now.

I flip the puck to Anna and she gets the honor of dropping the disk this time. Sweater guy is all over it, extending his entire body the length of the table and banging his elbows on the side rails.

My wrist is starting to stiffen up from hanging out in the same eight-inch square for over four minutes. I might have to shake it.

"Score!" sweater man yells, thrusting his arms in the air.

"We'll give you that one so you can still have a little dignity, face your children, and maybe get it up once a month for Lady Maura there," Alex says.

Anna shoots Alex a look that says enough of that young lady, but Alex is too Red Bulled up to care. Gainer grabs her and covers her mouth but she rib-jams him and screeches, "I will not be gagged."

Sweater man is so psyched up by his goal he conjures up energy he didn't even know he had and, in quick succession, scores on himself three more times.

I'm going in for the kill.

"What do you do for a living? What are you, a middleman for damaged goods?" I say.

"What? What are you talking about?"

Whap! Whap! Whap!

"You get the big SUV and house in Sugar Ridge by selling fruit to those Speedo-wearin' Canucks. Is that what you do—traffic in the nectar of the gods?"

"You're taunting him," Alex yells.

"You're the Taunter, " Gainer shouts.

"I suppose you own an Outback or two," I say, going lefty.

The guy awkwardly tries to pull the sweater off.

"Oh, look out. He's taking his sweater off. We're in for it now," Alex says, cupping her hands like a megaphone. "Stand back, ladies and gentlemen."

He's trying to one-hand the sweater up and over his torso without taking his eye off the puck, but he gets stuck and starts yelping, "Maura, Maura . . ."

Maura peels the sweater up over his face, but it jams when it reaches the crown of his head.

"Your head's too big for your sweater, man!" Alex says, putting the accent on "man" with a loud belch.

The striped sweater is hanging down the guy's back like the withered headdress of a disgraced Indian chief. I feel so disoriented but so powerful. Maybe it's due to being abruptly awakened. Sometimes we're boldest when we're caught off guard.

The score is 10-4 and for the heck of it I switch up and throw in a little offense.

Whap!

That was a mistake.

10-5.

"Let's go to fifteen," the guy says. "I'm feeling it. I'm feeling it now."

"We go to fifteen and you have to take the table and the pile of stuff I had left over from the garage sale," I say, pointing across the yard.

"Loser takes all!" Alex whoops.

Gainer directs a light he has attached to the side of his truck on a swivel toward the pile, landing on the green ice chest without a lid.

"Yeah, including the topless cooler," I say.

"Whatever. Let's go," he says.

"Honey."

"Shut up, Maura."

Ooo, somebody has a mean streak. The yard goes quiet. The crowd is motionless. We are bathed in light; my wrist flicks and suddenly the whaps have a strange echo.

Whap-wha! Whap-wah!

"Damn." The guy slams his hand down on the table at 14-6.

"You break it, you buy it. Oh, I forgot you already bought it."

"You could get a job as a master air hockey instructor," Alex says.

"Oh, are you looking for work?" sweater man asks. "I'm sorry to hear that."

"Don't try to distract me with pity," I say. "Too many . . ."

WHAP!

"Game time!" Gainer leaps off the truck. The jump sets the lights attached to the truck into a bouncy strobe and my arms shoot straight up into the air.

A thrill of barking like I haven't heard for weeks breaks out the front door and Alonzo comes frantically scrabbling down the walkway, charging into the heart of the excitement without so much as a trace of limp.

"Look!" Andrew yelps in amazement. "He's totally four-footing it!"

Gainer is charging at me, too, chest out. I didn't even successfully complete a high five until around 2004, so a chest bump is a long shot.

He goes up, I stay down.

"That's OK," Gainer says. "We'll nail it next time."

Even Anna has her hands balled up like tiny pompoms and is hopping up and down. I can feel Kristin tugging at my shirt, Alex pulling at my hair, and Alonzo leaping up for a chest bump of his own.

Everybody wants a piece of me.

Gainer kills the lights and it suddenly seems as if we've all been transported back to a strange, intimate moment. Anna wearing flannel pajama bottoms and a tank top, Andrew sporting kamikaze bed hair, Gainer with his arms draped over both Alex and Kristin. The night has closed in on us, forming a tight huddle.

I'd be ready to calm down if it weren't for Alex's crazed face. She's glaring at me as if she wants to gig me like a frog. "Awesome on air! Oh, wait. I got you something," she says, running toward her house.

"This all seemed like a blur," I say.

"I thought I was still sleeping. I thought I was dreaming," Anna says. "Especially when I got to the part about the nectar of the gods."

I collapse onto the front patio. "You know, I could go for those Red Lobster leftovers about now," I say.

"I'll heat some up," Kristin says.

Man, this feels good. I really needed this. I am a man of triumph in the shadow of a dead-end sign, his adulterous woman at his side. Maybe this is the kickoff, maybe Anna has one more U-turn in her. Maybe we all periodically disappear and then reappear as our old selves, like Kristin's psycho friend Olivia. Maybe . . .

"You deserve a prize," Alex says, standing before me with her hands behind her back. "Close your eyes."

Close eyes.

"Tah-duhhh."

"Oh, you're kidding me."

"Mach Threes, right? Those are the ones you were talking about, right?"

"You steal these?"

"I prefer 'snagged.'"

I shake my head and to my left catch a glimpse of Maura dragging the lid-less cooler through the darkness and across the far end of the lawn.

"Go," Alex says. "Have yourself a rich man's shave."

If anyone from the past happens to pick this particular Saturday to ques-tion what Jeffrey Reiner might be doing—right this second—this is it, my dear old friend.

I wheel back around toward the house. Every light is on, in celebration, and I can smell butter being microwaved into liquid for the four remaining snow crab claws. I eye Gainer. He *is* a brute—big, strong mitts. I wonder if he can lift me above all this, Bela Karolyi style. Up high enough so I can pull a Winnie and stay in the spotlight long after the action is over. Up where free-dom has no choice but to wholeheartedly agree with me. Up where I can see the steeple of the church Andrew and I will begrudgingly be attending to-morrow. Up where I can continue to live the soft-porn life, looking down through the Corvette's moonroof and the memory of the last time I ever made love to my wife (I'm still not sure if she gave me a rain check or not). Up where things are different. Up so, so high that if anyone really got to know me at that elevation—male or female—they would fall in love with me all over again. I just know it. Up high enough to be eye-level with the gallant graduation balloon tugging at the dead-end sign as if it could rip it from its cemented roots and send it sailing off to the Netherlands, or at least two blocks east. Up where no television shows ever, ever have dream sequences. Up where the statement "Jeffrey is going to try and do it himself" doesn't set off alarms. Up where we all take turns being smart. Up where I stop seeing the next twenty-four hours as the enemy. Up where we can all mightily survive forever on grapefruit and acai berries and a misbegotten check for seventeen thousand dollars.

We are high on the fumes of a real soldier boy's monster truck and every-body is still loudly conversing over one another and Alonzo's joyful barking; the energy is not subsiding. Anna is frantically rubbing at her arms, trying to erase the goose bumps of the night's chill. Alex is tossing Andrew a Red Bull and Kristin is reaching into a goldfish bowl, laughing hysterically and throwing scrunchies into the air like crazy confetti.

I can no longer hesitate. I can no longer wait for someone else to recognize my feats or make the first move. The safety is off. My bravado as false as my swagger, I tuck in my shirt, cinch up my belt a notch, and prepare to fly.

"Hoist me up!" I yell.

"Do it!" Alex screeches at Gainer.

"Yeah!" Gainer says, storming toward me. "Somebody hold my beer."

ACKNOWLEDGMENTS

I'd like to present crystal Excalibur awards to the following standouts:

To editor John Glusman, for constantly prodding my imagination with questions such as, "Terry, what if somebody goes missing?"

To agent extraordinaire Elyse Cheney for diligently seeking out a decent venue for my brand of humor and honesty.

To editor at large Tom Shroder for both raising my profile and always making each of my words look, sound, and smell better.

To Mr. Bob Weinberg for setting a standard of integrity that all mankind should follow.

To Jana Bielecki for the shady pizza delivery and the unconditional support all down the line.

To Shaye Areheart for her remarkable vision and a name that seems both mystical and mysterious whenever you drop it into conversation.

The following will receive either generic Lucite stars with green felt backing or Target gift cards:

To Ran Henry for the graveyard calls.

To Laura Recchi for the assist whenever I needed to be more witty than funny.

To Danny Shine for whenever I needed to be more funny than witty.

To NPR for the Tiny Desk Concerts.

To Brynn, Dante, Kaelik, and Nicole for all assuming I was doing absolutely nothing with my days while I was painstakingly laboring on this project—for an hour every other day or so.

To Hannah Elnan, Domenica Alioto, Tricia Wygal, Tom Pitoniak, Elina Nudelman, and Kevin Garcia for keeping everything on track.

Oh, to Laurieinthetree for the "suave."

And a big bronzed chunk of my heart:

To Chris for *all* the days, but especially today.

Loose endings:

Much hope that the careers of Laura Kokus, Terra Sullivan, Jake Cline, Joanie Cox, Colleen Dougher, Barbara Lester, Stephanie McMillan, Michael Farver, and Alyson Gold continue to thrive.

Thanks always to Mark Gauert, Al Hart, Robin Doussard, Stu Purdy, Dave Barry, and Johnny "99" Hughes.

Most of all, much admiration to those in front of and behind me in line— Traci, Len, Brent, Mosha, and Tara—at that last cattle call, when none of us made the cut. We were too good for Kohl's that day. We really were.

T. M. Shine is an award-winning journalist and author based in South Florida who has written on topics ranging from spending a week in fourth grade at the age of thirty-two to hunting down an elusive Lizard Man in the back-woods of South Carolina. He is a regular contributor to the *Washington Post Magazine* and his work has also appeared in numerous publications and been featured on National Public Radio's *This American Life*.